Sons Thunder

Gordon Stuart Collins

For Catherine, I love you

For all our friends and brothers, sisters, mothers or fathers that we've loved and lost.

Book Cover by Calum MacRae

A special thanks to Rab Elliott and his book 'No Rest for the Wicked'.

Thanks to everyone who helped me in the process of writing and editing this book, especially Julie for all your focused feedback and to Allison for saving my documents on numerous occasions.

Copyright 2012

Sons of Thunder

Prologue

There is far more than meets the eye, in the worlds which exist within a city.
The soul is a door which can open into manifold worlds of mind and spirit. Worlds of darkness and light, some of horror and of joy; worlds of dreams, visions, intuitions and the infinite imagination of a child; worlds where cruelty is the norm and where denial and insanity are the only ways to survive; worlds governed by subtle fear and secret shame; where sons and brothers, sisters and mothers, look for something to cling to- holding tightly to each other in their isolation and alienation.

Children absorb the energies of the worlds around them.
Unlike adults who can reason them away with clever words and avoid them with delusions and distractions, they can't do anything but run or hide from the invisible forces which press in on the soul, and faintly hope that some unknown good will keep them from the darkness.

At times these dark energies insidiously seep in and take root in the heart.
So much so that it becomes impossible to see where we begin and the shadows end. Yet against all the odds, even against hope itself, a smoldering ember of some happy dream may survive, rise up and become a scorching flame, burning its way out of the enveloping shadow.

For many, the world of their childhood can feel like a complete lie.

A perpetual Hallowe'en in which almost everyone is wearing a mask and not many are in reality what they seem. Children don't *think* too deeply about such things, usually. They just *feel* the hidden terrors and confusion, and let joy take them when it comes: If it comes.

Most of us quickly learn to hide the fragility of our existence.

There is vulnerability in being honestly human: the instinct to survive and to protect ourselves develops secretly, and in the deprivation of a city this becomes a necessity. This instinct sometimes seizes power as a cloak; sometimes the fragile heart retreats into the secret rooms of the mind; at other times the mind cracks, and unleashes a monster.

This is a story of many sons and brothers, trying to survive with all the worlds
>
which exist within a city, visible and invisible.

Sons born in a storm. Sons of Thunder.

Part 1

Chapter 1
The Storm Begins and the Lightning falls

The damp Govan home of young Joseph and James McShane should have been a safe place from the vicious storm outside, of howling Scottish winds and pelting Glasgow rain. The cold, grey tenements were closely compacted together like a useless fortress and seemed to absorb the battering storm rather than deflect its persistent attack. The boys were at home with their mum, Mary, and would soon be tucked up in bed. Not only would they be comforted by an extra woolly blanket on this dismal autumn night, but they'd even have an old duffle coat each, thrown over the covers for extra warmth. It didn't really matter to them that there was no central heating in their home, nor any heating at all in their room, as they'd be insulated by their nightly tea and toast and by the 'mad half hour' of carry on before ten minutes of pre-bed telly. Before bed they were oblivious to the anxiety that Mary was feeling and of the sense of impending doom she was trying to swallow. They contentedly sat in their paisley pattern pyjamas taking as long as possible to eat their supper.
"Right youse two, hurry up and finish that, it's time for bed." Mary tried not to let the fear slip from her voice,
"Och, Ma, can we no' stay up another ten minutes an' watch the telly?" James bargained, taking the role of spokesman as the older of the two brothers,
"No, I want you in bed before your Da gets in."
"But Ma, we're no' tired so how do we have to go to bed?" Joseph chipped in with their standard plea to stay up for longer.
Mary shrieked, "Because I'm tired! Get in and get your teeth brushed and get to your bed!"
How come we've got to go to bed if she's tired?
The brothers silently wondered as they knew it wasn't the time to ask.
The brothers were shaken by Mary's tone as she was usually gentle and patient with

their routine attempts for an extra ten minutes. In fact, she usually gave in with a feigned exasperation and a loving smile at their mischievous and cheeky wee faces. She found it hard to say no to the pair of gentle blue eyes that trustingly peered over the cup of tea, which almost completely hid their faces. The boys quickly gulped the last of their tea, jumped down off the couch and raced each other to the toilet, Joseph pulling the back of James's pyjamas to slow him down. A tear trickled from the corner of Mary's weary eye and she felt a pang of shame that she had spoken harshly with her boys, they were just being *wains*. They didn't know that John's drinking had been getting worse and that he hadn't brought a wage in for weeks. Neither did they know that the electricity company had sent a final letter warning that the power would be switched off if the bill wasn't paid before the end of the month. What was worse is that they couldn't understand the tremor of instability they felt during John and Mary's recent and ongoing arguments which contained a subtle seed of violence. At this stage it was only a threat, a menace and intimidation in John's voice, a hate and fear in his eyes which un-nerved Mary, but not enough to silence her.

As the boys gargled toothpaste water, spitting it on each other's backs for fun, Mary paced anxiously to and from the living room window to see if John was coming up the street. The 'Wine Alley' which the *scheme* was suitably named by the locals in Govan (due to its quantity of residents with serious alcohol problems) was dark and empty, apart from the discarded, empty chip packets and beer cans caught in the swirl of the wind. She could hear her sons giggling and arguing at the same time and as she turned to give them one last prompt to bed, the front door boomed like thunder. Before she could say a word to the boys they rushed past her and scarpered under their covers. She shouted, trying to appear calm,

"I'll be in in a minute to tuck you in."

Her heart was pounding in the chest of her fragile frame as she slowly walked to the front door, trying to calm herself by running a weak hand through her thick, dark waves of hair and forcefully breathing slower. As her hand touched the key in the lock, the door boomed again, accompanied by the demand of a drunken, angry voice, "Open the fuckin' door!"

Mary's spirit jumped. Anxiety filled her whole being. Her hands shook and she struggled to turn the key. The strength seemed to drain from her body and her muscle co-ordination faltered as if jolted with a bolt of electricity. She tried to muster feelings of bravery and self-respect but all she really felt was panic,

"I'm tryin' to open it, gi' me a minute, it's stuck. I was just puttin' the boys to bed." Mary unconsciously mentioned the boys in the hope that John's rage and impatience would simmer before the storm in his eyes gathered pace.

After thirty tense and fumbling seconds she opened the door to see John's foreboding figure leaning, one shoulder on the lintel of the door frame, using it to hold his intoxicated body as upright as he could, the gravity of alcohol and self-hate pulling him down. He tilted his head back to the centre of his body, his short, greying waves matted to his forehead by sweat and rain. He slowly slurred his bloodshot eyes in Mary's direction and brought a clumsy labourer's hand to his slobbering mouth, wiping the demonic, alcoholic froth from his sneering lips. And then he let the poison seep out.

"Whit the fuck is wrang wi' your face?"

On the surface Mary tried to maintain a look of disgust and disdain, but in the reality of her heart all she felt was a well of despair, streamed by fear and hate. She turned and walked away in the vain hope that the verbal abuse would end here and that the storm would be kept at bay by a closed door. She knew deep in her soul that this really was a vain hope, for it would take more than a lock and key to keep out the threatening thunder and rain which was going to pour down.

"I'm just goin' to tuck the boys in." Mary again reminded John of their children.

The boys peeked out from under the covers and Joseph, looking for reassurance but knowing there was none, asked,

"Are you awrite Ma?"

He had an overdeveloped sensitivity of responsibility to take care of his Ma, despite the fact that he was only four years old.

"Aye son, everythin's awrite, you two just get to sleep now and I'll see you in the mornin'." She leaned her delicate, pale face and kissed her boys on the cheek, as she dragged the old duffle coats over them from the bottom of the bed. "Now, don't get up even if you hear any noise, me and your Da are just talkin' about some stuff, awrite?"

The boys didn't understand the subtle warning but they knew it was there.

"Aye, awrite Ma, goodnight." James tried to be brave and show Joseph that there was nothing to worry about, sensing that his wee brother was going to start crying. As Mary turned the boys' room light out, the darkness and the silence thickened in the room, the restless calm before the storm. Joseph was frightened and he didn't know why. He knew that he had just been told that everything was alright, so was confused at the imminent terror he felt in the room. He lay wide eyed hoping the covers and the old duffle coat would protect him. As the voices began rising in the living room, and tones became harsher and sharper, the terror became more suffocating. He couldn't stay still under the covers and sat up. James knew what he was feeling and tried to calm him,

"It's awrite, just try and go to slee…"

But his reassurance was violently interrupted by a thunderous shout, followed quickly by a booming thud and Mary's yelp, like a dog being kicked as it cowered below a table.

Joseph jumped out of bed, not with any sense of bravery, but of desperation and confusion. James tried to whisper but shouted, "Joe!"

But it was too late.

Joseph was already standing powerlessly outside the living room door, not really knowing what to do, but unable to stay still in bed. James came up behind him and pleaded,

"C'mon back to bed."

But Joseph just stood there.

Unable to move, neither into the living room as he was afraid to open the door, nor back to bed, as he was afraid to leave his Ma alone. He wanted to know that she was ok but was paralysed with fear.

Is my Ma ok?

How can I help her?

He felt so powerless, even guilty! His emotions screamed inside.

What is this terror that I'm feelin'?

As these impressions bombarded his tiny mind and emotion the door creaked open. John's towering structure swayed and focused on the boys and for a moment he felt shame. He quickly cloaked it with anger.

"Get back to your bed, everythin's awrite. Your mammy just fell."

As he blurted out this incredulous lie, Joseph's eyes instinctively ignored him and scanned the room for his Ma, through the opening in the door. When he saw her lying on the floor, holding her jaw and trying to get on to her knees, her eyes blurred with tears and her face covered with humiliation, he burst out crying.

"I want my Ma."

John guarded the door, trying to conceal the violence which he had perpetrated.

"I told you to get back to your bed!" John's fear of exposure and self-accusation rose in anger.

To protect his wee brother from a slap, out of his own fear James acted, pushing his way past Joseph and attempting to get past John.

John grabbed him by the collar of his pyjamas and slapped his shovel hand across the side of his head. James cried but had secretly got what he wanted-for the attention to be away from Joseph. As John lifted his hand to strike James again, Mary jumped up and grabbed his arm,

"Don't! I'll put them to bed."

She turned the boys round with a hand on their shoulders, gently but firmly directing them to their room. They were both crying and Mary had swallowed her tears to try and provide them with some comforting illusion that she was alright, that they were alright, that everything was alright.

She put them back to bed and gave them both another kiss and a comfortless cuddle. She sat with them for a little while, stroking Joseph's hair, trying to wipe away the anxiety. But the fearful spirit which had entered the house with their Da began to seep into the secret corners of their minds. For Joseph, he felt that something had smashed inside; like his soul was a house and something had just shattered the window.

His vision of the world was broken. His spirit and his trust were torn. The fragmentation of his soul began.

The man he looked to as protector had become a destructive force; the inner world which he thought was safe was now filled with a wild fear and an insane dread. James dealt with the fear differently. He instinctively covered it with anger, pressing his nails into his palm until he could feel the pain. He was wounded more from his father's willingness to strike him with hate than the actual physical blow.
He felt the sting of rejection and wanted to punish someone, perhaps himself.
He inwardly made a secret, childish, wordless vow to exact revenge; on who or what he wasn't quite sure. He was only five years old and was already learning the false Glaswegian image of a 'real man'-minimal expression of any emotion other than aggression, the need for 'respect' and the fearful addiction to power in its most distorted forms. James fell asleep with his fist still clenched, Joseph drifted into the beginning of his nightmares.

Mary returned to the living room to find John half asleep, a quarter bottle of Johnny Walker falling out of one hand and the embers of a Regal King Size smoldering from the other. She silently sighed with relief and carefully took them both from his hand, hoping he wouldn't be disturbed. She stared at his strong, ruddy, jawline and tried to see the handsomeness and gentleness she had first met; all she could see was the ugliness of violence and hate. As sleepy silence descended on her home, she cupped her face in her hands and wept bitterly. Not only because her jaw was broken, but because she felt trapped and couldn't see the way out. She didn't know how this man that she had loved could do such a thing, how the 'demon drink' changed him beyond recognition. When sober he was a gentle, caring man, who loved his sons and cherished his wife. When he lifted the first drink he was like a man possessed, unable to stop the monster which it unleashed. They had married at eighteen with so much hope and now her life was so full of despair.
In the morning, once the boys were in school, she would take herself to the Southern General Casualty, telling herself this would never happen again.
For now, the damp windows of her red eyes closed and she prayed a silent prayer to

a silent God. She prayed for her boys, that they would find a refuge from this way of life. She wanted so much for them to escape this pattern of poverty, alcoholism and violence. Her own childhood had been marred with it, as was John's. It was accepted as normal, inevitable even. This was the way of life for so many in Glasgow's schemes, and despite the desire to change it and the fleeting belief that they could and would, Mary and John were circling the drain of the city's darkness. Mary prayed to a God she didn't know or even believe in, but hoped that he was listening.

Chapter 2
The Happy Hour

Despite the sectarianism which existed in 1970's Glasgow between Catholics and Protestants, reinforced by Celtic and Rangers fans, neither John nor Mary had any interest in it. John was brought up Protestant and Mary Catholic, both of their parents having direct descendants from Ireland, both north and south. They had listened to the bitterness of their parents which was always fuelled by alcohol and usually resulted in a punch up. The troubles in Northern Ireland were also prevalent during this time, which gave lots of Glaswegians more weight to their hatred and a cause to justify it.

John had sworn to himself that he would never become like his Father, that he would never be bitter or violent, that he would never pass hate on to his children. He managed to do so without the help of sectarianism. He seemed to carry with him the sins of his fathers and never really addressed or owned them. All the hate and blame and resentment had passed from one generation to the next as a poisoned inheritance. Mary also vowed to herself that she wouldn't become like her parents, particularly her mother. As she grew up in the schemes of Govan, moving from one to the next, she constantly told herself that she would 'find a man who wisnae a waster like your Da'. She looked at her mother and what she had to put up with-no wages, no respect and no hint of happiness. Mary pitied her Ma but she also resented her for putting up with so much abuse and neglect from her Da. Hadn't she been left time and again to bring up her younger sister while her Da went drinking and her Ma went crazy looking for him. She never brought any of her pals from school to her house, for fear that her Da would be drunk and her Ma would be screaming at him. Or that they would be scowling, screaming and clawing at each other in the street, in a drunken stupor. This was acceptable, even expected behaviour for some families in the Wine Alley, but Mary would escape from it, she'd find another way, surely.

John and Mary had met in the Barrowland Ballroom, 'the dancin' in The Barras', when they were sweet seventeen, young but not innocent. They fancied each other straight away and loved the idea that they were from different religions- that would really get on their parents' nerves! It was a time of excitement and optimism, they would be able to escape from their past by starting a life together. They could even leave Glasgow one day and live just outside the city, free from the schemes and all the shit that came with them.

If only it had been that easy. If only John would stop drinking. If only he could get a decent job and maybe even a house outside of Govan. There were a lot of 'if onlys' and not a lot of knowing how.

Mary fell pregnant with James at just eighteen and then had Joseph less than a year later. The boys had been born into a family inheritance of violence, alcoholism and poverty and both John and Mary believed that they would have something different. They truly did, despite the fact that history seemed to be repeating itself and the spectre of the past was haunting them. As John's drinking progressed, his time at home lessened by the day and was replaced with the ironically titled 'Happy Hour' in any Govan pub. Consequently, Mary's desperation for change increased. She went to the Housing and asked for a house outside of Govan-this would be the change that they needed.

To Mary's surprise she was offered a house within a couple of weeks in an area of Glasgow called Pollok. This area also had lots of problems, but it was a geographical change, which Mary hoped would be a new start. *It can't be any worse than the life I'm livin' just now... could it?*

She accepted the house and told John and the boys. John appeared neither up nor down at the idea and these days seemed resentful of anything that Mary did. The truth was that John was deeply unhappy with himself. He knew that he was ignoring his responsibilities, that he had a problem with the drink and that he had stopped loving Mary and the boys. But admitting this to anyone else would mean admitting it to himself, and he wasn't ready to do this. The drink had a hold of him and although he would glance at it with his mind's eye, he couldn't face it squarely as he suspected that it was more powerful than his will. He wasn't ready to admit defeat. He was constantly loaded down with guilt and shame but this always came out as anger, usually towards James. He seemed to leave Joseph alone, almost ignore him. His hatred seemed focused on James and for no reason he would often lash out at him. His twisted cruelty was never more manifest than when he was drunk, but not drunk enough to numb his hate.

The violence and hatred which John had brought into his home created a prison of silence in his wife and his two boys. To anyone outside they still looked, acted and played like two carefree brothers, but each of them had been touched by a malice which would grow within them as life unfolded. Mary had lost her trust and in its place she shielded herself with hostility.

The boys still had their mischief and daily torment of each other which brothers have, inventing new ways each day to inflict pain on one another. James would sneak up on Joseph, hold his body tightly and put one hand over his mouth, whispering,

"Die quietly."

He'd pin him to the ground, twist his arm up his back and demanded homage,
"Who is the king?"

"Aagh…No you ya big poof." Joseph squealed, trying to endure the pain and not surrender.

"I'm no' lettin' you go until you honour the king." James slowly jerked Joseph's arm further up his back until his fist touched the shoulder blade with a shooting pain.

"Aargh! Awrite, you're the king, leave me!" Joseph reluctantly surrendered.
James savoured the moment.

"Ma…Ma!" Joseph knew that when all was lost and he couldn't take it anymore he only had one option.

James released him and bolted out of the room, laughing from a mixture of adrenaline that he was going to get a slap from his Ma, and childish joy that he had gained another minor victory. Surely that was what wee brothers were for!

As John and Mary's fighting became more regular the boys need for distractions and their development of a kind of twisted humour progressed. The arm twisting game became simply choking each other to see who could endure the longest without, well, dying basically. They called this game 'evva'. This was decided simply because Joseph choked this out one day with James's hands squeezing his throat.

"Whit did you say there?" James asked his wee brother's reddening face, knowing that Joseph couldn't actually speak.

"Evva..." Joseph said

"Whit the hell's evva?"

Joseph was trying to say "Fuck off", but every time the word began to form James would squeeze a little tighter. The boys would willingly take turns to test the endurance of each other, finding great joy in the simplicity of watching each other's faces change from pale anticipation to suffocating red and blue.

The brothers were as close as brothers could be despite their torture games. They had to find ways to cope with, or rather distract themselves from, the tense atmosphere which filled their home.

One place they were able to do this without pain was aptly, like their Da's favourite time of day, called the 'Happy Hour'.Not the one centred on cheap alcohol, but a local get together for all the Govan kids, run by a small mission hall. Joseph and James didn't know or care about denominations or religions; they had at least been saved from one type of hatred by their parents. What they loved about the Happy Hour wasn't so much the free sweets for reading a Bible verse or for asking questions about God, but the way they felt when they were in this place. They loved the singing and sang their wee hearts out. There was nothing to think about that was horrible, no fear or hate or anger. They didn't really know why but they felt safe here, even loved. The 'Jesus wummin' who ran the Happy Hour always seemed happy to see them and would be so attentive. The smiling dirty faces were never washed with so much praise and encouragement.

Compared to the dismal clouds which most of these *wains* were living under, this felt like a bright blue sky on a clear day: a breath of fresh, lively, lovely air for wee souls who were drowning and didn't even know it. In this place there was the God of a child who is easy to understand and whose message was simple. He loved them just as they were. Protestant or Catholic, Muslim, Hindu or Jew didn't even come into it. These were complicated words and ideas created by big people. Joe and Jim, as they were called by friends, would leave the Happy Hour with a glowing joy in their hearts, laughing and forgetting, with not a care in the world. What a feeling this was to them, even if only for an hour.

Chapter 3
Dreams and Visions

Joe didn't know whether he was still in his body or out of it, but he was definitely flying.

The natural colours of this strange place, although recognizable, were much brighter, more vivid and alive. The pure air sharply pierced the nostrils and everything shone radiant with light. He was as light as a feather but still able to glide and control, soaring freely through mountains and over the surface of a calm bed of water. He moved without force but still had the feeling of being taken somewhere, guided even. He also had the certainty that someone was with him but there was no-one else in sight; he couldn't even see his own body! He was alone but felt curiously safe and wondrously happy. As he soared above a huge forest of Caledonian pine trees, his attention was drawn to something moving quickly through the trees with speed and grace. With joy his spirit instinctively accelerated and followed the subtle, parting movements of green, red and amber colours on the ground below. All of a sudden, his sense of flight came to a gentle landing and he found himself standing beside a young deer, although he didn't know that's what it was. He had never witnessed one in his life before, not consciously anyway. Yet he was unusually familiar with the whole situation, like an extended dejavu. The deer turned its gentle faun head and chestnut brown eyes and fixed its gaze on him, not with apprehension but with acceptance and serenity. This powerful gaze was so filled with a reassuring comfort that all trace of fear and shame seemed to empty from his soul-like a bright light pouring into a darkened cellar. It was like this creature had known him from some other life which he had forgotten about. He was beginning to remember the more he returned its gaze.

There were no words here, not in any sense of sounds, as the unbroken silence was as breathable as the air. Yet, as the deer browsed among the delicate, white lilies and quenched its thirst from the flowing brook nearby, it seemed to communicate with him, assuring him that all would be well. He had such a strong impression that he was here for some important reason which his mind had no words for. Despite knowing that he probably shouldn't spoil or interfere with this moment, Joe felt compelled to reach out and touch the deer. Instantly, the calf startled anxiously, a cracked twig splitting the silence as it turned its focus quickly in Joe's direction. To his confusion, its wide-eyes and pricked up ears attended not at him but behind him. The creature's four legs seemed to come together in perfect harmony as it sprung from its stillness and darted out of view. As Joe reluctantly turned to see what had penetrated this perfect moment of peace and light, he was engulfed by a formless flood of blackness and horror. It filled his lungs and in the panic of suffocation, before the moment of unconsciousness, his tiny blue eyes shot open and once again he found himself in the dimness of his bedroom.

His heart boomed in his chest and his whole body tremored with the shock. He felt that he had just returned not from a dream but back to his body from a different time and place-not only from a different geographical location but from another realm where time was irrelevant. Of course he didn't have these thoughts, but rather the sense of confusion and disorientation we could imagine such an experience may produce. He looked to see if Jim was still here; he was sound asleep, oblivious to the mixture of nightmare and joy which his little brother had been in.

As he readjusted to the dark reality of his room around him he became aware of a muffled argument. The high but fractured emotion, raised voices and acidic words, could be heard from the living room like the crack of a lashing whip. The familiar sense of anticipating chaos and the feeling of uncontrollability loomed in the atmosphere. He could hear the broken glass before it shattered; his sensitivity to it and the premonition of it resided in him now

Sure enough, a thud was heard as his Da jumped to his feet, and the smashing of a tumbler against the wall only served to confirm Joe's anxiety. It sadly didn't shock him anymore but only allowed his insecurity and his own broken trust to go deeper. This world which he now found himself in, not knowing any other except those of his dreams, was filled with anticipated trepidation.

The smashing of the glass startled Jim to consciousness with an immediate need to protect, strangely not himself but his wee brother. He too was acclimatised to the violent energy of his environment, his fear morphing in anger in order to fight the monsters in his head and in his home.

"Joe?" He whispered commandingly "You awrite?"

"Aye…I think so," Joe lied, trying to be brave and not wanting to feel ashamed of his fear.

"Do you want to sleep in here?" Jim knew the answer but also the need for his wee brother to be 'a big boy' as his Da would remind them when he sensed any tears from them.

"Aye…if you want," Joe returned, keeping his dignity in front of his brother. Climbing into the bed and under the safety of Jim's covers there wasn't a word spoken. They both knew the code: Don't talk about feelings or fears and pretend that all of the chaos in the other room is happening somewhere else.

"Just go to sleep," Joe played this tape in his mind until he couldn't hear it anymore. Jim wouldn't sleep now. He knew what was coming. He had to sit and listen…and think.

As the bumping of furniture and the whimpering of his Ma began, Jim knew he would have to go in and remind them that he was there. He didn't think for a minute that he could stop what was happening, he knew better than that by now. He just hoped that he could interrupt the hate by just standing silent, being present. He might get a slap, he would definitely get a burst of anger or a hateful look, depending on how much venom had intoxicated the atmosphere. He would go in anyway, not really knowing why. This was the routine and there was no other way to sit with the anxiety.

He opened the door slowly to the disturbing sight of his Da holding his Ma up against the wall by the throat. He looked commandingly powerful, but dangerous. John was so consumed by bitterness and drunk with whisky and power that he didn't even hear the door open. It was only when Mary's eyes fixed on Jim with a different terror and disgrace that John glanced round. He reluctantly let her go.

"Get to your bed!" John barked and would only give him one chance, if it was really in John's control. Jim tremblingly looked at his Da, his height, his strength, his dominion. He stared at his eyes which were the eyes of someone else, the reassuring blueness gone and now full of demonic hatred. Jim saw a shadow surrounding his

Da, not coming from him but hovering over him. There was a sheet of darkness around him, even above his head and about three or four inches around his whole body. This shadow was emanating from John and seeping into Mary. There was, in James's perception a connection between Mary's terrified eyes and the creeping darkness travelling through John. Once again he had no words to explain this, only images and impressions in the mind of a traumatised child.

"Let me put him to bed." Mary pleaded for herself and Jim.

John turned and slumped onto his chair and with a deceptive calm he poured himself another drink, buzzing with vibrations of power and the control which he thought he possessed, or which possessed him.

Mary took Jim's small trembling hand and led him back to bed. When she tucked him in, she gently cried as she held him close. He couldn't or wouldn't cry. A piece of his heart was closing more each day and becoming harder each night. She wept for her sons once again and in despair her heart prayed for help. She would ask her Ma to keep an eye on the boys for a couple of hours tomorrow. Tomorrow she would go back to the Housing and take the house in Pollok, whether John came or not. She hoped that he wouldn't. She prayed that she would make it till tomorrow.

This night had been worse than the others, not because John had been drunker than usual, but he carried with him an ominous insanity. He had come home from the pub during the day, around four in the afternoon which was early for him on a Friday. He came in quietly, deep in thought, brooding almost. His quietness and lack of animosity had un-nerved Mary, but she wasn't going to question it. When she had let him in he hadn't even made eye contact, but went to their bedroom without a word. Mary returned to the kitchen to get the dinner ready for the boys who had just came home from school and sat glued to the telly.

"You two'll get square eyes if you don't move back a bit from they cartoons"

The boys didn't even acknowledge their Ma's bizarre logic. About fifteen minutes later, just before Mary put the dinner out, she shouted through to the living room, "Jim, come in here and take these bins down before you get your dinner." Mary was once again ignored but this time not because Jim couldn't hear her but he wasn't there.

As she went in to reprimand and scowl at him, she passed the bedroom and John was perched on the edge of the bed. Coldly, with a clinical tone in his voice, almost trance like he declared,

"He's away."

"Whit?...Where is he? Whit do you mean he's away?" Mary was on the edge of panic but didn't know why; she just had the anticipation of bad news, like a bang at the door when you know it's the police.

"That guy took him."

"Whit...whit the fuck are you talkin' about?" Mary, confused, found anger, driven by maternal protection rise up from deep inside her. At this moment she didn't care if John felt *disrespected-* a common excuse for his aggression.

John had no reaction to Mary's anger, which really scared her. He just sat staring at the floor with empty eyes. She couldn't make out if he looked guilty or bewildered or both. Without any high emotion he declared again,

"I told you, that guy... him wi' the long black coat. He's been wi' me all day, followin' me. He said he was gonnae kill you and the boys if I didnae let him take Jim. I had no choice... he just came in and took him when you were in the kitchen. Jim was *greetin* but I told him he had to go."

"O my God, whit have you done?"

Mary's whole body weakened with panic but adrenaline rushed to her feet. As the cup she was holding slipped through her shaking hand and shattered on the floor, she bolted to the front door and ran down the stairs. She didn't stop to rationalise the situation or to ask the logical, even obvious questions which hindsight afforded. She just moved with as much speed as her panic allowed. She knew that this wasn't some sick practical joke; she could tell this by the sombre and convincing way which John had relayed the presence of this man to her. As she got to the front of the close, screaming Jim's name, she heard a whimpering voice in the back close; the sobbing sounded like someone struggling to breathe. She walked towards the back close, her heart in her mouth, in dread of what she might see. But to her confusion and relief all she saw was her wee boy, curled up in a ball, holding his knees, swaying and crying.

"O my wee pal, you're awrite…you're awrite sweetheart."

She would simply comfort him just now, no questions- just a mother's love.

Mary knew by the depth of his sobbing that he wouldn't be able to speak any sense. She took Jim home but he couldn't tell her what had happened. How his Da had called him into the bedroom within moments of returning home and whispered, "Get out." How he'd told him to go to the bottom of the stairs and wait there. He told him if he didn't wait there and go with the man with the long black coat that the man was going to take his wee brother and his Ma and never come back. He also said that if his Ma found out then it would be his fault if anything happened. Jim had left, trying not to let his Ma hear him cry, as he didn't want to fail and for his Ma to be taken away with Joe. He hadn't questioned his Da for a second. Why would his Da lie about such a thing? Jim hadn't fully learned that the things adults said weren't the absolute truth. Up until this day he still had some tiny fragment of the childhood innocence which believes that parents are always true, even if not always trustworthy.

When he had reached the bottom of the stairs he had waited, shaking with dread and unable to contain his sadness of not seeing his Ma and wee brother again. When he couldn't hold it in any longer, he had hid in the back close, waiting either for the unknown man with the long black coat or for his Ma. His relief at hearing his Ma's voice calling for him as she ran all the way down the stairs had also filled him with shame that he'd failed, and that his Ma would now be in danger because of his failure.

When Mary confronted John about sending Jim out, he maintained his story and had no remorse. He also quickly forgot the incident within half an hour as if it had never happened. Mary couldn't get her head around it and thought that John's drinking and his sick sense of humour and cruelty had thrown him over the edge of sanity.

She wasn't far wrong.

It turned out that John had been drinking earlier in the day with friends and one of them had spiked his drink, "for a laugh"! Throughout the day he had been experiencing disturbing visions of stalking figures, lurking in doorways, swarming his thoughts with paranoia, spitting hatred in puddles of blood and whispering murderous threats. He did in fact completely believe in this nameless man, who had filled him with terror and seemed to have some hold and control over his life. He strangely locked into a belief that the words and commands of this figure were binding and he felt no ability or will to refuse him. Mary only realised there was something seriously wrong , not when the violence started later that night, as there was nothing unexpected there, but when John had woken up abruptly during the night. Staring at the foot of his bed, he turned to Mary and with fearful inevitability declared,

"He's here!"

Mary's heart pounded with a wave of dread and for a split second of belief, asked, "Where?"

"There…he's just walked over to the corner of the room."

John seemed to be trying to simultaneously both convince Mary and to be contradicted by her of the 'reality' which was disturbing him.

In the small dark hours of this night Mary got up and phoned an ambulance, selectively telling them of the day's events and of the insanity which she thought had entered her home. The daily insanity which she lived with, she kept to herself. When the paramedics arrived, John was in the kitchen, staring out of the window and through the dim-lit Govan streets. His confusion amazingly and quickly changed to a sure confidence as he saw the paramedics.

"Thank God you're here. She's in the livin' room. I was really worried about her, that's why I phoned you. I think she's off her head."

Hearing this from the hiding place of the boys' bedroom, Mary jumped up to defend herself. She couldn't believe what she was hearing, and for a moment she questioned herself and all of the day's events, as they rushed through her mind together like a polluted river. The paramedic closest to Mary gave her a reassuring look and silently nodded, indicating his lack of belief in John's words, as if to say

"It's awrite *hen,* we know what's happenin' here."

Mary let slip a cry of relief that someone could see the reality of her situation, well, some of it at least.

For a moment she reluctantly felt the truth of her own anguish.

Months of hiding from people in the street, pretending to herself and others that things weren't as horrific and despairing as they actually were. It had taken an incident of insanity recognised by the medical profession for her to truly own, even for a second, the madness of what her daily life had become.

The paramedics had come from Leverndale Psychiatric Hospital in Pollok, and knew as soon as they looked at John's eyes that he was under the influence of some mind altering drug. They calmly and professionally convinced John, each taking an arm at either side of him, that they wanted to talk to him outside. They managed to persuade John, without provoking any aggressive action that they wanted to take him to the hospital where he would be safe to sleep for the night. Contrary to his usual, violent response when asked to do anything against his will, John went willingly, even gladly, perhaps suspecting himself that all wasn't well. John was in the hospital for three days, sleeping most of the time under heavy sedatives administered by the hospital until the nefarious visions passed. He was stalked by hallucinatory, foreboding figures staring calmly in corners of the ward and repetitively chanting words of death and destruction for his family. He was told they were not there but he could see them as clearly as he could see the doctors trying to convince him otherwise. And of a haggard old woman, a chronic alcoholic and psychotic in the hospital who wasn't a product of illusion but of the inpatient psychiatric ward. Her teeth and fingers covered in yellowy-brown, a slobbery froth dripping down her chin, she would avoid John as if she could see the angel of death on his shoulder. She grimaced every time he walked into the room and mumbled endlessly like a disturbed highland seer, "The Ravens! The Ravens will bring black rain."

The stupid utterings of a crazy old woman. He told himself without comfort.

At least Mary had three days of rest as well: time to make the arrangements for a move to another house. This night had been the culmination of months of chaos and madness, sealed by John's dark visions, which had touched the lives of her children in ways that she couldn't even imagine. She knew that Jim had been terrified of what he'd been told and burdened by the responsibility placed upon him. She also knew that Joe hadn't escaped untouched by these events either. He had no language to explain it away, but like a sponge he unknowingly absorbed the emotional climate and the twisted thoughts which he lived in. Mary would, as she had resolved, ask her Ma to watch the boys, perhaps even for a weekend. She had to make this move. She had to escape this madness.

Chapter 4
Loved by a mongrel dog

Joe and Jim loved going to their Granny and Grampa McDermott's. It was another world for them, a happier one, like an alcoholic Punch and Judy show with a slightly more sinister twist. Grampa McDermott was usually not in during the day but would arrive around dinner time, always drunk and with a bag of sweets in his pockets for his grandchildren. He never handed any money in to Cathy, his wife and Mary's Ma, but he always had money for drink and sweets. The boys loved the anticipation of him coming home, and unlike their own house, they were unafraid of the fights which would take place, as they intuitively knew that it wouldn't touch them, at least not physically, and that they were in no danger.

They would hear Auld Wullie, as he was known in Govan, coming up the street. Not because he had a particularly loud walk but he was always singing and making unintelligible words up when he was drunk. He had two favourite songs which he always sang, one which included the memorable line,

"Fuck King Billy, Fuck the Pope, Fuck the Queen, Fuck them all!"

He was impartial if nothing else when he had his satisfactory amount of Grouse Scotch Whisky. He also had his own trademark 'song' which contained a ludicrous chorus of "Eee Baa Baa Baa", which he chanted at the top of his voice. Although it was complete and utter nonsense, it never failed to throw Joe and Jim (and all the other cousins often present if it was a Sunday) into hysterics. It did not, however, have the same effect on Granny McDermott.

Cathy was a real Glasgow Granny; you know the type: constant curlers in her golden-grey hair, a kind heart and homemade soup that only a Granny can make. Her round and squidgy body had a hard exterior, particularly when talking to Auld Wullie, but she was softened by deep, caring emotions and a gentle spirit. However, she did not often display such gentleness to Auld Wullie, but was so frustrated at his self-centred alcoholism and his total disregard for meeting his financial responsibilities, that she would often fly into a fit of rage when he was mid "Eee Baa Baa", and then proceed to silence him with whatever was in her hand- usually a pot being used to prepare the dinner. Auld Wullie took this in his stride and pretended to cry whilst expressing his drunken love to her,

"Cathy, my darlin', you know that I love you."

This was then accompanied by Auld Wullie bellowing a spontaneous chorus of Patsy Cline's version of "Please Release Me." This was also a favourite song which, when intoxicated, he would phone the local radio station and dedicate to all of the prisoners in Barlinnie Prison.

Cathy would moan and wail but to Joe and Jim and even Auld Wullie himself, this was all part of the show. The boys would sit, wide-eyed, waiting for the next comical character to appear and right on cue, Suzie the cat, would stroll across the back of the couch, trying to leave the room un-noticed, cautious about being hijacked as part of the act. Sure enough, as soon as Auld Wullie spotted her, she would be snatched and lifted up from her tummy, kissed and serenaded for a couple of minutes, made to do a waltz, and then thrown from the first floor window to the dirty street below. The boys would howl with laughter, holding their solar plexus and roll about the floor, as they knew by now that Suzie always landed on her feet, unscathed. Even the cat had learned how to survive in an alcoholic home.

The boys would run to the window just to make sure Suzie was ok, hearing Cathy scold,

"I keep tellin' you, don't throw the fuckin' cat oot the windae!"

Only to be told by Auld Wullie that it was 'good for her agility.'

As the Punch and Judy show drew to an end, Suzie's dramatic exit being the climax, Cathy dragged Auld Wullie by the scruff of his urine-stained trench coat and made him go and lie down till she finished making the dinner. Joe and Jim loved dinner at their Granny's, it seemed to warm their hearts as well as their bellies. After dinner the brothers would go with their cousins Vinny and Ramie and would take Major, Granny's black and tan mongrel dog, to the Elder Park, which was only a five minute walk away and had a boating pond. They weren't so much interested in the boats as they were teaching Major how to swim. In fact, they weren't so much teaching him how to swim, as forcing him into the water and watching him scurry to the side, but not until he had retrieved the stick which they had thrown in. They loved the way that Major would do anything that they told him and that he seemed to be more of a pal than a dog. They would coax him to go places with them by asking with all sincerity,

"Major, do you want to go and get big juicy bones, that size?" Stretching their arms as wide as they could to illustrate the enormity of promised bones.

Major wagged his tail furiously and seemed to agree wholeheartedly. The joy of Major's excitement and his devotion to their adventures in the park, made him like a third brother, albeit one from a different species! Major loved them so much that he would often follow them home and would only leave when John came home drunk. He too instinctively knew the hidden dangers that accompanied the drink.

Jim and Joe also knew that their Granny loved them, and despite the occasional chaos that was her Govan home, she always had a reassuring smile and a loving glint in her eye for each of them. It was as if she knew that it was the Granny's job to impart to a frightened child that all would be well, that everything would be ok, that there was no hate in the world that was too much for love. Cathy intuitively knew that Jim needed this reassurance more than any of her other grandchildren, even more than Joe despite his shyness and timidity of soul.

When the boys stayed with her on a weekend such as this, when Mary needed time to breathe, Cathy would often let Jim get up from his bed once Joe had fallen asleep. She would give him a cup of hot milk and let him stare contentedly into the coal fire, while he munched on a slice of bread with sugar on it, an alternative to the luxury of a biscuit. He would look up at her and the delight on her face would let him know that he was safe, a feeling which had long since left his heart in his own home. He still believed that there was someone in the world besides Joe that he could trust, but only just. Before going to bed she would stroke his hair and teach him to say trusting prayers; prayers to God for his Ma and his Da and to help him 'be a good boy' to them. Jim knew that he was finding it hard to hold on to the last two but for his Granny's sake he would try. Sometimes he would open his eyes prematurely as they prayed and he would notice that his Granny was silently crying, tears dripping down her wrinkled cheeks. He never asked why but just held her hand a little tighter.

As Jim lay in bed, he would hear Auld Wullie waken from his slumber and start demanding his dinner, the joviality of the drink having now worn off. He would look for an argument, trying to blame Cathy for something, anything to offload the bitter taste which selfishness and whisky had left in his mouth. They would argue a while but Cathy would always give up on Auld Wullie, eventually. She knew the futility of reasoning with a drunk, despite the fact that she would always try and had done so for the last thirty-five years of their marriage.

Auld Wullie had put his hand to many jobs over the years-fruit-seller, milkman, porter, labourer and ironically a barman. But despite the ongoing change in employment, he never changed in appearance or in his lifestyle. His brylcreemed mane of white hair, his thick milk bottle glasses and his necessity for a suit and a tie, had made him look the same since he was in his early thirties. Even when the most devastating fear and horror of any parents' life tragically visited Cathy and Wullie's home, Auld Wullie never seemed to change, on the outside anyway.

On this fateful night, as Joe and Jim lay sleeping in deep childish dreams, having prayed for God to keep their family safe, there was an authoritative rattle at the front door. It was the police, which usually meant bad news. Jim listened to the muffled but serious tones of the police officers and his Granny wailing in response to their news.

"O my God… O my God…not my Thomas…not my Thomas!" She was uncontrollable and hysterical in her crying.

Jim got up and stood helplessly at his room door, watching his Granny fall apart. Once again he was powerless and felt a pang of injustice, helpless to rescue those he loved. Auld Wullie just stood there, stunned and silent, and then went to get a drink. Jim found out the next morning when Mary arrived, that his uncle Tam, Mary's wee brother, had been murdered. He was in *Geraldo's* chip shop in Crossloan Road, Cathy's street, and was attacked by two men, one with a knife. There was no previous argument. No exchange of angry words. Tam was in the wrong place at the wrong time and clashed with the wrong people. He was viciously stabbed in the chest and left to die on the chip shop floor. His heart bled from within.

Jim was told that it was 'a bad man' who had done this, as if this explained anything or alleviated the tremor which such an event unleashed.

Around this time, another incident took place near Jim and Joe's home which also leaked fear into the boys' minds, especially Jim's. There was a derelict building nearby which was being prepared for demolition, although one man and his two children were still living in it, waiting to be decanted to an appropriate new home. The substance of the local gossip was that the man had left the children in bed one night asleep, perhaps going to the pub or visiting a friend. He believed his children were safe, for it seemed that no-one would know that they were at home alone. Even if anyone did know, why would they make it their business?

I'm only oot for a couple a drinks?

The father returned home and was horrified at what he found.

His children had been murdered in their sleep.

The story spread like the plague across Govan and the Southside. Everyone was talking about it, many with judgement, and all with fear. So, when Jim overheard his Ma and Da talking about it and he saw the blatant newspaper headline 'Children murdered in Govan' he asked what happened and more importantly to him, who did it? Again, he was insufficiently told that 'it was a bad man'.

The seeds of fear began to grow and spread deep roots in Jim's heart, and the belief that evil existed in the world, and that some unknown and distant God didn't or couldn't always protect innocent children from bad men, left him with an ominous shadow inside. He had seen this shadow like a cloak over his own father. *Is he a bad man or a good man? Can a good man become a bad man? How can we protect ourselves from this bad man?* The confusion for Jim lay not only in the absence of answers about such questions, but in his subtle belief that this 'bad man' was no mere mortal; that this bad man knew things about children and could appear even in his own home. Children hear stories about 'bogey men' and ghosts but their fears dissolve as they grow up and realise that they are just frightening ideas. But to Jim this was something which he had felt and heard, and seen! He would keep this fear in his heart, for to speak about it would make it even more real, if that were possible.

Chapter 5
The Promised Land

In many ways a move away from Govan appealed to all in the McShane home. To Mary, it was the hope that a geographical change would mean an emotional and personal one in the way her family had been living. She hoped that it would be a change in her relationship with John and that they'd return to a happier time without hatred and fear. Maybe John would even calm his drinking down, now that he wouldn't be as close to his local pub and his drinking buddies. Behind his seeming indifference, John also had a small spark of hope and even the best intentions and the highest expectations. He imagined that when he got a new job he would be happy to finish the day by having a pint, then returning to a new warm home. He thought of his two boys running up the street to meet him (as opposed to hiding in the close when he came staggering up the street) and that he would be someone they were proud of- a symbol of strength and love to them. Surely, it was every father's dream to be the hero of his children, and the fear of failing this was a sick secret that crouched behind the door of every daddy's hope.

Jim and Joe wanted to move as well, even if it meant losing friends and being further away from their Granny's house. Deep within him Jim wanted to leave the terrors behind which he now associated with Govan, but in some strange ways he still felt bound to. And in Joe's heart he hoped that he would feel his family connecting again, that he would see his Da's touch as a tender hug to his Ma and his strength as loving protective arms, not as the hands of rage and destruction. He hoped that he would be able to come out from behind the anxiety which had crept into his soul. They truly wanted this; they didn't even know that this was what they wanted; they didn't know it in their minds and wouldn't have been able to tell anyone that this was what they desired. But their hearts knew and compelled them to grasp at some hope. So, with hidden anticipation and unconscious expectations they were glad to see the old blue transit van come spluttering and blasting round the corner to take their memories and their furniture away from Govan. Jim and Joe even broke off an intense moment of wrestling and darted to the window when Mary shouted to John. "That's Bertie here wi' that van…or is it an aeroplane? I couldnae work it out fae the noise". Mary even allowed herself a nervous smile, this nearly felt like a new start. "Aye awrite hen, I'll start gettin' the stuff into the van, you stick the kettle on for me and Bertie. Boys, you just play in your room just now and make sure that all your clothes and toys are in boxes ready to go."

There was warmth in John's voice which even Jim and Joe felt. Amongst all of his deep seated mistrust Jim glanced a glimpse of something in his Da's eyes which he hadn't seen for a long time-affection.

A few nosy neighbours were perched like nicotine addicted ravens at their open windows, curiously watching as if they'd never seen anyone move from this part of Govan. Of course, this wasn't the case, but to those who had accepted their lot and to whom the hope of real change had been long since abandoned, it always seemed a strange spectacle to them that someone would leave, actually believing that anywhere else in Glasgow offered anything different from the Wine Alley. In Glasgow schemes there was an overcast feeling which accompanied the dismal, grey clouds and settled on the minds of many of those living there. It was so prevalent and consistent that it was almost never questioned, never challenged. It was as if the cloud of oppression kept its inhabitants under the belief that this was normal, a subtle inescapable negativity which wasn't to be overcome but to be accepted, coped with and made the most of. To be fair, and in praise of the Scottish spirit, many of the people who lived under this oppressive gravity remained shining diamonds in the ebony night. The humour and love which many maintained in this place was incredible. It seemed to produce a tenderness and compassion in some which was encased in a hard exterior, necessary to cope and keep out the determined and insidious cloud. It was almost like a spirit of wartime, an affection and affiliation for those who found themselves in the same battle, fighting the same invisible enemies of thought and emotion on a daily basis. Many of these had lived through the Second World War and of even harder economic times than those living now found themselves in. Some had even, like Grampa McDermott, been born in the midst of World War One. What fears and love had been inherited from such atrocities could not be comprehended by the history books.

The feeling of forward motion and the street gradually disappearing from the windows of their blue van truly created a sense of leaving something behind. For this perfect moment they all really believed that life would be different now, as it surely would. Not only that, as John and Mary glanced into the back of the van to their two wee boys sitting on their mobile furniture, happy, carefree, it filled them with an elated feeling that different would be better.

Entering Corkerhill, their new scheme on the outskirts of Pollok, they weren't initially impressed, despite the fact that Bertie the driver was giving John and Mary what sounded like a local history of the origins of this place.

"You know this was built as a railway village after the Second World War, to house the workers for the railway depot just along the line there?" Bertie pointed with his chubby, sausage fingers along an old railway track, which ran the full length of the first street they had turned into.

"No, I didnae know that." John scanned the area like a curious, wild animal in a new territory, not making eye contact with Bertie as he continued to impart his knowledge to them.

"Aye, all they houses over there were lived in only by families of railway workers."

"Aye they're lovely wee houses they ones." Mary tried to sound interested so that the boys would have a positive first impression.

"But now they're filled wi' all sorts. They gi' these houses to anybody now. You'll probably find quite a lot of the families here originally come fae Govan, Kinning Park and the Gorbals."

John looked at Bertie with a sneering disdain and a speechless shake of the head for Bertie's lack of tact "Well, thanks for the history lesson Magnus, my specialist subject tonight will be pointin' out the fuckin' obvious!"

Although Mary smirked nervously at John's sarcasm and Bertie's bemused silent response, Joe and Jim felt an irritation in their Da's voice that they hoped had been left behind in Govan.

The boys got up from the old stripy chairs they'd been sitting on and looked through the windscreen at the towering grey tenements on either side. They were actually only four stories high but seemed huge to the boys compared to the two story tenements which they had left. Despite the dampness which seemed to stain the sides of the flat topped buildings, they had long red, green and blue verandas and the front doors of the residents of Corkerhill faced the open street, rather than the close type in the Wine Alley. The close was open for everyone to see the goings on of their neighbours as they stood chatting. The gardens were also a lot nicer looking, some with the grass and hedge trimmed for the wains to play in; there was even one with wee windmills, bridges and walls! It was bursting with rosy reds and brilliant whites, dotted with yellows and blues and lush with green. There were children of all ages littered through the street- mud spattered pre-teen girls playing with skipping ropes; a team of loud but jovial teenage boys kicking an old bladder ball high into the air and clambering over each other to header it when it descended; curious wee boys sitting at the side of the pavement with marbles or toy cars and wee wide-eyed girls with their mammy's high heels playing shops or cafes with neatly set out dolls and teacups. The dirty faces were free and happy ones and this place seemed to have a spirit, an atmosphere which was lighter and brighter. This first impression was a perception which the McShane family would try and hold onto, with both hands. Maybe this was the Promised Land that John and Mary had been searching for. To anyone staying in Corkerhill, the idea of it being likened to a promised land would either cause them to laugh with the absurdity or cry with pity for those who made this comparison. Yet to John and Mary, and even more to Jim and Joe, this was a place of hope and new beginning. Like the Promised Land for the ancient Hebrews, however, this was one which was going to be wrought with dangers, trials and battles before any real peace could be found.

Chapter 6
Pursued by Shame

Settling in to the new scheme, Corkerhill (or Hardridge, as it was known locally because of the name of the main street) was refreshing, despite the unfamiliarity of new neighbours, a new house and a new school for the boys. The boys were sent to a local primary, St. Edmonds, which sat beside the River Cart and led into Pollok Country Park. Not only was this an idyllic setting and a new built school which was open planned with many modern facilities, but it was completely carpeted! The boys couldn't believe it at first; the school carpets were nicer than the ones they had at home. All pupils had to take their shoes off and wear plimsolls, so as not to ruin the carpets. Luckily, Mary had been told this when she visited the school and had bought the boys new ones. It would have been deeply embarrassing to reveal their wet holy socks drenched from their leaky shoes. They had holes in their soles and were only allowed one pair of school shoes a year as Mary was given a government allowance for school clothes at the start of the term. The boys never questioned this as everyone in Govan was standing on holy ground with holy shoes and kids are oblivious to this being a reason for shame, until someone points it out.

After only a few days at his new school Joe overheard two girls giggling surreptitiously at something and when he asked what it was they confided in him, "See that boy Stuart? He's had the same socks on for three days... and they're wet and smelly cos he's got a hole in his shoes."

They laughed expecting Joe to join them in astonished mocking at such a degrading situation. To his shame and embarrassment Joe did laugh and pretended that his own socks hadn't been on for a few days and that his shoes were intact. This was the first time that Joe experienced shame from outside his home. This was a social convention, the false stuff which has to do with appearance and the judgements of others. What was normal to him was appalling to others from homes where they didn't need to hide their shoes, or sometimes put plastic bags inside them to stop their socks from getting wet! Joe didn't realise that his family were quite poor until he was aware of social snobbery. Joe now had something else to hide apart from his fears and sadness, a nameless shame which he didn't understand.

Mary was getting to know her neighbours and as Bertie had predicted, many of them were originally from Govan. The impression she was given about this scheme was mixed, depending on whom she spoke to. Betty, a kindly local community council worker, told her of the yearly Gala Day when the community came together and celebrated their area. They had floats with majorettes, dancers and people dressed up in weird and wonderful costumes, football and dancing competitions, demonstrations by the army and even bouncy castles and ice-cream vans to keep the kids happy. They even had a Gala Queen! A local girl, usually about thirteen years old would be picked and paraded about as the special princess for the day. Govan had its own fair too, which was much bigger and more well known in the Southside of Glasgow but for some reason this event seemed more intimate, perhaps due to the fact that the community was smaller and most faces were familiar.

Mary was also told by some more cynical (or realistic) neighbours of the growing problems with drugs and crime in the area. Many houses had been burgled and the local shops were broken into at least a couple of times a year. The local pub, 'The Cart,' named after the nearby river, also had its fair share of pollution and water rats. It wasn't nicknamed 'The Stab Inn' because of its cordial and welcoming customers. Hardridge was close to the larger area of Pollok which meant that many from other areas frequented the pub. This led to much trouble over the years, which Mary would discover in time.

For Jim and John there was a lengthy period of peace and stability in Hardridge. This was maybe due to the fact that they were in some ways similar in nature and would spend a long time surveying their new territory, keeping a low profile and remaining largely unseen. They both attempted to blend into their new environment and their new lives, genuinely trying to escape the ghosts of the past and to make this work. Jim went to school with Joe each day, keeping a watchful eye on his little brother and doing his best in school. The brothers had sharp minds and a thirst for learning in primary school, so they excelled quickly in most areas. They loved to learn and in particular reading as it was a realm of imagination and new information about all manner of things they didn't know about the world. Mary had been a great reader all her life but had seemed too distracted in recent years to concentrate on books; she had more pressing things taking up her mind and energy. This meant that Joe and Jim didn't read much at home, so they loved to read in class. Jim's teacher was a young female who was hippie looking, who wore long colourful dresses and large round earrings. Her name was Miss Currie and she looked like an exotic gypsy fortune teller, with sallow skin and sanguine eyes which sparkled with life. As she read Jim stories and attentively praised him for his 'great reading', she fanned a small flame in him- a zeal to know and a sense that there was so much more to life than his small perception of the world. Life felt good for Jim at this time and he glowed inside.

Joe's happiness showed itself in his dreams. It wasn't only the absence of nightmares and of waking up paralysed with terror during the night (a common experience for him), but he was actually having relatively happy dreams. He would dream of fearlessly climbing up, and then sliding down huge ice mountains with Jim on an old sledge, with great joy and exhilaration; of flying through strange worlds filled with beautiful but unusual creatures and atmospheres. He even dreamed one night that his family was actually The Fantastic Four from the Marvel comic books. This particular dream began with panic but seemed to end well. Joe was being chased by a huge brown bear at high speed and with much roaring and snarling by the bear, his emotion began to burn within. Much to his amazement he heard himself shouting, "Flame On!" and to his amazement he turned himself into the Human Torch. As he burned through the sky over his house, the bear pounding slowly in the distance to a defeated halt, he saw Jim in the street below with long stretchy arms like Mr. Fantastic, grabbing girls and throwing bricks at a boy who seemed to be tormenting them. As if this wasn't bizarre enough, as Joe flew down closer he could see that the bricks which Jim was throwing were falling from The Thing-brown rocks crumbling from his arms and head. The Thing looked up at Joe and its face resembled his Da's but was also different in some way, softer, kinder and faintly smiling. He was also throwing bricks, picking them from parts of his biceps and forearms and throwing them at Invisible Girl, who was darting behind cars and reappearing behind trees. As she reappeared Joe laughed as he realised it was his Ma, Fantastic Four Suit and everything, the whole set up. He shouted down,

"Ma, I'm over here, can you see me? Invisible Girl, I'm over here!"

Mary (or Invisible Girl) turned and smiled shouting,

"Watch out for the waterfall!"

Joe tried to turn round quickly as he heard the panic in her voice, but as he slapped into the towering wall of water he abruptly woke up, wet but happy. He had wet the bed again but for the first time didn't feel ashamed. Jim reminded him of the dream the following morning on the way to school.

"You shouted out 'Flame On' during the night and 'I'm over here Invisible Girl.' Whit was that all about?"

Joe exploded with a belly laugh and relayed his dream to Jim.

"You're mental wee man."

This simultaneously comforted and un-nerved Joe at the same time. He'd hold onto the comfort. John was also feeling quite pleased with himself that he'd same job for almost a year and had kept away from the Govan pubs long enough to have some clarity in his mind. John still felt very cautious about his life as if he was walking on a knife edge, always waiting for the moment when the storm would come and destroy all that he was trying to build. He hadn't ventured to the local pub yet and he didn't know why. He was still taking the occasional pint after work but he managed for a time to keep it under control, and away from his new unspoiled life. The restlessness inside him seemed to simmer for a time and he sat on a night and spent time with his boys, drawing dinosaurs on old wallpaper or kicking a ball about for half an hour on the grass verge outside. He also allowed his fondness for Mary to slowly emerge from behind his guilt and was grateful that she was there when he came home from work. There was no reason to suggest that this happy family life wouldn't last, other than an ominous feeling that there was an enemy watching them, crouching in cover like a bandit, waiting until an opportune moment.

Chapter 7
Who do you think you are?

As the primary school years unfolded for Joe and Jim, the threads of their home life began to unravel. They either seemed to ignore this or pretended that there was nothing wrong. In fact, the friendships which they had developed in the scheme and their impressions of their families, confirmed to them that alcoholism, violence and poverty were normal, they weren't words that were ever heard, but their reality was felt and unchallenged.

The old routines and patterns of drinking and fighting, followed by Mary weeping and silently despairing once again became the 'normal' lives for the McShane family. John became distant and somber; the boys rarely saw him and when they did they didn't want to. Once John decided to drink locally and the lie was again established in his mind that he was in control of the drinking, then his alcoholism accelerated. To most of Joe and Jim's friends there wasn't an obvious problem here as they were all living under similar circumstances. Men worked and went out and got drunk, always at the weekends, usually midweek and sometimes every day for months on end. Women worked even harder at home but didn't have the excuse or the warped sense of responsibility that a wage seemed to provide. It was apparently a man's right to drink and to forget his responsibilities to his family. So they told themselves. There were families who didn't have this lifestyle, but for whatever reason all of the boys which Joe and Jim gravitated towards had traces of violence and alcoholism in their lives. Some had even worse. Abuses and oppressions, sick spirits and malicious minds often spread like poisonous gases and slowly intoxicated the pure souls of innocent children.

The brothers and their friends learned to protect themselves from the fear and shame which lived in their homes. They all had their own ways of keeping the oppressive insanity and the dark depressions from cracking the walls of their minds, or at least trying to.

For Joe, he interpreted this abnormality as personal inadequacy and it filled him with nagging self-doubt. His most inner thought, his core belief, accused him that "there is something wrong with you". He couldn't see or understand that it was the situation that wasn't right. To be living in the constant threat of your Da smashing the house up or worse; to be hiding in the close because your Da, your desired hero, returned from the pub bouncing off every hedge in the street with urine soaked and ripped, blood stained trousers; to be living a constant lie to yourself and everyone around you, that you had a happy family and that you were in control of your own mind and emotions-this was the unquestioned existence.

Joe judged his own insides by other peoples' outsides.

Others around him never spoke about any feelings of falling apart or acknowledged any strangeness about their situation-they all seemed to be coping. Joe concluded that it must be he that was 'too sensitive' or he just felt ashamed of his fear. Without any conscious intention his reaction was to suppress all of these feelings and 'be brave'. He must never let anyone see that he was scared of anything. He must never show these fractured lines running through his fragile life. He must never let any sadness or depression seep out from behind the many masks which he would have to wear to feel safe. He would need so many different masks for so many different people. One for his home life to stay invisible and to please his parents, especially his Ma; one for his teachers to reinforce the illusion that he came from a happy home; one for his peers that he would be accepted and belong to them. This belonging was essential to have any roots and grounding in the 'real world', and to create a different world from the one which existed in his mind and emotion.

One way to establish popularity or gain recognition as a boy in Glasgow was through fighting. Joe had his first real fight in primary six, with a boy nicknamed Meeko, over nothing other than the need to establish who the best fighter was in his class. The boys burst into the fight with an explosion of energy and fists and after a few punches and kicks were exchanged they reached a stalemate of holding each other down by a two handed grip on the others' hair. Both boys had thick, dark brown curly hair so there was a lot to hold onto. They agreed to let go at the same time and since neither had lost any reputation in front of their classmates they were content to call it a draw. Meeko and Joe would have many fights over the next few years and it always seemed to end the same way. They were a good match and would also become great friends, like brothers even; they were similar in their slim, wiry athletic build which enabled them to employ violence to hide their secret fears. Joe realised that fighting enabled him to temporarily escape from his fear and it also had the benefit of gaining him respect from his peers, both male and female. He also felt a power in violence, the only place where he felt any sense of control in his life.

Jim also developed a propensity for violence, but seemed from the beginning to be drawn towards a more brutal and effective form, cutting out lengthy fights and disregarding consequences when he himself felt it was the right thing to do.

An incident to illustrate this point came in the form of a local bully named Richie Thomson. He was thirteen and his boy band blue eyes and blonde hair betrayed a cruelty of spirit which relished tormenting younger kids. He got away with it and his parents even seemed to approve of his behaviour, as they would disregard any complaints from neighbours accusing him of bullying. Like most bullies however, he picked on the wrong person one day, or perhaps it was the right person, depending on your perspective. Jim was the wrong person to bully and the right one to deal with such a character. Richie had been tormenting Joe and a couple of his friends, kicking their ball away and teasing them in front of a few local girls whom he wanted to impress. Joe never let on to Jim but he found out anyway, so Jim decided to join them the next time they played football when Richie was about. Now, although Jim was sturdy and muscular for an eleven year old, he was still small and unassuming in nature. He didn't appear aggressive and was quite quiet in manner. This drew Richie in to the trap as he scanned any possible opposition,

"Gi' us a kick of your ball wee man!"

Joe's pals felt the familiar shrinking feeling which Richie seemed to generate in them, but they had been told by Jim to ignore him and pass the ball to him when the moment came.

"Hey, gi' me the fuckin' ball a minute!" Richie's tone took no time to change to establish his superiority and impress the giggling girls hanging onto his arm and his reputation.

The second time he was ignored he had already decided that,

"One of these wee pricks is gonnae get a hidin'."

The freckly girls just laughed and anticipated a demonstration of Richie's dominance.

As he steadfastly made his way towards the small boy who was bending down casually tying his laces with the ball at his feet, his fist was clenched and his eyes filled with a mixture of rage and embarrassment.

"Hey, wee man! I told you to gi' me that fuckin' ball. Who do you think you are ya wee prick?"

When he was within striking distance he pulled back his right foot and arm to unleash a volley of punches and kicks on this 'wee prick'. Simultaneously, Jim took the large rock which he had hidden in his pocket and took a sharp, speedy step forward into Richie's space, smashing the brick on his clenched teeth. His mouth exploded with broken teeth and blood and he let out a yelp. Before he could gain his balance the brick came swiftly down and cracked the side of his skull. In two successive blows his confidence was shattered; the illusion of his superiority and intimidation were broken. Jim was poised to repeat the blows but as the bully looked up holding his head together, he knew by the pleading look on Richie's face that this was enough to end him. From this day on Richie never came near Joe or Jim or any of their friends for that matter. News of his humiliation and of Jim's willingness to 'go-ahead' and to use a weapon quickly spread. Jim wasn't seeking a reputation but the incident had provided an opportunity for him to unleash some of the rage he kept within and to exact a kind of personal justice, creating in him the feeling of satisfaction that some of the world's wrongs had been righted. Jim felt no remorse about his actions, for to him this was fear getting what it deserved-more fear. In his mind violence should reap more violence. He didn't consider for a second the fearful motivation behind Richie's aggressive persona. Nor could he see that his 'enemy' was himself a victim of paternal bullying. Why would he? How could he? His own teacher was violence, not truth. His vision was that of a child's.

For those pre-teen and teenage boys in a Glasgow housing scheme, who felt that life, the law and the adult world had nothing to offer them, there were many unsavoury elements which could bind them together. Violence and crime provided an identity when there seemed to be no other. Children's hearts are filled with an ocean of exploration waiting to be discovered, and there should be times of joy, excitement and a sense of wonder. The heart of every child knows this and for Joe, Jim and their friends this wasn't any less true. Their hearts and their lives were weighed down with so many clouds of despair which cast endless shadows of darkness over them. But their spirit refused to be extinguished, life within them was still bubbling like lava, waiting for its time to burst forth. For some, violence unfortunately provided a destructive channel for this burning emotion and the frustrated rage which simmered. Most of the friends whose lives were intertwined with Jim and Joe had the capacity for varying degrees of explosive and chaotic behaviour; such behaviour could not be contained by law, morality or authority. There was a rebellion in their hearts against everything which life had lashed out at them. Their lives were entangled by circumstances and geography, but over time their spirits were bound like brothers; fearing together, hating together and loving together in the only ways they knew how. What held them together they didn't even know-belonging, identification, humour, or even a mixture of love and fear? It didn't matter. They never thought about it or questioned it. They might have been labelled as 'a gang' and constantly reminded by those in authorities that 'they weren't good for each other'; all that mattered to them was that they weren't alone in this world. They could laugh and fight and discover themselves together, even if the law or life itself tried to get in the way. Together they would challenge it; together they believed they could overcome, maybe even leave a mark on the world; together they were as powerful as a storm-sons of thunder.

Part 2

Chapter 8
While we were Young

As Joe entered Secondary school, Jim, being a year ahead had already established himself as a sleeping dog you wouldn't want to prod. A couple of the older boys from other schemes (Pollok, Cardonald and Penilee) had discovered this, much to their displeasure. The result was usually Jim being suspended from school due to complaints of attacking or threatening other boys with a brick, a bottle, a stick or a classroom chair, depending on the availability of weapons at any given time.

Joe had also developed a propensity for fighting and a readiness to use it as a means of unleashing his rage and keeping his fears at bay. In both brothers there was also a secret pleasure in this as they were valued and 'respected' by their peers. This was something, unbeknown to them, which they craved; a secret substitute for the absence of self-esteem.

As well as fighting, Secondary school and the teenage years provided the boys with more pleasurable and exciting escapes, noticeably in the form of girls. Around the age of twelve or thirteen the pubescent teenager is a cauldron of emotion, desire and magnetic attraction. A new world awakens and the opinions of parents (and adults in general) become secondary, if not completely obsolete! This world is simultaneously exciting and terrifying; exciting in the emotion which it arouses and the pleasures which it promises, terrifying in its unfamiliarity and threat of humiliation. Joe and Jim were no different-no teeming Glasgow rain could put out this teenage fire!

When Joe arrived in First Year at Lourdes Academy he felt like a child in a sweet shop, but feared that he would only be allowed to choose from the penny tray-the one with all the rubbish sweets in it! He had a host of friends from the scheme, some who started at the same time as him and some who were a year or two older. So, he had both the safety of 'The Paka' (the name of his local gang) and Jim to back him up from any outside threat. Nevertheless, there were other fears now which required secret knowledge to overcome them and his friends were as oblivious as him, despite the apparent confidence of some. Boys from other schemes he didn't particularly fear; girls he didn't know were, however, another species which he hadn't a clue about. It seemed that everyone spoke about girls and sex and seemed to know more than him. Over time he realised that this 'seeming' was a pretense. Every teenager was clueless, except for those who had found the 'Holy Grail' of a young maiden who was willing to let a brave knight enter into her chamber, so to speak. Even unwitting relatives would draw attention to this lack of experience at family get-togethers. Joe and Jim had an old Auntie Lizzie, who would, without fail, always ask them in front of as many adults as possible,

"Are you winchin' yet son?"

Auntie Lizzie would scrunch up her wrinkled face and pat her white bun of hair as if it might fall off at any moment, expecting a detailed response to some private and mysterious aspect of their lives.

It took Joe about a month and some maneuvering twists in conversation to find out that 'winching' meant kissing with your mouth open. This lack of knowledge, and his first impression that winching had something to do with manual labour, evoked panic and left him feeling that there was some big secret that he wasn't in on. Despite his insecurities and sense of personal inadequacy, and much to his unawareness, Joe's spirit emanated a radiant smile and shone through his gentle sky-blue eyes, which caught the attention of many an explorative teenage girl. Yet, Joe was more than shy with girls and as much as he loved the attention of female admirers, and relished the physical affection when they played with his dark wavy hair, saying,

"I wish I had hair like that", he was caught between sexual desire and fear of anyone finding out who he really was.

What if they find out what my hoose is really like?

What if they saw past his bravado with other boys and realised how constantly vulnerable he felt? What if the people pleasing mask slipped and the rage or fragility of his emotions were exposed? This was the struggle which Joe had to contend with. He was by no means alone with such conflict-to some extent every teenager had similar fears. But he didn't know this. Everyone else emitted confidence and knowledge. Once again Joe felt confused- but love (or desire) would conquer…or at least give it a really good try; he had to.

The first time Joe was properly asked out, through the mediation of 'wee Katie McGloin' who lived across the road, was with the very direct and common adolescent communication that,

"My pal fancies you, by the way. Will you get aff wi her."

Knowing that 'Get aff' (or 'get off' if you were posh), was synonymous with winching, Joe had a good look at aforementioned pal of Katie. It didn't take him long to come to a decision. Marie Holden, the girl next close (Glasgow's version of the girl next door), was, to Joe's wondrous eyes, "absolutely gorgeous". She had shoulder length and silky smooth auburn hair, stunning ocean blue eyes and a delicately formed pair of rosy lips. Her high cheek bones and petite figure could hardly contain her exuberant spirit. Joe had known her a little from primary school and had always found her a joy to be with, full of life and laughter. She had always given him attention and seemed interested in him at school. Up until now she had been 'that nice lassie that stays in the next close'. Now she had become 'that really, really, nice lassie that stays in the next close'.

Joe's immediate answer was "aye awrite" despite the mixture of trepidation and adrenaline in his body. He also added, without really asking Katie or his brother, "Me and Jim will meet youse the night at the chippy… at 7 o'clock?"

Katie and Jim agreed. It was a date.

When they met at DeMarco's chippy that night it was a mild summer's evening (about seven degrees in Scotland), so they walked about the scheme talking, laughing and pretending to themselves that they weren't flirting. It was great! The boys even treated them to a roll and chips, a local delicacy of a Glasgow scheme. Joe was mesmerised by Marie, every little detail of her physicality and personality excited some new emotion in him. The way she stuck her bottom lip up to blow her fringe from her eyes; the way she tucked her hair behind her ears and bowed her head slightly to the left, whenever she was pleasantly embarrassed at

Joe's obvious expressions of fondness; the depth of emotion in her laughter at Joe's crazy antics and the vibrancy of her communication when she pounced onto some detail of the conversation, all left him feeling that this girl was without fault. She was perfect. Life was perfect. Well, for two hours of this night, while he was with Marie. At around 9.00p.m., half an hour before Joe and Jim had to go home, they both knew that the time to make a move was now. Joe was glad that Jim was there and bold enough to lead the way. For the longest three seconds in the world his words hung heavy in the air,

"D'you want to go in the back close?"

Katie and Marie glanced at each other and smiled knowingly.

"Aye, awrite then, but nae hands." Katie was as eager to experiment as the boys but girls weren't allowed to admit this.

"Of course, we're a couple a right gentlemen us two in't we Joe?"

"O aye, I could tell that when you bought us a roll 'n' chips." Katie gave a fond smile to Joe who couldn't say anything for the nervous giggling rising up from his belly.

"Right, c'mon then." Jim took Katie's hand and led the way into the mysterious darkness of the back close.

"O, there's an offer I cannae refuse." Katie mimicked Jim's decisiveness, 'Right, c'mon then'."

Marie and Joe followed holding hands and shyly smiling at each other. To Joe, Marie's hand felt like it was filled with a strange, pleasurable electric sensation, tingling with a mixture of sensual touch and rushing adrenaline, lighting up his whole being. He felt a fire rush through his body as if he could 'flame on', like Johnny from the Fantastic Four. This was the first time he'd ever held a girl's hand, the first moment of sensual, sexual pleasure. It was quite overwhelming, like being carried along by a huge tidal wave. He was just hoping that he wouldn't spontaneously combust from within, or in any other way.

Marie was also feeling really happy as she'd had her eye on Joe for a long time. And although she'd kissed a boy once before, it was never one that she'd felt such a fondness for.

In the dimness of the back close, Joe tried to keep his eyes on Jim to follow his lead. He could see the silhouette of Katie's straight brown hair and embracing arms and despite the lack of light he was sure he could see a glint in Jim's eyes. For a moment Joe felt the shadow of his fears trying to envelop and paralyse him, until Marie drew him gently towards herself with both hands around his waist. He sighed an inner relief and placed his right hand on her waist, embracing her closer with his left. Before he leaned forward to kiss Marie, he quickly glanced sideways at Jim and Katie to see the strange sight of their faces, interlocked in a slow circular motion which bizarrely reminded him of a washing machine beginning its cycle. The terror of the unknown gripped his heart. He didn't know what to do. He'd never kissed a girl before. What if he did it wrong? What if they laughed at him? What if they told everybody? He'd be humiliated. For a second he wished he wasn't there, especially with a 'more experienced' thirteen year old couple who seemed to have, as it were, a heads up. As the flood of emotion began to make him dizzy with nerves, Marie sensed his panic and took his face in her hand and kissed him. Her lips closed, placed gently on his, instantly stilled his panic and restored a calming joy to his heart. With a new confidence he returned her kiss, still with lips closed and cautious of moving into full *winching* position. Before he or Marie could take the proceedings further, the moment was interrupted by Katie's complaint,

"I said nae hands… it's like gettin' aff wi' a bloody octopus."

Jim slightly embarrassed but determined nevertheless, in the close proximity could be heard whispering,

"How no, that's whit you dae. I'm just puttin' my hand on your bum"

"Well, no the night it's not Mr.Fantastic. Keep they wanderin' arms to yourself!"

Joe and Marie held each other and giggled, knowing that today's events were sadly drawing to a close. Yet, they were both content and glowed with joy at their new found romance. This was the start of something beautiful and lasting, they were sure of it.

As Jim had led the way in to the darkness so it only seemed right that he would bring it to a satisfying close,

"We better go up the road Joe, before my Da gets in fae…work."

With romance brought sharply back to reality, Joe quickly agreed.

"Aye, awrite, will I see you the morra Marie?"

"Aye, we'll see youse tomorrow. I'll come up for you."

"Eh…no…I'll meet you at the swing park about seven."

"Ok, nae bother."

The brothers left the girls chatting in the close , Joe peered round to see Marie's admiring smile watching him walk away while Katie let Jim know that his attempts to further his quest hadn't blown it, shouting,

"Will you be there as well Jim? Will I come wi' Marie?"

"Aye, of course. We'll see youse the morra."

Jim was trying to play it cool but excitedly hoped that Katie's heart, and other parts of her anatomy, would be conquered in due course. He beamed at Joe,

"We're in wee man."

Joe beamed back, saying nothing. He was full of admiration for Jim, for his protective shadow. It was fantastic to have a big brother, sometimes.

"I'll race you hame." Jim sprinted as he said this and Joe followed on his heels.

As the brothers arrived at the front of their close and stopped to catch a breath, they looked up to their house to see a bottle of HP brown sauce, aptly called 'Daddy's', smashing through the kitchen window. This was followed by a full plate of what looked like mince and potatoes, although this was more of an assumption than an observation, based on what the boys had for dinner. The roar of John's rage accompanied the airborne meal. He obviously wasn't happy with the service. Mary couldn't do anything right these days, so John was always telling her.

"No wonder I fuckin' drink…havin' to look at your disgruntled face."

His best line of defence was attack. Before any conversation arose about his lack of time with the *wains,* his drinking or any other number of responsibilities he was ignoring, he would lash out at Mary, sometimes verbally.

Jim rushed up the stairs, in the hope that he would get in the way. Joe followed him, vainly trying to be invisible and wishing that his Ma would suddenly be endowed with this power too. Joe had learned by now to pretend to himself that this wasn't really his Da. He told himself that some other 'Thing' had taken his Da hostage and took his place.

This was the only reality he could cope with. He remembered his dream.

Chapter 9
The very 'Young Paka'

Joe and Jim had always been friendly with a host of boys from the street, some they went to school with and others who were just 'fae the scheme'. Corkerhill was a close knit community which was partly due to the fact that there were only three streets, closely compacted together in a relatively small area, and also because many of the families shared a similar social inheritance: deprivation in its various forms. As Bertie had pointed out on their arrival three years ago, this was originally a village built for the railway workers. Not many of the houses belonged to railway workers now, but the local railway depot provided endless amounts of mischief for wayward teenage boys.

There was an abandoned derelict railway signal house, previously used to assess the lights and tracks, which was referred to by the local boys as 'Corky No.2'. It had a black roof and white walls, made almost completely of large oak beams as its structure and long timber panels for its exterior walls. The brothers and their friends would often break in through one of the damp rotten panels and climb up to the second level, into a room filled with switches and wires. There were large windows at three sides used by the railway engineers to examine the lights, the tracks and the trains as they came from the nearby depot, only half a mile along the track.

There wasn't much to do here now, other than swing from the beams and smash the windows, but it was the thrill of being in a place which was out of bounds. Each of the boys seemed to harbour a kind of rebellious freedom and contempt for the law, without really knowing why. The Railway Police, in particular, were both feared and hated because the boys knew that if they were caught they would be simultaneously slapped about, whilst being given a lecture on appropriate moral behaviour! Something didn't add up but they were certain that this kind of abusive authority was not to be submitted to, certainly not in their hearts and minds.

The first time Joe was caught in Corky No.2, he experienced the long arm and back hand of the law, unfortunately not for the last time. Joe and Jim broke into the old railway house on the night of their arranged second date with Marie and Katie. Not the smartest idea they ever had!

About 6 o'clock, with an hour and some restlessness to kill, they met with their closest friends, who considered themselves part of a small gang 'The Young Paka' as they had been known for many years. There were also an older bunch of teenagers from Hardridge who resembled a more identifiable gang as they had been initiated into various acts of clan violence with other gangs from different schemes. This was commonplace in inner cities and the very 'Young Paka' was yet to discover this fully. Their particular clique included a trio they liked to call the 'Three Amigos': Meeko (his curly brown hair, freckled face and cheeky smile was brightened with gentle blue eyes which hid a bitter resentment towards life, although usually seemed to exclude his closest friends), Craigo (his Scandinavian looks-blonde hair, light-green eyes, thick lips and cherubic face belied his sharp mind and wit) and Gringo(who resembled a Mexican bandit with small piercing eyes and the adolescent traces of a fluff, blonde moustache, framed by immaculately straight dirty-blonde hair)- thus uniting the amigos . There was also Big Mooney (aptly named because he always seemed as if he was on another planet).Mooney was always a head bigger than the others and his face was as open as the universe. His wide, questioning eyes and his disjointed nose, broken in two places, struggled and strained to keep his gravity free mind from floating into the ether. Mooney seldom felt relaxed or at ease as he continually resisted the feeling of being a stranger on earth when amongst 'normal' people. With the McShane brothers and the Amigos, however, he sensed that 'normality' couldn't begin to describe their existence, so when he was with them he had a measure of identification and belonging. There were many others whom they associated with from time to time, an endless array of passing souls and intermingling lives, but the brotherly bond which existed was never as fully formed as with this mutinous tribe. Their fates were enmeshed in each other's. In their school photograph these boys looked angelic; they looked innocent but naïve they were not.

The boys were only just in and hadn't even the time to smash a window when Meeko shouted,

"There's the polis!" as he jumped for cover onto the level below.

Disastrously however, as he landed on the beam below, (the ground level being the only way out) he stood on a four inch nail which forced straight through his flimsy tattered trainers, pierced the soft skin of his sole and protruded from the top of his foot. His mouth opened like a cave and he tried to scream-nothing came out but silent agony. He just stared at the nail, eyes, mouth and whole face wide with shock and as the blood pouring from his foot drew the redness from his face, he fainted.
Joe was the only one who had noticed Meeko, as all of the boys had dangled like frantic chimpanzees, two levels to the ground below. Joe's mind raced as he watched the rest of the gang make their way along the railway track pursued by two burly railway police officers. He couldn't leave Meeko, but knew that he might get caught. His Da would kill him, hopefully not literally but he worried it might not be far off it. He lowered himself down to Meeko's level and tried to wake him, whispering, "Meeko, are you awrite mate?" He knew the stupidity of the question as it left his mouth but he didn't know what else to say.
Meeko had a four inch nail, which had broken from the damp beam, now lodged in his foot. It was excruciating. The pain was no longer sharp but a throbbing dullness. There was blood but not as much as you might expect. Joe asked again and as Meeko groggily came back to consciousness, sarcasm still intact, he replied,
"Aye, I'm brilliant, thanks for askin'…fuck…! You need to get me to my Ma or the hospital Joe."
The moment took on a profound quietness and even though it was only his foot, Joe was gripped with an eerie dread. A premonition of blood and fear and death rushed through his heart like a violent ghost. A cry slipped from Meeko's voice, but he refrained when he heard the voice of the law.
"There are still a couple of them in there George."
The boys sat silently staring at each other hoping that the police were bluffing.
"Right youse, we know you're in there! You better come out .If we've got to come in there we're gonnae kick your arses!"
Meeko and Joe panicked inside but tried, like a couple of losing poker players, to ride out the bluff.
"Ok George, just send the dogs in. If they bite them it's their own fault."

As Joe stood up on the beam, tiptoeing slowly to get a better look and to see if they actually had dogs with them, a large hand tightly gripped his ankle from the ground below,

"Got you ya wee bastard!"

He was pulled down from the beam and his arse was duly kicked. This was accompanied by a couple of slaps across the back of the head.

"How many of your pals are in there?"

"It was jist me…" Joe tried not to grass on Meeko, the Golden Rule in a scheme, but his lies were interrupted by his pal's cry for help,

"I'm here…I've stood on a nail and I cannae get down."

"Oh, that's strange, you thought you were up there all alone and you didnae even know that your pal was there to hold your hand. Lying wee shite." Another slap was applied like a painful full stop, ending the night's conversation with the law until they arrived at Pollok police station.

Meeko was taken to hospital by the railway police and Joe was charged with breaking and entering and vandalism. He was only twelve. He was scared. To his surprise, the police at the station were actually relatively kind, and simply went through the formalities of taking his details before placing him in a cell and telling him that his parents would be called to come and collect him. They had obviously been through this routine a million times before. One of them even stared at him sympathetically shaking his head and gently warned,

"Learn your lesson from this son…it'll lead you down a dark path if you carry on like this. You'll cause your Mammy grief and heartache… Worse things might happen to you."

To Joe this didn't seem like the usual lecture from authority, but a genuine, kindly wisdom which he wanted to accept and take to heart, but he couldn't. There was no room, for his heart and memories were still full of injustice and blame. As he sat in the police cell for the first time, wondering about the names scratched into the cold walls and pondering how old they were when they wrote them, he felt lost and alone. He worried about how his Ma would react; she'd be angry, but really heartbroken. He had let her down and he felt ashamed. He couldn't care less about his Da's reaction. He was scared about getting a hiding, but he told himself his Da didn't care about him so why should he care? He knew his Da was only concerned about his next drink and that he never gave them attention these days except to bark orders. Maybe if it was Mary who came to the police station she wouldn't tell him. Would it make a difference if she told him or not?

Why should I listen to anything that my Da said?

As Joe's resentment spun in his head like a whirlwind, a small tornado gathering momentum and indiscriminately scooping all trust and goodness from his heart, it was stilled by the gruff but gentle voice of the old 'friendly' police officer,

"Right son… time to go… your mammy's here."

Joe got up, glad to be going home, yet with a subtle bitterness at life, at himself and even at his parents, especially his Da, festering in him like a toxic disease. His shame was turning to anger. When he saw his Ma he didn't know if the look on her face was relief that he was alright (as she'd had a phone call from Meeko's Ma), or a weariness in her eyes that here was the city's darkness beginning to steal her children. She felt like it was all too much. Boys needed an approving and guiding father as well as an affectionate Mother. She had no control over the boys when they were outside, just as she had no control over John's drinking. She had in the last few months, lectured, scolded and even resorted to lashing out at her boys, but they seemed to look blankly at her, longing for another solution.

The whole bus journey on the way home was filled with sadness and silence. Mary stared out of the window and had nothing to say, this hurt Joe more than any words or belt. He would try and be better, a good boy, not the disappointment that he believed he obviously was.

Chapter 10
Freedom and Temptation

When he woke up the following morning the first thing on Joe's mind was Marie. He wondered if she'd still want to see him or whether she'd even be talking to him. Mary hadn't told John what happened and hadn't said a word to Joe other than, "Brush your teeth and go to bed Joseph."

He knew she was disappointed and these days she only called him Joseph when she was angry, but she didn't look angry. She looked tired and weary, like she was ready to give up on him. He quickly pushed that thought from his head and jumped out of bed. He'd get ready and go to Marie's house to try and explain. He would fix the relationship with Marie and then with his Ma. He'd do the dishes every night and even clean the cooker when it was his turn. He was going to turn over a new leaf. His spirit lifted as his ambitions and plans filled his mind.

He made a couple of slices of toast and was about to take them out the door with him when Mary appeared from the living room and asked,

"Where do you think you're goin?"

"I'm just goin' out to play wi' my pals."

"No you're not. You're in for a week. No telly, no sweets and no pals."

Joe felt angry and knew the punishment was fair but he still couldn't accept it. It was the summer holidays and he'd be back to school in two weeks. He wouldn't get the chance to explain to Marie. He was going to make it up to his Ma and take away her disappointment. His guilty frustration erupted and angry tears trickled out,

"I said I was sorry…it's the summer holidays."

"Well, you should have thought of that when you were bloody vandalisin' and breakin' into places last night!" Mary's anger began to rise at Joe and it exhausted her. She left the room as he threw his toast on the floor and turned away from her.

"And you'll pick that toast up too. Think yourself lucky I didnae tell your Da last night." Mary knew she had to be strong but still felt an overwhelming dread that she was losing Joe.

Joe went to his room and tore the sheets from his bed, punching and lashing at the

54

pillow as viciously as he could. Jim woke up, startled at Joe's outburst.

"Hey, calm doon Joe. Whit's wrang?"

Joe sat on the edge of the bed, "Ma's no lettin' me out for a week."

Jim stared at the floor; there was nothing he could say to make Joe feel better. Then he remembered some beam of joy from the night before,

"I felt Katie's arse last night."

"Did you!? You're jammy…was Marie there?" Joe perked up a little.

"No' while I was feelin' Katie's arse."

"You know whit I mean…did you tell her whit happened?"

"Aye, she was there when we met. I told her. She was on a bit of a downer after that. She went hame early." Jim didn't mention his delight at Marie's departure, knowing it would come out wrong.

As Joe sat brooding over his stupidity from the night before, wondering whether he'd blown his chances with Marie, Jim jumped up and got himself ready,

"I'll see you later. I'm meetin' Katie and goin' up the Big Hill…for a walk." Jim's excitement, although contained, was easy for Joe to decode, as the Big Hill (actually a small hill behind the scheme which led into Pollok Park) was the place where a teenage boy would take a girl for privacy. Not a lot of walking was required.

The week ahead was torture for Joe, well at least the first five days. He would slump down on the couch and skulk his way to the living room window, looking out like a lifer who had been unjustly sentenced, staring into the freedom beyond. He was unconsciously trying to wear Mary out and although she tried to pretend it wasn't bothering her… it was. She had enough sadness and anguish in her heart without Joe's cloud of despair filling the atmosphere. After five days of sighing, slumbering and slouching Mary couldn't take Joe's agitation any more,

"Right Joe, you can go out, since it's Friday night. But I'm tellin' you, stay out of trouble. The next time I'll be tellin' your Da."

Joe's face and his heart lit up,

"Thanks Ma."

He ran into his room, quickly threw on his trainers and bolted out of the door; he didn't want to risk the chance of Mary changing her mind. Mary didn't even get the chance to tell him to get his jacket on, but a tiny ray of joy pierced her heart as she watched him from the window. He ran until completely out of sight. She loved her boys, but wondered why this thought made her sad. The subtle stream of joy stopped as she felt the rock of failure damming her heart. Her thoughts weren't clearly laid out but she had a heavy sense that she should be doing more to help her boys, to nurture them, to help them become free to live their lives. Joe had burst free from the house like a rabbit unleashed from a trap. Why then did Mary feel that the trap still lay ahead and there was no way of stopping it? This ominous intuition had followed her from Govan and its roots seemed embedded within her home.

This melancholy reflection was unbearable. Mary sat on her chair, turned on the gas fire, switched the telly onto Coronation Street, picked up her knitting and placed her book on the arm of the chair, resolving to have a 'relaxing' night. The boys were always amazed that Mary could knit, read a book and watch the telly at the same time. For Mary it was the only way she could distract herself from the restlessness within her. The boys were proud of Mary but they didn't know it, and certainly didn't show it as teenagers. They knew she was coping with a lot and unlike John she was there for them. This was love, but it was never spoken. Like many Glasgow homes there was this enduring love but an inability or inheritance not to say it to children beyond the primary years, especially to boys. Occasionally drunk Daddies could say it to their wee girls, but very seldom to their growing boys. The only emotion boys were allowed to have and still be considered masculine was anger. Sadness, fear and the need for a mother's affection and a father's approval were frowned upon. For many this anger became an identity, the only foundation for personal power.

As Mary got up to make a cup of tea during the adverts, John came swaying and staggering in the front door. At least the boys weren't in. She could smell the reek of whisky and rage creeping up the hall like toxic waste. She tried to maintain some courtesy, "Do you want a cup of tea?" but it was swiftly demolished,

"No, I want my fuckin' dinner. Is that no' what a wife's supposed to do for her husband when he comes hame fae work?"

She knew she shouldn't have said it and knew that it was only going to cause an eruption, but maybe she wanted it over and done with. The anticipation of rage unleashed was as bad, if not worse than the outburst,

"Hame fae work? You look as if you've had a few hours in the pub?"

"So fuck! What if I have? I need a drink so that I can put up wi' your fuckin' moanin'!"

John didn't need a new excuse; the old one seemed to work just fine. Mary always fell into the trap no matter how much she prepared her mind to avoid it. The pattern of conversation played itself out like an old broken record,

"Have you got any of your wages left?"

Mary didn't know the exact response but she knew the answer wouldn't be 'Aye certainly, here you are dear.'

"That's all you care about eh? Fuckin' money!"

John could keep this up all night. The mutual unleashing of resentment and blame was exactly what his alcoholic stupor needed.

Mary couldn't keep it up; she was ground down, silenced and defeated. There was no rational conversation about responsibilities, only blame and hate. This particular argument ended like most of the others, broken glass and Mary on her knees, trying to clean away the mess before the boys got home.

John sat silently, slurping like a savage, drunkenly wolfing a chicken drumstick. Mary only glanced at him once more this evening; it frightened her. Like Joe had once noticed, she saw that this man before her wasn't John, but some deformity of him. Like the strange case of Dr.Jekyll and Mr.Hyde, here was a man transformed before her- all trace of the soul that once resided there completely hidden. Mary found herself wondering whether it was not absent entirely.

Unfortunately for Mary, a few chicken drumsticks wouldn't satisfy the restless rage.

Later on that night, when she heard Joe and Jim laughing and jostling through the front door, her heart sank. Not for herself but for what they were walking into. Joe sensed the atmosphere as soon as he walked in the door; Jim's armour also descended on his mind. The eerie silence crept up on them, having no trace of peace, despite the absence of noise in the house. Mary was sitting in the living room, eyes red and cheeks bruised blue.

"You awrite Ma?" Joe was worried.

"Aye son…I tripped and fell over that table."

The crack in the coffee table and the cup smashed on the floor didn't reinforce the lie, but this was the routine.

"Just go to your bed eh…I'm tired."

Something had changed in Mary's voice, a calm that unnerved the boys. They knew not to push the conversation but Jim added,

"Can we make a bit of toast Ma…I'm starvin'?"

Mary glanced with a despairing love,

"Aye, just get some, then go to bed, pal."

Mary hadn't called Jim 'pal' for years, so when she added,

"I love you boys…don't ever forget that", her lip trembling, they were really scared. The boys didn't know how to respond but just stood there for a minute. They looked awkwardly at each other then Joe walked over, Jim following, and each laid an unfamiliar hand on her weary shoulders. Mary wept.

"I'm ok boys, go 'n' get your toast before your Da gets back up."

When the boys were in the kitchen having their toast John woke up from his stupor and growled,

"Get to your bed!"

"My ma said we could have some toast." There was a pleading in Joe's voice, hoping to be left alone, as he noticed the sharp hatred in John's stare.

"Hurry up then."

Jim didn't make eye contact as he knew that he would become the target, but when John turned away he saw the shadow he'd seen before. His Da seemed to be carried by it, controlled by it.

The boys went to bed relieved that they'd got there unscathed. Yet, they knew something had changed, something was different in Mary. From their beds they could hear their Da provoking and berating Mary but there was no response from her, other than a lowly pleading in her tone,

"I can't take this anymore. Just leave us alone."

Eventually, Joe fell into a worried sleep and Jim's mind tightened with anger, looking for an escape from this problem and unable to see one. It was oppressive to him and the rage grew within him. Jim knew that if he allowed himself to be sad he wouldn't survive, so violent thoughts surrounded his heart like a fortress.

John eventually drank himself to sleep and Jim's angry thoughts exhausted him into an irritable unconsciousness.

Mary sat, once again in a cloud of despair. Yet, this time there was no anxiety. The dark shadow hijacked her thoughts and began to offer her a way out of this situation. She had asked John to leave and he wouldn't go. She knew that he would never stop drinking and that things would only get worse for them… unless there was some big change. What would happen to the boys if she wasn't here anymore? Would they be better off without her, without living in this chaos? *Maybe a care home would be better for them, away from John, from his violence and his drinking? At least they'd be sure of food and shelter. They might even be fostered out to a caring family.* This was all she wanted: for her boys to be ok. Her own life didn't matter now. *Things couldn't be worse than they are now if she wasn't here anymore, could they?*

It saddened her to think of her boys missing her, but it seemed like the only way out. This was the train of Mary's thoughts which carried her into the kitchen cupboard, where she kept the paracetamol and other pills. She was still in an almost hypnotic calm when she took the two bottles of aspirin from the shelf and a bottle of antidepressants, which she'd asked the doctor for a while ago but couldn't bring herself to take. Time took on a surreal quality now for Mary, as she took a bowl and poured the pills in as simply as she would have poured a bowl of cereal. Filling a glass of water, sitting at the kitchen table, she paused with the first handful of pills in her hand. Despite her feeling that God (if he even existed) had abandoned her, watching her coldly from a distance, she turned her thoughts to Him…for the last time on this Earth, or Hell. Her broken spirit prayed,

"God…" She cried. "If you're there and you can hear me, forgive me for whit I'm gonnae do."

She was breaking inside, words and sadness trickling through the fragments of her heart.

"Please…take care of my boys. Save them from all this mess. Gi' them a life that's better than this…please." Even a thought of compassion for John flickered like a smouldering wick, "Help John as well, he disnae see whit he's doin'."

As Mary tried to swallow a handful of pills, memories and images of her boys flitted through her mind in rapid succession-their births, their first time walking, their humorous boyish antics with each other, and their gentle smiles and the light in their eyes. The pain was too much, more pills were needed faster. She grabbed another handful but as she reached her mouth a shrill scream came from Joe's bed,

"Ma! Ma! Don't…"

He was having a nightmare.

Mary shot out of her own semi-conscious nightmare and ran into the room. Joe was still in the middle of his terror and he shrieked repeatedly,

 "Ma! Ma! Don't…"

Mary held him tightly,

 "It's ok son, I'm here. Joe it's awrite pal, it's jist a bad dream"

As Joe drifted back to reality, his heart reduced its pounding,

"I was dreamin' that you thought you could fly and I knew you couldnae…you were at the edge of a cliff…I tried to shout but you couldnae hear me. I started runnin' and my leg snapped. I was lyin' on the ground screamin'."

"Ssh…it's awrite…it was jist a dream."

Mary sat holding Joe for a few minutes until his breathing was normal and he was almost asleep again. He might have been twelve but he was still her wee boy. With a stroke of his forehead she left him to get some rest.

Mary returned to the kitchen and put the pills back in the bottle. She sat at the kitchen table strangely bewildered at her previous thoughts and how locked into them she had felt, and also how quickly she was snapped out of them. Mary had been stopped from taking her own life, but she still knew that she couldn't stay in the same house as John anymore. He wouldn't leave so she had to. As her boys slept she packed a bag and decided to leave for a few days, to sort out her thinking. Once again she'd ask her Ma to see to the boys over the next few days. She left a note for

John to send Jim and Joe to Granny McDermott's in the morning, and told him she'd phone in the next few days. She told no-one where she was going.

She went to Buchanan bus Station and got on the first bus out of Glasgow. It happened to be an overnight bus to Blackpool. Not exactly an exotic location to run away to, she thought, but it wasn't too far away from her boys and it was far enough from John, for now.

The boys woke in the morning to a sullen John and to Mary's noticeable absence. John told them she was gone and that he didn't know where she was or whether she was coming back. They both felt simultaneously angry and abandoned, yet their responses differed-Joe felt an emptiness which caused him to rush out the door, slamming it as he went; Jim felt a bitter pain reinforcing the ramparts of his heart as he calmly turned into his room and locked out the world. Joe was out of control and Jim felt that control was all he had. Both were trapped by this control and in the coming days and months it would reveal its grip on their lives.

Strangely, even to him, Joe found himself running to the chapel, perhaps because he knew it was a place he could go and get some peace and quiet or more probably as he knew no one would look for him there. As he entered the echoing emptiness he couldn't quite grasp whether the stillness made him feel safe or scared. He sat in the back pew with eyes closed as if this would shut out the screeching in his head. Agitated and unable to find any calm to his thoughts, he noticed that there were two old women sitting side by side in prayerful silence a few pews in front of him. As he wondered whether they had just received some devastating news as well or why they were here at all when there wasn't a mass on, a door opened directly beside them and a frail old man came out and nodded to them. He immediately stared at Joe with what seemed like threat or suspicion however, as if Joe had no place to be there, but he said nothing and began fumbling into the pew behind the old ladies. He glared questioningly at Joe once more and knelt down, whispering to himself. When the old lady nearest the door made her way through and into the adjacent mysterious room, Joe realised that it was a confessional room. The priest was in here receiving the confessions of the conscience stricken parishioners and offering them solace from the stain of guilt by means of disclosure and penance. He remembered how in primary school he had occasionally sneaked into the chapel for confession and found at least some peace of mind from the shame eating away at his well-being. Maybe he'd find some comfort in it now.

Joe waited until the second old lady had gone in and came out, and then he made his way into the confessional. The small room was dimly lit and smelled of old people; it had nothing but a chair and a stool for kneeling, and the meshed opening between this and the adjoining room where the priest sat. Although Joe had always been reassured of the privacy and anonymity of the confessional he couldn't shake off the fear of critical, glaring eyes as he entered and sat on the chair.

"Forgive me father, for I have sinned it's been…em, quite a while…em, a few year, since my last confession."

Joe waited for a response but there was none.

"Em… I've done quite a few things since the last time I was here…"

Joe felt a laugh nervously rising up but he quickly swallowed it as he realised it probably wouldn't lighten the mood.

"Em…I swore at my Ma, em… just once and I've been gettin' into trouble at school and wi' the polis."

Joe sighed in preparation for a lengthy list as the door of his conscience tentatively opened. However, before he even got through the first section of the list, 'stealing and lies', the deep authority of Father Wilkinson's voice cut Joe's confession with an accusing question,

"When was the last time you were at Mass?"

When Joe realised it was Father Wilkinson, that dark tower of a man whose smile never reassured him, he cowered,

"I've no' been to Mass for a couple of year Father."

"A COUPLE OF YEARS!" the priest blasted and his anger shook the whole room. God was obviously big on the whole 'going to mass' thing, although didn't seem too upset about the stealing, lying, abuse to parents and general rebellion towards life.

"I can't believe…" the priest began a tirade of condemnation and criticism and was barely started before Joe managed to quell his storm with two simple words.

"Fuck off!"

Joe simply got up and walked out. He'd had enough. He was afraid of Father Wilkinson which was apparently the desired reaction that he was looking for, but he slammed the door on the priest and the church. Wilkinson came out of the confessional with the imagined wrath of his God steaming from his ears and snorting from his nostrils, but it wasn't Joe's God anymore.

"Come back here!"

Joe reiterated his advice to the priest,

"Fuck off!"

Joe looked back once with hateful rebellion and never looked back again. He hadn't rejected a belief in a creator but wouldn't bow down to the one represented here, a Monster God in the face of an angry, frustrated, grey haired, middle aged man- who smiled for faithful parishioners and frowned on the 'sinner'.

Chapter 11
Separation

After two days of staring wistfully into the sea and feeling lost in melancholy on Blackpool Pier, Mary phoned John. He wasn't happy, but she wasn't going back to what she'd left.

"Hello…John…it's me." Mary anticipated anger but there was only a brooding silence.

"Oh, decided to remember your family did you? Where the hell are you, and when are you comin' back here?" John knew that guilt was all he had to bring her back.

Mary gathered enough strength in her to keep her resolve,

"I'm no comin' back unless you leave John. I cannae take any more of your drinkin' and your hate. I think my jaw was cracked… again. Just leave me and the boys alone."

Mary expected a verbal lashing but none came. She didn't know whether John's silence was the sound of a calculating mind or perhaps genuine guilt. Either way she'd had enough and knew she couldn't cope with either.

"Just leave John…I'm…"

"I'm sorry Mary…just come hame, please." He sounded convincing but Mary had no trust left.

"No John…it's finished. I cannae dae it."

John's tone changed when he knew he wasn't getting what he wanted,

"Well, this is my fuckin' house and they're my sons as well, so it's either all or nothin'."

Mary hung up. She whimpered a despairing cry and clenched her fist in anger and pain. What was she going to do now? How would she get her sons back? Was she a terrible mother, abandoning her children? Should she just go back and accept this life which seemed inevitable? Was this all she deserved? Was this all her sons deserved? Where was it all heading?

She staggered out of the phone box barely holding herself together. Her thick, brown, greying hair was blowing wildly around her head as she pulled her thin overcoat closer to her chest. To passers-by she appeared drunk or deranged, or both. The world was spinning. The drain was circling. Her spirit, her soul and her strength were leaving her. People were staring at her with worried looks on their faces; Children asking their mothers what was wrong with her. The world was out of focus, everything crooked. The dizziness became blackness and all Mary remembered was the sensation of falling, and sickness and the pavement rushing closer as she smashed into oblivion.

Mary woke up to the soothing smell of disinfectant and bleach, to the muffled voices of cheery nurses and to a reassuring quietness, broken only by the sound of caring doctors talking nearby. One of the nurses noticed that she was awake and looking around in confusion,
"Hello Mary, you're awake then? You must be feeling a bit confused? You're in St. Jude's hospital. Can you remember how you got here?
She held Mary's hand, seeing the panic in her eyes.
"Everythin' was dizzy. I think I fell…How long have I been here?"
"Two days", she fluffed her pillows as Mary sat up slowly, feeling various pains in her face and on her head. "I'm just glad to see you awake. I'll get the doctor to come and have a word with you and then we'll get you something to eat and drink. Is that ok Mary?"
Mary nodded, confused about how the nurse knew her name and beginning to feel dizzy again, as memories of her last conversation and the reality of her circumstances scrambled to reoccupy her mind.
The doctor told Mary what she already knew, about her falling, but suggested that she'd simply fainted, as they knew she hadn't been drinking. The reason for this they weren't sure about, but indicated that it could have been physical or mental exhaustion. The information from the paramedics (and from the old lady who phoned the ambulance) suggested that the crack of her skull on the pavement had knocked her completely unconscious. The doctor wasn't sure whether Mary had suffered a concussion or entered into a mild coma, as no obvious results had shown up on the brain scan.

Mary enjoyed the feeling of being taken care of in the hospital, and after another two days there was a part of her that didn't want to leave. Nevertheless, NHS policy couldn't really consider Mary's wants, only her needs. The nurses knew that they were under pressure to constantly shuffle patients out of the hospital to provide empty beds, and so the doctor decided that she was fit to leave, at least physically. She returned to the women's hostel where she'd been staying; they already knew what had happened, as the hospital had contacted them after finding their contact information in Mary's purse. She sat in her room, feeling more lost than ever, knowing that she'd need to call her Ma to make sure that the boys were ok.

"Hello…Ma, it's me." Mary decided to speak to the boys directly, she couldn't face John, and she was just too weak.
"O Mary, where are you? You'll need to come home. Joe's in the hospital."
"O my God, what happened?" Phantoms of fear and shame gripped Mary's heart.
"Don't panic, he'll be awrite. He was out playin' wi' his pals and he was walkin' along the side of a metal fence when it fell on top of him. His hip is broken…he's in the Southern General, they said he'll be in for at least a month." Granny McDermott was trying not to alarm Mary, hearing the fragility in her daughter's voice which worried her. She wondered whether Mary was on the edge of a breakdown. In the middle of one would have been more accurate. Granny McDermott didn't realise that a breakdown began on the inside while someone was still functioning on the outside, albeit barely.
"Where's John? Does he know?"
"Aye hen, I had to tell him. He's been down in Govan a lot. Not for the boys… for the pub. He couldnae handle it. He took Joe to the hospital but I huvnae seen him since."
"What about Jim, how's he?" Mary sensed that for some reason her Ma was deliberately not mentioning Jim.
"O Mary, just come home hen. Your boys need you. They need *somebody* to look after them. And you and I both know that's no gonnae be John." The resentment in her voice wasn't limited to John.

66

"I'll try and get hame the morra, but I'm no' goin' back to John's, I cannae Ma." She cried with a sense of her own failure. This pang of defeat wasn't just about her leaving the boys temporarily; it was the reality that her marriage couldn't be saved by her endurance; that her love couldn't overcome the spectres that had followed her and John all their lives; that all the dreams of a happy family, of 'normality' and peace, had been destroyed by forces beyond her control. She was beat, and it was a bitter pill to swallow.

Joe's face didn't reflect the joy he felt deep inside when he saw his Ma walking towards his hospital bed, with a bag of sweets and a bottle of lucozade. When she had been away he was disoriented by her absence- like a ship lost at sea, being battered by the waves and unable to anchor. He was happy to see her, and although he believed her when she said she was back for good and would never leave again, something in him had changed. He knew that the only person he could truly rely on was himself. This was more than independence; it was separation and rebellion growing inside. Rebellion towards all that he'd been told by his parents, priests, pastors, politicians and policemen. Not really in anger towards Mary, but more of a simmering un-named rage towards life. The belief that the world owed him, -that he had been given a raw deal, and that the only way to deal with this was to fight and take something back, even by illegitimate force-this was the shift which would turn Joe towards a different life.

Until this point in his life, Joe's behaviour had always been tempered and cautioned with a sense of respect for others, especially Mary. Even when he was getting up to mischief with his pals there had always been a line which he wouldn't cross, simply because he was thinking, *What will my Ma think if I get caught doin' this*? But now, there was disdain for those who were supposed to be there for him. Why should he care when nobody really cared for him? Why should he always be thinking about what was right and wrong when the adults around him seemed only to selfishly consider what *they* wanted?

He was wrong in his thinking, as far as Mary went. Her whole life was driven by the thought of doing her best for her boys, even at great physical and emotional pain. But

Joe was thirteen and had the perception of one only recently initiated into teenage life. His pain was the window from which he saw the world and it wasn't a clear sky he could see. The window of trust had been broken again and again and now it was completely shattered.

Mary knew there was a change in Joe but felt she had no right to question his hurt, after all, she felt responsible for causing it, at least in part. She visited Joe every day and he seemed to be enjoying the attention of the nurses, who always made a fuss over him. They would take him for a stroll through the wards in a wheelchair, and even take him outside if the weather allowed it. They all commented on his dark curls and his 'bright blue eyes'; he was used to this from the occasional girl at school but he felt pampered and special, being washed with attention and affection. They were like angels who had cared for him when he was in need. As a teenage boy, sexuality awakened, his fondness for them wasn't limited to his emotion, but he was working hard to hide this-his vulnerability and shyness couldn't own such thoughts, surrounded by so many affectionate women.

When he wasn't being wheeled about the hospital, both of Joe's legs were held upright by a type of stirrup, even although only one hip was broken. According to the doctors, this was to ensure that when Joe's broken bone reset he wouldn't walk with a limp, but would have balance in both his hips. Regardless of the reason for his legs in stirrups, this provided Jim, and even Joe's pals, with endless entertainment when they came to visit. They would take turns at smacking his backside which was exposed due to the position of his legs.

"Fuck off! I'm tellin' my Ma when she comes up Jim." Joe couldn't help a nervous, anticipatory laugh escaping, knowing that he would do exactly the same if the position was reversed.

"Awrite I'll leave you alone. Meeko, swap seats with me so that he knows I'll no dae it." Jim winked at Meeko as he walked around the bed. Slap!

"Aargh!…Meeko, I'm gonnae boot your balls when I get out of here." Joe couldn't even reach Meeko to push him away.

"C'mon Joe, it's my duty. When else would I be able to skelp you without any comeback."

"Fanny! …Gringo, you sit over here mate and keep they two away." Joe hoped that by appealing to Gringo's sense of loyalty that he might escape another slap.

Slap! Slap!

"Ya beauty, a doubler."

The three amigos and Jim were rolling about with laughter, completely forgetting that they were in a hospital. All of the other visitors looking at them with contempt; one even complained to the nurses.

"I'm sorry mate, I couldnae help myself. Your arse was…" Gringo zipped it as the nurse frowned towards them,

"Right youse, enough of that…and keep the noise down or yer leavin'."

"Sorry."

Joe apologised despite the fact that it was his arse that was being *skelped*.

The boys left with as much noise as they'd arrived in. Joe wasn't happy to see them go, even though they had tormented him the whole time they had been there. He'd been especially happy to see Jim, as he hadn't seen him since the day of the accident. When the fence had fell on Joe, Jim had ran away to get help as he couldn't lift it himself. For about ten minutes Joe thought he wasn't coming back and he had panicked. Apart from himself, Jim and his friends were the only thing he felt any fragment of trust in, even if this wasn't fool proof.

After two and a half months in hospital, Joe finally returned home. Mary took him home in a taxi, and Joe knew that her agitation and strained conversation was masking something. He didn't say much on the journey home, as he himself was hiding a deep sense of vulnerability, anticipating bad news and knowing that something profound had changed in his family situation. He wasn't going back to what he'd left, this he was sure of, yet he sensed that he was walking into some dark unknown. His anxiety nurtured the sense of losing control which was rising in his psyche.

Hobbling out of the taxi on his crutches, as the cab pulled up at his close, Joe noticed the brightness of the full moon, high against the bruised sky-shades of blue and black and purple. Part of the moon seemed blood red to him and the autumn chill sent a pang of shooting pain right into his bones. His hip and his mind seemed to ache simultaneously. His dread deepened.

Mary turned the key in the lock and opened the door to a silent, empty house. Joe still felt a little excitement at the thought of being back and seeing Jim and his pals. He even hoped that his Da would be in and happy to see him.

"Where's my Da?…Jim, are ye in?"

Mary looked at the floor, unable to look Joe straight in the eye, "Go into the kitchen Joseph. I've made ye some dinner and I need to talk to you."

Joe knew that his world was about to change. He sat down, and before Mary had the chance to put his plate on the table, he blurted out,

"Where's Jim?"

"Joe, this wisnae my decision, son, it was Jim's…he's away to stay wi yer Da."

"Whit do ye mean, 'stay wi my Da', where's he stayin'?"

Mary paused and tried to find the words which would hurt least,

"I'm sorry son…but me and yer Da are gettin' a divorce… and he's got himself a flat in Govan."

The word 'divorce' pierced his heart like a spear even though he didn't know what it meant, other than the end of something, of separation; a deeper alienation and isolation

Joe's abandonment fed his need to control, as waves of sadness and fear pounded his heart. Mary could see the pupils in his eyes expand as he forced himself to hold in his angry tears. She couldn't deal with any pause or silence.

"Yer Da left about two months ago… a few weeks after you were taken to hospital. When I told Jim we were getting a divorce he said he was goin' to stay wi yer Da. I don't know if he was upset or angry or whit, son. I cannae force him to stay…I don't know why he left…" Mary held back her tears, knowing that Joe had more than enough emotion to cope with for now. "I'm sorry son…"

Joe got up from the table, unable to sit with himself, his brittle world cracking like his hip bone.

"Will Jim be comin' back?" Joe knew the answer but couldn't help himself from asking.

"I don't know son…I hope so."

        He knew that meant no.

Chapter 12
Just for 'the Buzz'

Housebound and harbouring rebellious feelings and thoughts, Joe waited restlessly over the coming months for his hip to fully heal, spending most of the time in his room. Jim and his pals visited sometimes, to help him pass the time and to fill him in with what was happening in the scheme. Big Mooney told him, with a sinister excitement, about their recent exploits and new adventures down at the Railway depot and on the tracks. As Corky No.2 (the old railway signal building) had finally been condemned and a decision was made to demolish it, the boys from Hardridge had to be more innovative in their pursuit of 'a buzz'.

The need for an adrenaline rush or an activity which was either daring, dangerous or downright destructive, walked hand in hand with the adolescence of a Glasgow scheme. The 'buzz' was a way of escaping from the climate of negative and destructive emotion which shadowed their lives. This pursuit of a high took many forms over the teenage years-some were innocent in their motivation, but not in terms of their legality; it would not be an exaggeration, however, to say that some invited evil.

As Big Mooney told Joe about their most recent activity his eyes widened and Joe sensed that his mind was more spaced out than usual, although this was hard to comprehend.

"We've been breakin' into the trains when they come along to the station at night and stop behind the shops."

"Whit? When they're testing them to see if they're workin' awrite?" Joe was slightly confused.

"Aye. There's only two guys on the train, so we hide at the fence behind the shops and when we see an empty carriage we jump over the fence and onto the train." Big Mooney thought this was all self-explanatory.

"And…? Whit, are ye trying to tell me you're gonnae steal a train?"

"No, don't be stupid. We nick the fire extinguishers. There's at least two on each carriage."

"Oh brilliant, you'll come in really handy if the scheme goes on fire." Joe was feeling a little irritated, having been cooped up for several weeks.

Craigo could see the frustration and cut to the chase, "Whit it is Joe, is that when you've squeezed all the foamy stuff out of the fire extinguisher, there's gas at the bottom of it."

"Aye, and I squeezed it into my mouth for a laugh the other night and I was unconscious for about two minutes." Big Mooney beamed at this as if it were a statement of personal achievement.

Joe glanced at Jim, then looked back at Big Mooney and Craigo,

"Are you mental?...that sounds seriously dodgy to me."

"No, it was brilliant mate, it's some laugh. We've been doin' it every night since Mooney conked out." Meeko declared his position while Jim and Gringo sat silently, listening intently.

"He was doin' it the other night and when he was talkin' he sounded like that Darth Vader out of Star Wars." Big Mooney pointed to Meeko and let out a belly laugh.

"Aye, Star Wars sounds about right. Well I think it is safe to say that you three are actually on another planet…It's no' for me mate." Joe didn't want to appear scared but he felt a forceful intuition warning him that there was real danger here.

"Whit do you think Jim…Gringo?" Craigo wanted to ease his own timid conscience by reassurance from others.

"Does it always knock you out?" Jim inquired.

"Aye usually, but they're there to catch you." Craigo nodded to Meeko and Mooney.

"No' exactly reassurin' is it…Can you sell it?" This seemed a strange question from Jim, even to Joe.

"Eh, I don't know…who'd buy fire extinguishers?" Craigo seemed to be asking the whole group who now seemed totally befuddled.

"I know that wee Kenny and Rab fae the top of the scheme have been buzzin' glue and gas, the stuff ye buy for lighter fuel, maybe they'd be interested."

The boys paused to consider Kenny and Rab, as Gringo chuckled at the thought of selling fire extinguishers to two brothers who were well known for their arsonist tendencies when bored. In fact, they were so renowned for lighting fires that they had actually created an activity among the boys in the scheme which Craigo had aptly named 'Firebug Night.'

Firebug Night didn't require any great skill other than the daring to set fire to a bunch of newspapers which were strategically placed outside a member of the community's front door. This was usually a local busybody or 'grass', an older gentleman perhaps who was not averse to phoning the police when the boys were loitering or up to mischief. More often than not, the protocol was to place a dog's shit under the newspaper which had holes in it. The paper would be set on fire, the man's door would be chapped, and he would obviously stamp on the paper to put out the fire when he opened the door. It was always a bonus if he only had slippers or no socks on. A combination of fire and shit could not be a pleasant sensual experience. On a less focussed and malicious night, Firebug Night took the form of setting fire to any random target, from a streak of bin refuses throughout the back courts to the local woods. The fire brigade were seldom away from Corkerhill. The boys had no concept of the life threatening danger and the chaos that they were potentially creating; to them it was 'just a buzz'.

With a short consideration of entering into any business arrangement with Kenny and Rab, Jim abandoned the idea relatively swiftly,

"Aye, I think we'll leave they two to their own devices."

"Have ye seen they two on that glue, they're pure mental?" Craigo simultaneously told the gang but was also asking them to confirm his observations.

"Aye, I was wi' them last week and I went round to the back of the shops to watch them buzzin' it. They just started holdin' each other's hair and kickin' fuck out of each other. They said that's what they do all the time. It's no' a real fight but they just like doin' it when they're buzzed up." Meeko seemed bizarrely curious and amazed by this insane display of mind altered physical activity.

"Mental…pure mental." Big Mooney agreed but failed to see the madness in his own morbid attraction with losing consciousness.

"Whit have you been up to Jim? We've no' seen you about as much…You joinin' the Govan Team?" Gringo mischievously began to wind Jim up as the subject of 'being mental' was making him uncomfortable. He wanted to distract himself from any thought of mental health as he was living with his Da's insane rage and dark depressions on a daily basis. This was a matter of routine at home but he tried to erase it when he was with his pals.

"Aye, I've been hangin' about wi boys fae some of the schemes in Govan, mainly Teucharhill. We're always fightin' they boys fae Ibrox and the Riverside. Nothin' serious, just throwin' bricks and bottles at each other down at Govan Cross. They're all a couple of years older than me, but most of them are too scared to actually go ahead one to one. They're *gallas* when there's a big team of them, but shite-bags when they're on their own. They take liberties by settin' about one of us if we're on our own down at the Cross."

Joe noticed that Jim's eyes were unblinking and focussed when he talked about violence; this was his 'buzz'. Jim didn't want to be out of control or unconscious. In fact, he thrived on knowing exactly what was happening in his environment and sought to dominate it by mentally being a step ahead. The calculated sense of revenge and anger that seemed to filter into his speech was also felt by Joe, but he couldn't articulate the feeling into words, only into concern and anxiety.

"Aye, it's the same wi that Pollok mob. They only ever come over here when there's loads of them. Some of them are awrite, like Benson and Doc, but most of them are bad news." Meeko also savoured misplaced revenge, which arose from the abuses and injustices of his own home life.

Not only could Gringo not deal with topics of mental instability but control and violence also un-nerved him. Once again, he attempted to change the mood, "Who wants a game of blind darts?"

"Good call mate…first up." Craigo jumped up and grabbed the darts from the shelf on the wall.

Blind darts was the exact same rules as ordinary darts, except that instead of the dart board being on the wall, one of the boys held it in front of their face, thus rendering them figuratively blind. The game had come about due to Mary constantly giving the boys into trouble because of the amount of holes on the doors and the walls where the dart board had previously been. Blind darts solved this problem and had the added bonus of creating a more exhilarating game both for the holder of the board and the dart thrower. The aim of the game was supposed to be achieving the highest score of 180, as in normal darts, but on occasion developed more along the lines of trying to stick the dart in the other person's knee or leg. Joe had experienced the consequences of blind darts on many a bored night with Jim. It was always 'an accident' of course, especially when Mary asked 'how the hell' it happened.

Blind darts and 'Evva', the choking game, had been pre-teen attempts to enter into an excitement, which was both intense and at the same time something to laugh about. In the vacuum of their lives this had progressed into breaking windows, vandalising and Firebug Night, not so funny, especially to others. Yet in comparison to where the need for a buzz or an escape was heading now, this all seemed like childish mischief. Not to say that these former distractions were harmless, but pursuing unconsciousness, altering the mind through substance abuse or desiring vengeful violence were at another level. They didn't seem motivated by fun, but fuelled and filled with fear and mortal danger.

Chapter 13
Out of Control

It took only two weeks of *buzzing* fire extinguishers and occasionally gas lighter fuel, for Joe's inner warning to be realised. After the tragic night, which would be etched in their memories forever, the boys were rounded up by the police, charged with solvent abuse and breaking into trains. They were told at the police station that solvent abuse was the biggest and quickest killer of young people in Scotland. It had killed more young people than heroin, and the police were astonished that they had gotten away with this for nearly nine weeks.

The idea that they had 'gotten away with' anything was the furthest thought from their minds, for they had been face to face with death on that damnable night. Joe, Gringo, Meeko, Craigo and Big Mooney had broken into the trains and stolen two fire extinguishers. After spraying the foam over the shop windows and then playfully over each other, pretending to have immense powers of urination, they made their way to the swing park to take cover from the driving rain. Under a children's climbing frame, in the invigorating blackness of an early winter's night, they began knocking themselves unconscious with poisonous gas. The boys were accompanied on this night by four Hardridge girls who were also exploring the 'mad buzz' which toxic gas afforded.

Marie had reluctantly come down to the park and was only there to see Joe-she was worried about him and felt the need to watch over him. The other three girls were the senoritas of the three amigos. Craigo's new girlfriend, Danelle was as tall as any of the boys and slimmer than most of the girls with large, blue eyes which always expressed wonder and exploration-the true eyes of a child. Her fair hair, quiet manner and gentle laughter revealed a simplicity and humility of spirit which the words 'nice' or 'plain' wouldn't quite capture. Ruth was Meeko's 'on and off' girlfriend, and although her long, thick eyelashes flickered on a bright, pretty smile she had a fiery spirit and a stubborn mind. She certainly didn't listen to any advice from men, this included Meeko and the hierarchy of every man or boy she'd drawn her eyes across, beginning with her Dad. When she was around there was usually an argument close by. Carol-Ann was different. She wasn't only Gringo's girlfriend; she was also his best pal. They stayed next door and had known each other as far back as they could remember; they had started nursery and school together; they had played 'wee shops' in the muddy back courts, using leaves as currency and old toys as quality goods. Her dirty-blonde curly hair matched Gringo's in colour but not in manageability. It was wild and untameable and not at all like her personality when she was with Jamie (Gringo's real name). He always protected her with his laughter and his reassuring smile, and she adored him. They rarely disagreed on anything and when they did they could never stay angry with each other for long. Carol Ann loved to see Gringo's big cheesy grin coming round the corner and never doubted that they would be together forever. They shared everything, even the things that were forbidden. Like Adam and Eve they were inseparable. Even if Gringo was going to reach for the apple of deeper consciousness, then Carol-Ann would willingly take a bite.

"I'll have a buzz of that can after you Jamie." Carol Ann was the only one who ever referred to Gringo by his own name, even his Dad called him 'Gringo'.

Gringo held the nozzle of the gas can in between his front teeth and squeezed down as the gas hissed into his mouth like a serpent, taking his breath and replacing it with a toxic substitute. His eyes closed for about five or six seconds, the whole frame of his body became limp and lifeless and he slunk down against the ladder of the wooden climbing frame. When he slurred open his eyes and mouth, his voice was like slow motion, demonically and disturbingly deep,

"Wwwoow man, what a buzz…ahu."

His two syllable attempt at a laugh was disturbing to Joe and Marie in a way which the others didn't seem to notice. This wasn't surprising as both Meeko and Craigo had synchronically held the fire extinguishers to their mouths and blasted the dregs of gas, which lay at the bottom of the red bomb, deep into their heart and lungs. Their cardiac beating had slowed to an inch from death and their brains ceased to function. Unconsciousness seemed better to them than being awake. Big Mooney pushed both of them against the frame to stop them from falling, but in truth seemed more concerned about getting to their state of oblivion than holding them up.

"Right Craigo, geez a buzz of that!" Big Mooney shouted as saliva dripped from Craigo's mouth calling him back to the world of his senses.

"Meeko, you gi' me a buzz then! Pair of fannies."

Big Mooney was anxious that he was missing something.

Joe and Marie were feeling completely out of this world which their friends were in, and yet they reluctantly laughed at the total lack of control which they were seeing; senseless sentences which emerged from a surreal world, with distorted voices and bodies. But Joe was also deeply disturbed by something else, inexplicable, a horror in the atmosphere which frightened the life out of him. He wasn't unfamiliar with impending doom but this contained a danger and a dread which sharpened his mind and shook his spirit.

After about ten minutes of passing round fire extinguishers and lighter fuel, Joe had had enough. There was a selfish anger in the air, even between Gringo and Carol-Ann which was to him an obvious indication that the nature of reality had shifted. To Joe's mind, it was like a door was opened to a world of hostile spirits. His restlessness couldn't contain itself.

"Do you want to go for a walk Marie?" She nodded hastily and silently with relief.

"I'm out of here lads, I'll see youse the morra."

Nobody responded except Gringo and Danelle who said 'See youse later", at exactly the same time and then gave each other a dull acknowledgement which was less than a smile. The others were deep in their buzz.

"Carol-Ann, that's Marie away, are you gonnae say cheerio?" Gringo slurred and gave her a gentle shake to wake her from her slumber. Her face was turned to the side and she'd put Gringo's jacket over her head 'to stop any of the gas from escaping'.

"Carol Ann…?"

Jamie slowly pulled the jacket from her head and at first couldn't understand the dull blue colour of Carol Ann's cheeks, and the darker blue of her lips. He thought that he was still in his buzz and tried to adjust his eyesight. Marie and Joe had just turned to walk away and as Joe glanced to see Gringo shaking Carol Ann silently and furiously, his eyes were transfixed on the image of death which had replaced her youthful face.

"For fuck's sake!" Joe darted to Carol Ann just as Marie noticed her lifeless pal. "O my God!...O my God!...O my God!". Marie held her quivering hands to her widened face.

The rest of the gang were shocked into awakening by the repetitive screams of Marie and then Danelle. Gringo was hysterically crying and shaking his wee pal like a rag doll, trying to bring a spirit back to her empty body. Meeko and Mooney held him back at Joe's frantic instruction and Craigo ran to get someone to phone an ambulance.

As they waited for the ambulance to come, huddled together in their loneliness, their panic slowly descended into a shocked silence. They didn't fear the trouble they were in, but only how they would live without their pal. *How would Gringo live without her?* He had run into the woods of Pollok Park like a terrified rabbit fleeing from a fox, seconds after Mooney had let him go. Joe stared at the ground the whole time and Marie held tightly to his arm and cried silently into his shoulder, hoping to wash the image of Carol-Ann's face from her thoughts. Joe didn't even know she was there.

When the police and the ambulance arrived there was no anger, only a rapid series of questions, while they rushed the body onto a stretcher and turned their flashing lights on, as if they could save her. There was a sombre tone from the police but no harsh words, not really. Well, none that touched the numbness which had wrapped itself around their hearts

Chapter 14
The Lost Boys

From the moment of Carol-Ann's death, Gringo was lost. At the funeral he was present in body but absent in spirit. He didn't shed a tear and his greying face was like stone. Regardless of how many people, friends, family and even Carol-Ann's parents told him that 'it wasn't your fault', he still felt the sentence of death on his own heart. He had condemned himself and refused to hear any conflicting evidence. The jury and judge which resided within him had been firmly established by his own expectations, his love for Carol-Ann and the despair that now filled his soul.

On very few occasions, over the coming years, a glimpse of the carefree, light-hearted, optimistic Jamie, which had once shone like a radiant star, escaped from the darkness through a chink of light. To others outside of the gang he looked as though he was functioning normally as much as anyone does in the midst of deprivation. But to Joe and Jim, to Big Mooney and especially to Meeko and Craigo (his two amigos), a part of Gringo was gone. The times where he seemed most alive were when he was in the midst of destruction and robbery. A vacuum grew inside Gringo which was insatiable and greedy and he sought in vain to fill it with material goods, the treasure of ill -gotten gains.

Gringo's skill and acumen for stealing was matched with his enthusiasm and fearlessness to pursue any opportunity for a robbery. From shops to big houses, from warehouses to factories, and from hold-ups to hijacking, his desire increased exponentially. Nothing could satisfy the black hole in his heart which was powered like negative gravity by loss and the feeling that his life (and his love) had been stolen from him. He would take back and nothing would stop him. He had no desire to harm others; it wasn't within his gentle nature. Yet he justified to himself any fear which was generated or any human obstacles which were in the way when he sought to steal something or rob someone. He was more comfortable stealing from those in society who, in his mind, wouldn't miss losing a couple of grand's worth of goods. He never stole from anyone in the scheme (except the local shop owners who fitted into the previously mentioned category in his eyes), and if he could avoid it no-one would be harmed. But this wasn't always something which could be avoided.

The rest of the gang-Joe, Jim, Meeko, Craigo and Big Mooney-were also propelled into a new way of being after this encounter with death. It wasn't that they believed that it was anyone else's fault other than their own, but there was another level of fear and anger in them. This anger fuelled the rebellious passion which was consuming them like a forest fire.

Most of the gang were in their second year at Secondary school and the teachers couldn't control them. They tried hard discipline, they tried ignoring them, they even tried being supportive to them. The boys were apparently unreachable and many wrote them off as lost causes. They were 'cheeky, insolent, rude, un-cooperative and unwilling', according to report cards and headmaster's comments.

Joe managed to keep a level of respect towards some teachers, although the only opinions that mattered to him now were his friends. Despite his intelligence and his obvious academic potential, he was indifferent to the approval or disapproval of any kind of authority figure. In his eyes, teachers, priests, policemen, social workers and Children's panel workers all had the same agenda and message-Control.

For all of the boys and many others, from every scheme in Glasgow, the teenage years became an unconscious attempt to feel free and happy by throwing off all restraint. This meant 'risk behaviour' and run- ins with the law and authorities, and every institution which represented them. The deterioration became obvious in school but this was only a symptom of the problem and not its cause. School didn't always help, in fact sometimes it reinforced in them the sense of their own failure and worthlessness; but the storm of emotions which they had been born into, complicated with the brokenness of their own families and the tempting evils which lurked in every city, had prepared them for the chaos which would follow.

This wasn't a cop out which they used to refuse responsibility; it wasn't an excuse they held onto for their behaviour. There were many teenagers who did well at school, who were focussed and 'mature young adults' as some teachers comparatively referred to them. The boys knew such people, even some from the scheme, but they were simply acting out what they had absorbed from their environment and family climate. Yes, there were issues of attitude and anger, and those of maturity and responsibility, but there were also those of the emotional, social and perhaps even spiritual realities which hid like sick secrets within their souls.

Joe knew he was acting 'wrong' and that he was a disappointment. His friends all knew the same was true of them, and yet being free from control and escaping from fear and shame, prompted a mutinous anger in them. They would be constantly reprimanded by everyone but would listen to no-one.

"Your son thinks that he can take the law into his own hands and exact vengeance on whomever he feels deserves it!" Mr. Conroy, Joe's 'Guidance Teacher', was referring this particular time to the most recent incident of Mary's son assaulting another pupil.

Mary didn't know what to say as she felt that it was her that was being given into trouble.

"I'm sorry Mr. Conroy...I don't know what to do. Ever since his Da left Joseph has been angrier and...well...out of my control."

Joe resented this explanation, "It's nothin' to dae wi' that. He kicked me on the football pitch in P.E., so I hit him back."

"No, McShane, a kick during a game of football does not merit you snapping a large piece of wood over another pupil's head, outside of the school gates and twenty minutes after the game had ended! You should have reported any incident to Mr.Miller and he would have dealt with it promptly."

"I dealt wi' it quite promptly." Joe's calm tone was filled with contempt and he hoped he'd get an infuriated response. He hated the way Conroy spoke to him- another angry man.

Mary was mortified at Joe's attitude, "Joseph, shoosh! You're in enough trouble."

"Yes, that's very true, as the boy's parents want to press charges, and I have no choice but to tell them that I will be suspending you from school for two weeks. I will also be referring you to the Children's panel in the hope that they might reconsider. Maybe they'll have some compassion on you."

"I don't need their pity."

Mr. Conroy was exasperated by Joe's disregard but had the sense to realise that goading him any longer was like prodding a tired, cantankerous dog.

"Well McShane, you do need something to help you son."

"I'm no' your son." Joe was now completely docked in the harbour of his hostility. Both Mary and Conroy chose not to react to Joe but he knew he was having an effect.

"I'm sorry again Mr. Conroy but just to let you know Joseph will be grounded for this and I will be letting his Dad know."

The mention of his Da sharpened Joe's mind and hardened his heart.

"He disnae care…so tell him if you want. I don't care."

Mary had no intention of telling John and it made her heart sink to realise that in some way Joe was right. It wasn't that his Da didn't care but John was lost in an alcoholic fog and Joe hadn't seen him for about three months. They left the school in silence just as they had on the last two occasions. This was the third time Joe had been suspended in two years and he was apparently unreachable by anyone.

The Children's panel felt like a court to Joe, with three people sitting sombrely behind a long intimidating desk, asking him probing questions about his personal life and recent behaviour. He sat and listened for the first ten minutes as they read his reports and spoke about him as if he wasn't there. In some strange way he felt like he wasn't there or maybe he was wishing himself away. When they questioned him he played along and acted sorry, knowing that they did have the power to suggest that he be taken out of the family home if that seemed appropriate. He had no belief that they were actually trying to help him, but they were. All he could hear and see was failure and punishment. He didn't want to hear it as his damaged soul told him this every day.

So, when they put him on a Supervision Order, and told him that he would have to visit a social worker once a week for a year, he felt that this was a sentence and not a support. The process of becoming institutionalised was beginning and it had its roots in both the institution and in Joe's mind.

Chapter 15
Catch us if you can

Joe sprinted home from school pursued by three 'skinheads' from Pollok, his head bleeding from the nail which had punctured his skull. The three boys were waiting for him when he walked out of the school gates, fence posts in hand, hoping to exact revenge for Jim's attack on one of their friends. Joe didn't know them, nor had he ever met them. He knew them only through the rumours that Jim had smashed a bottle over one of their heads, at a local dance in the Church Hall. Needless to say, that the priest wasn't too thrilled by this and had barred everyone from Hardridge as a result. Joe wasn't surprised that they had attacked him when he found out who they were, but they had caught him off guard. It wasn't unusual to target the family member or friend of someone whom you were after, if you couldn't locate the target themselves. There was no right or wrong about it in Joe's thoughts, it was just the way it was. He accepted it, and knew he was more vulnerable now that Jim stayed in another scheme, after being expelled from Lourdes for bringing a knife to school. Luckily, Joe managed to outrun his pursuers this time and escaped with only the initial blow to the head which was administered from behind, accompanied by the shout of their war cry, "Pollok Krew". There were many gangs in and around Pollok with weird names such as 'The Kross', 'The Bundy' 'The Young Priesty' and 'The Young Nitsy' to name a few. However, 'The Krew' were the biggest gang in Pollok and Jim often had conflicts with them, especially now that he was considered an ally of two tribes, "The Paka" and the "Govan Team". Jim didn't mind the confrontations with gangs or their notorious members. In fact he thrived on it. He seemed to draw to himself those who had reputations for violence and secretly delighted in 'clashing swords' with bullies.

Joe had also developed a reputation for fighting in school, and wasn't slow in attacking anyone who lashed out at him or even threatened to. On more than one occasion, older boys had barely finished their threats and Joe had pounced on them and viciously assaulted them. Like Jim, it didn't seem to matter to Joe that a certain pupil had a reputation for fighting. As he was so determined not to be dominated or intimidated by violence that his strategy was often to carry out a pre-emptive strike, just in case someone got the better of him. Nevertheless, even although Joe had been in at least six fights in his first two years at Lourdes Secondary, he was in confusing contrast quite happy-go-lucky by nature. It seemed unusual to others when they had known him for a short time to see him lash out at someone with such velocity. It was like watching another person, a part of Joe's shadow which he kept hidden until the moment required it. Joe loved to mess around and had a playful spirit, usually. He loved to be the class joker and wind the teachers up in school. For a select few (those who seemed to look at him without hate in their eyes) he reserved a cheeky grin, for the others he was relentless in his often manic and bizarre humour. His off the wall antics were seldom attempts to simply undermine the teachers, but rather a source of distraction from his restlessness and of self-esteem for his emptiness. Other pupils often delighted in his bold disregard for the system and the consequences which it threatened. Class teachers threatened him with Principal Teachers, who then threatened him with Guidance Teachers, who in turn threatened him with Deputy Head teachers, whose only threat was the Head teacher. Joe was often passed from pillar to post ignoring every threat along the way. The more aggressive a teacher was with him, the more likely he was to pay little heed to them. He knew that they couldn't physically harm him and he would have quickly retaliated if they had. Some teachers were seen as bullies and neither Joe nor Jim, nor any of their friends for that matter, ever reacted well to bullies. The contempt in his heart hadn't begun with teachers, but as this was the biggest part of most of his days as a teenager, so teachers became the front line enemy.

Education wasn't really something which Joe associated with school; most of what he was learning in his life at this time was focussed on girls and his gang, so he decided to concentrate on these and gave them his full attention. School seemed like a distraction, something which he had to endure. It was frustrating for many of the teachers to watch this deterioration in Joe as they knew he was intelligent and creative, but he didn't seem to care. His contempt for all adults and his mistrust in almost everyone easily projected into his feelings and thoughts about school. Most teachers had given up on him and those who hadn't didn't have a clue how to help him, if he even wanted to be helped. Part of the problem was that Joe didn't consciously know that he needed help, as he had put his brokenness and deep vulnerability out of his conscious awareness, and had cloaked himself in a persona of humour mixed with violence and recognition from peers. This persona took on many forms and enabled Joe to keep running away from his fears and shame; sometimes he had to run faster than others, literally.

Joe had just begun his second year, after another summer of 'freedom' had left him even more disheartened about school than he had been previously. Despite being arrested on more than one occasion, Joe had felt a sense of freedom from the watchful and judgmental eyes of a system which he felt deeply at odds with. He did a lot of running during the summer holidays and it wasn't an attempt to increase his fitness levels.

As much as Joe and his mates loved being out from under the restriction of school, they were often as restless and bored outside as they were in. They sought to resolve this problem in habitual behaviours which were perhaps not considered conventional hobbies, but seemed to organically arise from their need for adrenalin and their desire to have more than what they had. What they really wanted they didn't actually know, but breaking into the local shops seemed as good a place to start as any.

The older guys from Joe's scheme would often break into the shops by breaking down the back door, away from the glaring eyes of local residents. On one particular night, Meeko and Joe decided to break in by using an iron crow bar to wedge the shutters off from the front, for the entire world to see. It wasn't so much an act of bravado but simply that it seemed to them the easiest way to get into the shop. To their surprise the alarm didn't go off once the metal shutters had been wedged from the rail, although they weren't exactly light-fingered silent bank robbers. Craigo kicking a football against the shutters as an attempt to mask the noise of Meeko and Joe ripping metal from metal wasn't even remotely conspicuous. The numerous faces peering behind curtains and the occasional shouts of,
"Right you lot, get away from there. I'm phonin' the polis…" from the braver

neighbours, didn't deter the boys either. They would continue until Big Mooney, who was standing at the corner of the street and able to see the police coming from any angle, shouted "Edgy"-the Glasgow lookout warning. They weren't the Great Train Robbers, nor had they ever been praised for 'diligence' in school but they were certainly showing admirable staying power on this occasion.

It took them about seven or eight minutes to completely derail the shutters and push them up far enough to see the shop window. For a few brief seconds it was a glorious sight, and for the first time all year the boys felt a sense of achievement, working hard to ignore the small nagging conscience and the growing fear of being caught. As the silver shutters rolled up Meeko and Joe's hearts and minds accelerated with fear and adrenalin, quickening them to complete the mission.

"Joseph McShane and Stephen Meechan… I know your mothers. I'll be havin' a word wi' them the morra!" Old 'specky' Lily's last brave attempt to prevent the boys from going any further, by naming and shaming them, wasn't enough to simmer the mercury rising within them, drawing them to their crime. However, they knew now that time was short before someone actually phoned the police, if they hadn't done so already.

"Joe, we're no gonnae have enough time to burst the door open." Meeko was really asking Joe to do something more immediate and effective.

Joe instinctively understood and didn't allow second thoughts or fear to have any time. He took three or four steps back and with two hands picked up a large rock. Without any communication, Meeko, Craigo and Gringo all moved to the side as Joe sprinted forward and hurled the boulder through the exploding window. The shattered window of opportunity invited them to jump through, in contrast to the blaring alarm which had gone off warning them to run from this forbidden place. But it wasn't time to run just yet. Joe was helped up by standing on Meeko and Gringo's cupped hands and he entered with nervous ecstasy. Inside the shop he felt exhilarated to be in it alone for the first time ever, not to buy something but to take what he wanted. He knew it was wrong, but it excited him to be breaking the law. For a moment he was transfixed just looking at all the goods available to him, rows of sweets and small sections of cigarettes behind the counter were for the taking; he was free to take and no-one was there to stop him.

"Hurry up Joe, the polis will be here in a minute!" Meeko had lifted himself up and was peering through the broken glass. He couldn't prevent a smile and a laugh escaping from his face as he saw the wonder on Joe's.

Joe's mind felt a little unravelled as he started stuffing Twixes and Mars Bars into his pockets and then passing boxes out to Meeko, who was also slightly bewildered. "For fuck's sake Joe, get the fags… and the money out the till. We're no' gonnae get much for a box of fuckin' Mars Bars."

"O aye…right enough." Joe also laughed, as he cleared the shelf of every packet of cigarettes and scanned behind the counter for any larger packs.

There were none so he turned his attention to the till; it was locked. Although his mind was racing and his heart beating quickly and loudly in his chest, he couldn't ignore the strange enjoyment he felt from being behind the counter in the shop. He felt like he was working there and providing a service to the community. To his pals he was, but I'm sure the rest of the community and Khan the shop owner took a slightly different position. Having emptied the contents behind the counter Joe rushed to the back store of the shop to top up his supply. He immediately picked up two cartons of cigarettes, but before he managed to do a thorough search, he heard Big Mooney's voice faintly shouting,

"There's the polis! Run!"

Meeko reinforced this in case Joe had missed it and bellowed, "Joe! Bolt!"

Joe kicked the fire bar on the back door, and felt the freedom and fear of reality as he jumped over the railway fence. His heart thudded in his chest and drained the moisture from his mouth, as he furiously ran along the railway tracks, making his way to the gate near the top end of the scheme. This would lead him to the opening to Pollok Park, where he had pre-arranged to meet the gang if they had to scarper. Joe was at the 'wee woods' by the time the police had arrived, and they had quickly checked the shop to see if there was anyone still in it, giving the boys another few minutes head start.

"There he is…the Great Chocolate Robber." Meeko couldn't resist a wind up as Joe slowed to a panting halt.

Hands on his knees to catch his breath, he let out a belly laugh,

"I know…I panicked for a minute…I must have been a wee bit hungry and forgot that we were lookin' for stuff we could sell."

"Did you get anythin' from the till or the back shop Joe?" Gringo was hoping for a more substantial reward than chocolate and cigarettes.

"The till was locked mate." Joe panted, "I got a couple of cartons of fags, two hundred smokes in each carton. How many did I pass through the windae?"

The boys gathered together to look at their takings collectively and to divide them equally. As Craigo was working out how many cigarettes (and chocolate bars) they each had, and how much they would get for them, their momentary bubble of joy was burst by a blaring angry voice,

"Right youse! Run!"

Panic filled the air and joy once more became adrenalin and fear.

"It's the polis!" Big Mooney stated what was obvious to his fleeing friends as they simultaneously threw their incriminating treasure behind the trees. Joe felt as if he was only running for about thirty seconds before a burly black uniform wrenched his jumper from behind,

"Right, got ye!"

"Shit!"

Joe looked around to see that the woods were filled with about eight or nine uniformed policemen, many of whom had apprehended his partners in crime. The police had known that they would throw their stolen goods away as soon as they saw them, and that they would deny all knowledge of the break in. So, they had shouted "Run", as the boys running was apparently evidence of their guilt. The police retrieved all of the stolen goods as they had only been about fifty yards away when they had shouted. The boys had stupidly thought that they were home and free under the cover of the trees. Even now, however, they would maintain their innocence.

"Hey, Jack, wait to hear this…this one said he doesn't know anything about the shops…he was out looking for birds eggs." Every officer in the back of the police van sniggered and chortled at Big Mooney's lame attempt at an alibi. The boys sat in the back of the riot van facing each other, Joe and Mooney on one side and the three amigos on the other, book ended by the law. Despite their discouragement they couldn't help see the hilarity.

"O aye…wait a minute, let me see. Right, you were looking for birds eggs…" The fat sergeant pointed at Mooney, but each of the boys knew his prodding finger was going to target each of them one by one. "You were looking for golf balls…You were looking for flowers for your mammy, and youse two were gonnae arrange them for her and wrap them up in a nice wee bundle."

The other three constables were in knots and the boys shook their heads at Big Mooney, smirking incredulously at him.

"And not only that, you were all totally unaware of each other in the woods and just happened to be running in the same direction? What a marvellous coincidence!"

The gang would refuse to confess and were relentless in their refusal of all blame, despite the overwhelming circumstantial evidence. As far as they were concerned it was the law's job to prove their guilt. At some deep level of denial they even told themselves that they were innocent. After all, they hadn't been found with any stolen goods on them! They were reminded by the police that they had seen them throwing stuff away which had been found. "It wisnae us!" was the automatic response of almost every teenager in a Glasgow scheme. The boys held to this with stony faces hiding shame filled hearts.

It wasn't the only time that Joe used this during the summer of 1984. The battle at Car-D college between his scheme and the Glasgow skinheads, who congregated from a variety of schemes (and were united by a common bond of baldness, bad attitudes and the BNP), also required the universal denial of involvement.

The battle was organised by the older members of The Paka (those around sixteen to nineteen), due to a dispute which Joe knew nothing about. This didn't matter, as the scheme rule was that you showed up for a fight even if just to increase the numbers and throw the odd brick or bottle. This was exactly what Joe and his friends had done, leaving a clash of knives and other contact weapons (hammers, baseball bats, golf clubs, etc.) to the older boys who led this particular conflict. The skinheads looked intimidating but were just flesh and blood like everyone else, which became obvious as it spilled onto the road. The actual point of contact only lasted for two or three minutes, enough for one or two people to get severely injured-slashed, stabbed or struck with a weapon. Joe watched this from a blurry distance and was content not to be on the front line, as his spirit absorbed the violence, regardless of the space and time between him and his unknown enemies. He could hear muffled shouts, then thuds and yelps, as youthful flesh met wicked wood and malicious metal After the initial clash, and once a couple of casualties had been witnessed, the sirens were heard in the distance, and then both gangs dispersed.

As they began the twenty minute run home, they deliberately scattered and separated, as an individual had a better chance of denying involvement than a group of two or three. Yet, Joe's aloneness as he ran home (or perhaps his inability to cover the guilt on his face) only served to make him stand out to the patrol car as it passed him. He slowed down as he saw it coming and tried to act as if he was casually returning home from a visit to a friend. The car did a U-turn and drew up beside him. As the window rolled down Joe's heart pounded faster. He was annoyed as he was only five minutes from the safety of the scheme, where he didn't need an alibi and had plenty of places to hide.

"Hold on a minute son…" Joe stopped at the officer's command but would have to make a split decision as to whether he was going to make up a story or make a dash for the scheme. He paused to try and quickly gauge their suspicion.

"Aye, whit is it?"

"Where are you coming from?" The officer in the passenger seat asked this while opening the door of the car, seeing in Joe's eyes that he was poised to sprint, like a runner waiting for the starting pistol. The click of the opening door was all that Joe needed to hear; and he was off! The officer slammed the door shut and pursued him across the busy main road, as Joe stopped and started to avoid the speeding cars. The officer was shouting something about stopping and 'only making things worse', but once again Joe was beyond the point of considering consequences and listening to adult reason. He'd make his own decisions and all that mattered to him at this stage was getting away from his pursuer. He ran down the stairs which led to the train station at Corkerhill, his escape route clear in his mind. The burly officer chased him and, knowing that Joe was faster, was now beginning to curse and swear. Apparently, thought Joe, he wasn't as civil as he had first seemed. Joe reached the railway platform and to the officer's fury he leapt onto the tracks and ran straight across, not really giving a second thought that a train might be coming. He was focussed on escaping; he wasn't going to be caught.

As he began to climb the fence behind The Cart pub, he glanced back and gave a cheeky smile to the irate policeman. He was radioing his colleague, as he knew that he was never going to catch him alone. Joe came out from behind the pub and breathed the atmosphere of the street like the smell of freedom. Many of the older team of boys, who had returned about ten minutes before from the fight, (alibis sorted) were sitting on the wall outside of the pub and had been watching Joe's elusive antics. Some of them had cheered as he emerged. But he wasn't free yet, for the driver of the police car came screeching round the corner and slammed to a halt, just as Joe was about to take a victory seat. As the officer fixed his glare on Joe, he knew that the chase was still on. Joe ran into a nearby corner garden, facing the pub, followed closely by the policeman who was more than slightly chubby. Joe realised that he would be caught if he tried to run on the open road, so he decided to weave in and out of a gap in the hedge. The officer followed and Joe wasn't aware of how hilarious this sight was to the older boys observing. One minute they could see Joe, and then he disappeared back into the garden, each time closely followed by the law, only to continue reappearing through the gap. To the boys it was like a weird live Jack in the box, popping in and out. He could hear them laughing hysterically and simultaneously hear his pursuer cursing him. The boys began to cheer him on and goad the sweating policeman.

"Come on wee man! You're nearly there…he looks as if he's gonnae take a heart attack any minute."

However, despite beginning to feel the pleasure of entertaining the older boys at the expense of the police, Joe knew that time wasn't on his side and that he'd need to make for the back close and run through the back courts before more police arrived. After one last dash into the gap in the hedge, he ran into the close and into a trap, as he forgot that the door of this particular close was often locked. There was no way out! The humiliated and angry constable raced in at his back and immediately struck him over the head with his radio.

"Got ye, ya wee bastard!"

Waiting in the empty silence of a cell at the police station, Joe's mind was still running, not from the law but from himself. He knew that Mary would say very little when she arrived, but would ground him for at least a week. Her discipline had little effect on him now, not as a reflection of her ineffectiveness as a loving mother, but because he was past the point of punishment altering his behaviour. Something more was needed for Joe to even consider changing the path he was now running on. Mary didn't know what it was and she was filled with despair and confusion. Joe had no awareness that he was even running; he couldn't slow down enough to look at himself. In his weekly probation meeting the social worker would ask him about his behaviour, about his family or about his thoughts and feelings. He had no language to answer her questions, even if he trusted enough or was willing to, which he was not. His still small voice, his inner compass, his conscience and even his self-honesty, had been pushed down so often and ran away from so many times that he didn't know how to return or connect to it .He was running fast, accelerating through the teenage years and away from the innocence of childhood. He was repeatedly being initiated into a more destructive way of being, which required darker lies, more shadows and a continual running from the truth. Perhaps, without knowing it, he hoped that someone would catch him…and bring rest back to his soul.

Chapter 16
Where are you now?

Joe's heart sank at the thought of returning to school after the holidays, but there were three things which lifted his spirit and moved his body to get there at nine o'clock. The first and most important to him was Marie, the second was the new image which included school clothes (courtesy of the Provident cheque lady) and peroxide blonde hair which he was sporting, and the third was meeting his friends, some of whom he had hardly seen all summer.

Joe had hardly seen Marie either during the summer and he did miss her. But the whirlwind of adventurous activities which he'd been caught up in, and the aftermath of being grounded, had swallowed up all of his time. She was always on his mind and he knew that she had been asking his friends about him, which made his spirit rise a little. Yet, despite the energy and excitement which his recent exploits gave to his sinking heart, the truth was that he was becoming more and more isolated and alienated: a feeling of exile and separation from others. This led to an avoidance of anyone or anything which heightened his vulnerability and forced him to connect to his own feelings. Joe had been running all summer, avoiding the law, his parents and even Marie.

When he entered the school gates at ten to nine, his friends were all behind the smoker's shed sharing a cigarette between four of them.

"Hey, Blondie…where have you put Meester Joe?" With a cigarette butt hanging from the side of his mouth, Gringo put on a Mexican accent like a stereotypical spaghetti western villain.

"You look like a light bulb mate." Big Mooney didn't see this as a criticism, just as an observation.

Joe had resolved to take the initial comments about his altered image, knowing that resistance would only prolong it. His friends knew that it was their duty to wind him up, but they also knew that criticising and humiliating Joe was a risky business. He had become more volatile in recent months and most of the time his mind seemed to be somewhere else. And when he *was* present he had a growing unpredictability about him.

"I think it suits you Joe." Craigo beamed and took his hood down to remind Joe that he wasn't the only blonde in the gang.

"Who done it Joe…tell me and I'll get them for you mate." Meeko always took it to the edge.

Joe laughed it off, "It was my three cousins fae Dunfermline, remember them- they're mental."

"Aye we can see that mate, but why did you let three lassies near your head?" Meeko tightened the wind-up to see how far Joe would go.

"I stupidly let them talk me into lightenin' my hair wi' a bottle of peroxide. They didnae tell me they were gonnae use the whole bottle…and two blonde dyes. There's no way I was lettin' it stay that ginger colour it went at first!"

"What did Marie say? Did she like it?" Craigo knew Joe was becoming uncomfortable being the centre of attention and tried to steer the conversation in another direction. But when he mentioned Marie, Meeko and Gringo both looked at each other, then stared at the ground. Joe noticed their reactions and felt an irritating twist in his own gut.

"Whit's wrang wi' youse two?

An awkward silence permeated the atmosphere.

"Gringo, whit is it?"

Gringo sheepishly responded, "I wisnae sure if you knew mate, but Marie's goin' out wi' that wee Murphy fae Penilee."

Joe immediately pretended that he was indifferent to this news, despite the bomb which had just exploded inside.

"So, that's cool. It's nothin' to do with me, I'm no' goin' out wi' her anyway. She's just my mate."

The words hung empty in the air, devoid of meaning and truth. Joe's friends intuitively accepted the lie and played the game, talking about the madness of the holidays.

"Here Joe, that was some laugh breakin' into Khan's…" Before anyone could respond to Meeko, Big Mooney blurted out,

"I heard that she was movin' to Penilee, that's probably why she's been hangin' about wi' Murphy."

Big Mooney was the only one who didn't fully get the need to totally avoid the topic of Marie, and that the code was never to mention her again. The three amigos silently sighed.

The bell blared and provided an escape from the moment, for everyone.

As the boys separated and went to their own class lines the camaraderie was renewed. They knew that they had to arm themselves with humour and carry on, in order to cope with the sombre tone and controlling authority of school.

Joe went to class and seemed to be placidly listening to the teachers, but his mind wandered all day and he escaped inside daydreams and fantasies. Some teachers thought that perhaps he had miraculously calmed down over the summer and had returned to school with a new attitude. They didn't know that he had only returned in body and that his mind and spirit were somewhere else. Joe had woken this day with only a small thread of willingness and hope attaching him to the tortuous prospect of another year of school. The revelation about Marie had cut that thread and he felt like he was floating through his day. He had a melancholy and uncaring reaction to the stress and drama and crazy antics of the first school day: timetables, coursework, reminders of school rules and classmates discussing excitable memories about the summer-all held no importance to him.

The first few weeks of Joe's third year in Secondary school were pretty much the same as the first day. He would usually start off the year with best intentions and attempts to tune in to what teachers were saying, despite the fact that most of the time school felt like a foreign country. He could hear his teachers talking and was able to get by with a general sense of what they were on about, even although school left his head buzzing and disoriented. It was like another language was spoken, one that he rarely used outside and found it difficult to connect to. He felt his way through school rather than listened to what was being said. The problem with this, despite the obvious confusion for someone with such intense feelings, was that the emotional message which Joe heard was usually that he was failing or not trying hard enough.

"Joseph! Joseph McShane! Joe!" Mr.Carroll, Joe's registration teacher, peered over the desk, elevated himself by pushing his short, stubby legs up by the tiptoes and frowned in Joe's direction as he was usually someone who could at least gain his initial attention.

Joe looked at him with an empty expression.

"Here."

"Are you sure you're here Joseph?… Are you feeling ok?" Mr.Carroll was one of the few teachers who had a genuine concern for Joe, and was always happy to see him return after a holiday, or in more recent cases, after a suspension from school.

"Aye, I'm awrite. I was thinkin' about somethin'."

"He was usin' his glowin' head to contact the mother ship Sir." Meeko's jibe sent the whole class into hysterics. Even Joe and Mr.Carroll reluctantly laughed as the volume rose to riotous.

"Ok, calm down…Right! Enough! Let me finish the register or some of you'll be marked off." Mr. Carroll could also sense Joe's discomfort when any focus was on him.

"Aye, but would anybody notice if we wurnae here Sir?" Meeko's question was met with a silent, but compassionate frown from underneath Mr.Carroll's glasses.

Meeko was joking, but his question sowed a seed of opportunity in Joe's thoughts. Joe became more and more detached from the sounds of teacher's voices, and even lost any willingness to participate in winding the teachers up as an avoidance tactic, more than he had ever been. It only took until the beginning of the fourth week of the new term, for the seed which Meeko had unintentionally planted to fully bloom.

"I'm *doggin'* it the day." Joe's statement about bunking off school was also an offer or request for company.

"How are you gonnae dae that?…You'll get caught…If you're marked off at registration the school'll phone your house." Craigo hoped that his logic could be refuted and that Joe had a strategy.

Joe didn't disappoint, "I know, I'm goin' into *regi* and after that I'm gonnae jump over the fence at P.E. Then I'll come back and go to *regi* in the afternoon. It's only your registration mark that goes to your Guidance teacher."

"I'm up for that. You up for it Meeko?" Craigo was excited at the prospect of doing anything more stimulating than going to school.

"Aye, sound. We'll try it for a couple of days and see if anybody gets suspicious. We're all in different classes for most subjects. You and Joe are in wi' the geeks and me and Mooney are in remedial wi the dafties." Meeko's interpretation of his own dyslexia and Mooney's difficulty with language and in social communication would nowadays be viewed as politically incorrect. But to them it was an accurate assessment of their current state of affairs; this was unchallenged and sometimes reinforced by the school, however self-defeating and demeaning it may have been. Joe was ready to do anything to fill the growing void, and he had no fear of consequences to his 'educational development', which teachers harped on about. He just needed some excitement and adventure, or even a distraction from the emptiness.

In the weeks leading up to his decision to take some 'unauthorised absence', Joe saw Marie once or twice. They chatted about her moving to Penilee and about the summer holidays but they both avoided any discussion about her new boyfriend. Joe couldn't bear it and Marie felt that she had betrayed him, even although they hadn't been going out, officially. The distance which Joe felt between himself and the world was even more acute when he spoke to Marie. He often felt that he wasn't a real person; as most of the conversations he had with others were like an act. When he was messing around with friends, his own personality and humour were still evident and gushed out of him, but he seemed to have a contradiction between his inner and outer worlds. To some extent he had unconsciously created a persona to guard his heart and to feel safe. This persona had no reality or grounding in Joe's most authentic thoughts and true emotions. So, it caused him to wander ghost-like through certain aspects of his life. The harsh reality of his life, he didn't have the means to come to terms with; it was easier to be somewhere else other than in the moment. Joe had drifted from the ground of his own being; he was still there, lost inside himself and disconnected from the truth. Of course, as a teenage boy he didn't have such thoughts, but rather a deep feeling of exile from himself which could only be countered by intense emotions and experiences outside of himself.

His spirit, soul and body propelled themselves over the school gates and out into the world.

There was a freedom in this to explore and search for some meaning, to try and find an answer to the questions of his heart. This 'freedom', however, was fraught with danger. It was exhilarating for Joe and his friends to be without boundaries and control. But without any direction and with a desire to escape (not only from school but from every aspect of their existence, even themselves), this would take them down many hellish paths and dusky valleys. Like brothers they would watch each other's backs and stand beside each other, when necessary and if possible. Yet if they had known that some of them would not return from these paths which began in naivety, perhaps they would have taken different routes in life.
Perhaps.

Chapter 17
The Valleys of the Shadows

Two days of *dogging* school became two weeks, and then nearly two months, before Joe, Meeko, Gringo, Craigo and Big Mooney were finally caught. The boys had randomly and infrequently attended certain classes to diminish any suspicion which the class teachers had. The head teacher was amazed that the system of attendance which was in place could be so easily defeated. The subject teachers, who had all assumed that the boys just had poor attendance (and were secretly happy not to have them in class as they were usually disruptive and difficult to deal with), hadn't raised the alarm at first. Only a coincidental staffroom conversation with Joe's Art teacher and Mr. Carroll had made them realise that the boys had been extending their summer holidays somewhat.

The school was embarrassed when it came to light that five pupils had outwitted them for so long. The boys, although gutted to be caught, were secretly pleased at having beaten the system for a time in their own way; in the only way they knew how. When they returned they were given attendance cards and all teachers were alerted to their magnetic propensity for the other side of the school fence. This came after a three week exclusion for playing truant! This was obviously bizarre to everyone, except to the policy of the school, which held that pupils should be excluded as the final punitive measure. Even Joe and the gang knew this was weird but they weren't going to complain-another three weeks off school! Even if the first week involved being grounded and having to wear their parents out before they were let outside the door, it was still worth it.

The form of punishment primarily used by Scottish schools, 'the belt', had been banned in Joe's second year at Lourdes. This was not before he had received six of the belt on numerous occasions, usually for fighting and winding the teachers up. Yet as much as the belt was painful-especially during the winter months when your hands were freezing- for boys like Gringo, Meeko and Joe it was never a deterrent. Most of them had experienced much harsher violence than this, and on occasion were content to have an immediate punishment which only lasted a few seconds. In fact, on occasion, Big Mooney would deliberately do things to get the belt in order to heat his hands up on a cold morning. This was insane, even to the boys, but there was at least some logic in his lunacy.

During their dogging days the boys had to find or create places to go to avoid the police and stay 'off the radar'. At first they would find a close or the stairs in the Tarfside high rise flats and would share their two single cigarettes. They would keep themselves from being bored by humorously goading each other in various ways. One activity that they engaged in was simple yet effective for humour and annoyance. They would take turns at copying each other, where four of them would repeat everything that one of the group said, whilst continuing their own conversation. To the uninitiated this sounds like a mindless and uninteresting activity, making no sense and having no inherent entertainment value. But its power to annoy the victim and provide the perpetrators with an endless feeling of control over another person, had to be experienced from the inside, to appreciate the hilarity it could generate. Joe was usually the instigator of this annoying practice as he hated the empty silence of the high rise flats.

"Meeko, you still goin' out wi' Ruth?" Joe asked partially from boredom and partly to see what he could find out about Marie.

"Meeko, you still goin' out wi' Ruth?" The three amigos harmoniously conspired to give Joe a taste of his own medicine.

"Fuck up…are you?"

"Fuck up…are you?" The amigos tried to maintain this with straight faces, the only way to make it last as long as possible.

"Awrite then, I'm no' that bothered", Joe knew that at least ten to fifteen minutes of being annoyed were coming his way, "Mooney have you got a bird yet?"

Awrite then, I'm no' that bothered…Mooney have you got a bird yet?" Meeko laughed, knowing that Joe's apparent indifference was the sure sign that he had Joe exactly where he wanted him.

"On ye go then ya bunch a fannies, see how long you can keep it goin'."

"On ye go then ya bunch a fannies, see how long you can keep it goin'."

"My name's Meeko and I'm a complete fanny." Joe began his first of many strategies to break their consistent and persistent repetition.

"My name's Meeko and I'm a complete fanny." The amigos continued, Meeko included, smiling with anticipation for Joe's next move.

"My name's Gringo and I'm gay, these are my two bum chums, Craigo and Meeko." Joe said this with his best 'gay voice' and even made a camp limp handed gesture, touching Gringo's shoulder.

His friends couldn't stop laughter escaping from their determined, focussed faces but Meeko motioned for them to keep going, copying everything as the rules required, even the intonation and body language.

"My name's Gringo and I'm gay, these are my two bum chums, Craigo and Meeko." Big Mooney was doubled up, clenching his stomach with pleasurable pain. Joe kept this strategy going for about two minutes, even reverting to extreme lengths of involving family members of his friends in the conversation.

"Hello, I'm Meeko. I didnae want anybody to know this but I fancy Big Mooney's Ma."

Barely holding it together in the pause between Joe's expressions, the amigos continued,

"Hello, I'm Meeko. I didnae want anybody to know this but I fancy Big Mooney's Ma."

Joe realised that both he and the gang could keep this going for quite a while so he took a pause and allowed his kaleidoscopic mind to take his friends on an even more surreal trip. If what followed had been witnessed by anyone other than the five boys, they would possibly, in fact probably, have been sectioned under the mental health act.

Joe let go of all control of language and with full lungs shouted, "Hoorymahaw!"

The boys followed,"Hoorymahaw!"

"Mahamaraho!"

"Mahamaraho!"

"Maheemara Hamara Haw!"

"Maheemara Hamara Haw!"

Big Mooney stared at his friends with a mixture of both joy and terror as something

about this strange language, which sounded to him like a primal form of Gaelic mixed with Native American, disturbed him deep in his gut. He laughed reluctantly and somewhat fearfully, sensing a fear of losing control in the core of his soul.
Joe journeyed from these gibberish utterances to a fully developed song, as if it sprung from some past existence when he knew this language from another place and time. This was sung to the tune of 'Bibbidi-Bobbidi-Boo', the magic song from Cinderella.

"Hoorymahaw! Mahamaraho! Maheemara Hamara Haw
Hoorymahaw! Mahamaraho! Maheemara Hamara Haw…"

As Joe entered into his second chorus, with a freedom of spirit and an unexplainable joy, having lost Gringo and Craigo, and Meeko clenching his solar plexus barely holding on, he suddenly became aware of another presence.

"Hoorymahaw, Mahamara…!" Joe abruptly stopped and his pals thought this was just another turn of Joe's madness. As he slowly turned his head, looking up to the fire exit door, through the small rectangular window, a wrinkled frowning pair of red eyes stared at them, with a mixture of anger and bewilderment etched on its face. When eye contact was made and Joe realised they were not alone, the door creaked open. Only at this point did the amigos and Mooney stop laughing and shot a glance towards the door.

"Whit the fuck are youse doin' in here!? Get yourselves to f…" Before old Alcoholic Archie, the Concierge of the flats, was given a reasonable explanation as to the presence of the Glasgow Navaho, the young braves flew over each other, pushing their way past him as one entity, knocking him on his arse.

Their joy and laughter began to return as they leapt down each flight of stairs. and heard the echo of his threats fade.

"I'm phonin' the polis… wee arseholes!"

At other times the boys would create hiding places which were closer to home and where they wouldn't be disturbed. They spent nearly a whole week during this time, playing cards and telling jokes in Meeko's cellar, which was in his back close. They had turned it into a den, which simply meant that they stole some cushions and blankets from Meeko's Ma's house and candles and matches from Craigo's. For extra comfort Gringo also brought an old mattress, which in hindsight wasn't the best health and safety choice when combined with candles, teenagers, a confined space and a locked door. It took them five days and nearly burning down Meeko's whole close, before they considered that it wasn't the greatest idea. But they did have fun, and they did feel free, in some ways. Nevertheless, this freedom, the absence of any structure or stimulation led them, once again, to create their own stimulation.

At fourteen years old, five sons caught in the murky confusion between childhood and adulthood, descended obliviously into the valley of drugs. The boys had closely observed drug use in the lives of those a few years older. At this stage in their journey, they didn't know many drug addicts and despite having been touched by death in the solvent abuse incident, they told themselves that it was different. In some ways it was different; some people seemed to do it as a lifestyle choice and were apparently gaining lots of pleasure from it. There didn't appear to be any obvious consequences to their young minds. They were only experimenting and it couldn't be any worse than drinking all the time like their Das. Not only that, a lot of it was 'natural', 'plants and herbs', *so it couldn't be that bad, could it*? These were questions and considerations which came as they delved further down into the valley, not when they were at the edge looking in.

Gringo's Da was working and wouldn't be back till ten o'clock. He had taken the back shift in his taxi and would probably go to the pub for a few drinks afterwards.

"Here…you'll never guess whit I got fae Div Logue?" Gringo was excited and felt a pride in having interacted with the local drug dealer.

Meeko was in a foul mood, having been shouted at from his Da just before he 'left for school'.

"Whit is it? I'm guessin' it's no' a quarter of sherbet Bonbons."

Gringo's eyes widened with anticipation in seeing his friend's admiration, as he held out to them a small, oily, brownish substance, wrapped in Clingfilm.

"Look…a deal!" Gringo thought this was self-explanatory to the whole group.

"Did you get a bargain?" Mooney looked confused "Whit is it?"

"It's a bit of hash ya *numpty*." Meeko had seen his brothers smoke cannabis over the years and even knew how to roll a joint. Well, sort of.

"Let us see it Gringo. Do you have any fag papers? Whit about fags?" Craigo felt a hunger and a haste in him to enter into this experience before something had the chance to ruin it. Although he knew that there would be no concierge peering into Gringo's living room window, and that the chances of burning his house down were minimal, he still felt something driving him to quicken the experience. Joe was also intrigued and felt the adrenalin of an opportunity, which offered initiation into another aspect of scheme life, but he was scared. Perhaps the others were also, but as is the human experience, he was only acutely aware of his own fear. His spirit, his intuition, knew that this was the first step on a path which was unknown, unfamiliar and unpredictable.

As they all sat down, almost in a circle, with the drug in the middle holding the status of the room, all attention was fixed on every detail of this experience. This felt like the beginning of a ritual which would take them into another world. Their senses were on high alert before the cannabis had even been burned to soften it. As Gringo crumbled it into the carelessly joined, cigarette filled Rizla papers, their eyes were transfixed on this small substance as it released its sweet herbal odour into the room. The smell was intoxicating and although a completely different aroma it reminded Joe of the incense burnt in chapel. More than the scent it was the atmosphere which it seemed to evoke, a sense of the attending congregation bowing down in reverential submission to some invisible force. This was as weird to Joe as it sounds to us, yet he couldn't shake off the similarity. Both rituals felt like shadows of some reality to Joe and he strangely felt more comfortable with the drug initiation than the religious one. All the drug ritual seemed to require was engagement and it invited (or even seduced) the individual to come just as they were. To Joe the church often felt that its acceptance was conditional and that it required him to be more than he was, or to feel guilty for not being more than he was. Bizarre as this comparison was, it continued for Joe as he was passed the first joint.

"Here mate, take a few puffs of that." Gringo handed Joe the joint, holding in the inhaled smoke until he had finished his sentence. He then blew it out as if it was both painful and pleasurable. He coughed and spluttered and sunk back in the chair.

"Whit's it like Gringo?" Joe hesitated, half hoping that Gringo might say something to stop him. Gringo just stared at him for about five seconds (which to him felt like five minutes), and then he burst out laughing.

"Aha…Gringo? I didnae realise my name was so funny." Gringo was totally unaware of how slow his speech was and how incomprehensible he sounded to the others. He couldn't understand why they had never realised how funny his name was. They all laughed at him and with him.

"Hurry up Joe, geez a puff." Craigo was anxiously waiting for the door of perception to be opened.

"Calm down, I'm savourin' the moment." Joe smiled and put the joint to his lips, and then he sucked the smoke into his mouth. It burned his throat as it raced to his lungs. He instantly felt his eyes and his mind expand and lifted the joint to take a second puff, quickened by the eager eyes of his pals. His throat couldn't take it and he broke into a fit of coughing.

"Looks like good stuff." Nobody could tell if Big Mooney was being ironic as he sounded genuinely approving of the effects of the hash. Its ability to produce fits of coughing were apparently proof to him of its inherent goodness.

Craigo took a couple of puffs and his naturally contemplative mind embraced the experience, like a spiritual disciple absorbing the wisdom of his guru. He then passed the joint to Meeko, who in turn completed the circle by giving it to Mooney. For a few moments they all sat in silence, unable to connect the contents of their minds with their lips. Their thoughts took on an entirely new quality; they were slower, longer and clearer. Thoughts seemed more tangible, more real and in some ways more present. Their visual, audio and even tactile perceptions were sharper and more acute than usual. To adjust to this strange and initially peaceful feeling, they each tried to focus outside of their heads by concentrating on something in the room. Joe happened to be staring at Mooney's face and found it fascinating that he had never actually had a good look at him. He noticed the largeness of his oval eyes and how they seemed to cover almost the full breadth of his face. He didn't mean to offend when he broke the thick silence,

"You look like a fly Mooney."

The rest of the boys turned in a kind of slow motion and stared at Mooney. They could all see it and one by one they started to giggle. The laughter accelerated and continued for about five minutes until they couldn't even remember what started it. Mooney laughed as well, but once again he felt disconnected from what the others seemed to be experiencing and the seeds of paranoia which lay dormant in him, began slowly to creep in his mind like weeds.

"Sorry mate, I didnae mean to embarrass you." Joe felt protective and sensitive to the disconnection he saw on Mooney's face .

"It's awrite, it was funny Joe." Mooney tried to convince himself that what had happened to him was insignificant and he desperately tried to be at peace with himself. It wasn't really Joe's words which had caused this feeling, but they had served to draw Mooney's attention to his sense of separation from himself and others. The cannabis had taken the boys into a different experience, which presented itself as a way out of boredom and a disassociation from reality. For Mooney it awakened a dormant restlessness which like a sleeping snake had appeared dead and harmless. To Joe, Meeko and Gringo it provided a comforting dullness to their raw emotions and a lightness and humour to the melancholy of existence. Yet for Craigo, who sat silently for most of this experience, it was a combination of both; it elated him but also deflated him. His mind could now go deeper and his intellect was sharper, but his emotions and his spirit were deadened. He had descended into the valley, and had stepped onto a path of belief that the only way to ascend was more stimulation. To ascend this valley would not be without cost, nor would drugs provide a guide or a way out.

Chapter 18
Fear No Evil

The first time that Joe and his friends smoked cannabis was the beginning of a relationship with drugs which would last for many years. For some of them it was sadly the beginning of the end of their lives; the knife which would cut their lives short. Like all long term relationships, there were good times and bad times. Ironically (and somewhat hypocritically), adults who smoked, overate and intoxicated their bodies with alcohol on a weekly basis would lecture the boys on the danger of drugs. There was even a campaign set up by the government with the simplistic and ineffective strategy of 'Just Say No'. However, the complexity of forces at work on the minds and lives of many young people in Glasgow wasn't usually dispelled by a simple 'No'; it was rather more complicated than that. The truth about drugs is that no-one would take them if they didn't offer intense pleasure or sweet release-but as Joe and his friends came to believe, they did.

Like the first experience Joe and his friends had, there were many nights of intense laughter, *the giggles*; many times of heightened sensual pleasure ranging from *the munchies* to their first sexual exploits on drugs. Also on this spectrum of experience was the acute attention and pleasure in music, television and for some even physical activities and sports. For Craigo and Big Mooney there was also great pleasure in discovering a world of strange and hidden knowledge in books. This knowledge, accompanied by smoking increasing amounts of cannabis, promised keys to unlock the mysteries of this world and perhaps provide a glance into other possible worlds. To the boys any way out of this world, even temporarily, was inviting. Drugs offered avenues and a connection to the world of ideas which seemed a lot more effective and quicker than going to school. This was how it seemed to Joe and his pals.

In the early stages of their relationship there was no telling these boys that drugs were 'bad' or even harmful. In fact, they often believed that drugs were the solution to the problems of existence. The seductive and subtle power of drug use began to develop from desire to habit; then in time from habit to dependency; and for most the journey led from dependency to addiction. No-one who begins to take drugs ever believes that it could end in addiction or even death. 'Junkies' are judged and condemned by a society of dependents; even by those who are simply 'further down' on the ladder of addiction-food, alcohol, sexual and emotional dependencies. The deceptive power of addiction partly lies in its ability to convince the individual that he or she, in some unnamed way, has a power which will enable him or her to avoid the pitfalls of drugs common to the rest of humanity. The delusion rests on the lie that we, as individuals are different, that we are in control of our dependencies. The absence of foresight, and the eager desire to be free from the here and now, embraces the lie and often welcomes it as a support, rather than as a 'dis-ease'.

With their combined experience, as well as the depth which already existed in their own minds, there were also nights of incredibly intelligent conversation that many philosophers would be proud of. These might have been 'poorly educated' young people (partly through choice and the limits of the system which they were bound to), but they were in no way unintelligent or lacking in insight. Their psychological tapestry of consistent broken trust, living with traumatic emotion and an intuitive sense that not many adults were what they seemed to be, created a discerning and astute mind in them. They each possessed a 'bullshit detector' and with varying degrees of accuracy and unrivalled wit, they reduced the theories of mortal men to where they truly belonged -in the dust. Reflecting on many subjects, the drug induced philosophical enquiry flitted from whether ghosts existed to the origins of the universe. Their perceptual abilities had been sharpened by their experience and the brokenness of their minds and emotions enabled them to question all appearances. They didn't trust and it quickened their minds.
"Where did dogs come fae? How do they fit in to the equation?" Craigo stared at Shane, Big Mooney's Alsatian dog and it returned his curious gaze as he questioned its existence.
"Whit are you on about Craigo?" Joe had been tuned in and lost in the Bob Marley song 'Is this love?' and his thoughts couldn't even register a question about the origin and existence of dogs. He tried to tune his mind to Craigo's wavelength.
"No, I mean, I know about evolution and shit, but did everythin' come fae the same

substance? I thought we came from somethin' out of the water. So, how did dogs evolve fae that?"

"Oh right, you know about 'evolution and shit', the two pillars of our existence. Why are you pickin' on the dugs then?" Meeko felt the need to clarify Craigo's motivation for raising the question as he passed the *spliff* to Gringo; his small piercing eyes actually looked shut due to the three hour session of smoking joints, pipes, bongs and water bottles. These were all attempts to deepen the stone, take them into new depths and alter the consciousness further, which, judging by the conversation which followed, had reached their desired effect.

"Did they no' all come fae wolves?" Big Mooney chipped in, although quickly realised by the unanimous frowns and blank expressions that he was missing the main thrust of the argument.

"Aye mate, but Craigo wants to know how a fish became a wolf." Joe's ability to articulate ideas visually brought them back slightly from the conceptual argument.

"I don't get it. I'll need to read that book on evolution again. I must have missed somethin'." Craigo's need to know things was in itself a type of addiction which soothed his anxiety about losing control. If he knew things, if he could work everything out, then things would be ok.

"Aye mate, you're definitely missin' somethin'." Meeko didn't even look up from building another joint as he said this, and only Joe picked up on his sarcasm.

"Never mind the dogs, where did the fish and the water even come fae?" Gringo emphatically expressed his question which startled Shane, who released a tiny yelp of disapproval and looked slightly offended at the negation of his species.

"Oh look, Gringo's pickin' on the goldfish now. Whit's wrang wi' you?" Joe tried to keep things light as his mind felt so heavy and cloudy.

"No Joe, he does have a point. I hear whit you're sayin' mate. Where did anythin' come fae, even the stuff which caused the Big Bang and evolution?" Craigo wanted to explore this further, his way of holding on to some pursuit of 'reality' or meaning. He needed things to be explained, but for Joe he wasn't ready to face any ideas of reality, he was doing his best to run away from it, to hide from it.

"It's always been here has it no'?" Big Mooney's succinct and simple opinion was self-evident, at least to him.

Craigo took a deep puff of the joint, not even allowing the residual smoke around his nose to escape. He breathed in and allowed the cannabis to act as both a preparatory pause and also a steam train on which his thoughts could travel further into the essence of this argument.

"No mate, that disnae seem right to me. Everythin' must have a beginnin'. Everythin' must have started somewhere. It disnae seem right just to say that it's always been here. That's just no' right. There's got to be an explanation."

"Maybe, it was actually a big dog that created the world and that's why your first question was about where dogs came fae? That ties in with that thing that people say 'a dog is a man's best friend'. Whit do you think mate?" Joe said this with such conviction that for a split second Craigo actually considered that there might be some validity in it. His bullshit radar, however, navigated him back to detect Joe's wind up. He laughed and allowed himself to humorously entertain the creator dog theory.

"That would be mad wouldn't it? A big hairy Creator, munchin' some Cosmic Chum."

The gang exploded into laughter; they loved Craigo's mind and how it could freely float from philosophy to fantasy. There didn't seem to be a big divide between them at times, only a single thought and shift in perspective.

"I know, maybe that's why dog is God spelt backwards." Big Mooney was still at some level, holding the creator dog theory as plausible, and in the haze of stony reflection his question did make sense to Meeko.

"Aye, do you think God's got hair?" Meeko laughed but again the question seemed to hold certain validity.

"The Rasta's better hope so or they've got that whole dreadlock thing seriously wrang." Joe laughed, yet slightly uncomfortable at the image developing from the creation of dogs to Creator dog, and then returning to the idea of a plausible Creator, albeit a hairy one.

In some respects, the boys began to use drugs in much the same way as others join clubs, take up sports or engage routinely in hobbies. In one sense they were just 'something to do', a way to relieve feelings of boredom, melancholy and emptiness.

The use of drugs wasn't always exciting and fun and in fact sometimes prolonged the feeling of emptiness. The boys would often take drugs and hang around closes or walk the streets when they were moved on by the police. And like many hobbies or pastimes they become routine behaviours and established ways of distracting the mind from the difficulties and realities which they all had to face. Yet, for many in the schemes of a city, drugs become so much more than an additional activity of their lives.

The roots of drugs creep deep in to the mind, the body and even the spirit. Their persuasive nature is to offer a freedom which both expands the mind and alters perception to make it a more palatable experience; whilst at the same time, its roots entangle themselves around some part of the human soul and slowly strangle out the very essence of life. As the vines of drugs began to choke their young lives, the everyday normality of their lives became even more unbearable. The only way to counter the emptiness, quietness, boredom and restlessness of the days, was to get more stoned. The need for oblivion, to take the edge from life, grew into a paradoxical way of being: endless, restless activity without any real substance. Despite the exploration of every topic from politics to religion, and every fantastical idea from a universe governed by a dog to the existence of spirits and ghosts, the subject of drug dependency or any of its negative repercussions never arose. Perhaps, those who engage in drug use intuitively know that questioning the long term fruits of the experience might close the door through which they're trying to escape. Or at least make it a more restricting experience.

In a short period of time the boys moved through different experiences of consciousness as they experimented with different drugs. From cannabis, the next step was magic mushrooms or acid tabs, then powders and pills such as Amphetamines (Speed), Temazepam (Jellies), Vallium and an endless list of others- uppers, downers and trippers. However, despite being drawn to the altered consciousness of being stoned, Joe always made his excuses and avoided the hallucinatory drugs (like acid and mushrooms). He didn't know why but he feared that his mind would begin to unravel if he allowed it to enter into a more vivid world than the one which his spirit already occupied. His dreams, his nightmares, his daydreams, the intuitions and impressions of energies all around him, and even the intensity of his emotions, were so vivid and disturbing to him that he knew he didn't need anything else to heighten his sensitivity to other invisible or thought realms. There was an unwritten natural progression in the world of drug use, and although almost all began with smoking cannabis, very few remained there. Once they had entered this world it was as if the initiation into different (and more powerful) drugs was an inevitable part of the process. It was never discussed or even deeply considered by those involved. Most of the time it wasn't even peer pressure, but simply that in this world, opportunities (or temptations) were offered freely and routinely. Joe often thought of Jim during this time as he had made himself scarce since being expelled from school. Jim wasn't interested in drug use as he liked, or needed, to be in control. Watching his Da and his Grandpa's addiction to alcohol was enough to steer him clear of this particular poison. He would occasionally come up from Govan to see Joe and to look in on the boys from Hardridge. He had a fondness for them and would have been there for them if needed, but he kept his distance. Joe sensed this distance and yet could see that Jim had his own initiations to go through. This wasn't about becoming a man or any warped *rite of passage,* but the inevitable unfolding and fruition of the seeds which had been sown in them as small, receptive and innocent children *would* reap a harvest.

The brothers had a connection which went deeper than speech; they each knew that the distance between them would grow and they had some hidden longing that they would arrive at the same place, hopefully together.

Chapter 19
Baptism of Violence

While Joe and the gang were coming under the subtle, controlling influence of drugs as the predominant preoccupation of their daily lives, Jim was being seduced by another form of control-violence. Jim had been a 'good fighter' from his early days and was known, both in Hardridge and Govan, as well as in school, as someone to be cautious of. Adolescence was a laboratory for releasing all of the potential energy stored up since early childhood. Sometimes the catalyst which unleashed this energy was accidental or coincidental; sometimes it was intentional and premeditated.

Since John and Mary split up, Jim stayed with his Da and Joe with his Ma. And like any divorce or separation there was a great sense of loss, pain and confusion. Joe was angry at his Da for not being there, and even when he was there he felt a deep resentment simmering. As usual these feelings had no place or space to be acknowledged, never mind expressed. So, they were displaced into other aspects of life-school, the gang, criminal activities and most of all, Mary. Joe was in constant conflict with Mary and used every means possible to avoid any responsibility for his behaviour. The world owed him and someone was going to pay.

Jim also possessed a volcanic rage but most of the time he appeared calm and controlled. Jim was living with active alcoholism- neglect, absence and an emotional climate of blame, accusation and constant criticism. Sometimes the criticisms were subtle, at others they were cloaked in venomous words, hateful expressions and the constant threat of violence. Jim was now the buffer between John's alcoholism and his failed responsibility. At home Jim had no place to express his anger or act it out like many teenagers do. He would have been beaten senseless. So his rage grew inside. It was only a matter of time before the violence in him could not be contained any longer. Although he knew better than to lose his temper as this meant he had lost control.

Two events acted as the keys to unleash this pain and this rage. The first was fuelled by loss and love, the other by revenge and the desire for 'respect'.

Jim was always the closest grandson to his Granny McDermott, Mary's Ma, as she had always given him the extra attention which was absent in his home. Granny McDermott had a tribe of grandchildren as Mary had two brothers and three sisters, all with their own wains. She loved them all and showed them kindness and care whenever they came to visit. But she intuitively knew that Jim had a unique place in her heart and she in his. Yet, when Mary and John first separated, and Jim went to stay with his Da, he felt that he had to take a side. There was no middle ground on which to rest and be at peace. There was a war and everyone was caught in the crossfire. The tension between John and Mary and between Mary's family and John filtered down into the hearts and minds of their sons. Jim felt a warped obligation and loyalty to John, despite his Da's propensity for lashing out at him, verbally and physically. He felt that his Da needed him in this time and with his distorted mix of loyalty and obligation he made his choices. Jim hated hearing the criticisms of his Da and his blame for what had happened was clearly focussed on Mary. To him, it was her fault that their family was torn apart. One outcome of this was that Jim refused to visit Mary for a time and even refused to visit or speak with his Granny. He chose his side and with determination he resolved to stand his ground.

In the confusion of divorce and of the history which had gone before, the mesh of secrets, lies and shadows fed the fears and shame in Jim's heart. He guarded his heart like a stronghold, so that he would not be shaken in his stance. He wanted to prove to his Da that he was a faithful son whom he could be proud of, and to show Mary that she had caused him pain. An opportunity arose for him to demonstrate his loyalty to his Da and gain his approval. It was in the middle of Govan Cross, at the bus station on a busy Saturday afternoon. It was exactly three o'clock as the Old Parish Church bell called the world to attention. Jim's mind was particularly stilled by the church bell as his eyes fixed on two jet black ravens scarpering and squawking like an omen from the Parish Tower. The hustle and bustle of Govan's centre always had an air of excitement mixed with the potential and anticipation of trouble; the boys were out of their own territory as Govan was separated by different schemes. Jim was standing with two friends from Govan, wee Davie and big Ramie.

"D'you think we'll see any of they Govan Casuals doon here Jim?" Wee Davie was trying to act as if this was something that he invited, but really hoped that there wouldn't be any trouble.

"Aye, I hope so. They set about wee Dunky last week when there was a big team ae them. We'll see if they're as bold when there's only one or two of them." Jim genuinely invited, even searched for the opportunity for violence. He had recently become quite obsessed with knives and his Da was always telling him about the 'Glasgow Hard Men', with a kind of pride or admiration. There was a mixed message to both stay away from violence and trouble but to honour it and respect its power. This 'respect' was paralleled with the many nights where Jim had to stay in the house on his own, either because his Da was working late or had gone to the pub straight after work and wasn't back until the early hours. His imagination began to foresee someone breaking into his house and attacking him; his spirit was filled with murderous visions and images of bloodbaths. He started placing weapons in strategic places all around the house-knives, hammers and a pick shaft handle which his Da kept behind the front door. This was to make him feel safer!

In the darkest places of his memory the 'bad man' who had murdered his uncle Tam and the two abandoned children in their innocence, still lurked and stared. To him, this was the same bad man that his Da told him to go away with as a wee boy-the one who threatened to kill them all if he didn't do something about it. His distorted sense of protection and responsibility had grown from a frightened child into a teenager with a mind heading down the path of violence.

"Aye, I hope we run into that Kenny MacDonald. He slashed wee Healey a few months ago. I wouldnae mind givin' it back to him." Big Ramie was also keen to be the first of his gang to use a knife and knew it was only a matter of time before it happened. His heart was set on it.

As Jim scanned the bus station and Govan Cross to see if there were any of the Riverside Casuals nearby, out of the corner of his vision he was aware of someone staring at him. At first his heart jumped at the thought that someone was looking for him just as he was looking for others, particularly as he knew his own intentions. However, as he turned and focussed he realised that it was his Granny, smiling and carrying two shopping bags. She put one of them down and waved over. Jim didn't wave back but said to his pals,

"Hold on a minute, I need to see somebody."

"Where are ye goin'?" His pals were more concerned about their own safety than they were about Jim's.

As Jim walked over to his Granny an icy pain covered his heart. He thought of his Da.

"Hello son, whit are ye doin' doon here?" His Granny was so glad to see him as she'd been worried about him since the breakup.

"I'm just down wi' my pals." Jim's heart was completely closed and he couldn't look her in the eye.

"Eh…when are ye gonnae come up and see me. I've no' seen ye for ages. I was gonnae come doon to your Da's to see if you were awrite. How have ye been? I'm missin' you pal." Granny tried to reach beyond the wall that Jim was quickly building. She could see his pain and could never have been angry with him.

"I'm awrite. I'm no' comin' back up to see you, or my Ma. And don't come down to my Da's. I don't want to see any of you." Jim's pain could only show itself in anger and his Granny could see it. Her heart cracked a little but she understood that Jim's anger would pass and that she shouldn't try to push it. Even in Jim's bitterness she loved him even more. There was no trace of judgment in Granny and she had only compassion in her heart for what Jim had been through.

"Awrite son, if that's whit you want." This was both a way of letting Jim go whilst allowing him the freedom to come back to her in his own time. She knew he would because she knew that behind all the confusion, behind the teenage hardness which he felt obligated to maintain, he loved her with the sweet and trusting love of a child.

"Aye that's whit I want, so you can tell my Ma as well." Jim walked away and never looked back. He knew that the look of sadness on his Granny's face would be too much for him to carry back to his pals.

"C'mon, let's go back to the scheme." Jim left a part of himself at Govan Cross -in due time he would return here to find it, not even aware that he was searching.

If only Jim had known what was around the near corner. If only he would have known that our pain may become regret if we hold onto it. If only he had been alone this day and ready to open up when he had met his Granny. If only he had been aware and free enough when he saw her. Free to be honest about the turmoil buried inside.

If only he had known that he would never see her again in this life, he would have done something different.

This last thought buzzed in his head like an angry bee.

The fact that the news came from Mary didn't help.

"Jim…I'm sorry son, but your Granny died this mornin'." Mary sobbed but sensed that Jim didn't want her affection or her attention. The words felt like a tonne weight had been dropped onto his chest. He sat down under the weight and stared at the ground, trying to hold back the flood of feelings battering against him like a tsunami.

"Get out!" Jim turned on Mary and she had nothing to say. She left, holding her tattered coat and heart.

Jim's head told him that he should be crying and that he should feel something. This was irrelevant. He told himself that what had happened had happened. There was nothing that could be done about it. He was a fifteen year old teenage boy from a Glasgow housing scheme. To him, this simply meant that crying wasn't part of the picture. This was just another pain to be swallowed, another memory to be ignored.

Jim never spoke to anyone at the funeral except Joe, and even to his young brother he had very little words. Joe knew that Jim was deeply troubled by his Granny's death but he didn't have the words to comfort him. He just let him know that he was there.

"You awrite Jim?"

"Aye... are you awrite?" Jim's deflection of the question was a mixture of his brotherly protection and his denial of his own feelings.

The funeral service passed; people got drunk afterwards; voices got louder in the Chapel Hall and Granny was forgotten. This was how it seemed to Jim. The days and weeks which followed were infused with numbness as Jim considered life with a stinging bitterness. Jim was angry at his parents, himself and the world that he found himself stuck in. He needed to burst out of it, to break the oppressive sadness which was clouding his mind.

On another busy Saturday afternoon, in the middle of Govan Cross, three weeks from the day of Granny McDermott's funeral, Jim's violence awoke as the Church Bell once again struck its third chime. He was aware of a feeling similar to déjà vu but its gravity felt more like the hand of fate, driven by some dark desire. Once again the two ravens fled the tower and hovered over the bus station, like vultures lurking for carrion. As Jim's eyes scanned the bus station they landed and fixed on Kenny MacDonald, the leader of the Govan Casuals.

Jim's accomplice on this particular afternoon was one of the Hardridge gang who had unexpectedly yet somehow aptly gravitated towards him in the weeks leading up to this ominous day. His name was Rab Pollok and was one of the glue-sniffing brothers who had a propensity for fire (and was in fact the originator of 'fire-bug' night) and other forms of mindless destruction. He had a cruel streak and emptiness in his eyes which Jim saw potential in. This emptiness was the kind which could be filled with violence and Jim had plans to beat Big Ramie in the race to use a knife first.

When Jim saw Kenny MacDonald his heart didn't race, nor could it be said that there was high emotion or adrenalin. Rather than any sense of panic or drama, he was taken over by a calculating and focussed mind, which prepared to clinically and effectively execute a bloody act.

"There's MacDonald. You wait here because he'll bolt if he sees the two of us walkin' towards him." Jim was adamant that even Rab wouldn't get the chance to be baptized into this violence before him.

"Whit are ye gonnae dae?" Rab's greedy eyes wanted in on the violence but for now he was quite happy to stay in the shadow and let Jim's anger come into the broad daylight of Govan Cross.

"Just wait here. If anybody else appears, *hander* me. If the polis appear, shout."

With commands delegated, Jim set his face like flint and made his way towards the carefree Kenny, who was enjoying the company of two giddy teenage girls.

The three of them were laughing and Kenny with his deerstalker hat, his top designer labels and his shiny white trainers was caught in the illusion of safety and invincibility. He saw Jim pacing towards him but because he was in his own territory, in the middle of the day, with scores of witnesses, he vainly held on to an air of confidence and security. To show his unconcern for the threat of this 'wee guy', he turned round and kept speaking to the girls. It was almost as if, in his unassuming manner and the lack of terror in his eyes, Jim was cloaked within the shadow of his intention.

In his mind Jim could 'see' the event before it took place. He pre-empted and played out reactions from victim and witnesses and had at least two possible escape routes in the eye of his mind. When there was a distance of about fifteen feet between him and Kenny he reached for the wooden handle of his blade.

It felt cold. He was ready.

He quickened his pace enough to accelerate his force but not too much to be noticed by the bustling shoppers.

Kenny, still smiling, turned to face Jim and was met with a blade fiercely plunging under his rib cage. He thought he'd been punched and winded and he clutched his side, as if to stop the burning pain travelling across his side and his stomach.

It was warm. He was cold. He collapsed. Blood spilled. People screamed. Jim ran.

Jim's mind felt clinical and clear; he almost felt as if he was someone else, like his mind was possessed by another body which was carrying out these acts. His sharp, expanded thoughts guided his body, which felt that it was too small and vulnerable for this powerful mind.

Keep running. Keep running. Don't look back.

There was no feeling of completeness or satisfaction which Jim assumed would come with this act. In fact, if he would have truly been in touch with his body and his own mind he would have been acutely aware of feeling deflated, dissatisfied and even of a tear in his soul. He had ripped through flesh and his hands were smeared with blood. He had pierced through the reality of the material world, and in doing so he felt like he'd torn himself from it.

Rab from Hardridge had witnessed the event with an uncomfortable excitement.

Although he had fantasised about knife crime, as many young boys in Glasgow do, observing this incident dispelled many of the preconceptions. This was simply a disturbing home movie, not a Hollywood action film. He may still have been drawn to it in the days to come by his own self-destructive spirit, but the false glamour had been removed. Only when he committed a similar act two months later did he see the emptiness of this experience from the inside. There was a seductive power with committing an act of violence like this. Nevertheless, the fruit of the experience was always a growing sense of the perpetrator's inadequacy to live authentically. Like a bad trip on drugs, many would try this experience and never return, but some would continue to seek more of the same and chase it until they felt contentment. This never truly came.

Initially, Jim didn't retell this story, but Rab did, to everyone he could. This retelling was a way of making it more exciting and palatable than it actually was. Talking about it was another way of removing himself from the real feeling which it had left him with.

As expected, Jim was woken the next morning to his Da telling him that the police were at the door and they wanted to speak to him. The process of coming under the hand of the law was systematic and impersonal. They silently searched his room for a knife and took two which were under his bed. He was silently taken to the police station. He silently sat as they asked him various questions and then charged him. Attempted Murder.

Even in the court room, hearing the charges being read out by a judge and the echo of his own plea of 'Not Guilty' bouncing off the walls of the court and his mind, there was no sense of shock or terror. Jim felt inevitability about the whole process. Not so much that it *had* to happen but rather that it was *going to* and therefore was no surprise. It had only been a matter of time before the desires conceived had become thoughts, which in turn grew into fearful fantasies and then birthed dreadful actions.

Rab was also charged and made the same plea. He didn't even look at Jim when they were brought into court from the cells below. This un-nerved Jim slightly and his gut twisted inside. They were released on bail and free to tell their tale to all. Rab assured Jim that he hadn't spoken to the police and had done the sensible thing, which was to say nothing until they came to trial. And only then would speaking be a final measure to secure a release. The boys from Govan and Hardridge eagerly asked them about every detail and were satisfied that one of their own had made a mark on the Casuals.

The Casuals were gangs of designer-label wearing youths who initially formed together as football fans of the same teams. In the mid 80's and early 90's they would go to football matches solely for the purpose of fighting and not really to support a football team. They had developed a certain level of violence at the games and this spilled out into their lives outside of football. Many of the teenagers from schemes hated them, perhaps because they were intimidating due to their large numbers or maybe it was because they could afford expensive clothes. Moreover, they seemed to be shrouded in arrogance and most of them were actually quite cowardly without the shield of a crowd behind them. Jim, in particular, always had contempt for The Casuals as they took liberties with people, often innocent passers-by. Yet, knowing many of them individually from living in Govan and going to school with some of them, he knew that their violent activity was limited to their identity within the group. Warped as it was, he felt that his own violent activity had at least an element of authenticity. He was willing to face people alone and even at this young age of fifteen his frame of mind was such that he would have taken it to its limits and faced the consequences if necessary-death or prison.

Joe was beginning to realise this about Jim and although he felt a pride by association, that his brother was gaining a reputation as a force to be reckoned with, there was sadness in it which he didn't fully recognise. But it was there. It was the sadness that Mary felt also, one which could not be articulated but filled her with despair. The despair that her son, and many sons in Glasgow were so filled with emptiness, worthlessness, anger and fear that they lived with complete disregard for throwing their lives away.

It was only three months later that this baptism which Jim's spirit had been immersed in at Govan Cross, took the next step into this new way of being. This time Jim was back in Hardridge, visiting Joe and the gang. He sat with them in the close as they rolled a few joints and had a laugh with each other. For the time being Jim put the impending court case out of his mind and enjoyed the light-hearted camaraderie of his brother and friends. As much as the Hardridge gang were capable of violence, they were more drawn to the hilarity and carry on which often accompanied getting stoned. They were skilled at distracting their minds from the world, and even from themselves. As they spent most of their time either hanging around the streets or on a good night finding a house to get stoned in, they found themselves mingling with other like-minded drug users who were often more hard core. From time to time each member of the gang would bring others into the usual company, some from the scheme, some from the many surrounding schemes on the South side-Penilee, Pollok, Govan, Ibrox, Kinning Park, Cardonald, Priesthill, Nitshill, Arden, Thornliebank, Carnwadric, Kennishead, Pollokshaws, and a host of other smaller areas with their own gangs, their own drug problems and their own levels of crime and violence.

Hardridge was only a small scheme but many teenagers from other areas liked to mingle with The Paka, perhaps because they were not seeking violence and were willing to share their territory as long as there was no threat of dominance. They were happy to co-exist as long as others knew that this was *their* scheme. Like many inner city areas Glasgow's was very territorial and young people, particularly boys although not exclusively, felt a strong sense of tribal identity within their own area. Some 'tribes' welcomed others but were also defensive and aggressive if there was a perceived threat or aggressive attitudes towards them. Depending on the level of insecurity and subsequent violence within a 'tribe', or within an individual, an 'aggressive attitude' at more subtle levels could range from being present to looking at someone in 'the wrong way'. This was known as *growling.* An individual or group may be perceived as growling simply due to a certain facial expression, usually involving a prolonged stare with a hint of anger and hostility. There were obvious difficulties with this, the most apparent being the lack of ability to accurately discern what the intention of any individual was, just by their facial expression. A teenage boy looking at another with fear, anger or simple curiosity would often be met with any number of rhetorical questions, all of which were confusing and had no obvious answer. These included,

"Whit are you fuckin' lookin' at?"

"Who are you fuckin' lookin' at?"

"Whit's your fuckin' problem?"

And the absurd ones which asked the recipient if he would like to be the victim of violence.

"Do you want a kick in the balls?"

"Do you want your jaw ripped?"

"Do you want your head kicked in?"

A simple 'yes' or 'no', or even 'I don't know' always seemed an inadequate and inappropriate response. In fact, although in the form of questions, they were actually just statements which could be translated as

"Stop staring at me or you will be on the receiving end of violence in one form or another."

This was terrifyingly disorienting for someone when asked this, especially in the middle of someone else's community.

The upshot of this strange territorial and defensive behaviour was that thousands of young people (and even those who never grow out of this narrow thinking), were trapped in an endless hostile world of suspicion, where staring contests had a much sharper edge. If you could *growl* longer at someone, then in some way this was an indication that they were more afraid of you than you were of them!

Bizarre as this was to the outsider, almost every teenager from a scheme in Glasgow had experienced this, especially when in another territory. However, if someone came in to your territory from another area and was growling, even from a distance, this was an act of war, an invasion, an openly hostile act.

Such was this night when the stoned laughter of Meeko and Joe was abruptly halted by the content and tone of a passing stranger's words,

"Who are you lookin' at ya prick?"

Immediately alert to the threat of violence, the bravado of this individual suggested one of three things to Jim-that he was mentally unhinged, that he was intent on violence or that he wasn't alone. It turned out to be a combination of the last two, as the large blade slid from the sleeve of his jacket, calling his baseball-bat and knife-wielding comrades to appear. There were five of them and had the Hardridge boys been armed they would have stood their ground. They weren't, so they waited for Jim's lead.

"Who are you lookin' for?" Jim attempted to open the lines of negotiation before open war, but talking was not on the agenda.

"We're lookin' for Weaso, but you'll dae just now." The intruder burst into a sprint and his cohort followed. Jim noticed that the two members of this gang weren't boys but middle aged men. This threw him a little as it didn't fit the usual picture. Before he moved himself he shouted to Joe and the others.

"Run!"

Leaving unrolled joints and the lightness of the night behind, they scampered through the back close and jumping over fences and bin recesses they ran as one through the back courts. They knew they were to stay together and they all knew where they were heading. Despite the pumping hearts and the fear of falling when a machete or a baseball bat is twenty feet behind you, they were confident that they wouldn't be outran or caught in their own scheme. They knew every broken fence, every open back close and every possible door to chap for refuge.

When they were safely back at Joe's close and the panic died down, Joe and the Amigos let out a burst of relief and laughter. It was always a rush to get away when the violence was so close. Yet Big Mooney and Jim weren't laughing. Jim was fuming that these characters had been ready to attack them, even although it wasn't their fight. He'd been angry with himself for not carrying a knife- a decision he had made whilst out on bail. Big Mooney had become more and more anxious as the quantity of smoking hash had progressed in the last few months, and he was overwhelmed at even the presence of violence these days. He couldn't be near it anymore as it terrified him and made him feel that he was breaking up inside. He tried to contain this from the rest of the gang but felt like he was holding a time bomb inside. He trusted the gang but didn't understand what was happening to him, so he kept it in the dark-just until he could work it out in his own head.

"Right, whit are we gonnae do? I'm no' lettin' this go." Jim was restless and his mind racing to plan and execute an attack before this gang left the scheme.

"We could go up and see Weaso…and tell him that they're here. We could get *tooled up* and tell him we'll hander him, if he wants." Joe's simplicity made sense and appealed to all except Big Mooney.

"I'm gonnae go up the road Joe, I'm no' feelin' too good." Big Mooney was kind of asking for permission as well as telling them what he wanted to do.

"Nae bother mate, we'll see you the morra." Joe could see the terror in his eyes and he knew it wasn't cowardice but some fragility in his spirit.

"You takin' a whitey big man?" Meeko's reference to the prolonged state of sickness which sometimes accompanied smoking hash provided Big Mooney with a get out.

"Aye mate, I think I might be." It was usually embarrassing to admit this but on this occasion Mooney was happy to accept.

However, before he left the boys couldn't let him go untouched, it was their duty.

"You *are* lookin' a bit chalky Mooney." Gringo knew that a commentary on a whitey would quicken the experience and he wanted to see it before they entered a night of violence. It might lighten the mood.

"Aye mate, your lips are even white, that cannae be good." Craigo mischievously smiled at Joe as he said this but Big Mooney was happy to take the bait.

"Aye, I'm gonnae go. I'll see youse later."

"Right, c'mon Joe, let's get a hold of Weaso. We'll go through the backs."

Weaso was the same age as Joe and he stayed in Meeko's close. They had known him for years and were on really good terms with him, they considered him a friend and ally; they often smoked hash with him or joined him in other minor criminal activities. There was even a lengthy period of time when Joe in particular considered him a good friend, although there was always a small warning in his gut as he also had an element of the cruel bully about him and had even taken a few liberties within the scheme. He slashed a harmless local thief, making up a story that he had *bumped him* for money they had stolen together. Jim knew that this was not because of any sense of justice, but simply knowing that it was designed to generate fear in others.

His desire, like the typical bully, was to establish an air of intimidation. His small, piercing eyes and short stubby nose were features which reinforced his nickname as one which should be avoided. He was small, athletic and muscular for his age, and could handle himself in a street fight, not unlike Jim. Not only was he shrewd but he could be devious and malicious when insecurity ruled his heart, which it often did. He also had been touched by the dark fears which permeate the broken soul.

Jim didn't really know why he was drawn to him, perhaps, like his unusual connection with characters such as Rab Pollok, it was apparent that there was the potential for a level of violence. Or perhaps, even more strangely, it was as if unseen forces out with Jim and Joe's control were drawing people, places and events together to send them in a wayward direction in their lives. As they drew nearer to the age of legal responsibility it seemed as if the path of crime, drugs and violence was an inevitable route which they were being led or driven in to. Events in their lives were accelerating and although they were making daily choices and adopting new and more dangerous frames of mind, there was no questioning or caution as to where this would end. That it wouldn't end well lurked in the caves of their minds. By the time they reached Weaso's door they were ready for a fight. So, after hearing that there were five individuals with weapons prowling the streets for him, Jim was still surprised to hear Weaso say,

"Eh…I'm just stayin' in the night. I'm gonnae wash my hair."

Thinking that he was not making his offer of support clear, Jim reiterated,

"No…we'll *hander* you. Just gie us a couple of blades, or whatever you've got. Me and Joe and the Amigos are up for it." Jim was more interested in exacting his own revenge rather than supporting Weaso's cause.

"No…eh, I'm too tired I'll sort it out wi' the McMahon's in school." Weaso was adamant and Jim and Joe found this incredulous. They just looked at each other. This was a guy who carried himself as an aspiring hard man; he even had connections with some notorious local drug dealers and was distributing small amounts of cannabis for them. But he didn't want to confront these pursuers who had come right into their scheme and declared a challenge-because he was washing his hair!

"Well, any chance of givin' us a couple of blades or somethin'?" Jim wasn't going back out unarmed. "Who were the two guys that were wi' them?" Jim gauged every detail of Weaso's facial expression, body language and voice intonation.

"Whit? Eh…I've no' got a clue Jim." The lies dripped from his lips like honey. Weaso told them that earlier on that day he had beaten up one of the McMahon brothers and taken some money off him at school. He said that they wouldn't have realised who Jim was and would probably run for cover if they were confronted with weapons. What he didn't tell them is that he'd found out that their Uncle was apparently quite capable of violence and would be looking for Weaso.

Weaso happily armed them with various weapons-a six inch lock-back knife which Jim took for himself and an assortment of hammers and chisels from his Da's toolkit, which the others shared. He was happy to wash his hair while Jim, Joe, Craigo and Meeko fought his battle.

By the time the boys returned to the street it was dark and empty, about nine o'clock. They circled the scheme but there was no-one to be seen. Joe was glad and although Jim wasn't particularly looking for violence on this night, he was irritable. It was almost anticlimactic; as if the night had offered an event and then went back on its promise.

Jim decided he would return to Govan and Joe and the boys walked him to the bus stop. For Joe, the relief that he wouldn't have to engage in violence lightened his spirit and his mood. Yet Jim still had a brooding sense that the night wasn't over. A heavy premonition hung over his head which he couldn't shake. So when he saw two middle- aged men standing at the bus stop, his mind quickened and the controlled violence within him prepared itself. It was them, the two men who had accompanied the McMahon brothers. Joe had heard about the incident at Govan Cross and had imagined it in a detached sort of way, without emotion and the rawness which an act of violence possesses. So when Jim looked at Joe and his friends, and with a simple nod of his head, motioned to them, "Get Ready," they weren't sure what was going to happen. But Jim had played it over in his mind as if it had already happened.

It was clear that the men were completely oblivious to the identity of these teenage boys or to the threat which came with them.

The boys stood on the outside of the bus stop as the men continued chatting inside.

Joe assumed that nothing was going to happen as they waited for Jim's bus. The men glanced round a couple of times and although a little unnerved at the presence of the boys, there seemed to be no threat. Perhaps they'd been mistaken. Maybe this was just two middle- aged men going home after a few pints. Jim could smell the drink and one of them even reminded him of his Da. When, the bus came round the corner Joe was relieved that either Jim or these guys would get on it. Jim stood motionless and silent.

The two men put out their hands, indicating the bus to stop. As the doors opened they moved forward to step on and simultaneously Jim stepped forward decisively. Without warning and even to Joe's surprise and shock, Jim plunged the knife violently into the side of one of the men. There was a yell from the man and a holler from the bus driver. In a panic the two men tried to run back into the scheme, the victim fleeing like a wounded animal into a lion's lair. Jim and Joe pursued the injured man who had by this time produced a large, glittering blade. As they reached him, this aging and terrified man whose fear flashed in them images of their own drunken father, he was flailing his arms and cursing, not with violence but more with terror. He lashed his knife at Joe whose youthful energy and focussed fear was far superior to a bleeding, drunken and dying forty two year old. To his unacknowledged shame, Joe kicked him to the ground. Jim stepped behind him and mercilessly plunged the knife into him again.

He lay motionless.

Both Jim and Joe couldn't shake off a flashing memory, an invasive image of seeing their Da, lying drunk in the street. A fateful seriousness gripped their hearts but their conscience was seared as to what they had really done. A man lay dying and all they could admit was that they'd been challenged and won.

The other man had ran into the pub and asked the barman to call the police. Jim knew he had to leave.

"Joseph. I'll no' be here for a few days. I'll see you when I come back." Jim smiled but Joe couldn't tell whether it was victory or defeat he was feeling.

The morning came and although on the outside of Joe and Jim's life nothing seemed different-everything had changed. With dread Joe awaited the police knocking at his door, but it never came. A phone call came to say that Jim had been arrested and he had two co-accused: Weaso and Colin Pollok (the brother of Rab who was arrested with Jim in Govan). This was bizarre to Joe until he found out that Jim had met Colin on the way home and told him what had happened. Unfortunately for Colin, someone had witnessed the two of them walking along the street and assumed that they were together previously.

To Jim's suspicion and surprise the police were even more silent than the last time. They never even questioned him! They mechanically charged him with another Attempted Murder. But this time he wasn't released; he was sixteen so he was sent to Barlinnie Prison for one week, and then remanded(for the standard one hundred and ten days) in Longriggend Remand Institution for Young Offenders.

The police did question Joe a few days later and his alibi was an unbelievable pack of lies involving Jim, the Amigos and a card game which went on all night. They hadn't been out in the street and they didn't have a clue what the police were talking about.

Even although Jim hadn't spoken to Mary in weeks, her heart was shattered. Her fears of failing as a parent had now come to pass. Her beautiful wee boy had nearly killed another human being and she was filled with anguish and despair-he had thrown his life away. What would become of him now? And what about Joseph? How could she help them? She fell down on her knees and sobbed.

Chapter 20
Captive Children

Longriggend Remand Centre was a mixture of petty criminals who had made one mistake too many, repeated young offenders and those who were taking their first serious steps towards a life of violence and crime. Jim fitted into the latter but he was by no means alone. The recent regeneration of the building with white tiles on some of the walls, and almost luminous white paint surrounding the barred windows didn't cover the tension and often the terror which lurked in the hearts of those waiting for a trial date. The young offenders' institution swarmed with boys from Govan and they stuck together. Jim wanted to patiently wait for his trial and keep his head down whilst on remand. So, he maintained his quiet, unassuming disposition and wasn't without hope that he would still be released after his appearance at Glasgow's High Court.

Unfortunately for Jim and for those who didn't know him, not everyone on remand had a quiet and long-suffering nature. Out of their fear and need to control, many individuals in prison were loud and aggressive. Eddie from the East End came in barking like a vicious dog and attracted lots of attention to him. He was tall and muscular, his lived in face, hard green eyes and ruddy face was devoid of the youth which he still possessed in years alone. He was under the illusion that loudness and aggression would cause everyone to be afraid of him. He had committed a serious violent crime and wanted everyone to know what he was capable of. Jim avoided him, or at least tried to.

Nevertheless, Eddie like others before him misunderstood Jim's quietness as weakness and tried to intimidate him one morning in the canteen, puffing himself up with angry, empty words.

"D'you think you're a fuckin' wee ticket because you've stabbed a couple o' people, or because you're surrounded wi' all that Govan Team?"

Jim put his head down, trying to diminish any threat.

"I'm no' lookin' for trouble so I suggest you get to fuck." Jim tried to be firm but fair as he really wanted to keep a low profile but his gut told him that he was heading for an unavoidable conflict.

"Aye, I thought as much ya wee prick. Youse are all the same fae Govan, you think you're untouchable because there's a big team of youse in the jail." Eddie thought Jim had already surrendered so he thought he would humiliate him in his 'defeat'. The boys from Govan were furious at this outburst, and although slightly intimidated they wanted to attack Eddie there and then. Jim told them to leave it as there were too many screws there and he wanted to resolve the issue in his own way. He had already decided that this was another bully who could only be dealt with one way-quickly and severely. Contrary to his show of strength and power, Eddie was unnerved by Jim's lack of reaction and decided not to go for a shower and stayed in his cell for the rest of the day. Jim had a jail razor made (a razor blade melted onto a toothbrush) and carried it down to the canteen with him the next morning. The calm, calculating mind of violence which he was now more familiar with, accompanied him as he deliberately moved up the line for the canteen, in order to get closer to Eddie. The East End growler tried to maintain his illusory status by staring angrily at Jim in the line. However, once again his resolve was crumbling inside as he saw something in Jim's avoiding eyes which shook him to his core. The blink of Jim's eyes triggered an image for Eddie of an alligator he'd seen in a nature programme, waiting to snap at a victim. Jim waited patiently for the precise moment as the screws were always present and on the lookout for trouble. They had heard that Eddie had been mouthing off the day before and were expecting retaliation from the Govan boys in one form or another.

The screws, Eddie and even some of the Govan boys were on edge but Jim was resting in the confidence of violence. As the prison officer nearest to them glanced at his colleague to see if the all clear could be given to proceed to the canteen, Jim stepped forward and like a wicked surgeon ran the razor down the full length of Eddie's face. He suddenly felt the sharp scratch of metal against his cheek and with a mixture of anger, terror and realisation he lifted his hand to his face. As the line of prisoners slowly started to move so too did the line on Eddie's face. The line was thin and faint until the blood rushed to the surface and forced the soft flesh of his cheek to open like a dam.

The blood gushed through his cheek and neither his hand nor his anger was unable to stop it.

"Ya fuckin wee prick! He fuckin' slashed me! He fuckin' slashed me!"

Eddie's panic wasn't addressed to anyone in particular but the screws quickly descended as the blood started to pour. As he tried in confusion and desperation to attack Jim, not knowing what else to do to take back all the growls and the words of the previous days, the screws wrestled him to the ground shouting,

"Right! Fuckin' calm down."

They were more concerned about the blood spilling onto their shoes and pristine uniforms than the gaping wound on Eddie's face. This was just another boy who had mouthed off at the wrong person. There was no thought from most of the screws or Jim, certainly in this moment, of the bare fact that this scar would last a lifetime. In his fear Eddie was loud and intimidating but this was another childish mask, one which would never cover the physical and mental scar which this experience had left him with. This was a lifelong reminder of the ugliness of violence and fear, even if he managed to rid them from his heart and mind. Every glancing stranger would double take with suspicion and judgement for the stupid choices of childhood. This was the world that Jim and Eddie were part of and there was no justification, despite what they told themselves.

Silently and calmly Jim handed the razor back to his friends who quickly disposed of it. He remained expressionless as the screws surrounded him, laid hold of him and dragged him down to the *digger* for solitary confinement.

Naked and alone he spent the next few weeks here. He was content to have peace and quiet and felt a certain satisfaction, a kind of justice to what he had done. There was no remorse or trace of guilt. He didn't replay the event in his mind as he knew that it was finished. He could tell from the terror in Eddie's eyes that he was finished. It wasn't so much that he could feel the power of violence but his mind told him that it was a solution to certain problems. A solution which he felt he could excel in and which seemed to be seducing him, particularly in this world which he now found himself in. Eddie was taken to the hospital to have his face stitched. There was now no solution to the problem of violence etched on his shocked and shattered face forever. He had been a perpetrator and was now a victim of violence. The violence was indiscriminate and fulfilled its purpose-to steal and destroy.

Joe and Mary came to visit Jim while he was on remand and it was a strange experience for all of them. For Mary, seeing Jim in his pristine prison clothes-a light blue shirt and navy blue trousers- and appearing calm and even light-hearted while he chatted to them about nothing and everything, was more disturbing than if he'd been crying or worried. His apparent acceptance of this situation and her awareness that he was surrounded by other criminals, some of them violent offenders, made her fears concrete realities. Mary couldn't endure the whole visit but tried to hide her discomfort.

"I'll let you and Joe talk for ten minutes son. I'm just gonnae go out and have a fag." To Mary, there were no words which made sense in this environment. "Eh, I'll be there when you come up to court. Take care ae yoursel'." *Whit a stupid thing to say,* Mary thought, but anything was inadequate when your son was at the edge of a cliff and showed no emotion.

Jim had shown little emotion out of protectiveness, of Mary, Joe and himself. He didn't want Mary or Joe to worry any more than he knew they would already. He had protected himself for so long by pushing his heart into some dark place within and this wasn't the time or the place to let his guard down. Despite a flickering hope, Jim had no thought that it was time for him to leave this path that he was on. On the contrary, this felt like a beginning rather than an end. He couldn't allow his thoughts to regret or even reflect too much about where he'd arrived at. He was only sixteen and he could be facing a long time in prison, particularly if his last victim didn't recover, which was a strong possibility. His mind was on the task at hand-endure this time and be strong. What other option did he have?

Joe looked at Jim across the table of the visiting room and they discussed the previous events, working out their alibi together. Jim asked many questions about what his co-accused were saying, trying to prepare him for what might unfold in court. He didn't trust Weaso or any of the Pollok brothers but he was now entangled with them. He was vulnerable; they could betray him.

The High Court in Glasgow had a weighty air of authority and power. Jim sat in the oppressive cells waiting to be brought to trial. The lawyers and QC's (Queens Counsel) with their flowing black robes and prisoners' lives in folders under their arms scurried about with a vibrant arrogance, discussing amongst themselves 'who was who' in these two cases, and who was going to pay for the crimes that had been committed. Jim was on trial for two counts of Attempted Murder. His co-accused for the Govan stabbing was Rab Pollok. For the Hardridge stabbing his co-accused were Colin Pollok and Weaso. Joe and Meeko were witnesses for Jim's defence and there were other unknown witnesses summoned by the courts.

Before and during the trial, the Pollok brothers, Weaso and Jim were kept in the cells and all of the witnesses were in a separate waiting room. The tension throughout the trial was palpable and nerves were getting the better of many, particularly Weaso and Colin Pollok. They were both being pressured by their lawyers to 'turn Queen's evidence', a fancy way of saying 'grass' on your friends. The trial went on for three days and on the last day it was clear to Jim, Joe and his lawyers that he was facing a prison sentence. As the trial unfolded it was revealed that Colin Pollok had made a statement on the night of his arrest which completely handed Jim over. He told the police everything that Jim had relayed to him on the night of the stabbing, leaving out no details. Due to this revelation Jim's Counsel urged him to make a deal, to accept a plea bargain. This would tie up the case and allow everyone else on trial to be released. However, Jim wanted to force Colin Pollok to take the witness stand and speak out his betrayal in front of him. He wanted to look in his eyes and for Pollok to have to look into his.

As Pollok took the stand his small nervous frame shuddered like a child being reprimanded by an angry parent. He was ashamed, but not so guilty that he would retract his statement and help secure Jim's release. Jim stared at him unflinchingly and marked this moment like a tombstone in his memory. He embedded the details of his shamed face and the darting eyes which wished this moment had never come. Once Colin had uttered his betrayal, Jim made a decision to accept the plea bargain and fully admit to the Hardridge stabbing. The Crown accepted his guilty plea and the Govan stabbing was dropped. The victim of the Govan stabbing had made it difficult for the prosecution to sustain Jim's guilt and in fact tried his best to help Jim's case; this earned him a lot of respect among the Govan boys. Colin Pollok and Weaso left the courts in freedom but not without a certain sense of foreboding. Weaso hadn't betrayed anyone but Jim knew that if he hadn't admitted to the Hardridge stabbing it might have been a different story. Jim was a shrewd and discerning judge of character and was able to see the fear in Weaso's eyes which might have caused him to break under the pressure of a potential prison sentence. The trust between them would remain forever fragile. The trust between Jim and Colin Pollok was completely broken.

As the Judge declared with condemnation the sentence of

"3 Years in a Young Offender's Institution", it fell like a millstone around Jim's neck.

He remained emotionless. His eyes were still fixed on his co-accused and Pollok's disloyalty burned itself into his memory. When the courts were silent and Jim waited in the cells to be taken to prison, the high emotion and tension of the week had left with his 'friends'. He was alone and the emptiness of the cell mirrored his soul. He prepared his mind for what lay ahead, as much as this was possible.

Chapter 21
Chasing the Dragon

Joe left school two months after Jim had been convicted. The last couple of months had been a complete blur and any motivation for school had ended for Joe a long time ago. He refused to sit any exams and to him school felt like a sentence that was almost complete. One or two of his teachers, Art and English, tried to persuade him that if he just turned up for the exams he would probably pass, but Joe had lost all care. This was the heart of the Thatcher years and there was hopelessness and deep disillusionment about work prospects and the future. So, Joe left with no qualifications and no real hope for a job. He feared the future but didn't even know it.

All of his friends had left school and none of them had jobs, well, not legally. Meeko worked with his Da temporarily but couldn't handle the daily interaction with close family members which this required. So he left and joined Gringo and Craigo and countless others on the dole queues. Big Mooney wasn't working either and occasionally met up with the gang for a smoke and a laugh but he wasn't the same anymore. In fact, since Jim had gone to prison, the deflation of leaving school into the nothingness of an unemployed routine became a daily ritual. This spurned the gang deeper into numbness to keep depression and anxieties at bay. Joe had been under the illusion that when he left school everything would be different and he would feel better. He didn't ever really think it through as to how this would manifest itself but he just had a faint optimism that maybe something good would happen.

Regardless of being unemployed, without qualifications and in the worst political and social climate Scotland had found itself in since the Second World War, Joe and the gang still managed to have a laugh. Sometimes humour was the only coping mechanism available. To them this was usually enhanced by drink, drugs or an often potent combination of both.

By now, cannabis was an accepted part of their daily intake of drugs and this became as important to them as food; they very rarely missed a meal. Yet as their tolerance of hash increased so therefore their need for something extra also grew. To Joe, Meeko, Craigo and Gringo this came in a lethal form: smoking Heroin. Joe knew that Jim would disapprove, as he had a different view of powders and pills compared to Cannabis. But Jim wasn't here and to the gang drugs were drugs. They were only experimenting.

"Anyway, you cannae get addicted wi' just chasin' the dragon; it's only 'jaggers' that are junkies."

As much as Joe had always been cautious with drugs which made you trip, like acid and magic mushrooms, he seemed to be drawn towards substances which helped to numb his feelings. Meeko and Joe were the first to buy *kit* and quickly realised why it was nicknamed *smack*. It hit them fast and powerfully from the moment it entered their mouths and made its way to their lungs, their nervous system and their sense of oblivion. Like smoking hash the ritual was all part of the drug's seductive power. The sense of being in control of something which could induce a powerful state of numbness, and so drastically alter the nervous energy which accompanied scheme life, was alluring. The whole journey of allowing the forbidden thought to take up residence in the mind and then conspiring with trusted friends to search out this ancient, mysterious substance became a concrete reality for Meeko and Joe when they found themselves at McKinnon's shabby tenement door.

They were out of their scheme and out of their depth but they were carrying knives, as usual, and felt an adrenalin rush at the prospect of this new drug experience. The rumour was that injecting it was better than sex. However, this wasn't a comparison that Joe and Meeko could fully appreciate. They had only had one significant sexual encounter which had taken place about a year ago when two girls from the scheme had offered the gang the opportunity of losing their virginity. This took place over a period of three weeks where all of the boys had 'dated' these girls in succession. The two girls seemed to be in competition to see how many of Joe's gang could be counted as their personal conquest. The gang were more than happy to oblige due to the growing pressure of being initiated into this particular form of scheme 'manhood'. The boys had fumbled their way out of virginity and into the freedom of sexual experience. This was more a freedom from the wind up of older and more experienced guys from the scheme rather than any actual feeling of liberation. Nothing much had changed, other than the thought that they could now answer 'yes' to the fearful inquisition of their older 'role models'.

When they returned to Meeko's house they opened the small paper pouch wrapped in Clingfilm, the brown powdery substance seemed unimpressive and even insignificant to Joe. *What was all the hype?* The boys didn't really know what to expect but thought that they might be a little more excited. Despite the initial lack of enthusiasm they did begin to enter into a sense of silent danger as they divided the brown powder 'equally' onto two small pieces of tinfoil. They then made *tooters*, small tubes made out of a cigarette coupon with which to inhale the smoke when they burnt the tinfoil. Meeko went first.

He held a lighter underneath the tinfoil and the powder began to change its form from a soft powder to a slithering liquid, and then to a bitter-sweet smoke. Meeko chased the smoke as it rose and he invited it into his lungs. He was only aware of the bitter taste for a second until its power numbed his head, moved through and invaded his whole body. He had 'chased the dragon' but was now stunned and stilled by its power of paralysis. His eyes rolled back in his head and he remained transfixed as if he was suspended in time and out of this place. The heroin had indeed taken him to another place, an indifference to worry and fear, responsibility and shame; he had a sense of not caring about anything, even his own life. Sad though this was, he preferred this to the oppression which he lived under most days. When Meeko slowly began to open his eyes he looked at Joe and formed what to him was a smile but to Joe there was no happiness in it, only the absence of pain. This seemed more like medication than recreation.

Putting his restless unease aside Joe took the lighter from Meeko's limp hand and chased his own dragon. He too entered a dark calmness which was quickly followed by a rush of the most uncomfortable sick feeling he had ever experienced .He jumped to the window and violently vomited. His body tried to reject this alien substance. There were even traces of blood in his vomit but this didn't stop him finishing off the little brown powder. Nor did it stop him over the next few weeks to keep chasing this elusive dragon which promised freedom- from what he wasn't sure.

Joe enjoyed the numbness, the lack of anxiety and even a fleeting sense of unity with himself which accompanied *smoking kit*, but he knew there was something counterfeit about it. In the depth of his being the whole thing carried with it a sense of inauthenticity. There was a disparity within and he knew at some level he was deceiving himself.

Meeko on the other hand had very little sense of any discrepancy. To him this was the perfect escape from discomfort and a possible solution to the restlessness which had accompanied him his whole life. Meeko and Joe continued to *have a wee burn* and although they perceived the experience differently, neither of them once started had any intention of stopping. In fact, they brought their 'new friend' and introduced him to the rest of the group. Craigo and Gringo trusted Joe and his sensibilities and judgements. If it was good enough for Joe then it was good enough for them. They entered the experience and almost as one entity the boys had accepted this new ritual as part of their daily pursuit. This was another distraction from their restlessness with themselves. Craigo, like Joe, felt the deception in the whole process and like Joe ignored it. Gringo had never been able to even simmer the burning pain in his heart since Carol-Ann had died, until now. This was a way of being without feelings, at least while the drug was still potent. Its impact would decrease as their tolerance developed. More of the drug would be required as time went on. It was a costly habit but not only in monetary terms. Any spark of optimism about life which the boys had always relentlessly maintained began, very slowly and insidiously, to dissipate. This hadn't been a real hope but more of a coping mechanism, a youthful refusal to be depressed and an affinity with each other which held a feeling that at least they had each other. Heroin was a jealous lover and wouldn't share its affections with anyone. It was both possessive and voracious in its desire to be possessed. It didn't want a relationship, it wanted prisoners.

Big Mooney watched his friends, his only brothers, as they continued to develop their relationship with heroin. It was obvious to him that from the outset this was a partnership that wasn't going to end well. He had been hiding away recently but invited Joe and the boys round one Saturday night for a heavy *puffing* session and a few drinks, and felt a joy as the night unfolded and a sense of the old companionship began to emerge.

"Gringo, I heard it was a full moon tonight, show us your toes." Joe wound his facially fluffy friend up with the common jibe that he was in fact a werewolf and that was why he always went home early these days.

"AOOOOW!"

Gringo howled for real, and then with laughter. He didn't want any focus on the fact that the recent entrance into heroin had caused him to spend more time alone with his dark and depressing thoughts.

"Hey Mooney, whit have you been up to mate?" The vodka and coke, complimented by the sweet aroma of *Afghan black,* tapped into Joe's recently forgotten affection for his pals.

"Eh, no much Joe, I've just been stayin' in and havin' a puff. Wee June fae Pollok has been comin' over and havin' a few drinks wi' me." Big Mooney focussed on something external and hid his increasing anxiety and social phobia which had been feeding on his isolation. This was a monster he wasn't ready to face.

"*Wee* June, mate? She's about thirteen stone and she's only four foot eleven." Meeko laughed as Craigo was alerted to a wind up and shot out of his *gouch.*

"I know big man, a couple of drinks? Two straight whiskies, each served in a pint tumbler? She can drink like a fish that lassie."

"Fish don't drink a lot." Gringo was too stoned to even open his eyes as he had sneaked a *wee burn* before he had met up with his pals.

"You know whit I meant…she lives in the bottle. I've never seen somebody that young lookin' so rough." Craigo wasn't criticising Mooney's choice of company he was just speaking his mind, unaware that such comments had a disproportionate power to alienate Mooney these days.

Mooney shrunk back and Joe noticed.

"Fuck up youse two. Whit were you sayin' Mooney?" At Joe's light-hearted rebuke Gringo and Meeko returned to building a few joints in preparation for a lengthy card game.

"Och, no, that was it Joe, just keepin' myself to myself. Whit about you? You're no' still takin' that shite are ye mate." Mooney was looking for an opening to warn Joe. "Och, just now and again mate, nothing serious, it's somethin' to dae i'nt it?" Although he knew that he was diluting the seriousness Joe was glad to feel someone's concern. In fact, for him, taking heroin was in some ways the clichéd cry for help. Although he could see that he was important to others (his Ma, Jim and his pals) and that he'd be missed if he was gone, he needed something else, more than he had to fill some gaping hole inside. He was trying to fill this need with heroin and hoped that someone with 'the real deal' would come and show him another way. The night continued and even in the midst of drink and drugs a real closeness returned between the boys which each of them had noticeably missed. The laughter and the mad conversations had never been so infused with a thread of affection. Yet, along with this each of them had a strong intuition that in a very short time everything was going to change. To Joe it was like a going away party where each of them, in secrecy, would be driven to follow or pursue something in an unfamiliar place. The sense of something slipping away or of coming to a point of no return lingered in their hearts. The premonition was real.

    Everything would soon be changed. There would be no going back.

Part 3

Chapter 22
Happy New Year

In December 1986 Joe turned seventeen while most of his pals had reached their eighteenth birthday. For three months he had been smoking heroin and it had already stolen most of the hope from his spirit and the spark of light from his eyes. Jim had been in prison now for more than a year and for the most part was keeping a low profile. He was in an open prison in Dundee and was biding his time, hoping to be released in less than a year. Meeko, Craigo and Gringo had gradually and unconsciously became entangled in a prison of their own-the addictive personality of a mind which needed heroin to function. Big Mooney hadn't been seen since the last night they had met in his house. He had in fact fled to London, trying to get away from the disturbing inner voices which he could hear through the cracks in his mind. In the past year most of Joe's days had begun by Mary shouting at him to get out of his bed and look for a job. She wasn't just moaning, she still cared for her sons and would never give up on them. However, that's not how Joe interpreted it. Fortnightly he would leave the house and sign on the dole, looking through the irrelevant boards at the Job Centre, and then return to the scheme and spend most of the days getting stoned. He was accompanied in this by what seemed like thousands of others across the city. It was a depressing sight to see so many young people wandering aimlessly through hopelessness. Joe and many others had left school with no qualifications and had never been convinced by the benefits of education. School success wasn't for the likes of him and he had literally never even had a conversation about University or further education. No seed had ever been sown and it was assumed that boys like Joe, from schemes like Hardridge and Govan, would have to find some other path. They did.

 Envy and resentment fanned the flame of rebellion in Joe's heart. In his eyes the lucky ones had apprenticeships, usually because of someone they knew-a friend or a relative, perhaps even their Da who had a trade. It didn't seem to matter how clever someone was, it was as if the path was already laid out. The lucky ones got jobs, the unlucky ones didn't and the desperate ones took the YTS (Youth Training Scheme) jobs which were nothing more than exploitation in Joe's mind. He wasn't going to work for £25 a week, knowing he'd have to give his Ma at least half of that. He'd find another way to make money.

Three months after his seventeenth birthday an opportunity presented itself to Joe through a conversation with a long-time acquaintance from Hardridge. His nickname was Bull, apparently due to his broad, muscular shoulders and solid frame which had proved itself often in response to many violent red rags waved in his direction. Bull had known Joe for many years through growing up in the scheme and they often shared a wicked sense of humour created by the need to let go of the malice eating away at their hearts. They were mutually respectful to each other, and like his interactions with Weaso Joe considered him a friend. Joe had an accepting and light-hearted spirit and no malice in his heart for those who didn't wish him harm, but he was uneasy with completely trusting Bull, despite his apparent openness. Joe put this down to his own uncertainties with others and ignored the caution which his darkest thoughts generated. He wanted to see the good in others and hoped that if he treated others with respect then that would be enough. He thought he could control others' bad feelings towards him with his own 'niceness' to them.

But an intuition warned his soul.

Bull was a serious puffer, smoking cannabis every day and a good source of locating and acquiring hash when there was none in the scheme. He was tall and strong and he could take care of himself in a street fight. He had a constant frown on his wrinkled forehead which was clearly visible due to his prison style crew cut; he always seemed to be brooding about some dark thought and he could easily see the worst in others, never the best-even in himself. Bull's brother was also a notorious criminal in the South Side of Glasgow and had even been involved in Prison Riots which gained wide media coverage. His brother's reputation gave him a certain credibility which undoubtedly created some type of security somewhat -by providing the proud illusion of protection which accompanied a family not alien to violence.

Nevertheless, he could be relied on to find a smoke when there was a *dry up*- always a good quality to possess in a scheme.

During one particularly bad dry up, when the puffers in the scheme were reverting to even smoking cigarettes, and malicious rumours abounded among the hashish community that smoking banana skins and tea bags could get you high, Joe visited Bull. He did indeed have some quality *solid* and even some *grass,* apparently both from Pakistan. As exotic and interesting as this sounded, Joe was only concerned with one thing.

"How much can you get us Bull? Me and the boys are strung out. We never had a puff at all yesterday."

"Not even banana skins…you should try them." Bull laughed as he passed the strongest and sweetest smelling joint that Joe had ever smelt.

"I tell you mate, my head was beginnin' to drift off and before I knew it I was even considerin' oranges… and then grass! Not the stuff fae Pakistan, the stuff the cows are eatin' in Pollok Park." They chortled as they shared the common affinity of needing *weed* to take the edge from existence.

"O man…I've been tellin' everybody about the banana skins. I'm tellin' you, two wee guys fae Kinnin' Park were trying to convince me last week that it actually works. I was ready to sell them a bunch of bananas yesterday instead of a tenner bag of grass." Bull paused, laughing to himself and then remembered Joe's request.

"Much do you want Joe? A quarter is usually twenty five quid but you can have it for twenty."

"Or we could half in and buy a quarter pound and smoke our brains out." Joe laughed but immediately and simultaneously they were quickened by the prospect of lots of drugs and making money out of it.

"Much would a quarter pound actually cost?" Joe always had a keen mind for a business venture but had never considered selling drugs.

"My brother knows a couple of guys who would probably gie you one for three hundred quid."

"O aye, get me two then, and I'll keep one in the cupboard for next week." Joe's financial situation brought him back to reality. How would he ever come up with three hundred pound on the dole?

"He'd probably gie you *tick* if I ask my brother to put a word in for you. He gave me two ounce once cos he knows I can shift it. It's only another two ounce." Bull raised Joe's hopes.

"It's worth a try i'nt it? See what you can do, I'll *square you up* if he gies us tick." Joe felt like a door was opening here and he was optimistic about the idea of making some money.

The time it took for Bull to phone his brother's friend and to arrange a quarter pound of cannabis on credit was quick and it all seemed so easy. Before he knew it Joe was given the lump of Afghan Black, wrapped tightly in cellophane and aromatic to his senses and his ego. He couldn't believe that he'd been given credit but Bull had acted as guarantor and vouched for Joe's reliability. For the first time since he had left school he felt motivated and hopeful. It was the hope of having some focus to his life, something to get him out of his bed in the morning. It was also the hope of providing a useful service to his friends, his own distorted approach to community involvement. He was aware of the illegality but considered it was low risk if he was careful and watchful. The mistrusting element of his nature and his hyper vigilance which kept him constantly on guard would enable him to be both effectively. He was also aware of the immorality, or at least the social disapproval, but he refused to pay attention to either. He felt that he almost had a right to do this; perhaps even a responsibility to make something with his life. After all, hadn't every adult who ever reprimanded him lectured him about taking responsibility for himself and to make something with his life? Ok, this wasn't a conventional career path but perhaps this was the path which Joe was meant to follow. The fact that it only took two days and everything fell smoothly into place spurred him to pursue this new career opportunity.

Joe hastily did the footwork for his business venture by buying a set of scales and a good cutting knife, a roll of food wrap and a small box to keep it all in. When word spread that Joe had hash the puffers swarmed to him. He refused to give out any credit as he knew that if he couldn't pay Bull's supplier then it would be the end of this money maker. Joe sold the quarter pound in two days, making a quick profit of one hundred pound. He eagerly paid for the first and ordered another which pleased both Bull and his friends. By the end of the first week he had sold another and had two hundred pound. If he'd given tick he could have sold more as most smokers operated on the basis that they could run up a credit bill until they got paid or it was Giro day. Yet Joe was smart enough to know that he could only be more lenient with his own money and from the outset he pre-empted that this might bring some trouble-either having to chase people up for money or occasionally slapping someone about who hadn't paid on time.

So, by the end of his first two weeks he had made nearly four hundred pound. He couldn't believe it but he didn't let the success go to his head. He had known a deep failure all his life and didn't want to go back there; his feet were firmly on the ground. He asked Bull to get him another quarter pound, only this time he was paying.

Joe built a reputation in the scheme and surrounding area as a reliable source of cannabis, who didn't unduly tax his product. This meant that the weights he sold were accurate and where he could he would give good customers, mainly friends from the scheme, a good deal. A little bit extra here and there and tick to anyone from the scheme immediately gained him loyal customers. Word of his good business spread rapidly and after the first month he was buying a half pound every week. Joe was happy, his friends were happy and the local puffers were delighted that they had found a reliable dealer that they could go to without threat, intimidation or robbery.

It was very common around this time, particularly in certain areas of Govan like the *Wine Alley* and *Teucharhill* for hash smokers to get robbed either from dealers giving them *rubbish gear* or their cannabis being taken off them at knifepoint, two minutes after they left the dealer's house. This was usually an act of desperate drug addicts, independently stealing hash to pay for heroin; but it was also the case that some drug dealers told the local heroin addicts to rob those they had just sold drugs to, and then they would receive a cut when the hash was returned. It was sometimes a vicious circle of buying drugs and robbery where violence would be exacted, usually by a slashing or stabbing, if a victim refused to hand over their drugs. So the Hardridge and Govan boys felt safe going to Joe, but Joe didn't feel so safe in this world. This was a desperate and dangerous world which Joe had entered into. He wasn't naïve to this and although he had no intention of being drawn into violence he sensed a subtle threat was always lurking. Joe's only ambition was to make money. He wasn't interested in notoriety or reputation. He did have a feeling of usefulness and liked being needed and sought after for his commodity; he also enjoyed the interaction with most puffers as they were usually laid back and jovial, not looking for trouble. But there was always the threat of being ripped off or unpaid debts by people who thought there would be no real challenge from Joe. More than this he was aware of other drug dealers in the area who maybe felt threatened or even jealous of his success and might try to shut his business down, one way or another. Joe started to carry a knife almost everywhere he went, just in case. He didn't want to stab anyone and that level of violence never sat well with his spirit, if it really does with anyone's. It was like a jacket which didn't fit him but that he had to wear if he wanted to do this job. He weighed up the pros and cons of this endeavour and resolved to steadfastly build up his business, regardless of possible obstacles. Perhaps Jim would join him in a business partnership when he was released from prison. He trusted Jim with his life and believed that they could work well together. They had always been so close and always looked out for each other. They would risk their lives for each other, literally. If Joe had foresight he would have seen that this thought would be tried and tested. Joe would feel safer with Jim by his side but for now he would pursue this path on his own.

As his business became more and more established so too did new relationships and friendly alliances, as well as genuine enemies. Joe still spent time with the Amigos and on the odd occasion Big Mooney (who had recently returned from London) would make a show. These were indeed 'odd' occasions and this was often a show which unnerved Joe. Big Mooney's speech and behaviour became more and more erratic and he seemed intensely anxious and paranoid. He found it difficult to make eye contact and where in the past he would have found certain conversations light and funny, he developed a seriousness and an angry defensiveness.

Thoughts that no-one really liked him and that their intentions and motives were bent on harming him dominated his mind. The sense of fracture and separation which Mooney had glimpsed the first time he took drugs was growing. In fact it was almost established as a new way of being within him. A perception began to form of the world as a terrifying vacuum which could steal his soul if he didn't stand guard over the door of his mind. Or a sense of his soul imploding, turning in on itself and crumbling into non-existence. And yet, no matter how much he tightened up security over his mind, speech and behaviour the fragile walls of his psyche were cracking. The falling rubble of fearful thoughts clouded every moment of clarity. Joe and Craigo could see the desperation in his eyes of the prisoner who was being carried away helpless but under protest. They compassionately tried to reach out to him but like Othello's green eyed monster 'which mocks the meat which it doth feed on', he saw suspicion and heard harm in even the kindest gesture.

"Are you awrite big man? You're no' lookin' too good." Joe paused but the attention filled silence in Mooney's littered room provoked the voices in his mind to shout louder. These voices were constantly telling him that he was hated and therefore no-one could be trusted, not even Joe or Craigo, the two people he had trusted most in the world.

Big Mooney just stared at the floor, his eyes darting to and fro while with all his will he tried to believe in his friend and accept his reaching out.

Craigo could also see the vulnerability in his big pal and it terrified him. For in the mirror of Mooney's eyes he could see himself, or what he might become. These fleeting impressions were never rational thoughts, never psychological theories, but powerful intuitions which were more influential than the physical evidence of their senses.

"You know we're your mates Mooney. You can talk to us if you need to mate. We're on your side big man."

Silenced by confusion, not at Craigo's words but at the manifold voices inside his skull, all Mooney could hear was "There are sides! You have enemies! Choose carefully, your life depends on it." And from here he descended down the spiral staircase of negativity, his mind ablaze with flaming arrows of fear and hate, like an Escher painting with no way out. This was a mind touched by hell and it seemed that no-one could help him. He would strangely and unpredictably come out of this chaos at times, and in these moments Meeko and Gringo thought he was just slipping in and out of a low mood or depression. But Joe and Craigo could feel the unravelling of his mind and empathised with his brittle heart. The gang were at a loss to help him and they mutually agreed to try and ignore it and just encourage Mooney to have a laugh. This was easier said than done.

As the New Year approached the boys were all invited to a party in Hardridge and Joe thought that this would be an opportunity for a 'right good laugh', which might bring the old feelings and trust back to Mooney. Joe knew that he could also do with a lift because the occasional *burn* of heroin he was taking was surreptitiously sowing dark thoughts and hopelessness into the threads of his existence. Joe was making plenty of money and had started to buy expensive clothes and jewellery (a gold sovereign ring and a chunky gold bracelet which cost him six hundred pound).He looked the part. Although the gold and designer labels provided him with a fleeting ego boost and a feeling of status without substance, it wasn't enough. He still unknowingly held onto the idea that money could remove the stain of shame which he always carried, but the more money he had the more obvious the illusion was. He wanted to feel clean, to feel pure, to be free from shame. He did love money and buying things as it at least gave him the means to distract himself from his hollowness. The idea of being the local drug dealer also enhanced his status among his peers. He also had a constant supply of drugs to alter his fluctuating mood.

The boys arrived at the party and it was already jumping. As the door opened, the waft of alcohol and smoke, mingled with the faint but potent varieties of perfume and aftershave, was a disturbingly comforting aroma for the boys. This was an indication that the pursuit of pleasure, rather than the anticipation of violence was the prevailing mood of the room. The loud and free laughter competed with the blaring rave music beating like a jungle drum. The music wasn't so much in the background but a booming heartbeat stirring the passions and quickening the intoxicated minds to a refuge of forgetfulness. Small groups of three or four individuals, mostly men were spattered among corners and sofas in the room and gave a relaxed, fleeting glance to Joe and the boys as they came in. The absence of growling, suspicious eyes was a reassuring sign. Every girl in the room was dressed to impress, or seduce- immaculately applied make-up and enough hair spray to kill a rat; sparkly tops revealing just enough flesh to stir the imagination and keep most guys in the room hanging hopefully and helplessly.

Mooney told them that he'd meet them in there as he wanted to arrive after the bells. He was too self-conscious about the way he looked and had always believed that he was ugly and undesirable, so a New Year kiss was a terrifying anticipation. Not only that, he couldn't handle the New Year as it contained a whole history of family fights, verbal abuse and being silenced with violence. A 'happy new year' was something he didn't quite get. Nevertheless he did promise to make the effort to be there. It was half eleven and the anticipation of 'the bells' was imminent. The party had been going since ten o'clock so the alcohol consumption was significant and the emotion was high. After initial greetings and acknowledgements the Amigos found a corner to gain a vantage point from which they could safely intoxicate themselves and still keep an eye on any activity. There were strangers in the party who were by no means acting in a threatening way but they were not from the scheme and were therefore to be watched. This wouldn't destroy their ability to have a good time, this was normal. It was unspoken and yet a completely agreed code among the boys. Glasgow was a violent city and alcohol was so often the fuse which ignited the explosion. The boys had lived this, they knew the drill. Joe mingled with the guests and was well received when the word spread that he had plenty of hash to sell. He sold a half ounce in about ten minutes. He felt pleased with himself and was relieved to get rid of it from his possession. The New Year was usually accompanied by the police in his experience and even more so these days he didn't want to find himself in their company.

Having sold his last *half quarter* he decided to 'reward himself' and take the edge off his nerves by smoking the last of the heroin which Meeko had given him in exchange for some hash. He knew it was too risky to smoke it in the party so he nodded to Meeko and Craigo to come outside onto the stairwell. As they huddled together on the stairs to keep their lighter from being blown out by the wind, and to guard the light powder and any precious smoke from being lost, they didn't notice the two girls cautiously coming into the close. The boys had their backs to the girls and were *tooting* their way into numbness when a shocked, angelic voice cried out.

"Joe? Whit are you doin'?"

Joe turned round and the contrast between the heaviness in his body and the joyful hope in his heart when he recognised who it was quickened his spirit.

"Awrite Marie…how's it goin'?" Even saying her name and seeing her bright eyes and beautiful smile evoked a contrast of both joy and sadness in him. The sadness was where he found his life in this moment; the joy was a storehouse of memory and experience which he'd long forgotten.

"I'm awrite Joe. Hi Craig…Jamie." There seemed to be a compassionate but sorrowful question in Marie's hello which asked "Where are you all and how could you come back here after what happened to Carol-Ann?" To Marie, seeing Joe and his friends, her friends, the rims of red eyes and the heroin hiding behind their smiles, reminded her of the face of death which so painfully scarred her heart from the night of Carol Ann's death.

It looked exactly the same.

For her there was no difference between buzzing gas or smoking heroin, both contained within them a seed of death. This death began in the soul and ended in the body. She could hear and feel the decay in Joe's words. She was still so happy to see the boys, especially Joe and tried to retrieve some of the old fondness. She knew she couldn't judge them. She knew that they had all lived with horror and had been lost boys for a long time. Yet this couldn't hold back the sadness and love which she felt for them.

"Are you goin' to Katrina's party?...This is Kristy by the way."

The boys said their hellos and vainly tried to hide what they were doing and clear up their mess.

"Aye, we just popped out for some fresh air, it's blarin' in there." The irony of the air around them being fresher wasn't lost on anyone. Marie looked at the ground, struggling to say something to reconnect them.

"Well, you better hurry up Joe. The bells are just about to go and I don't want to be kissin' any of they Pollok boys."

"No, me neither." Gringo's ear to ear Cheshire cat grin brought a smile to everyone's face, even Kristy's. She walked up a few stairs and took the safety of Gringo's arm. She could feel his goodness, even through the trouble in his eyes and the paleness of heroin's shadow.

"Well, you can take me into the party and keep an eye on me then. The lassies fae Penilee are far too good for they Pollok boys." She laughed and smiled and her affection made Gringo forget about everything for a moment, even Joe and Craigo. Joe escorted Marie into the party and as the bells' chimed to welcome the New Year her warm lips on his cold face were like healing to a wounded soul. He had missed her so much and he told her so. She had missed him too and had forgotten what good pals they were. She noticed the gold and commented on his expensive clothes, but knew not to inquire too much. She could tell that Joe's reluctance to give details wasn't just his natural shyness. She could see the shame in his eyes and she just wanted to comfort him. She did. They talked and laughed all night, oblivious to anyone else in the party, except when Craigo or Meeko passed him a joint. They knew there was no point asking him to roll one as they could tell that he'd found something he'd lost and he wasn't going to let it go, not tonight anyway.

Gringo was also locked into the fine, feminine form that was Kristy. He was bombarding her with all his patter and shouting playful profanities at everyone in the party just to make her laugh. Craigo stared at Gringo and Joe and it brought a glow to his heart and a smile to his face to see them happy. It had been a long time since any of them had felt anything remotely like happiness. They had fun, pleasure, ecstatic drug experiences and great times of having a laugh but happiness was something much more full than this. Happiness was what he could see in Joe's eyes as he sought to charm Marie back to himself. Her laughter at his antics filled the room and contained a fullness which made the alcohol and drug fuelled emotion empty by comparison. They were the only ones in the room who really looked like their joy would last. Craigo hoped that it would.

As the party diminished and there was no-one left but the host and a few crashed out stragglers, Marie and Joe lay on the couch in each other's arms. They felt safe and carefree, not wanting this day to end but for time just to stay still, even for a little while. The light of dawn broke through the drawn curtains and called the New Year into the reality of the day. The party was over but it was the first time in God knows how long that Joe had woken up with a positive thought in his head. This positive thought required no effort as she lay beside him asleep in his embrace. She was so beautiful and peace radiated from her. Would it last? Would she stay? Or would Joe be saying goodbye again and have to readjust once more to the feeling of loss? Marie woke with a dry mouth and struggled to sit up but when she realised she was with Joe her lips puckered to welcome a kiss. Joe responded and moistened her lips with his; joy gently trickled through his body. This was indeed a Happy New Year! They quietly left the comatose asleep on floors and chairs and made their way out and down the streets. Hardridge had never felt so good nor seemed so bright. The air had never seemed so lively nor the sound of morning birdsong so clear and melodic. It was a beautiful day and the walk to Penilee took only a moment in Marie and Joe's minds. In reality it took about forty five minutes and had they not been walking like happy conjoined twins, unable and unwilling to separate, their feet would have been weary. Nothing much was said but they both knew that this feeling was love, regardless of how imperfect and clouded by the previous night's drugs or alcohol that it may have been.

As they neared Marie's home she broke the inevitable silence.

"It was great to see you again Joe."

"Aye you too. It would be really good to see you again." Joe hoped this wasn't a goodbye but the fear of loss crept up his spine.

"Aye…I'd love to see you again, I really would, but…"

"Are you goin' out wi' somebody?"

"No, it's no' that. It's the drugs Joe. I mean…I'm no gonnae try and tell you how to live your life but I just couldnae handle watchin' you on that stuff. You're a great guy Joe. Your life's worth a lot more than that. It just reminded me so much of…" Marie's eyes filled and a before a tear escaped Joe reassured her, feeling a new hope in his heart.

"I'll stop it Marie…" Joe held her close, his hands reassuringly on her shoulders and hoped this would be enough, but Marie looked at him with doubt and caution.

"I mean it." Joe did mean it with all his heart, he knew that this night had been the best he'd felt in so long. He didn't want it to slip through his grasp.

Marie's eyelashes flashed like a switch turning on her wide smile. She was so beautiful, so lovely and gentle in spirit. This thought washed over Joe like a refreshing wave. They arranged to meet the next day and Joe floated home. This was a new start, he could feel it. He would definitely stop taking heroin and this was a relief, as he had begun to feel its insatiable grip over his emotions and apathy about life permeating his core. His spirit had been lifted and he was on a high. He wouldn't tell Marie about his drug business, not now anyway. His fantasies about being in love, or being loved, about becoming rich (and his associations with that idea-status, freedom from shame) and from financial insecurities, these were vague impressions within but they still stirred fire in his heart.

Joe returned to the scheme as those with hangovers slumped like zombies to Khan's newsagents for a fix of food or fags. Rolls and sausage or Ten Regal King size would take the edge off the Hogmanay obliteration so that the drinking and drugs could continue, for at least today, maybe tomorrow and for some until the money and tick ran its course. Joe could see it but for once since he'd left school he was detached from it.

Greetings of "Happy New Year!" resounded throughout the day and this year it was real for Joe. He thought of all the 'parties' which he'd endured as a wee boy, cowering behind the couch or under his covers, feeling that there was something wrong with him, something missing inside as all the intoxicated adults were 'happy' and he was so sad. Maybe this was his time to shine. He reflected on last night's party and Gringo's hilarity and antics; it made him smile. He thought of Craigo and Meeko lying wasted, at peace and safe. His mind turned to Jim and although his thought was tainted with sadness, the fire in his heart couldn't be quenched today. He had a positive slant even on this; even Jim could share his happiness when he got out, or at least his business. Joe wanted to lift everyone up with him and wished happiness on his friends and family. His desire to rescue others was strong, obsessive even. When he helped others he felt good about himself. Big Mooney flitted through his heart and he wondered why he hadn't shown at the party. He hoped he was alright but the thought un-nerved him.

Mary filled Joe's mind and he made his way to her house to wish her 'All the Best' for the New Year. On the way to Mary's he met Craigo looking quite sombre but approaching steadfastly. It wasn't just a drug and drink hangover, he had something to say.

"Did you hear about Mooney?"

"No, how, whit happened?"

"He got the jail last night and I heard he's been locked up in Leverndale." The disproportionate terror in Craigo's voice reflecting his own fear of insanity.

Joe was confused.

"WHIT? Whit d' you mean? Arrested for whit? How did he end up in Leverndale? Whit did he dae?" Joe expected Craigo to answer all the questions in one nicely packaged explanation.

"I'm no' a hundred percent sure but wee Billy that stays next door to him said that the coppers and an ambulance arrived at his house last night just after the bells. He said that Mooney came out all strapped up and escorted by the ambulance guys and the polis. He said there was blood all over him but he didnae seem that hurt."

"So, whit did he dae? Whit did he get the jail for? Whit's the rest of the story?"

Joe's impatience and anxiety made Craigo feel a bit responsible.

"I'm no' sure mate I've been tryin' to find out all mornin' but I don't want to go to his house. You know whit his Da is like. He's mental." Craigo looked at Joe and a nervous and slightly uneasy laugh escaped from both of them at the sinister irony of referring to Mooney's Da as 'mental'.

"I'll go round to his Ma's later and kid on that I don't know anythin' about it. See if I can get any info. If you find out any more I'll be about. I'm just goin' up to see my Ma just now. I'll see you later."

"Awrite mate, see you later." As Craigo walked away he turned back and as if the previous conversation had never taken place he shouted with an unashamed joy, "O aye, I meant to ask you... Did you get your hole last night?" He beamed and started to jog not expecting an answer but hoping the thought would leave Joe on a better note.

"Shut up ya fanny!" Without a trace of anger but with slight embarrassment Joe giggled. His mind raced trying to make sense and work out this bizarre information. For now he'd hold onto the happy thought of Marie and try to take some joy into his Ma's house for a change. *"Happy New Year! Happy New Year!"* Joe thought if he kept saying it to himself it would make it so. Why was happiness so fleeting in this scheme? Why could he not just hold onto some good...just for a while?

Chapter 23
A Table Prepared ...

Joe arrived at Mary's house and she was so happy to see him. She'd been crying, her heart still breaking for Jim but seeing Joe unexpectedly and knowing that he'd survived through Hogmanay safely evoked a surge of relief. Not only this, she felt a dim hope as she noticed the light in his eyes and the lightness in his spirit. She had heard about Mooney as word quickly spreads in a small scheme. Her heart could start beating again as she knew more than Joe about what had happened and it had filled her with worry and terror. All of her fear cleared like a passing rain cloud as Joe's happy face appeared at her front door.

"Happy New Year Ma."

Joe gave Mary the biggest hug and kiss as his childlike affection for her fluttered. His own depressive state since leaving school had closed his mind to the love and respect he had always kept hidden for Mary.

"O son, Happy New Year, it's great to see you. Thanks for comin' up."

Mary was surprisingly joyful.

"You're my *first foot* as usual. That's got to be good luck, my tall, dark handsome boy bringin' in the New Year...I'm just glad you're awrite. Did you hear about Big Iain?"

"Aye, Craigo just told me he got the jail last night but he wisnae wi'us."

Joe knew Mary's nervous disposition always required some extra reassurance.

"How did *you* know?"

"O Sadie phoned me and told me whit happened...she was all over the place, hysterical."

"Did she tell ye whit happened?"

"Aye, once she calmed down she told me that Iain came home and went straight into his room. She said she tried to talk to him, to wish him a Happy New Year but he just stared right through her...said his eyes were like golf balls...manic. Anyway, she said she left him for about half an hour and then he walked into the living room covered in blood, holdin' his hand. He had chopped his own finger off!... with a lock-back knife that his Da uses for fishing. He wisnae screaming or anythin'…nothin'. He just stared at her and said 'It's a wee bit quieter now.'"

"For fuck's sake…sorry Ma."

Joe was shocked but he knew it wasn't an excuse to swear in front of his Ma.

"So, whit did his Ma dae?"

"She phoned an ambulance, but when she told them the details they sent the ambulance from Leverndale…and the polis came wi' them. She found out that they had actually been lookin' for him anyway as he'd went into Marks and Spencer's earlier on yesterday, the one in the town, and just started smashin' bottles of wine off the ground until the polis showed up and then he ran."

Mary was starting to get tearful again, partly her compassion for Mooney but more with another surge of relief that Joe wasn't with him.

Joe sat in stunned silence. He didn't know what to say. He could feel the walls of last night's joyful hope starting to crack. A casualty from the gang was an ominous sign and another fear was realised. There was no comfort in having seen this event coming but only another reinforcement that life for the gang may unravel and that the forces they had felt pressing in all their lives may be greater than they could eventually bear.

The secret sins and dark thoughts were catching up with them.

Joe would find out more about his big pal and try and make contact, but for now he forced the dark cloud from his mind. He needed some happiness, some positivity. Mary needed it as well and Joe knew that they'd sink without it. He tried to steer the conversation in a more positive direction and Mary knew she had to try and let a glimmer of light in. He told Mary that he'd met Marie at the party and that he was going to see her again. She was so happy for him and she also shared with him some good news. Apparently his Da had stopped drinking and was going to some type of meetings to help him stay off it. She told Joe how she'd met him a couple of days ago and that he was sober. In fact he hadn't had a drink for two months. Joe knew that Mary had also been going to some type of meetings for families and friends of alcoholics for about a year now but he hadn't really paid much attention. He was too absorbed, too consumed in his own mind and emotions, trying to find some direction in his own life. It had been like trying to find a light switch in the dark and he hadn't found it yet. He was glad to see Mary not depressed but he felt no affection for John. It was there but it was still too painful a wound to open.

Joe spent the whole day with Mary and she cooked a traditional Ne'er Day meal- homemade steak pie, mashed potatoes and cabbage. Gringo came up and Mary invited him to stay for dinner, knowing that his own house wouldn't be a jovial place after a night of booze and brawling. Gringo was still feeling great from last night's 'romantic liaison' and although worried about Mooney something had also lifted from his mind.

Eventually as the day unfolded Craigo and Meeko appeared looking for Joe, partly just to see him but mostly because there were numerous punters in the street waiting impatiently, jangling from the night before. So the boys left Mary's, wishing her well and remembering how they envied Joe.

"Your Ma's crackin' Joe. She's always dead kind. She's always happy to see us. The only time my Ma's happy is when I'm on my way oot the door."

"I know mate, she's awrite i'nt she?" Joe agreed and held onto this thought as he prepared himself to get to work. He had business to attend to and he wanted to make money. He needed to focus as he was aware that he had to be constantly on guard as he was often in the presence of potential enemies.

Over the coming months he maintained his service to his own customers and even expanded his business by 'employing' two boys from other schemes, one from Govan and the other from Pollok. He gave them each a quarter pound on tick and they paid him back once they had sold it. He was making at least a hundred pounds from each of them and with his own dealing business was booming.

The cream on this cake was Joe's relationship to Marie. With each passing day they became more intimate, emotionally and physically. They shared their hearts and their bodies with each other and were so free and relaxed in each other's' company. They went clubbing together, for romantic meals and movies and even spoke about going on holiday together. Joe had never been outside of Glasgow and he was beginning to see that the world was so much bigger than his family experience, even than Hardridge.

Joe's life excelled at this time not only in terms of financial success but also with a feeling of connection, closeness to another human being-Marie. She was the love of his life and he was so protective of her. Well, he liked to think of it as protection when in fact it was more like his obsessive possession. He did love Marie but the fears and shame which lay dormant in his heart, bubbling under the surface of appearances, were threatening with restlessness. Joe still hadn't disclosed his affairs to Marie but she wasn't deaf or stupid. She quickly found out what Joe was up to but decided to turn a blind eye to it. After all, he had stopped smoking heroin and he was really good to her. Joe's gentleness and kindness when he was with Marie was in sharp contrast to the growing violence within him which was part and parcel of the path of drugs and crime which he was waywardly wandering on. From week to week there was always someone who would try it on by not paying their bill, just to see if Joe would respond without Jim. He did, usually by a violent attack, hiding in the shadows of a back close and unleashing a volley of punches and kicks on some desperate puffer. Luckily at this stage Joe hadn't been in conflict with anyone who required a more serious attack, someone for whom hands and feet would not be a strong enough deterrent. But it would come. Joe knew this and was hopeful that when Jim was released he would accept the business invitation.

Marie was satisfied that Joe had stopped taking heroin and he himself thought that he should be content. He had a beautiful girlfriend, money in his pockets, designer clothes and he was dripping in gold. His status and desirability among the drug community was growing and he even began mingling with other criminals when there was a mutual benefit. Housebreakers with video players and jewellery for next to nothing were a quick way for Joe to earn money. He knew they were desperate and despite being reasonable to them he was clued up as to how to make a lot of money from them. Joe loved money but it was never enough. He wanted so much more. The more he had the more he was aware of the emptiness that he was trying to fill. Not even money or Marie could still this hunger.

Heroin was gone for Joe but not for Craigo and Meeko. They had quickly descended deeper into the valley and taken on an unquestioned role in life as young people with a primary focus-more drugs. A combination of unemployment, unemployability (through lack of motivation and qualifications) and their own internal emotional gravity was driven by heroin's destructive power which rendered them lifeless. Their day was filled with thoughts of getting *wasted* and every second idea or feeling revolved around meeting this need. They didn't consider themselves junkies, just recreational *tooters*. They were deep in denial and under the delusion that the absence of needles meant the absence of addiction.

Smoking hash for Joe still took the edge off the rawness of life but he also needed more. At this time, Temazepam capsules, or 'Jellies' as they were commonly known due to their similarity with jelly sweets, were common among both serious and moderate drug users. Joe would often take one or two jellies to calm his accelerating mind and like heroin they were accompanied with a sensation of indifference. Being on jellies was similar to having a carefree attitude but not with optimism, more with resolution and acceptance. Listening to someone who had taken lots of jellies (and many users would take up to thirty or forty at a time ,some even injected them as they came in liquid filled capsules), was like listening to a madman who was completely convinced of his own insane opinions and was continually trying to persuade others of his insights. Joe was happy to take no more than three at a time and even these could put him into a deep semi-conscious state. He was both awake and asleep simultaneously. He could talk and even do business but he usually needed Gringo to be around as he'd forget when he had given a customer drugs. The jellies stole his memory and a part of himself each time he took them. Jellies also produced a bravado in others which came from the false sense of safety which they provided. This could be a lethal concoction for desperate drug addicts, willing to do whatever their fear and dependency required. Joe had to be on high alert, even more than usual when customers were *bouncing* on jellies.

Marie did notice the difference when Joe was on jellies and she tried her best to tell herself that it wasn't that bad. She didn't want to lose Joe but he was slipping through her fingers once again. He became aggressive and defensive when she confronted him about his drug use. Not because she was wrong but because she was right. She was telling him the truth because she loved him and he didn't want to hear it. Joe had always vowed in his heart to be everything that his Da wasn't. This was a vow that he wasn't keeping and his conscience reminded him, particularly when he was with Marie. She was the only one who could see it and her love for him was stronger than her denial.

In the passing of time all things changed.
Nothing stayed the same as Joe began to experience that life is to change and grow, and if not grow then to decay. The two street-crossed lovers didn't understand how it happened and didn't see it coming until it had fully arrived. The process wasn't static, nor was it completely hidden but they had repeatedly closed their eyes to aspects of their relationship which they didn't want to see. Joe turning up to Marie's house late at night, stoned and bouncing, looking to take and not to give anymore; turning up and being moody and resentful that Marie couldn't take away the discomfort he felt within himself; turning up with blame in his heart and twisted perceptions, refusing to take responsibility for his own emotions and reactions; more frequently not turning up at all because his need to get stoned and forget himself was greater than his need or desire to be with someone who loved him. Joe was blinded by his own history which he refused to own or even acknowledge. He literally and figuratively set his course on 'getting out of his head' as his mind was becoming more and more unbearable. Strangely, the simple and pure love of someone who had nothing but his best interests at heart was the poultice which drew his pain to the surface. Marie took all the flack but her love could only take so much. There were still times when Joe's true nature, his own gentleness and kindness, still shone through but the drugs and the shadows which were engulfing his life were too much to bear. They wanted so much to believe that they would be together forever and their longing caused them to overlook the mistrust, fear and even resentment which had begun to take root. They still loved each other for sure, and they had believed that they were 'meant to be' together but they began to question whether they were supposed to be together forever.
In the midst of all this Joe's childhood brothers –Meeko, Gringo, Craigo and Mooney-as well as his own big brother and best friend Jim-were all set on their own

course. They would still meet and their paths frequently crossed but nothing stayed the same. The seeds of childhood experience would once again be nurtured and grown in the soil of their new reality. This had, like all experience, the potential for either life or death.

In the space of three months Joe was arrested three times, once for carrying a knife and twice for assault, one with the use of a bottle. He was also confronted with the violence of his past one night when he was out with Marie.

Joe and Marie were at a hypnotist show which in itself disturbed him slightly as the antics of the hypnotist and the trance- like consciousness of the on- stage volunteers provoked a childhood memory of his Da being physically present but mentally or spiritually absent. There was laughter and incredulity at the strange nature of the mind and how foolish people would let themselves be in a hypnotic state, but Joe couldn't throw off a sense of danger or threat in the atmosphere of the Pavillion Theatre. He had safely guarded his mind all his life but this threat came from deep within him and told him that he was in physical danger.

During the show's interval his intuition became clear when he was alerted at the Pavilion bar by uneasy, friendly words.

"Awrite Joe! How's it goin'? Enjoyin' the show?" The McMahon twins, the sons of Jim's victim stood at either side of Joe with wide, unnerving smiles and held an air of power, realising that Joe was alone. Joe turned round, self-controlled and alert, holding any fear deep inside.

"Aye, I'm awrite. Whit do *you* want?" The fear in his voice morphed into anger as he prepared for violence, the pint glass in his hand already dedicated to the temple of the nearest brother.

The boys quickly exchanged a glance and played down any threat.

"Look Joe, we're no' lookin' for any trouble. We saw ye wi' your bird. We just thought we'd come over and let you know that everythin's cool. All that stuff is in the past." They were almost believable had the warning in Joe's belly not been so strong.

"Aye, awrite." Joe played along and walked between them, two glasses in hand, each willing to be used as a weapon.

Joe scanned the boys as they walked away and sat down beside another friend who had been standing at the front door.

"Who was that Joe? You awrite?" Marie saw the violence beginning to sharpen Joe's mind, his eyes narrowing, his brow hardening, his face and heart changing to stone.

"No, that's they McMahon brothers. Remember…Jim stabbed their Da."

"Wht did they want? Whit did they say?" Marie's anxiety accelerated as Joe appeared calmer, resting in the shadow of violence.

"They said everythin's cool and they don't want trouble. That's obviously a lot of shite. I'll need to phone some of the boys, Craigo and Meeko maybe."

"Aw, Joe just leave it. We'll leave early and just get the bus. I'm not bothered anyway…do you *want* to?" Marie was almost pleading as she was terrified at the thought of violence, especially if Joe was going to be the victim. "Don't phone anybody Joe…please… I don't want any trouble."

Against his better judgement Joe decided to try and take the path of peace, for Marie's sake. As the audience were requested to return to their seats for the second half of the show, Joe and Marie hung back and made a sharp exit onto Renfield Street. It was a bustling Saturday night and the Summer sky was high and clear for a change; the town centre welcomed them into a blast of Neon lights, overwhelming wafts of alcohol and the vast mixture of oriental, Italian and Indian foods hung heavy between the tenement office blocks.

It felt good to be out of the confined space of the Pavilion Theatre as there was more scope for either fight or flight. Marie thought that they were in the clear but the threat never left Joe. He turned to see if they had been followed and was not surprised to see the three boys smiling without joy and approaching with intent. Marie turned also but had a different picture; they were gone and she took a sharp and clear breath. The town was filled with all levels of intoxicated individuals, from those lying in the gutter to those staggering and arguing- sometimes even with other people. There were also the happy couples who'd had a couple of drinks, and perhaps a nice meal or gone to see a movie or a show, just like Joe and Marie. But unlike these other couples Joe and Marie were not being followed by a night of happy memories and a safe walk home.

"Leave my hand a wee minute Marie."

With the hyper vigilance of a wild animal Joe pre-empted the strike.

"They're away Joe. It's awri…" Marie had barely finished the last syllable when Joe heard a rush of pounding angry feet and a wide green cider bottle thumping the crown of his head. Marie screamed as she realised what was happening. She even lashed out with her bag viciously and repeatedly. She was caught on the edge of the whirlwind. Joe's rage that they had attacked him in front of Marie released a surge of adrenalin and revenge. In a flurry of kicks, punches and grabbing he tore the shirt of the tallest brother from the collar to the waist. As the blood streamed down Joe's back his mind accelerated with panic and survival. As kicks and punches came in and out like a violent 'hokey –cokey' he was wrestled to the ground. Surrounded by three young men with an audience of passers-by trying to ignore what was happening, Joe tried to quickly scan from which side each consecutive blow was coming. His focus was on the bottle and his main defence was his face. He didn't want a scar; being slashed was considered a defeat, a second prize unless the opponent was in an equal or worse condition. *Why did I not carry a blade tonight?* So many thoughts and impressions raced through Joe's mind and his perception seemed strangely quickened and external reality slower than usual. *Was this shock? Was this a near death experience? Why were people not shouting at them or going for help? Was that Marie's scream he could hear?*

Later on that night, neither Joe nor Marie could adequately explain to his friends how he went from being on the ground, defeated and surrounded by his enemies to chasing them up Renfield Street with the bottle in his hand which they had struck him over the head with. There seemed to be a few frames missing from the film of their memory and although Joe dreamily remembered feeling an inner strength lifting him to his feet, he couldn't explain it as a simple act of will or adrenalin. Marie just remembered screaming out "O God! O God, help!" Not in a spirit of prayer, but with the threat of death once more gripping her heart. She was such a gentle creature that she just couldn't take this way of life, regardless of her love for Joe.

Both of them were shaken by the experience but as Joe retold the story he allowed the nervous energy to become exhilaration at having escaped the violence which had pursued him. Marie had no such reward. She was just exhausted and wanted to cry. She feared this violence hadn't run up Renfield Street and left for good. She was right.

Chapter 24
Bitter Roots and Poisonous Weeds

There was no classical music playing in the background, no dramatic climax and no real shock or surprise when Joe and Marie broke up. In the most truthful place within them they had seen it coming for a long time. Marie didn't want a life of worry and loneliness and Joe didn't know what the hell he wanted. They parted with sadness and affection not with arguments and anger. They each knew that they were letting go of something which was precious, beautiful, sacred even, -but let it go they must. "You take care of yourself Joe." Marie couldn't stop the well of bitter tears from forcing their way past her resolve and her eyes.

Joe hardened his heart, not out of hatred but to shield his vulnerability.

"Aye, I will. You as well. I'll hopefully still see you about." He knew this just wasn't going to happen and he drew his eyes to the ground. Joe held onto Marie and squeezed her close to him, fully aware that the smell of her hair and perfume would fade as she left. Marie left crying, unable to say any of the things that were in her heart. She knew that they would fall on deaf ears. As Joe let her go and the warmth of her embrace departed, a chill spread over his mind. He was alone but would not allow any self-pitying as this would be disastrous. He needed to harden to keep going and this was what he did.

Everything changes. Nothing stays the same. Everybody leaves eventually.

Joe kept himself active with business and emotionally numb with drugs in the weeks that followed. He took *jellies* every day just to keep the pain of another loss at bay. Each night he would smoke until his mind was too tired to think and he accompanied this by drowning his sorrows. This wasn't a wilful intention but just a coping reaction. Life was secretly and subtly turning and the path which he was on was becoming more crooked and blurry than it had ever been.

Fortunately, Jim's release from prison, shortly after Joe's break up with Marie was timely and quickened Joe to refocus. He resolved to invite Jim into partnership with him and to commit himself to making his business a success, perhaps branching off into other areas of economically appealing criminal activities, if the opportunity afforded itself. Joe had a great sense of anticipation before Jim's release, not only because he would be delighted to see his brother but also the thought of them pursuing life side by side and embarking on a journey together. Joe and Jim had been separated too long and they missed the trust they shared. Jim had been in an environment where trust wasn't a luxury which could be enjoyed. Joe had let his guard down and trusted in the safety he felt with Marie, even trusted life to work out. It wasn't Marie's fault that it hadn't but Joe felt the bitter sting of loss and was ready to retreat back into a world of self-will and denial.

To Joe's surprise Jim initially refused his offer and decided to try and get a job, staying away from violence and crime. He really tried. He didn't want to go back. For the first couple of months Jim moved back in with John who was now sober and staying in a notorious scheme in the East End of Glasgow, Cranhill. John reckoned that a move away from his old drinking buddies in Govan and the Southside would be better for his sobriety, and perhaps even for Jim when he was released. This suited Jim as he had befriended a guy from Cranhill *inside* who was well known in this area. He was known as Spike, due to his long thin physique and sharp facial features, as well as his propensity to use a knife in a conflict. Nevertheless, like John and Mary had found out when they moved away from Govan many years before, that the unaddressed issues of the heart would follow them and look once more for residence in the soul.

John was working on a building site and managed to secure some work for Jim, labouring for a couple of months. Jim was content to go to work, pick up his wages and generally keep a low profile. He occasionally dropped by to visit Joe who seemed focussed and excited as his business was accelerating. The offer to come on board was an open one and Jim appreciated the invite, but for now he would continue on a straight path.

Jim had spent more than two years in prison and didn't want to go back. Neither did he want to enter into the spirit of violence which had taken him there in the first place. Jim's intuition forewarned him that the appeal of money and engagement with the drugs world would come at a price. Violence would be part of that and he sensed that it was always close, looking for a way in. This became apparent one night as Jim took a young cousin to the cinema in the city centre. *What could possibly go wrong there?*

On their return it was about ten o'clock and they decided to get a bag of chips at the Blue Lagoon beside Central Station, before catching the bus home. The town was relatively quiet as it was midweek, a few devoted drunks and groups of two or three friends out for a few drinks after work. There was nothing external in the atmosphere to suggest danger, so Jim was confused as to why his spirit was deeply disturbed. From about fifty yards from *the chippy* Jim could see through the large well lit window that there were a few people in it. Like an eagle scanning a rat from a distance, his eyes fixed on a guy who appeared intoxicated but jovial and who was attempting to engage those in the queue in unwanted conversation. Jim put his head down and slipped into the back of the queue hoping to go un-noticed. His wee cousin Daniel was trying to talk about the film but Jim felt the need to be alert.

"D'you think Batman could batter Spiderman Jim?" In wee Daniel's eight year old mind this was a serious consideration.

"Aye pal, nae bother." Jim wasn't really giving the question ample thought as the 'jovial' drunk turned and squinted his rolling eyes in their direction. He looked at Daniel, then at Jim.

"Awrite wee man! Whit team d'you support?" The question didn't seem as innocent as the smile on his face. Jim knew that the answer could open a door of false affection or verbal abuse. As his wee cousin looked to him to see whether he should respond, he squeezed Daniel's hand as if to tighten his lips.

"We're no' interested in the football…A bag of chips please." Jim tried to quicken his order and hoped that his serious and formal tone would be enough to end the conversation.

"Don't talk shite! You're fae Glesga. You must support either Celtic or Rangers. C'mon, who do ye support?" The man interpreted Jim's avoidance as fear and the alcohol evoked a false bravado in him.

Jim made no eye contact although he was watching his every move. Jim had made a decision not to carry a knife anymore as he knew this would be tempting fate but at this moment he felt its absence and worried of a different fate.

He thought of his uncle Tam, stabbed to death in a Govan chippy.

As the drunk came uncomfortably closer into Jim's personal space, the stench of alcohol and the shroud of intimidation which emanated from his body and spirit evoked in him the instinct to protect and lash out.

"I'm askin' you a fuckin' question. Whit's wrang wi' ye? It's a simple fuckin' question."

Daniel's presence and the nervous onlookers made it impossible for Jim to act. He wouldn't be able to make a secure exit with glaring witnesses, especially with a distraught child with him. Once again he was powerless and vulnerable in the venomous face of alcohol and violence. In his emotion he felt an intense fear and a vicious rage but flashes of the High Court, the alienation of prison and the loss of his freedom provided a harbour onto which a spirit of shrewd and patient control rested. His focus sharpened as he left the shop without his chips, holding Daniel tightly and ignoring everyone in the shop. Daniel's confused moan would be answered in due time,

"Why are we not gettin' chips Jim...Eh...Why are we not gettin' any chips?"

"There's a better chippy down here pal, ok?"

Standing at the Union Street bus stop after leaving the 'better chippy', Daniel's satisfied and chip filled face was oblivious to the images of revenge and violence which were weaving their way into the neural pathways of Jim's brain and deeper into his heart. Jim had seen too many victims of violence in his life and he wasn't going to be one. He couldn't stop the projection of his mind which was imagining various scenarios in which he was attacked and unarmed. In other words the resolve to carry a knife began to grow in him again.

Once he had dropped Daniel back home at his Uncle Shuggy's (his Mum's wee brother), he made his way to Hardridge to visit Joe. Joe sat and smoked a few joints as Jim relayed the night's events and let out a little of the anger that he was feeling. After listening intently (or rather with stoned silence), what surprised Joe was that the upshot of these events had led Jim to two conclusions. Firstly, he needed to carry a blade at all times. Secondly, he reasoned that if he was going to return to a crooked path he might as well go the whole way.

"So, anyway…is you're offer of a partnership still open?"

Joe's ears pricked up and he sat upright from his slouch with a wide grin.

"Of course it is mate…brilliant!" Joe was immediately excited and enthusiastically began to fill Jim in on his current status and future plans. Jim was impressed at the work which Joe had put in-he had three people selling hash for him in three different parts of Glasgow's South Side. Nevertheless, Jim also had plans. He wasn't the type to half-heartedly commit to an enterprise. It was all or nothing.

Joe quickly explained to Jim the weights, the prices, the acquisition and distribution of his commodity. It came almost natural to Jim; he was always good with organisation, especially when it came to money. Poverty had equipped the brothers with the drive that money was a way out of their problems and had given them the shrewd organisation skills required to pursue this.

"Awrite Joe, who are ye gettin' your gear fae?" Jim was eager to get involved, not just to put up some money.

"Well, Bull's been gettin' it fae a guy he knows but if you know anybody else?" Joe was eager to become independent and not rely on anyone except Jim. He knew that as business increased the risk of sabotage or robbery increased as well.

"I do actually. I know a couple of guys I met in the jail that should be able to help us out. Leave it wi' me."

And with those simple steps a new business partnership had been established, with family and friendship at its basis. This was an unholy alliance which the brothers embraced wholeheartedly. Both Joe and Jim were interested in only one thing- making lots of money. They weren't interested in intimidation but suspected that selling drugs, even at a street level would invite trouble. Within a few months Jim was buying a pound of cannabis and Joe had his punters shift it weekly. They were making quite a lot of money, but it still never seemed enough. It was enough for Joe to buy expensive clothes, feed his own drug lifestyle, and furnish his room at Mary's house until it looked like a display at Curries or Dixons. His room was filled with the latest large screen televisions, sound system and even a tropical fish tank to *gouch* into in the small hours after a smoking session.

Jim, however, saved his money, lived frugally and kept under the radar of the law. Yet, he lived as if he was waiting for an enemy to come out of the shadows. Most of the time he only visited Joe when they needed to talk or do business, although he would hang around on the odd occasion to listen to the stoned conversation of Joe and his friends.

During this time, Joe was usually joined with a friend from the scheme whom he had known his whole life in Corkerhill. He was a well-respected fighter and amateur footballer whose dark hair, handsome looks and soft blue eyes were reminiscent of a young Frank Sinatra. All valuable qualities for an eighteen year old testosterone filled guy from a housing scheme.

His name was Bongo.

Well, obviously not his real name. His real name was Allan and he had been referred to once, when he was about eight or nine as 'Ali Bongo', a well-known comedy magician. The name stuck. He was always referred to by Joe and others in the scheme as 'wee Bongo' which must have been a term of affection rather than any reference to his height as he was about five foot ten! Wee Bongo usually had a gentle nature and loved a good laugh. Although he was also known for his cheek and sharp tongue, but only with those from other schemes who thought they were *wide*: a wise guy, a smart-arse but usually with a more malicious connotation. He was also a devoted and committed *puffer* as well as a loyal and trustworthy friend. These were the qualities which Joe connected to and their friendship developed deeply and quickly as they spent almost every day together. Surrounding Joe's business, their days consisted of dealing, puffing, munching, hysterical laughing, loitering, walking round the scheme, winding people up, puffing, dealing, drinking, munching and of course puffing. This was interspersed with the occasional harsh word or back handed assault for punters who were late with payments. Joe thought of himself as fair and lenient with those he knew but was quick to pick up on whether an individual was trying to 'get wide'. He knew that if he was to let one person rip him off then this would be permission for all and sundry to do likewise.

Craigo, Meeko and Gringo were still around on occasion but not as frequently as they used to be. Craigo's drug lifestyle which began as a social experience was now predominantly carried out in isolation. He would emerge from the darkness of his book –filled room at times to glance into the outside world and to keep the creeping spectre from enjoying rent free room in his mind. Craigo, like Mooney, was restlessly aware that his thoughts were an inner monologue which often seemed malicious and didn't always seem like his own. In the company of heroin and cannabis, his thoughts like unfriendly voices would often accuse, criticise and scratch away at his dwindling self-esteem and self-confidence.

Like Mooney had experienced with drugs and Joe had also known, Craigo felt like an exile from himself. He sought to regain this connection in two ways: Firstly and ironically by altering his consciousness through taking more drugs, and secondly through knowledge. Craigo was a highly intelligent individual whose intellect and memory enabled him to consume books with ease. He began with psychology and philosophy. He believed that self-knowledge would come as he understood the inner workings of the mind and then the invisible world of ideas. For someone on drugs who was already a natural introvert and a highly sensitive and perceptive spirit, this became a spiral staircase delving further into the mazes of the mind. Like Mooney he would also keep his nagging fears as sick secrets but they were always looking for a way out, like an angry dog barking behind a broken fence. Craigo loved to read and felt exhilarated when he explored new ideas and unfamiliar ways at looking at the world. Some of the philosophies and theories even made great sense to him and he identified with them. Like R.D.Laing's 'The Divided Self' or Chomsky's 'Manufacturing Consent' or any one of Dostoevsky's classic novels, Craigo perceived the essence of 'truths' in them but knowledge didn't seem to quieten the aloneness he felt within. Craigo ate up vast amounts of academic and classic literature texts voraciously, more eager than any hungry university student. He would sit up all night, stoned and thinking. He continued into the morning, stoned and reading. He would sleep during the day, stoned and dreaming.

The initial reading of a new text filled him with hope and he loved the expansion of his mind and a new horizon for his inner perception. But as the book faded and time passed he was left feeling emptier than before. He needed more than the growth of his mind and consciousness, so when psychology and philosophy lost their shine Craigo sought solace in the foolishness of Faust. Craigo's family had a history of interest in occult reading and there were many books in small, dusty cupboards around his house with titles like 'Witchcraft and Demonology' and 'Esoteric Mysteries of The Occult'. To Craigo these were just books, just more knowledge to explore and hopefully still his hunger. He couldn't see that his motivation for reading them was fear and control. He was compelled by the deep fear which separated him from his own spirit and the need to control his mind, and possibly even his environment.

As he explored these forbidden secrets he simultaneously and paradoxically began to feel weaker and stronger at the same time. His mind felt stronger whilst his spirit and body were drained of energy and life. His ego was boosted by the acquisition of unfamiliar knowledge about a world of spiritual rituals and psychological powers and influences, but he couldn't shake off a deeper unease which dominated his emotions-shame. The seeds of self-condemnation were present in Craigo since early childhood just as they would be with any child living in an environment of secrets, silence, fear and blame. His sensitive soul absorbed his environment by emotional osmosis. His own actions and pursuits to try and free him from this shame had ironically become an even greater source of self-condemnation. He still had a smile painted on his face for the public world but in the lonely room of addiction he truly hated who he had become. He didn't know how to free himself.

Meeko had also gone deeper into the Babylon of drugs and was enslaved by his own desires and cravings and the character defects which they had created in him. Unlike Craigo however, he didn't retreat with caution into the development of his mind but sought refuge in any criminal opportunity on offer. He wasn't a specialist but open to everything from housebreaking, to car-theft, to wheeling and dealing in every form to eventually selling class A drugs for some local would- be gangsters. Meeko didn't have the mind, the memory or the language skills which Craigo possessed and neither did he have the sensitivity of spirit which compelled his amigo to retreat from public interaction. On the contrary he pursued his identity on the outside, to be 'somebody' in the criminal world. This opened him up to manipulation and trickery by those he imagined to be successful and influential, regardless of their character or their trustworthiness.

Meeko had a good heart but it began to be suffocated by deception and even malice in his dealings with others. He occasionally did business with Joe, selling stolen goods or bringing customers to him for larger quantities of hash. And as much as he never robbed Joe or ripped him off, the trust between them was more fragile. Joe's intuition warned him that sometimes he was dealing more with the addicted personality than his childhood friend. There was sadness in this but also acceptance. Acceptance that the friendship bond remained but that life was more complicated now; they were each carrying more despair and loss. They weren't children anymore and this city could be cruel, it demanded survival skills governed by self-interest. Meeko and Joe would always have an affinity as close as many brothers, but for now caution was required.

Gringo, on the other hand was absent due to other distractions. He stopped taking heroin but still took a puff and consistently engaged in various activities surrounding the removal of articles which were not technically his, without the intention to return them at any given time. He couldn't help himself. He was still trying to fill the void and pay an inner debt which he felt Carol –Ann's death had thrust upon him. Nevertheless, he was generally happier as his relationship with Kristy was still blossoming and he was calmed by her affection and her laughter. He even considered getting a 'real job' at one point but the thought left as quickly as it had arrived.

The last of the gang, Big Mooney, hadn't been seen much since he had been released from Leverndale Psychiatric Hospital and although Joe had tried to visit him he just sat as vacant as an empty shell. After cutting his own finger off, smashing up Marks and Spencer's and attacking the police on several occasions, Mooney was under constant supervision by a CPN, a psychiatric nurse who visited him daily. Big Mooney had been ordered by the court to accept these 'visits' and was on a Compulsory Treatment Order. This meant that psychiatrists saw the solution to his problem as medication, which left Mooney comatose but calm. The last conversation that Joe had with Mooney was the most bizarre and unsettling he had ever had in his life. Joe tried to make a connection and was met with a silent stare. Mooney seemed to be looking to Joe, boring his eyes into Joe's face, searching for something he had lost. There was a hopeless longing in his eyes and Joe felt powerless to help him. After filling Mooney in with what was happening in the street and rambling for five minutes about nothing and everything, he tried to elicit a minimal verbal response.

"How's things been mate?"

The awkward silence was thick with Mooney's paranoia.

He stared at Joe, acknowledging that he could hear him but unable to say anything intelligible. Joe looked with trepidation around the room and saw, among cigarette douts, roaches and beer cans, a selection of unusual pamphlets and books.

'Scientology', 'Tarot', 'the Esoteric Mind', 'Astral Projection'…

"Whit you been readin' mate? Whit you been learnin'? It looks a bit heavy." Joe felt as if he was opening a door which he wasn't sure about entering, but he had to try. His hope lifted a little when Mooney slowly looked up, as if poised to speak and wiped the white film of foamy saliva which had formed around his lips. When he spoke, however, his voice was detached and lifeless; his eyes were manic and cold. This wasn't his pal sitting before him.

"God is in the stray dog."

The bizarre and random phrase might have been a previous starting point for a stoned topic of conversation but Joe was terrified. Never before had he felt such a threat in his psyche, even in the presence of violence. Mooney was completely somewhere else, perhaps on the edge of some un-nerving psychological world. Like Joe had seen in his Da when he was a child, the person he loved wasn't completely there in any real sense- he was taken over, influenced and controlled by some dark energy and thought. Everything inside Joe was telling him to leave and yet from somewhere inside an expression arose, which although true he would never have dreamed of saying. He stood up nervously as if to leave and his hand rested on Mooney's shoulder.

"I love you mate…"

Mooney seemed to hear and receive as his head went down further, ashamed at his own inability to fight the inner demons controlling him. He still couldn't respond but Joe was glad he'd said it.

"I'll see you about mate. I'll pop back up and see you when I get a minute." Joe left, not really knowing if he'd return and Mooney's only expression swam around inside him.

'God is in the stray dog… God is in the stray dog… God is in the stray dog'.

How mental was that? He tried to understand it and to imagine what was going on inside Mooney's mind. *How could there possibly be any sense or meaning in something so random?* His pal had truly lost it. Joe wanted to stop thinking about it but he couldn't let it go until a memory made him smile and suddenly connected to Mooney's voice in his head. He remembered the crazy laugh the gang had when they were younger, discussing The Creator Dog Theory and the concept of God in general. What Joe remembered more than the content was the feeling; he remembered the affinity he had with Mooney and the amigos, the sense of closeness and brotherhood; the feeling that this would never change; the feeling of belonging, of not being alone or friendless.

He also thought of Mooney as wandering around in his mind, not belonging to anyone, unkempt and un-kept. Like a stray dog which no-one wanted, barking at passers-by and running from every threatening sound, acting in the only way it knew how. Perhaps he was crying out for help in the only way he knew how-through his madness and his isolation. Perhaps Mooney was also trying to remember this feeling, a time in his life when he felt at least some connection, if only a little.

Chapter 25
Betrayal

When Jim began working with his brother their enterprise accelerated and took a new turn. Once again, everything was changing and moving quickly. Their established customers and employees were still generating business steadfastly and faithfully and the money was coming in. Changes came in various forms and Jim watched the synchronicity of events with caution and curiosity. Jim liked Bongo and had a strong intuition that it was good for Joe to be around him as he sensed that there were others around him that were not as transparent as they professed.

Joe had recently given Weaso a job, *shifting gear* for him and enabling him to pay back a debt which he'd run up over a couple of weeks. Weaso, like Meeko had recently been working with a local drug dealer who controlled most of the drugs in the south side of Glasgow and who was territorial and controlling by nature. His name was Bradford and he had been watching Joe's business with a keen and jealous eye. Through Bull and then through Meeko, Bradford had offered to be Joe's supplier and did, to be fair, offer a very reasonable price. On both occasions Joe declined, however, knowing that a deal with Bradford meant he'd be tied up with him, reliant on him. Joe and Jim also believed that competition was healthy. Joe wanted to continue expanding his business. He didn't want to be drawn into a trap so he let Bradford know that Jim was on board and that he was able to secure sufficient supply in terms of quantity, quality and price.

Jim knew Bradford's reputation. He knew that he was responsible for a number of serious violent assaults in the Govan area, usually in connection with business rivalry between him and other drug dealers. He also knew his character. He knew that he enjoyed the power and status which his small empire afforded him. The desire for power would inevitably create conflict so Jim was preparing himself, like a chess Grand Master, for a subtle move from his opponent.

At first Weaso generated lots of money for himself and Joe as he had his fingers in a lot of unsavoury pies. He mingled with all sorts of criminals from areas around the south-side, so he had quite a few connections. He began selling at the street level but quickly moved to selling ounces and quarter pounds to up and coming dealers or small groups of smokers who put their money together to buy in bulk, saving a few quid. To some extent he gained Joe's trust over a couple of months until Joe was happy to give him *tick* for larger quantities. At one point his bill reached around six hundred pounds and he promised Joe that if he would give him one last quarter pound he would pay his entire bill at the end of the month. This took his debt to nearly a grand and Joe was starting to get worried. He could smell a rat.

Jim had been paying very close attention to the situation and occasionally popped in to ask Joe how it was going. He also had other things on his mind that he wanted to discuss with his brother. Jim was a very secretive person and he lived by the principle *'you're only as safe as your secrets'*. The darkness of some secrets, however, had a purpose in being brought into the light, or at least into the shadow of his brother's confidence. In this case Jim wanted to declare to Joe the path which he was on and perhaps to prepare him for what he could feel was coming. They were in this together.

"Did you see that picture in The Times last night of some guy that got slashed in the town last week?" Jim's smile had a guilty pleasure.

"Aye, that was a belter man. He looked like the joker out of Batman." Joe tried to make light of a subject which always disoriented him.

"That was me!" Jim contained his pride as he wanted to see his brother's reaction first.

"Whit! Whit do you mean it was you? Whit happened?" Joe was shocked but wanted to appear eager to know as it did in fact feed some deep fear in him to have the availability of violence.

"Remember I told you a couple of months ago that some drunk guy was gettin' aggressive wi' me in the chippy at Central Station when I had wee Daniel at the pictures?"

"Aye."

"Well I couldnae believe it .When I was walkin' through the town last week on my way back to Cranhill, I spotted him. He looked as if he'd had a couple of drinks and he was wi' a couple of women…I had a Stanley blade on me. The polis were circling the block and I just waited and timed it. I walked past him wi' my head down and when I got close enough I belted him right across the jaw. He was fuckin' shocked." Jim began to relive the pleasure of revenge and the thrill of the unsuspecting violent moment. "He started screamin' and I bolted. Threw the blade in the Clyde and ran to the bus stop."

Jim had indeed done what he'd said and he'd deliberated intensely before it, knowing that once this line was crossed he was firmly established in the way of violence once again. The line was crossed, the door was opened and violence had entered his soul once more. Joe wasn't really sure how to respond so he said what he thought was the right thing.

"Well, he got whit was comin' to him. He shouldnae be fuckin' aggressive to innocent people in the street, especially when they've got weans wi' them." The word 'innocent' didn't ring true to either of the brothers.

Revealing this incident enabled Jim to let his brother know that violence was back in and it might be closer than they thought. He also wanted Joe to know not to be concerned about Weaso. Jim suspected that Weaso was a spy in the camp right from the outset. He had been sent by someone, perhaps Bradford, to infiltrate their business and sabotage it from the inside. If Joe wasn't going to work with Bradford there was treachery at work which meant he wasn't going to work at all.

"Tell Weaso that it's me he owes the money to and that I want all of it by the end of the month. Nae more tick!"

Joe followed the instructions and Weaso subsequently made his promises. But from the moment Joe had drawn the line with Weaso and forced him to make a decision, whether to pay his debt or enter into conflict, malice slithered into a corner of Weaso's mind and a series of events were set in motion. What Jim had suspected all along and Joe was now beginning to see more clearly was the deception and the betrayal in Weaso's heart. From the outset of working with Joe, Weaso was being used as a pawn, although he thought he was a king. Weaso had been persuaded by Bradford that if he sabotaged Joe's business then he would be rewarded with a little piece of his kingdom, and that he'd have an aspiring business of his own. This seduced his ego enough to prompt him to act as a Judas to those who trusted him.

Not only this, but he was also encouraged by Bull to gain Joe's trust enough to get at least a half-pound on *bail.* Bull promised him that he would shift it for him at a reasonable price and that if there was any comeback from Joe or Jim that he and his brother would back him up in any conflict. This was a soundproof plan, how could he lose? Money, power, reputation and the means to achieve it were all offered to him. He met Joe in the street and covered his face with an angry frown. He made his move.

"Tell Jim he's not gettin' his money. Tell him that if he wants to go ahead, I'm up for it."

Weaso told Joe this with a façade of confidence but Joe knew he was nervous. Joe stared at him, his mind quickening and hardening to harbour the violence docking in his mind. Joe's initial anger at the betrayal was swallowed as he looked down and noticed Weaso's clenched fist clutching something in his pocket. He had a blade.

"Aye, I'll tell him." Joe's concise and emotionless reaction couldn't hide the sting of betrayal burning his eyes. Weaso saw it and knew this wasn't the time for violence. He had made a choice which was going to have serious repercussions. There were the possible consequences which might come from Jim but also the fact that he had destroyed an alliance with someone who had been nothing but a good friend to him. Joe had backed Weaso up over the years with various small conflicts with other gangs and had shown him nothing but fairness and even kindness. Weaso had made a serious error of judgement and in his own lust for money and status, driven by drugs and malice he had now invited a violence which he could not have foreseen. Weaso and his *back up* had underestimated the measures which Joe and especially Jim would take to maintain their business. This was their way out of the scheme and they were ready to *go ahead.* When Joe told Jim that afternoon even he felt a shudder of fear at Jim's reaction.

"I'm no' gettin' my money. Is that fuckin' right?" Jim was standing rigid, his body began to tense as he stared at the ground, thinking. Jim was usually very controlled in his anger, especially since he'd been in prison but the rage he felt bubbled like lava over the edges of his mind.

"Well, that's awrite…cos I tell you whit…" The violence filled Jim's face and anger burned his eyes and found itself in his hands, he began viciously stabbing the air. " I'll fuckin' stab fuck out of that wee bastard…and that fuckin' Bull and Bradford…if they've got anythin' to do wi' this I'll stab fuck out of them as well."

The spirit of violence filled the room and consumed the brothers with hatred and revenge. Joe knew these were not idle threats and was anxious at the murder which was empowering his brother's body. He had never seen Jim so angry and for a second he was anxious that Jim wouldn't be able to control it and might be reckless in his revenge. Now it was Joe's turn to underestimate his brother's effectiveness with violence. Jim was just releasing the valve a little in the safety of Joe's confidence. Jim was well aware, having filled his later teenage years in prison with books about paramilitaries, organised crime gangs, assassins and other 'effective' violent criminals, that control and intelligence were necessary to avoid the law and defeat potential enemies. Jim's mind had been nurtured by this violence and now it would begin to reveal its potential.

"Aye, we'll do him just don't dae anythin' stupid. We don't want to be gettin' the jail." Joe attempted to calm his brother before he left Mary's house in case he bumped into Weaso in the street and unleashed his fury.

"Don't worry, I'm awrite. Right don't you dae anythin' just now, leave it wi' me. I'll sort it out." And with that Jim got himself ready and said his goodbyes to Mary as if nothing had happened.

The next day Jim appeared at Mary's house early, intent on gathering intelligence on who his enemies were and what he was up against. He strongly suspected that Weaso would never have had the bottle to challenge him on his own. He told Joe to get up as they were going to visit Bull to see what he knew.

The moment that Bull opened his door and invited them in Jim's spirit was disturbed and he knew he was in the lion's den. His mind, however, was calm and controlled. They told Bull what had happened and he feigned surprise, but the smirk escaping from the corner of his lips revealed his involvement in this treachery. Bull believed that his brother was in a different league from Jim and Joe and that they wouldn't consider harming him because of this fact. He believed that he was untouchable. He was wrong.

For now Jim would play along and pretend that he had been deceived by Bull. He had suspected that Bull had a growing jealousy of Joe's success and that a bitter root had grown in him. Maybe he was right.

Joe listened intently and let Jim do most of the talking. He listened not only to the words of his enemy but also to the slight tells in his body language and in the betrayals of his tone. A memory of a poster in school, a phrase on the wall behind a teacher's deck in RE, flashed into his mind,

'Out of the overflow of the heart, the mouth speaks'.

The brothers left Bull's house with the appearance of friendliness and gullibility but they knew his involvement. Jim would bide his time and exact revenge in his own way and under his own terms. He felt disrespected and undermined.

His enemy's estimation of him would change in due time. His violence was patient.

Within two days of confronting Bull and preparing to attack Weaso, word was sent to the McShane brothers that their betrayer had fled the country. Weaso had indeed gone into hiding and Joe was told that he had gone to London with the money he had made from selling their drugs. This didn't seem to upset Jim in the slightest although Joe was more impatient. He had lost face in his own scheme and had been made to look foolish. He had been ripped off by a so-called friend and wondered if anyone else would try it on. He filled his vulnerability with rage and fantasies of revenge. When Weaso returned, and Jim confidently reassured his wee brother that he would, they would be quick and callous in their attack. For now it was a waiting game and a new way of learning to be. Jim had learned that with violence it was always safer to bite before you bark.

Many people were expecting the McShanes to be ranting and raving about what they were going to do, but they remained silent. The violence in them could grow stronger in the silent darkness. They had both been unconsciously preparing for this moment from the day they first set foot on this path. Once again there was inevitability in the unfolding of these events. Joe and Jim wanted to avoid violence, or at least they consciously told themselves this. Yet it was as if they were drawing towards themselves, people, places and happenings which enabled them to play out the suppressed material hidden in the recesses of their minds. Not only was this violence inevitable, it seemed unavoidable.

Chapter 26
If the ski mask fits

Weaso's betrayal left Jim and Joe even more wary and untrusting than they had been before. Their childhood had taught them not to trust adults and now they were part of a world where even 'friends' had to be watched closely. Despite the setback of this betrayal, Joe and Jim redoubled their efforts to keep their business on track and also began to look into new opportunities to make cash faster. Money from cannabis was steady but Joe was spending it as fast as he was making it. Money to get stoned and drunk, to buy expensive clothes and jewellery as well as trying to save for a car(as he'd recently got his licence), were all swallowing his 'wages' hungrily. Joe had dreams of buying a house and getting away from the city, of having enough money to retire from this business before he was thirty. He couldn't see that his greed and insecurity, where money was concerned, wouldn't be satisfied no matter how much he acquired. He told himself *'If I can make a couple of hundred grand then I could get out and live a good life... a happy one'.* Under this false hope, Joe knew that it might take years to make this sort of money selling cannabis. *How could he make money quicker, even if there's a bit more risk?* Almost as if Joe was sending this question out telepathically to anyone or anything that could provide an answer, two opportunities came into his path. The first one came from Bongo's exhaustion at the end of a hard days' work as a delivery driver for an electronics company.

"You want to have seen the tellies we were deliverin' the day Joe. Absolute beauties... four hundred quid, forty two inches, Toshiba. We had six of them, plus we had four of these top of the range Technics music systems. You want to hear the sound aff these things, Amazin'."

"Aye? Whit else did youse have?" Joe immediately saw his new car materialise in his mind as Bongo was talking.

"All sorts of shite. Different tellies, music centres, eh...whit else?" Bongo was asking himself as his cannabis induced short term memory loss was kicking in, even though he had initiated the conversation.

"Hurry up Boy Goucher. It was only three hours ago you were deliverin' them." Joe laughed, "Ya fanny." He was fond of Bongo but couldn't resist winding him up, it broke the boredom of standing around in closes generating business, which was the main part of each evening.

"Tell me this. How much is all that gear worth?" Joe's focus made Bongo realise that he was scheming.

"I don't know, probably a few grand." Bongo deliberately played this down as he could feel a proposal coming which might put him in a predicament. And sure enough the proposal came in right on cue.

"We could bump youse? Me and Jim could wait until you've got a delivery near the scheme and then hijack your van. Who do you work wi'?"

"Wee Martin fae the top of the scheme. I don't know if he'd be up for it, cos it was him that got me that job." Bongo knew this might be his only way out.

"That's awrite. It disnae matter if he's keen, as long as he disnae stick us in."

"No, he widnae dae that."

"No, I'm sure he wouldnae, especially if we make it look real. I'll mention it to Jim."

"Aye, but nae real violence or anythin'." Bongo wanted to clarify what 'make it look real' entailed.

"No, don't be daft we'll no' touch *you*…" Joe smiled mischievously, "We might slap wee Martin about a bit but, we don't want anybody gettin' suspicious."

"No, don't, Martin's awrite Joe." Bongo was aware of Jim's capability but unsure of his ethics.

Joe burst out laughing, "I'm kiddin' you on… we'll not touch any of youse…honest."

Bongo wasn't exactly reassured and he knew that if anything went wrong then he and Martin might even get arrested or lose their jobs.

"I mean it Joe, I don't want anythin' happenin'."

"Calm down mate, I'll tell Jim just to bring the *wee* machete." Joe knotted himself and Bongo couldn't help laughing at Joe's sick humour, but he fluttered with worry.

A few days later Jim came up to Mary's for his weekly visit and he was beaming with contained excitement. Joe couldn't remember the last time he'd seen him looking so pleased with himself. Joe told him about hijacking Bongo and Martin and he was very eager and interested, but he was itching to tell Joe news of his own. "Wait to you see whit I've got." Jim opened the small holdall he'd been carrying and delicately removed its contents which seemed to be wrapped in old oil stained towels.

Joe's excitement diminished slightly as he couldn't imagine anything of great value wrapped up so shabbily. As Jim unfolded the towel Joe had a strong sense of danger and power, not dissimilar to the first time he opened a bag of heroin. When it was fully opened the brothers just stared silently at the two heavy, dull, metallic weapons. The sawn off shotguns were compact, containing within them the potential of power and death. Jim revelled in the moment and Joe was also restlessly excited.

"Wow…where did you get *them*? They're belters!"

"I got them off an old crook I know fae Teucharhill…wee Boxer."

"How much were they? Is it one each?" Joe laughed, as he wasn't sure whether his own question was serious.

"Aye, of course, a hundred and fifty quid each."

Joe picked the shotgun up and held it firmly in his hands, trying to imagine the experience and the feeling of firing it for real. But the whole situation felt anything but real, it was like a fearful fantasy, a violent movie where you were actually inside the movie. There was a deep sense of being carried along here for Joe, of time moving out of his control. Not that he believed it was ever in his control but a premonition haunted him ,that unseen forces were influencing events and shaping his future. *What were they going to do with these weapons? What were they for? Were they actually going to use them?* Jim timely provided some answers.

"That wee Weaso'll get a surprise when he comes back. One of these starin' at him in a back close…And if any of his back up want a wee battle then we'll be ready for them."

Joe was still stunned with silence as he tried to absorb this new direction. He was under the same spell of violence as many young males in Glasgow. This was woven with the promise of power over, and respect from others. The dreams which filled his mind were starting to materialise, whether he wanted them to or not. There was no other alternative reality which seemed a viable option to him.

"We can use them to *do turns* as well. Look at them as an investment."

The shotguns were stored in Mary's cellar and left until their assistance was required. For now Joe and Jim focussed on hijacking Bongo and wee Martin. They decided to leave the guns out of this particular robbery; they would have been an unnecessary risk. Plus the fact that Martin was already in panic mode that something was going to go wrong. He was more concerned that he was going to potentially lose more than his job.

So, a date and a time were decided. The plan was that Bongo would phone Joe whenever they had a delivery in Hardridge, preferably at the start of the day when their van was full. The day arrived and Joe and Jim were excited. Their intention was to use Jim's old transit van which he'd bought from a guy in the street. It wasn't exactly the cool getaway car but was reminiscent of Bertie's blue transit van which took them away from Govan as wee boys and into the new stage of their youth in Corkerhill. It wasn't fast, it looked shit and it was not for the boy racer, but it was big enough to get quite a lot of gear in. This was their only concern.

Bongo phoned Joe when he left the shop with a loaded van, his hand shaking a little despite his willingness.

"Awrite Joe, it's me. We'll be down in the scheme in about half an hour. We've got a delivery up near the swing park. The van's full of gear."

"Awrite Bongo, we'll be there mate. Don't worry, it'll all be sound." Joe reassured, hearing the tremor in his pal's voice.

The McShane brothers got ready. They simply got into their van, parked at the top end of the scheme and waited for the delivery van to come round the corner. When it arrived they drove down to meet it, reversing the back door of the Transit to the back of the delivery van, about six feet away. Bongo and Martin got out of the van and unlocked the treasures inside, Jim and Joe were delighted but didn't allow themselves time to ponder. As planned they told the delivery boys to help them transfer the gear and then 'forced them' to get into their empty van. Jim then tied them up with plastic tie straps and locked the door. Martin and Bongo were just relieved that this part had gone without incident, although they would still have to tell their boss and be questioned by the police.

Jim and Joe took the televisions, music systems and other electronic devices to Gringo's house where he had arranged for a buyer to come up and have a look. He offered them three grand to take all the stuff from them. They were delighted. This was much quicker and more exciting than standing about the scheme waiting for punters to buy hash.

They duly gave their accomplices a cut, once they were released, having spent most of the day explaining to their boss and the police about the robbery. The story was convincing enough as the police had been initially alerted by a phone call from a clueless old lady, telling them of some strange shouts coming from a delivery van parked outside her house. She told the police that she did find it strange that some of the items from the van were being removed and put into another. She had started to get impatient as she thought they were delivering her new telly when she saw them arrive at the close. However, after fifteen minutes of waiting she went out to see what was happening and heard the shouts to call the police. She did so promptly. "I mean…" she said, feeling guilty that she hadn't called them sooner, "I just thought they were being really careful bringin' the stuff oot."

The delivery company boss, nor for that matter the police, had any reason to suspect the boys unduly. Robberies and hold ups were quite common in this area and in fact many companies wouldn't deliver to this particular part of Hardridge because of the risk.

They were away scot free. This was something which Bongo and Martin didn't want to repeat but the brothers were enthused. This was the start of something exciting. They knew that the next time wouldn't be so easy and it would be the real thing. They would actually have to dress for the part, accessories included.

It wasn't long before Jim had planned a new robbery, one which would be just him and Joe, and that they'd be guaranteed *'at least eight grand'* between them. This was undoubtedly a step up, both in terms of the amount of money and the risk involved. The location was a bookie's in the East End where their Aunty Maggy, John's sister, worked as the cleaner. When Jim 'innocently' quizzed her about it she told him that she was there to open the doors at 9a.m. and that the boss would arrive at 9.30a.m. Every day without fail he emptied the safe and an average day's takings were between eight and nine thousand pounds. The plan was for Jim and Joe to arrive after Maggy had opened the doors, go in through the back door, tie her up, wait for the boss to arrive and then force him to open the safe. There were a couple of obvious considerations to ponder before acting out this crime. Firstly, there was the risk of arrest and the seriousness of a gun crime. Secondly, the bookies were owned by a notorious Glasgow crime figure who would seek to find the robbers and punish them. And thirdly, the boss might not give up the money so easily if he knew that the owner of the shop might suspect him of being in on it.

So, the brothers weighed up the obstacles and decided to go ahead on the following basis: One, they were willing to risk time in prison for such a considerable sum of money. Two, they would make the robbery appear real in all ways possible and not tell another soul about their plans. And three, Jim decided that if the boss put up any resistance he would waste no time in shooting him in the leg to let him know that they were serious.

Only three weeks after hijacking Bongo's van, Jim and Joe put on their old oily boiler suits to make them look like workmen, and then took their tool bag to do their job. If the police had stopped them and checked their bag they would have discovered that its contents were slightly less conventional than your typical workmen. The traditional apparel of ski masks, a crow bar and a sawn off shotgun probably wouldn't be much use in fixing your boiler or central heating but were 'essential' requirements for a certain line of work. Joe thought that the shotgun wasn't loaded and that it was merely a frightener to persuade the boss of the seriousness of the situation and to get things moving quicker. Jim thought it best to allow Joe to believe this; this would avoid unnecessary anxiety, although watching someone being blasted in the kneecap with a shotgun at 9.30a.m. would surely bring its own stress.

Aunty Maggy had been persuaded and reassured by Jim that there was nothing to worry about, but she was still petrified. Nevertheless, Jim's forcefulness of will and determination were difficult to resist. She would go ahead with this but every second would be torture, not literally she hoped. When Jim and Joe arrived at the bookies they drove into the lane which led them to the back door. The street was unusually quiet as they put on their ski masks and armed themselves. Joe was nervous. Jim was focussed. For some reason Jim was almost comfortable with this, like the present form of his mind could be easily adapted to this level of criminality. The ski mask was terror, violence, intimidation, darkness, secrecy, and the threat of cruelty, power and force. As Joe pulled it over his face it was like becoming someone else to adapt into this other world. There was both a thrill and a terror in the power. There was both a safety and a falsehood in the secrecy.

"Are you ready Joe?" Jim spoke with clarity and decisiveness as he knew that he should take the lead.

Joe breathed deeply as he held the cold steel of the crow bar and glanced furtively at the shotgun resting on Jim's lap. His lust for money prompted his heart as he took a deep breath.

"Aye, let's dae it."

They quickly checked the mirrors and the windows on every side and jumped out of the van, looking around to see if there were any witnesses. The streets were empty and there was not a sound except for the occasional car whizzing by on the main road at the front of the shop. They used the crow bar to force the back door open and Maggy was standing at the other side as white as a ghost. When she saw the two figures with boiler suits and ski masks, weapons in hand, she was momentarily paralysed. *This wasn't her two wee nephews who she used to baby sit.* She had a drained anxiety on her face as she pleadingly said,

"I have a really bad feelin' about this. I think we should leave it Jim."

By this time Jim was completely in role, his mind fixed on the task at hand.

"Who the fuck is Jim? Don't fuckin' talk. Get o'er there and get under the counter. When your boss comes in don't say a fuckin' word."

Jim was so convincing that Maggy actually wondered if this was someone else robbing the shop. Jim knew that she'd have to be convincing to the police and her boss. The robbery had to look real.

Jim directed Joe to hide behind a side wall as he hid behind the one closest to the back door. The boss would arrive here in about five minutes and he had been perfectly punctual every single day in all the time that Maggy had worked there. Five minutes passed and the brothers prepared their minds for a moment of violence. When he arrived he'd be forced to open the safe and give the boys the previous day's takings. The waiting was a strain and Maggy silently wept as she couldn't believe that she'd been talked into this. *No amount of money is worth this level of fear.* When seven minutes passed, then eight, then ten, the silence had to be broken. Jim could sense the tension in the others as he shouted over.

"Joe just stay where you are, we'll gie it another ten minutes! You just stay where you are as well missus."

In the next ten minutes every worst case scenario and fearful thought swam around Joe's head.

Why is the boss not here if he's never been late before?

What if they'd been seen coming in and someone had phoned the polis?

What if the polis had stopped the boss and they were waiting outside for Jim and Joe?

There would probably be armed response. What if they opened fire when they saw the gun?

Even if they didnae open fire, if they are there we're going to jail for a long time.

The thought of a long time in prison seemed worse to Joe than the possibility of them coming out shooting the gun and trying to make a getaway, like the final scene from Butch Cassidy and the Sundance Kid. As Joe's anxious mind flitted between the past, the present and the future, a memory flashed in his mind of himself as a wee four year old boy on Christmas morning, swaggering outside his close with a full cowboy suit, hat, holster and silver guns, imagining he was the Lone Ranger as John and Mary knotted themselves with laughter from the window. Jim shouted over, snubbing out this little fantastical light and bringing Joe back to the moment.

"Joe! Let's go…somethin''s no' right." He quickly cut the tie straps on Maggy's wrists and prepared for what was outside. To their relief and surprise the world outside was the same as they had left it, quiet, empty and uneventful. They got into the van, put the ski masks and weapons in the holdall, threw it in the back of the van and returned to the south side. As the anti-climax descended and the adrenalin dissipated, the brothers were relieved but also disappointed. They wouldn't be getting the jail but neither would they be getting any money.

However, later on that day they found out from Maggy that the boss had actually arrived at the bookies on time and realised that he'd forgotten the keys for the safe. He then quickly got into his car and made his way home to get them. Was this coincidental? Was this good fortune or bad luck? Whatever it was, Jim viewed it as an omen and wouldn't try to rob this particular bookies again. Perhaps if they'd gone through with the robbery they would have had another enemy to clash with, not knowing that there were already some pawns being moved in the shadows, being put in place for a battle at their own doorstep.

Chapter 27
Shifting Shadows

Six months after he had made his escape and gone into hiding, Weaso returned and brazenly strolled down Hardridge Road as if he didn't have a care in the world. Gringo brought Joe the news and he in turn told Jim that he was back.

"I think we should do him straight away and waste nae time before he gets a chance to make a move." Joe wanted to regain the credibility he had lost and exact revenge on his betraying friend. But Jim was extremely calm, controlled and collected.

"No. Don't dae anythin' daft. Send word to him that I want a truce. Tell him I want to talk to him, to gie him the chance to pay back his debt."

When Joe had told Jim that Weaso had returned and was calmly parading the street, Jim knew that one of two things was happening. Firstly, that Weaso was either being watched by the police or secondly that their former friend believed that he had *back up* suitable to protect him. So, Joe sent word to Weaso and assured him of no hijack but that they just wanted to talk to him. Weaso agreed as he had quickly spread about the news that he was working for Bradford and let others believe that he also had support from Bull and his brother. His mind was confident but when he eventually met up with Jim he couldn't stop the rush of nervousness streaming through his body.

"Awrite Jim. Listen…I just want to say that I'm willin' to try and pay back whit I owe you if you gie me a chance."

"Awrite…relax. All I'm interested in is gettin' my money back and if I do anythin' to you then that's no' gonnae happen…is it?" Jim sat down on the stairs of Mary's close and immediately communicated that there was no threat. Weaso thought that Jim's attempt to make peace was a combination of his good sense in getting his money back and maybe even a little sign of being intimidated by his connections. Jim was happy for him to believe this. The fly was buzzing around the web.

"Awrite Jim…that's brilliant…I'm glad we've sorted this out…I just got myself intae a mess the last time but I will pay you back. I could even dae a wee bit o' work for youse?" Weaso put his feelers out to see if there was another opportunity for a rip off.

"Well, I'll tell you whit…I've got an even better idea. This is between us…" Jim let Weaso feel that he was not only forgiven, but trusted. "…me and Joe have done a couple of turns recently, robberies. It's much quicker than punting weed. I've got two lined up if you're up for daein them wi' us?"

Weaso was not only reassured but excited at the prospect of hold-ups and robberies. "Aye, that sounds brilliant, right up my street. When and where?"

"Well, I'll let you know the details next week but it'll be soon. Are you definitely up for it? Have a think about it and if you decide to pull out before next week let me know." Jim's tone was calm and reassuring without a trace of control, manipulation or malice. The fly was trapped.

Throughout the conversation with Weaso, Joe sat silently providing the appropriate, reassuring nod and smile. Despite the fact that Weaso had ripped him off he believed Joe to be an honest and fair friend, someone he could rely on, who would forgive and give a second chance. Forgiveness was far from Joe's mind. He was sick of trusting only for it to be crushed.

When Weaso left the close he genuinely believed that all was forgiven and forgotten. His pride told him that the McShane's reluctance to attack him was a result of their fear and gullibility. He believed that he was so much shrewder than them. He felt a sense of victory. His return to the street and to his desired reputation as a feared, aspiring criminal was re-established to his deep satisfaction.

Jim's demeanour changed the moment Weaso was out of sight, like a brilliant actor exiting the stage; he turned to Joe with malice and murder in his mind.

"If he agrees we'll tell him it's next week. I'll tell him that the turn is a Post office in Ayrshire and that all he's got to do is be there wi' a blade and wear a ski mask. I'll tell him it's a cert, there's no way we'll get caught. We'll drive out to the countryside somewhere…in the middle of nowhere. I'll produce the gun fae the back of the car. Tell him to get out and walk away fae the car a bit…then I'll blow his fuckin' leg aff." Jim's anger burned in his eyes, "… and leave him to bleed to death."

Joe tried to get his head round what he was hearing. He wanted Weaso punished and to have his revenge but the sound of 'Murder' was hard to comprehend. To take another's life, to enter into this level of violence, scared him. Of course he didn't voice this but showed compliance and full agreement to Jim's plans. There was no doubt that Joe wanted Weaso shot, now that they had the means to do it. He knew that simply attacking him might invite retaliation, but using the gun was more definite and decisive. Jim's talk of killing him helped to break Joe's fantasy and illusions about the fruits of violence. Joe knew that his brother wasn't making angry threats but would carry this out effectively and clinically. Driven by his own rage and revenge, Joe had fantasised about the feelings of power and the acquired perception of others when one committed violent acts, but this wasn't a fantasy. They were planning on killing someone.

The responsibility for ending a life would be on their souls, even if they didn't get caught. Jim's focussed, violent mind had pierced the blindness in Joe's-he could now clearly consider that to use violence, even when the intention wasn't murder, could lead to it. To the rational, objective observer this may have been a glaringly obvious point, but to Joe (and countless other young people in Glasgow) the truth of violence wasn't so transparent. There was a falsehood, a fantasy of violence which seared the conscience and removed them from the reality. This fantasy was driven by fear, rage and the desire for power, and was often only realised for many when they sat in the prison cell for the first night after being sentenced. In some quiet place within him Joe could feel the reality of where he was heading pressing in on him, but he still chose to silence it and continue on his way. He would take revenge, if this was what it took.

Joe told no-one about this and Jim stayed away from the scheme, waiting for Weaso's confirmation. Joe went about his business and skilfully conveyed to others that a truce and reconciliation had taken place between them. He even told Bongo that he was giving Weaso a second chance as he pre-empted intense police pressure and interrogation when the deed was done. He wanted the rumours and gossip in the community to support his alibi when it was needed.

In the vacuum of waiting for this plan to be exacted, there seemed to be a steady flow of activity within the scheme. A young, aspiring criminal who had recently begun to distribute cannabis for Joe, had his own run in with Weaso. Gally, as he was known, was only sixteen years old and had spent most of his childhood in youth detention centres and even a year in a secure unit. He had a helmet of straight dirty-blonde hair and although his face was that of a child's, his eyes were as war torn as a mercenary's. His agile and athletic physique had been developed through years of fighting his way through detention centres and running from the police. His small piercing eyes were cold even when his smile beamed. It wasn't that he didn't have goodness in him but the absence of love and the shattering of trust had buried it deep inside. He was known for being prone to violence and quite 'mental'. Not in a medically diagnosed sense but in that he was not averse to committing acts which required a total disregard for consequences. Despite his reputation Joe had a real fondness for him and saw him like a younger brother. Joe knew that behind all the madness there was still a soul there, and at times even a good one. So, when Gally appeared at Mary's door full of rage and revenge, Joe saw an opportunity.

"Whit happened to you?" Joe pointed to the blood stains on the shoulder of his tee-shirt.

"That wee prick Weaso stuck the heid on me cos I widnae gie him tick." Gally was up to provide more than information, he had a question and a proposal.

"I would have attacked him, there and then but I knew he had a blade on him…an' I've heard that Bradford is backin' him up…so Weaso is puttin' about anyway…" Gally paused in preparation for his proposal, "D'you think Jim can get me a gun?"

"Whit?" Joe tried to feign innocence but Gally was sharp. He knew that the truce Jim had declared was a hoax.

"C'mon in and have a couple of joints and calm down." Joe ushered Gally in and stepped back in his mind to scan whether his young employee was as bold as he was angry. He had used a blade on a couple of occasions and wasn't someone who shrunk back from the threat of prison. He'd spent half of his life being passed from pillar to post in government institutions.

After smoking a couple of joints and assessing the extent of Gally's genuine willingness to shoot Weaso, Joe could see another option at work, other than the original plan of murder. Without disclosing any information about their own plans or even about their possession of firearms, he told Gally not to do anything just now but to leave it with him.

As soon as Gally left, Joe phoned Jim and asked him to come up. He hoped that Jim would see the sense in removing themselves from any involvement in Weaso's fate.

When Joe told Jim about this new opportunity he was initially suspicious. *Was Gally really as genuine as he claimed? What if Weaso had actually got him on board and had sent him up to gather information?* Jim knew that he had to be careful, he knew in his gut that a Judas spirit was in the air. Whose heart it would enter was still an open question.

Jim immediately visited Gally as he knew he'd be able to read any duplicity if he questioned him. But there was none. Jim was satisfied and started to put the plan into motion. It had to be perfect. He wanted to be as patient, as devious and as brutal as he could be, whilst at the same time avoiding any heat from the police. He still wanted to make some money. Jim was aware that if they were to allow Gally to do this now then they'd lose his employment, his custom and a wicked opportunity. He told Gally and Joe that the element of shock and surprise would be much more effective than a public declaration. They would bide their time and distance their whole crew from Weaso. A date was set-three months from now, Bonfire night. This would be a night of loud bangs and screams. One more would go barely un-noticed, for most people at least.

Chapter 28
Pirates-Lost at Sea

Joe's life had always been one of perpetual change, nothing ever stayed the same. He often felt his life was like a ship caught in a storm, being tossed to and fro by the pounding waves. The tumultuous waves of violence and fear, of anger and shame, battered against his mind. He kept this well hidden and held on close to his own independence and the distorted freedom which came from forcing solutions and trying to control people or events whenever he could. He was familiar with change so when 'wee Manny' appeared on the scene looking for drugs, Joe wasn't particularly fazed by his expressive and erratic manner. Manny was surprised, however, that the local drug dealers were these 'wee guys' whom he had watched growing up in the scheme since they were *wains*.

Manny pulled up at Joe's close in his old ocean blue Vauxhall Cavalier and bounced out in his usual confident manner. Manny was about six or seven years older than Joe and Bongo but he was well known in Hardridge as someone who used to sell drugs and ran about with the older Paka boys in his youth. His tanned, shaved head and the curious expression constantly etched on his round face strangely reminded Joe of a turtle for some reason, but slow he was not. His large, puffed up chest and powerful shoulders were supported by a short pair of runner's legs and a confident swagger. His reputation as someone who could fight preceded him but he was known in recent years as someone who had experienced some sort of spiritual transformation. So, Joe was surprised at his request when he sauntered into the close.

"Awrite boys? Hows it goin'? I'm lookin' for a bit of hash…where can I get some?"

At first Joe was reluctant but business was business. Bongo moved closer to the baseball bat which he'd hidden behind a small wall nearby.

"Much are you lookin' for?"

"A quarter."

"Aye, we can get ye some." Joe produced a matchbox with four lumps of dope in it and handed one to Manny. "Twenty quid."

Manny handed over a score whilst analysing his hash with the eye of a seasoned buyer.

"I thought you didnae touch this stuff anymore?" Joe was slightly suspicious, but more curious.

Manny's usual confident mask slipped and Joe recognised the mark of shame on his face.

"As a dog returns to its vomit… so a fool returns to his folly. What can I say mate I'm a fanny."

Joe smiled.

"Not only that…" Manny paused for effect and clothed himself with his mad persona, "I'm the King of the Fannies…and you better no' be tryin' to take my reputation."

Joe laughed as Manny gave a broad, cheeky smile and warmed to these 'wee guys fae the scheme', immediately recognising in them a couple of good souls.

"Have youse two got any skins?"

Joe searched his pockets and pulled out two packets, giving one to Manny.

"There you go mate, enjoy. That's good gear by the way."

"Aye? Do youse fancy smokin' a couple of *doobies* wi' me?" Manny's warm smile was disarming.

Joe and Bongo looked at each other and simultaneously responded.

"Aye, c'mon then."

"Are youse two Siamese twins or somethin'? Right, let's go to the Bounty."

"Whit are ye on about? *The Bounty*?"

"That's whit I call my motor. To get in it ye need to talk like a pirate."

The idea of sitting in a car and out of the rain for a while appealed to the boys but Joe and Bongo were bemused; this guy was obviously a bit unhinged, but interesting. They welcomed the change, especially if they were going to get a smoke and a laugh out of it.

"Pirates? How dae ye talk like a pirate, d'you stand on one leg or somethin'?"

Manny explained the language of pirate talk by telling them that they had to speak out of one side of their mouth and whenever they wanted to express curiosity, doubt or disagreement they were to say in a Long John silver styled croaked voice, "That'll be right." He was clearly mad, a screw loose, mental. He had the playful spirit of a thirteen year old boy who didn't care about the opinion of others but only that life should be fun. Every opportunity for madness should be grasped with both hands. Joe and Bongo saw a bizarre contradiction within him which they couldn't quite pinpoint. There was definitely something different about him compared to their usual clientele.

Joe saw something childlike and unfamiliar but also honesty in Manny, his self-loathing and derogation were inviting. Joe had heard many stories of Manny fighting for the Paka and yet he felt unthreatened by this larger than life character. Manny was clearly a bit crazy but Joe liked him.

As they got to know him over the first few weeks of the summer months, they realised that his spirit always wanted to expand and he was never satisfied with sitting around stoned, gazing into the emptiness. He was always looking for more, enjoying the drugs but usually with a bitter taste in his mouth. In a very short time Joe and Bongo became acquainted with wee Manny's way of life and how bizarre it actually was. Not only did he have an insatiable capacity for various drugs, any drink and every other form of pleasure whenever it was available, but he even had his own kiss-o-gram business!

Before long, Joe and Bongo were escorting Manny and his kiss-o-gram employees, big Tom and Audrey, to pubs, clubs and private parties around Scotland. This was exciting and often hilarious as the boys would watch with disbelief the manic antics of boozy hen parties and salivating stag dos, hooting and howling at the scantily clad physiques of Tarzan Tom and Amazing Audrey. This was a lot more entertaining than standing in closes and getting stoned.

In addition to the kiss-o-gram nights, wee Manny enlarged Joe and Bongo's daily experience with long drives around the lochs, over and through the mountains in the Trossachs of Scotland. The newly found trio would get seriously stoned and 'head for the hills'. Joe loved this time so much that he began to feel alive again for the first time in years. He loved the sense of freedom and the expansion of his mind and spirit which the mountains seemed to evoke in him. Before this time Joe and Bongo rarely left their own scheme and even more rarely did they leave Glasgow. Yet, in the depth of his being Joe connected to the greatness, the beauty and the invisible qualities of the natural world. The stillness of the lochs, the power of the mountains and the freshness of the mountain air refreshed his spirit.

Manny, Bongo and Joe would often pick up hitch-hikers on the country roads or chat away to strangers in the Loch Achray Hotel, and it became apparent that everyone had a story to tell. So many people with unfulfilled dreams and guarded broken hearts were scattered everywhere like ships lost at sea. Joe didn't know he felt lost but the empty way of life which had been handed down to him, mixed with the acceleration into drugs, crime and violence, formed a mutiny in his heart which wanted to pillage and steal. He didn't really want to harm anyone but did feel a rebellious rage at life. The world owed him and he would take what he could.

Joe could usually adapt to the shifting sands of experience with some skill, as long as he had some hash to calm him and an element of control to anchor him, even if both were fleeting and illusory. It wasn't just the material mightiness of the mountains and the sensual silence of the lochs which were opening Joe's perception but some unseen energy, separate from his own self-consciousness was present in the periphery of his mind.

Even the interaction with others, whose experience was radically different from his own, had a new and enriching quality about it. In this unusual time, as Joe spoke to hitch-hikers and strangers in pubs, observed the drunken and drug infused self-medication of himself and those around him he could feel a shift on the shore of his own heart: a softness, a tenderness, a feeling of compassion and mercy towards himself and others. He couldn't understand this; it was freaking him out! This was alien to Joe, a contradiction with the bitter anger which was about to bear fruit in the shooting of a childhood friend. *What's happenin' to me? Am I losin' my mind? Am I losin' control? Am I just scared or guilty?* It seemed to be more than this as it wasn't just about the wrongness of what was happening, but the reality of what was happening. His mind was shifting and his heart was more open. *What's this life all about and is death the end?*

In the midst of this paradigm shifting and emotionally softening change Joe reverted to what he knew-drugs and madness. Joe and Jim had recently begun to expand their drug enterprise into powders and pills, in the form of amphetamines and temazepam. They had always told themselves that they would stay away from class A drugs but their greed told them that 'it's only speed and jellies'. At this time this was justification enough.

Jim never took drugs but Joe needed to calm the rush of experience and emotion which constantly streamed through his soul. Joe bought an ounce of speed each week and sold enough to make a profit, but as new emotions emerged he needed to run from himself even faster. A gram of speed every other morning and a joint to start the day became the alternative breakfast which enabled him to do this. He would have his breakfast and head for the freedom of the hills with wee Manny and Bongo. Jim would sometimes accompany them but more with a watchful eye, rather than a spirit of mutiny and adventure which his brother had taken hold of. Jim was even more untrusting and cautious than Joe, and was particularly vigilant in the weeks leading up to Bonfire night. He didn't want anyone or anything to sabotage his plan. He could see a change in Joe and he wasn't certain it was a good thing. Jim had a suspicious eye on Manny as he knew that he had the *gift of the gab* and he could see his insatiable appetite for drugs. He was concerned that Manny was using Joe as a supply of drugs and he wondered whether he had a hidden agenda. Jim had his brother's best interests at heart and was still quite protective of him, even although Joe was in his eighteenth year and could usually sift out the presence of an enemy or trouble. He was still Jim's younger brother. They needed to have each other's backs; this was a treacherous world that they were part of.

As Icarus fitted his wings and flew towards the sun, so Joe and his friends snorted their speed and tried to flee from the earthly mind. They accelerated as fast as they could go, Joe trying to get away from the tenderness which was drawing near to him and the still, small voice within which called his conscience and perception to come back to his spiritual senses. The pirate minded madness propelled them into pubs, clubs and into dark corners of criminal plots and schemes. Joe didn't care about consequences or morality. He told himself this so often that it became his reality. His days were filled with drugs and anything which provided escape. The daily business activities of selling drugs were left mainly to Gally and Joe's other buyers. During the summer months he would often hire a car, which Manny would drive and race to the refuge of the mountains. Any opportunity to get away from the city was grasped wholeheartedly and passionately. These times were exhilarating and infused with laughter. They would go swimming in the Bracklin Falls in Callander, get drunk in the Rob Roy Hotel and try to chat up the bar staff. Not all of the bar staff, just the females. Although when reminiscing at the end of a week's events, once they'd arrived back (in what seemed to them the dullness of Glasgow), Manny would say in a Grampa like tone,

"Aye, we had great times this week eh? Aye just like the old days…when men were men…and wummin were men…and we had a gay time…Stop hoggin' that joint you. Do you want a bottle o'er the heid."

Bongo would always take the bait,

"Aye, on ye go ya fanny."

Manny would then proceed to very slowly lift the beer bottle above his own head and smile,

"There ye go then, a bottle o'er the heid. I got ye ya prick…and remember…I'm no any fanny I'm the King of the fannies…stop tryin' to take my reputation."

Manny's comical self-reproach knew no bounds sometimes but Joe could tell that there was an element of belief in it. So, when Manny used to call himself 'Captain Bullshit…at the helm of The Bounty', Joe noticed a deep sense of loss in him, as if he'd found some treasure in the past and had now squandered his takings. There was tangible sadness and rejection in him despite his propensity for mad conversations and his willingness to do anything for a laugh.

Joe and Bongo grew very fond of Manny and he of them. It was as if time was condensed and intensified and that they'd known each other their whole lives. There were many others who joined them on their escapades to the hills, punters from the street who were friends of Gally, but to Joe much more than this. Surrounding Joe, there was a whole generation of up and coming puffers and criminals; children of alcohol, poverty and violence: some of neglect and some of manifold abuses; some simply of emptiness and loss; many and most without any real meaning or living hope for their lives. Joe was very fond of them as he could see in them his own broken humanity. This wasn't a thought in his head, just brotherly affection in his heart. According to the tradition of the schemes every one without exception had a nickname imposed on him by others. Among the many there was Crums, Lovey, Woody, Hammo, Geo and Keenan (also known as Spock). Manny had told Keenan that his pointy ears, black hair and sharp features reminded him of a young Leonard Nimoy and so began calling him Leonard on a regular basis. Everyone except Keenan found this a funny reference when stoned but this was firmly established one night when leaving a house party in the Tarfside High Rise flats (notoriously developing as a haven for drugs and crime). Joe and all the boys, about ten of them in all, were squeezed into the lift heading home to Hardridge and were very deep in their stone as Keenan stood nearest the buttons. In the deep silence of a heavy stone, when the air is thick with thought, Manny dryly instructed,

"To the Engine Room Mr.Spock." The lift exploded into a roar of laughter and even Keenan couldn't contain the joy of the moment. The name stuck and Mr.Spock became a native not of Vulcan but of Glasgow for the rest of his days.

Manny, never being content with just being stoned would look for any opportunity to catch one of the boys off guard and bring a sense of hilarity to their drug proceedings. He would quite often, at the end of a session, turn to one of the boys if there was a lull in the communication and randomly ask,

"When?"

So, Joe knew what was coming when Manny turned to a very stoned Keenan one night and said,

"When Spock?"

Oblivious, Spock replied,

"When what?"

To which Manny retorted, "When are you gonnae get your act together?"

This went on for months and Keenan and many others, with their depleted, stoned memories were often caught off guard as Manny tried to amuse and entertain himself from the emptiness of drugs. Although it ended for Keenan one night when Manny thought he was too stoned to remember he asked,

"When Spock?"

To which Keenan looked up slowly and decisively replied,

"Monday."

He had obviously been thinking about getting his act together!

Joe was quite protective of the 'Young Team' just as Jim had been of him. They were only a couple of years younger than him, sixteen and seventeen year old boys. But like the generations before them they had been shaped enough by scheme life to have lost a large part of their childhood, and certainly of their innocence or naivety. Joe had a strong sense of brotherhood with those he had grown up with-Meeko, Craigo, Gringo and Mooney as well as Jim; but now there was an individualising of the paths which they had taken. However, the friends and the connections which he had developed in the last few months, with many whom he had known for many years, also held extreme significance to him. There was always the bond which territory created in the Glasgow mentality but it was more than this. Again, an impression that their lives were inextricably bound together forged invisible ties of loyalty and closeness. Men and boys in Glasgow don't talk about such things, but they were tangible and real. There was a real spirit of hope moving among the boys and despite the devastation which their own history, their social environment and Thatcher's politics had brought to Scotland, they still believed that life could turn out good. Joe unconsciously hoped that it was more than the drugs which had created this optimism.

Chapter 29
The Shadows begin to fall

As the presence of some dim hope and fluctuating joy arrived in Joe's life it didn't come alone. The new energy which he felt hadn't solely been the consumption of a daily gram of speed, but of some inner change taking place within him. The growing awareness that life was more than flesh and blood, that he had an intangible mind, a soul and perhaps even 'a spirit' began to grow within him. *Is this the drugs? Am I goin' over the edge?* Joe had heard about ancient tribes and peoples expanding their consciousness and reaching ecstatic spiritual heights through drugs, but he certainly wasn't seeking any enlightenment! He just wanted to get stoned, make loads of money and be happy.

As well as the new awareness and heightened sensitivity which Joe was experiencing, a conflict accompanied it, both inwardly and outwardly. His constant companions of secret fear and explosive anger were manifesting in a number of ways, despite his attempts to avoid all restlessness and find some lasting happiness. A rage was bubbling under the surface of appearance and violence was in his face, literally.

At the end of the summer Joe found himself in a conflict which he paradoxically did and didn't want! He didn't want it because it propelled him into fear and violence, but some impulse within him yearned for it to unleash the storm within him. He also didn't want it as he knew about the upcoming event on Bonfire Night and didn't want any distractions from this. But regardless of his need for control and the illusion of manageability, Joe would once again have to learn that life was not under the power of the human mind or will.

Greggo from Ibrox, a boy racer with a flashy car also thought that he was in control as he sped through Hardridge, glaring and growling at Joe and Bongo as they stood in the street sharing a *spliff*. He only ever left the car to go into his brother Billy's house, which was conveniently on the ground level of a tenement close. Billy was a drug addict who had spent time in and out of prison, wheeling and dealing for years. He was originally from Govan and considered Joe and his associates to be small time drug dealers who were in a league below him as far as criminality went. Nevertheless, he was in fact on friendly terms with Joe, selling stolen goods to him on a regular basis. So much so that Joe had recently given him a quarter of dope *on tick*, knowing that he was dependable as a regular supplier of worldly treasures. Their business relationship was productive but slightly strained when Joe put the sole of his boot through Greggo's Ford XR2 window for growling. Joe saw Billy from Mary's kitchen window and made his way to the street to resolve the problem, or at least tie up all debts and conclude their business.

"Awrite Billy? Have ye got that twenty quid you owe me?"

Joe immediately noticed that Billy was *bouncing on jellies*; he had a defiant and semi-conscious glare in his eyes. To Joe his face seemed more distorted than usual, blurry, like he wasn't completely in this world. His prominent mop of hair was jet black and shiny but the blueness of his eyes was dull, trying to return from another place. It reminded Joe of Star Trek when someone was entering the transporter room from another planet and only some of their facial features were in focus. *Bizarre!*

"Twenty quid! Whit about my wee brother's car windae? Who is gonnae pay for that?"

The aggression rose in Billy's tone and as his shoulders slowly rose and his torso puffed out Joe sensed the danger. Billy was a rogue but he wasn't usually aggressive. Joe knew that this was the temazepam talking so he tried to negotiate an agreement.

"Look, that's got nothin' to do wi' you or the money you owe me. Whit if…?"

Before he could offer a proposal Billy interjected angrily.

"No, fuck that! You either pay for his windae or you're no' gettin' your money."

The temazepam, despite dulling Billy's good sense and slurring his speech had triggered an unresolved violence, at this moment directed at Joe. Before Joe could say,

"Is that righ…?"

Billy struck him on the face. Instantaneously, Joe's mind shifted into violence mode and he took a step back to prepare to fight, but alarmingly he felt a hot liquid running down the side of his jaw. As he glanced at Billy's fist and saw the top two inches of a lock back blade protruding, he immediately lifted his hand to his face meeting the redness before it ran onto his shirt. He was enraged but knew he had to get a weapon to be sure of winning this fight. Joe sharply stepped back, shouting,

"Ya fuckin' prick! D'you want to fuckin'go right ahead. Stay there ya prick"

Joe sprinted up the stairs and into Mary's house, grabbing the first weapon he could see, a hammer lying in the hall behind the front door. By the time he returned to the street Billy's induced bravado had worn off and he was sprinting up the street and into his house. Joe ran after him and was met by Bongo and Manny who had been sitting in the car in 'the middle street' smoking a joint. Billy locked himself inside as Joe began to kick his front door. The violence possessed Joe and he had lost any sense of witnesses or consequences. He just wanted revenge. Billy's girlfriend came to the door, holding a toddler and the sight of her stopped him in his tracks. But he was still full of rage.

"Tell that prick to come out here!"

"He's not in. He jumped out the back windae. You can come in and look if ye want."

Despite his rage Joe was momentarily embarrassed at having brought trouble to this girl's door. He turned away, not knowing what to say or do.

"Tell him if I see his face in the scheme again he's gettin' done."

The bedraggled girl with a worn out face stared fearfully and silently, an expression which didn't remotely ease Joe's discomfort.

As the day unravelled and Joe calmed down he was still determined not to let this go. Even although the cut in his face was only a nick he felt that he had to do something about it. He wasn't going to wait for Billy to return. He phoned Jim and told him of the situation. Jim agreed that something had to be done and suggested with clinical prognosis that they should shoot him. They were clearly in another world now and the purchase of two shotguns was simply a series of violent acts, potentially even a murder, waiting to happen. Joe was pleased with this suggestion and plans were made to act swiftly. Billy would probably be waiting for things to calm down but Jim knew that it would send a stronger message to any other challenges to him or his brother, or their criminal aspirations.

Within two days Jim had found out where Billy was staying and where to find him during the day. If Billy thought that Joe and Jim might seek revenge he would be expecting an attack in cover of darkness and certainly not out of their own scheme. So, when the McShane brothers conspiratorially drove past Billy in the middle of Ibrox, it would be fair to say that he was shocked and outraged. He was standing with an older man in his fifties. Joe and Jim would later find out that this was his uncle and a local gangster. But for now they didn't care, their minds were set on violence.

Joe drove the old transit van around the corner and they prepared for the attack. The brothers got out, put on their blue boiler suits and sat back in the van. Jim knew what he was going to do and felt no anxiety. He had a shotgun, he was in control, and this was the 'right' thing to do. Yet he knew Joe was worried and wondered if he was having second thoughts.

"You ok Joe?"

"Aye, gi' us a minute."

Joe lifted his hands to indicate that he needed to catch his breath and without really knowing it, shut down his emotions. The reality that they were about to shoot someone, possibly dead, in the middle of Govan, during the day, was flooding his mind. The reality of prison if caught was banging on the door of his mind but he refused to let it in. He took the leap.

"Awrite, let's go."

With ski masks on their laps Joe started the van. The plan was 'simply' to drive round the corner, where Jim would approach Billy from an advantageous point and blast him with the gun. But before Joe even pulled away from their parking spot, a black ford escort screeched round the corner, parallel to them on the opposite side of the road, and two men jumped out. One of them was Billy, the other an unknown accomplice.

Billy and his friend had spotted the brothers and decided to take the battle to them, believing that their courage would crash. Without any time for words or the ski mask, Jim opened the passenger door with the shotgun firmly in his hand and ran towards the two bold men. Their faces turned from anger to panic in the same second.

Looking down the barrel of a gun can evoke that experience.

With a determined and focussed stare, Jim blasted the gun at Billy who had begun running in the other direction. His friend was back in the car trying in a panic to start the engine, but as he saw Jim approaching he decided it was better to exit the vehicle and make his way to the nearest hiding place. This was probably behind or under one of the cars which Billy was also stumbling towards. Jim believed that he had hit the target as Billy had let out a scream and seemed to be staggering. Jim, being someone who liked to finish a job, let loose another blast of the gun and as it reverberated through the Govan tenements, Billy lay still on the ground. This all took place within seconds and Joe was standing beside the car trying to take it all in and mentally preparing the getaway route. As Jim returned, quickly but calmly, the brothers got into the car and drove away, towards the city centre.

"Did ye get him?" Joe was unsure what answer he wanted to hear.

"Aye…I think so. I blasted him twice and he was within range. He was lyin' on the ground after the second one."

Joe was pleased, excited even, others would hear of this and think twice about launching an attack. His ego was elated and his sense of power heightened but once again he couldn't shake off the feeling that revenge was more bitter than sweet to him.

Jim was simply pleased with the outcome and knew that a certain frame of mind had to be maintained to carry the weight of such acts. The police might be involved. There might be a murder charge. The conscience would try and dilute their resolve. Yet Jim knew that if they were in this world they were in it with all their hearts and minds. There was no room for doubt.

Chapter 30
Wake Up and Listen

It didn't take long for Joe and Jim to find out about Billy. There was no visit from the police and no come-back from Billy's friends or family. He had been sprayed by the shotgun blast but wasn't seriously injured. He was, however, mentally distraught and a nervous wreck after the event. He was never seen or heard from again. The brothers were satisfied with the outcome and word spread in the scheme that Billy had been a victim of a shooting. Joe and Jim denied all knowledge but everyone who heard about it knew they were responsible. They were learning more and more about how to be devious. The Machiavellian intellect, mixed with the deceptive 'art of war' was becoming more and more their normality.

Darkness was growing in the soil of the soul's secrets.

This was the first time that they had actually used the shotgun and it was an egotistic rush. It wouldn't be the last. They weren't considering consequences or morality. Their seared consciences and justifications were established on the notion that anyone who was part of this world they were in understood the rules. If you were willing to live by the sword then you had to be willing to die by it. They didn't have a single thought for the anxiety which would now fill Billy's mind for the rest of his days; they didn't have a single reflection about his motive of standing up for his family and his own sense of Joe's injustice; they had no compassion or care for the fear which they had planted in him and perhaps in the lives of his girlfriend and wee son. All they could hear was the loud voice of their own vengeance and the silent satisfaction of their self-justifications.

Despite the suppression of all emotion, the shooting of Billy seeped into their nervous systems and strengthened the foundations of fear which violence was built on. They weren't deterred from using the guns. In fact, they were more ready when Bonfire night arrived.

However, a very unusual change continued to take place among the boys in the scheme, and in Joe in particular.

A strange wind of transformation was blowing in the hearts and minds of many young people in Hardridge.

His recent trips to the mountains and attempts at freedom from the darkness of the city, combined with the intensity of violence drawing closer, were catalysts for a gradual but radical altering of his worldview. It wasn't simply the external experiences themselves but a growing attention to other forces at work in the world, influencing events. Joe had always carried a strong sense of the energies around him, especially the dark and malicious ones which had seemed so present, not only in his dreams but in his real life. He could see these energies or forces (he didn't have labels for them) entering through the human heart and mind, wilfully influencing human choices. It wasn't control or possession but the notion that what we gave ourselves to, what we surrendered to, what we opened our hearts to, would have some sort of power over us. Not unlike the curious Dr.Jekyll wilfully taking the potion until he was taken captive by the distorted Mr.Hyde. Although Joe knew there was always an element of free choice he couldn't let go of this idea impressing upon him that there was more than meets the eye in the worlds which he existed in. Yet, it was not all darkness.

Driving through the Trossach mountains one day with Manny and Bongo they stopped to smoke a joint and take in the breath-taking autumn view. The landscape was more beautiful than any artist's painting, with golden browns, crimson reds and mustard yellows mixed with every fading rusty shade and the evergreen pines. The wind was blowing hard on this October day and gently forcing brush strokes across the canvas of the world as the leaves fell from the trees. Joe noticed that many of the trees in the glen below them had been torn up from the roots and lay lifeless across the stream riveting into the mountains. As he stared at these uprooted giants of nature a lightness of mind and spirit rested on him and his thoughts started to drift with the wind. *The invisible force of nature, the gentle or powerful wind, can tenderly change the colour of the world like a brushstroke or be the instrument of force to overturn the mighty. The wind blows wherever it pleases…an axe at the root of the trees.* Joe's daydreams seemed to be floating with the wind as he questioned its mysterious and unpredictable nature, its invisible qualities and immense power. Following the movement of the wind as it swept down the mountainside and into the valleys, Joe's thought was broken by the swift but graceful movement of a young deer sprinting through the trees and grass. His mind flickered to a fading dream he had long ago and he was instantaneously overwhelmed with a rush of ecstatic hope and faith in some unseen power, guiding his life and trying to reach into his consciousness. He felt lifted from the limits of his perception into something more expansive, more real and infused with more clarity than the narrowness of his familiar mind. He didn't exactly welcome it as he had spent years not allowing any feeling which might overwhelm him, especially hope. Joe had no sense of the time which he'd been 'daydreaming' but the feeling of something awakening within him was freaking him out, so he turned to Manny to break the silence, surprised at what came out of his mouth.

"You used to be into all that God stuff didn't ye? Whit was that all about?"

Joe tried to appear dismissive and only slightly curious.

Manny had been sitting silently as Joe's mind had been wandering. His attention quickened when Joe mentioned God as it was the first time that the topic had ever come up in their conversation. Before answering he turned his head to the ground and seemed to deliberate carefully before he spoke. Joe could see shame in his eyes which he'd noticed the first time they'd met and many times since. It was well hidden but an oppressive shadow behind his eyes.

"Everybody's lookin' for love Joe…some people look for it in sex, some in drugs, some in money, some in power…some even in religion or politics, all sorts of places. The last place most people would even think about lookin' for it is in God…but that's where it's found."

Joe didn't know how to respond to this. He just stared, uncomfortably.

Nobody from schemes spoke like this, especially men!

Love? God? I've had enough of that shit…religion!

As Joe's eyes glazed with coldness Manny empathetically intuited his rejection.

"This hisnae got much to dae wi' religion Joe."

Joe guarded his thoughts closer as he hadn't meant to disclose them in his expression.

These didn't seem to be elements of the world which Joe lived in. It resonated true but he didn't know why or how. In fact, it connected to some part of him which had long been abandoned and forgotten. He wanted to entertain it, welcome it or accept it but his trust had been broken so many times and his hopes crushed so frequently that he didn't have the ability to receive it. His fear of being deceived, mixed with a hunger for the truth, filled him with questions and curiosities.

"Well, if that's whit everybody's lookin' for, the meaning to life an' all that shite, then why are you no' followin' it? Whit are you daein sittin' here gettin' stoned wi' us?"

Joe hadn't intended to evoke and heighten shame in Manny but that's what happened; he knew Joe didn't mean to hurt him.

"I told you when I first met youse. I'm the King of the Fannies, Captain Bullshit and you better no' be tryin' to take my reputation."

Manny laughed but there was a sincerity and seriousness in him when he said,

"If you're no' livin' in the truth Joe you're livin' in lies. It's as simple as that mate. We've all got free will mate, and we all fuck it up. Don't look to me as an example of love or how to live. His love is real but I'm full of bullshit. If I'm no' talkin' about His love then I'm probably talkin' a lot of shite. So the only time you're ever gonnae get the truth out of me is when I'm talkin' about him. *He is the truth.*"

This was the first time that Manny had ever sounded remotely serious. Joe was sensitive to some hidden pain in Manny and instinctively knew it wasn't the time to ask him to explain why he was running away from his past life, but he had so many questions. It was like he'd been quickened to listen and found himself looking at a new world, a new version of reality.

"So if God is real where is he and where was he when I was growin' up?" There was a sharp edge of pain and anger in Joe's tone even although he was trying to contain it. Manny's mind slowed and deepened as he looked for a simple way to explain the inexplicable as if to a child.

"It's like the wind Joe. You can see its influence but you cannae actually see it wi' your eyes. God's love and influence are everywhere if we're lookin' for it and listenin'. That'll only happen if we want it."

Bongo and Joe hungrily listened but it was tempered with suspicious caution. They didn't know if this was something they wanted. They wanted to know more about it but were reluctant that the truth they might hear would change them; it would change everything. Joe was used to everything changing but it was usually for the worse, filled with loss and sorrow. Joe was making good money and he was well respected by his friends and useful to his punters. His business was steadily growing and he believed that he could become rich if he pursued this life. He had clawed back some semblance of self-esteem by establishing himself in what he was doing. All this talk about spiritual matters might ruin everything. The conflict within him began to grow. He wasn't ready to change but in the coming weeks Joe continued to ask questions about these ideas of a spiritual realm, the love of this unknown God and the alternative realities which these belief systems seemed to explore. Manny emphasised to Joe and Bongo that this was not only something to be believed in but something to be experienced.

"God isnae a figment of imagination or thought Joe, but somethin' we can experience."

As well as constantly asking every conceivable question to satisfy his need to know and feel safe, Joe *was* experiencing this, but he was finding it hard to accept it. *How can I ever admit to myself or anybody else that there might be a God?* From this first day of questions, gentle waves of emotion like an incoming tide, continued to wash over him despite the awareness of his own shame. Even although he had justified every dark thought and selfish motive to himself many times, his conscience had awakened and he was acutely aware of his own waywardness. This wasn't just about society's frowning condemnation, his criminality and propensity for violence, but of how far his heart had drifted from some truth within him about who he was. This wasn't just about wrong actions but about the soul or spirit separated from its source. As Manny had so eloquently put it, 'we all fuck it up'; Joe knew he was not alone in his going astray. Joe's life would have been easily judged and condemned by others but he began to see this same separation from some spiritual truth, even in the most law-abiding and 'moral' citizens. We had all fallen short and each of us had gone our own way.

He thought of Big Mooney. *God is in the stray dog.*

Boys like Joe, from schemes like Hardridge, weren't interested in talk of spirit or anything remotely to do with religion. This was for old woman with blue hair and woolly jackets or wee kids at Sunday school who didn't know any better, and with childlike trust believed everything they were told.

This cannae be happenin'! This shouldnae be happenin'!

In Henry Africa's bustling nightclub, in the midst of weeks of heavy puffing sessions and even in his rage at punters or life in general, with unsettling clarity Joe continued to hear a gentle voice within his consciousness; the voice always surprised him as it was not one of condemnation but of kindness and forgiveness. He knew that his behaviour was often deplorable and his lifestyle in general was often a reason for guilt but some force of grace was pursuing him at every turn. The feeling of being loved, even in his madness and immorality, was tearing him apart. He would need to run faster to get away from this grace because its offer of healing was accompanied by a niggling torment at the same time. He was losing his mind, just as Big Mooney was losing his.

Maybe this is how it started!

Speeding into Glasgow one night, eyes wide with drugs and reflections after an intoxicating day in the hills, Joe was wondering how he would ever be able to accept these bizarre ideas and how he would ever be able to let go of this life which he was entangled in. As they sharply turned the corner onto Great Western Road with the rain blurring the neon signs of pubs and take away shops, Joe was confronted by a damp, crumbling sign hanging loosely from the doorway of an old gothic church. It read

'You Must Be Born From Above."

It struck his soul like lightning!

His mind was elated and he experienced a disorienting epiphany which resounded within. As his jolted nervous system returned to calm an unexplored faculty inside him quickened to life.

Whit does that mean? But how can that happen?

What Joe failed to consider was that like any birth there would be discomfort and pain. Despite his struggling, obstinate will trying to reject this experience, all of this 'spiritual stuff' called to some core experience in Joe but he was set on a course of self-will, driven by revenge; controlled by fear, shame and violence. His mind and heart felt that they were going to explode inside. Hash no longer had the power to dull his senses in the way that it had done previously and speed couldn't make him run fast enough to evade this ever present energy. Bonfire night was approaching and plans were in motion to exact revenge. Joe could hear his conscience and a cautionary voice. He ignored them.

Chapter 31
Hallowe'en: Whit's under that mask?

As Joe walked through the forest the only light on his leafy trail was the fading blue radiance of the moon. In his mind he knew he was looking for the Amigos but he didn't know where to find them. His thoughts, like the branches he was pushing from his face, were irritating and mildly painful as they snapped back at his forehead. He tossed and turned. When he came to a clearing in the woods it wasn't exactly an open space but there was a visible pit which had been dug out, about six feet deep, with a shovel lying at its edge. He pondered the thought that the Amigos were hiding in here and waiting to jump out on him. *Bunch of fannies!* He couldn't help smiling at the thought as the childish hide-and -seek excitement bubbled up in him. He quietly crept over to the edge to peer in and maybe even jump on them with a scream.

It was empty.

There was no sight or sound in the whole forest.

A numinous dread began to fill Joe's body from his toes to his throat. He wanted to speak, but he couldn't. He wanted to shout for his friends but he was suffocating with fear. Dizziness swirled around his head. He stumbled and fell into the pit and landed on his back with a thud. He was still conscious but dazed as his thoughts prompted him to push himself up. He was aware of two moonlit shadows encroaching on the brim of the pit. He smiled, believing it was Meeko and Gringo. He sat up, resting on his elbows as two hooded figures appeared at the edge of the pit. They turned to glare down at him. Horror choked on his heart and throat. The face which drew his soul towards it was cavernous and skeletal and silent. The other guarded its identity with a monstrous hand with bulging veins, grasping the hood at both sides of a face which oozed slimy worms and toxic bile. As Joe bellowed out an unheard scream the pounding red muscle in his chest exploded. His eyes shot into the consciousness of his room. He was soaked with sweat and covered in anxiety. But he was glad to be awake.

In the weeks leading up to Bonfire night Joe met up with Jim to discuss their plans and to tell him about these strange new perceptions that were growing in him, despite his best efforts to block them out. Joe arrived and noticed that Jim's face was inscribed with a grave expression; a morbid reflection had been carving itself into his inner vision.

"Awrite Jim, how's it goin'?"

"Aye, I'm no' bad, cannae complain. Whit about you?"

"Och aye, I'm no' too bad."

As the trivial formalities of reconnecting were taking place, Joe instinctively glanced around the room and felt inquisitive, although he didn't know what he wanted to ask. His scanning eyes caught the edges of an image which was underneath a book about the IRA hunger strikes. Joe walked over and curiously picked it up. It was a drawing of a child, holding its knees and crouched in the corner of an empty room. In the centre of the room there was a hooded, skeletal figure with a sickle-The Grim Reaper.

"Whit's this? Happy thoughts?"

Joe tried to lighten the obvious tension.

"Och, it's nothin'. I was just doodlin'"

Jim didn't want to talk about it and Joe kept his dreams to himself. He quickly turned to a more positive emotion and began to describe to Jim the recent uplifting experiences he'd encountered among the mountains and hills.

Jim could clearly see that his brother was changing and that he'd found some new kind of optimism, maybe even hope. Hope was dangerous and Jim wondered whether Joe's resolve would change concerning Weaso. However, Joe reassured him that he still wanted to *go ahead*. Nevertheless, Jim could see a spark of light in Joe's eyes when he talked about this new found 'awareness', but talk of love or anything remotely religious was also dangerous and therefore approached with a calculating mind. If people were to hear about this their business would be seriously undermined. Jim didn't have a problem believing in the existence of spiritual forces but trusting them was another issue. He had always believed in some notion of a creator, ever since his first prayers with Granny McDermott but he believed that this uncaring deity had abandoned him a long time ago and he wasn't going to let his mind entertain such thoughts now. He was also concerned that Joe was being played by Manny. Jim didn't trust anyone and was always looking for hidden agendas. He looked to see what was behind the mask of peoples' personas. He would keep a close eye on Manny.

As far as the shooting was concerned, all was still in motion. Gally was still keen to pull the trigger and was determined to go through with the revenge attack and Weaso was still waiting for the promised robbery opportunity which Jim had offered him. He was making enough money selling drugs for Bradford to keep him in a permanent stone and oblivious to the imminent threat on his life. He was carefree and carried himself with an arrogant swagger. He was exactly where Jim wanted him to be. This suited Joe and Jim as the peace was maintained and the past was forgotten about for the time being.

Even although he wanted to contain his new epiphany, as it might bring slander and contempt from his enemies, Joe couldn't keep it from his friends. Bizarrely he didn't have to; they were strangely having experiences of their own which paralleled his. This became apparent when Craigo invited the Amigos and Joe round for a smoke. It was Hallowe'en.

Joe felt uneasy as he walked through the streets in the midst of witches, ghouls and demons. As much as he'd enjoyed the preteen days of dressing up for parties with friends, trick or treating and *dookin'* for apples, Joe had always felt that the energy of Hallowe'en was quite intense. He was usually on edge and had a strange sense that some other aspect of the human mind or spirit which was normally hidden was made manifest. He made his way to Craigo's as speedily as he could, looking forward to sharing recent events with him.

"Awrite Joe, great to see you man. Take yer jacket off mate. Whit's happenin'?" Craigo had buoyancy in his spirit and a spark in his eyes which Joe hadn't seen for years. Joe gave his wet jacket a shake and threw it on the floor.

"Awrite Craigo I'm no' bad mate…bit of a mental time."

"Aye tell me about it, it cannae be any madder than whit's been happenin' wi me. I'm really glad you're here mate…I need to talk to you. I think I'm goin' aff ma heid"

As Craigo passed Joe the joint he slowly sat down, not taking his eyes off his pal but with a deep feeling of synchronicity and awe. The twist in his gut told him that the conversation about to unfold was not to be dismissed. Joe kept his own secret to himself so as not to influence Craigo's story

"Aye? Tell us all about it then. Whit's been happenin'?"

Craigo hadn't shared this with anyone but he knew he could trust Joe.

"I don't know where to start mate…em…you know I've always been interested in mad ideas, readin' and shit."

"O aye, the twin pillars, 'readin' and shit'?"

Joe lightened the mood sensing that Craigo was struggling to let go of any control. Craigo laughed at his own intensity and took a puff of the joint.

"Well…the last few months I've been readin' all sorts of stuff –witchcraft, astral projection, tarot…anythin' to do with the occult…anyway, all sorts of mental stuff. I don't even know why I've been daein' it. At first it was givin' me a real buzz…I even felt as if it was really openin' my eyes to stuff… I felt like I was seein' things clearer, understandin' people and things a bit better. Anyway…as much as it was takin' ma heid to another place…and ma dreams have been mental… I started to become really full of fear…an' Joe I don't just mean scared that something was gonnae happen to me, but I felt as if I couldnae breathe. It wisnae just a physical feeling but it was something worse, I don't know what to call it, like I was being drowned in a dark pool."

Craigo was paranoid, imagining Joe's silence as suspicion of his insanity.

"I know this all sounds mental mate, but it gets even more mental than this. I know I'm blabberin' on, you awrite wi' me talkin' mate."

"Aye mate, keep talkin'…I'm just listenin'…you're awrite."

"Aye, well, this is been going on for months Joe and at first I thought it was just a mad side effect ae bein' wasted but it was really takin' over, even when I was completely oot ma nut and…"

Craigo paused to stop his tears as the fear he'd been hiding reached his throat.

"I thought I was havin' a nervous breakdown or somethin' Joe. I kept feelin' this weight on ma chest, like somethin' was trying to crush me. I know that sounds mental but I couldnae stop thinkin' about Big Mooney. I could see the same thing in him the last time I met him. I could see him drownin' as well, only he seemed further under the water. Then one night, about two in the morning I woke up out of this dream that I was suffocatin' and…I switched the light on cos I was shitin' maself. You know? Pure shakin' an' sweatin' like a maniac?"

"Aye, I know that one mate. I had one…"

"Aye, Jim used to tell us about your mad dreams…"

Craigo was happy for identification but he hurried on as his story was bursting out. "Anyway…turnin' the light on usually calms me down, but when I turned it on the fear just wouldnae leave me and I had that horrible feelin' that there was somethin' or somebody in the room wi' me…I know it sounds like somethin' out of a horror film but…

Craigo stopped, realising that his story sounded insane, his worst fear.

"Keep goin' mate, it's awrite."

Joe prompted, knowing there was more.

"Aye, well I don't know whit made me dae it but I started talkin'…oot loud! An' you know me mate, I've never believed in anythin' like that, I'm fae a long line of sceptics and atheists."

They laughed.

"Aye, I cannae even remember what I said but it was somethin' along the lines of 'If you're there, help me…, an' the fear just lifted aff me. The room seemed really bright an'… I've never felt peaceful in my life Joe, even when I was stoned, but the whole room was just still and silent. It was freakin' my mind out cos I could still hear the thought that I had finally went mad. I eventually went to sleep and had the best sleep I've ever had in my life. And no' only that, when I woke up the next day I still felt the same…I huvnae touched kit since. I'm still having a puff but everythin's changed Joe. Whit dae you think of all that? I know people are gonnae say I'm aff ma heid wi' drugs Joe, but the way I feel just now is out of this world, without smack! I've never felt so happy in all my life…"

Craigo paused hoping for a positive response.

"Wow mate! Just to reassure you, you're no' mental by the way. Well, maybe a wee bit, but if you are you're no' alone. I've been gettin' all sorts of mad thoughts and feelings to do with God and shit."

"O aye, God and shit, the polar opposites of life."

They sniggered.

Joe went on to tell Craigo all about his recent paradigm shifting experiences and how it had awakened hope in him, but also a strange conflict. They began to get excited as they shared these strange new thoughts which they hadn't remotely sought. It seemed as if the experience had come to them, initiated from outside. It also appeared to be perfectly timely, like events and uncontrollable circumstances of their lives had led them to this significant moment. Just as they acknowledged the bizarreness of this weird time the door rattled.

Craigo opened the door and was faced with the grim reaper and the devil. He invited them in, delighted to see them. He knew it was Meeko and Gringo even before they lifted their masks, as he could hear them laughing and fumbling outside, trying to adjust their faces.

"When are youse too gonnae grow up? Couple of fannies."

When Joe saw the two messengers of death he experienced a pang of dread inside, even although he knew it was Meeko and Gringo. The grim reaper and the devil had obviously smoked more than a few *spliffs* before they came up as they were giggling like a couple of schoolgirls. They took off their costumes and greeted their pals.

Joe and Craigo began cautiously to tell them about these 'mad experiences and thoughts' and at first Meeko and Gringo stared in disbelief, questioning the sanity of their pals. Joe tried to explain that this wasn't about religion, certainly not the way they had been taught in RE. It wasn't about 'being good' or going to church or priests and rituals but of something much more dynamic.

Gringo turned his head trance-like in slow motion and in his best 'Exorcist' voice he croaked,

"Don't... talk... to me... about God."

He had sneaked the devil mask back on and again propelled himself into fits of laughter. They all tumbled into hysterics with him; even Joe as he tried to explain what had been happening, but he couldn't talk to them about love or forgiveness or grace -the impressions which had been breathing through him recently like a strong wind. When Gringo realised that this wasn't a Hallowe'en joke he eventually calmed down and asked some genuine questions. He was open-minded but Meeko sat untrustingly and vigilant. His mind and heart were still captive in the dark grip of heroin's deception. Heroin would not let him go easily even although he could see that there was some radiance in Joe and Craigo which drugs could never afford. His soul wanted freedom but the drugs in his body resisted any exposure. This light and energy that was shining through his friends was blinding and scary; for the time being he had to look away.

"Anyway, ya couple of Bible Bashers, me and Gringo have got a dozen ecstasy tablets we got off Fritz and we're gonnae get mad wi' it."

"Aye, brilliant. I've heard that they're amazin'. Whit's in them anyway? I heard there was smack mixed in wi' them Meeko?" Craigo was still subconsciously caught in Heroin's hook and would not get away without a struggle.

"Aye, I heard that tae. Fritz said there's some kind of acid in them as well, so who's for a wee trip?"

"Aye, I'll take two to start aff wi'."

Gringo put out his hand, hasty to regain some good feeling now that he was with his old friends.

"Joe? Craigo? Youse up for a couple before we have a puff?"

Meeko opened the bag and passed them out, assuming that there would be no conscientious objectors.

Craigo and Joe took two each and together they all began another journey. They didn't know that this was the final journey they would take together. They all felt a deep connection between them this night and thought that this was the beginning of something new. Perhaps in a way it was, but it came with a cost. Their delight to be together in each other's company had never been so evident. They each built a joint with a great expectation of an exciting night.

"Hey Meeko, whit happens to you when you take these? Do you trip or do ye just get wasted?"

Craigo wanted to prepare.

"I don't know mate an' I'm up for anythin'…I don't really care what happens…" He looked at Joe impishly and smiled. "… as long as we don't start believin' in God."

They all burst into rapturous laughter.

Chapter 32
Bonfire Night

Bonfire night arrived and true to its origins the night was filled with treachery. As a way of exploring his new found experience Joe had recently sought some clarity or understanding in the only way he could think- a small local community church called The Street Mission. Manny had been part of this small gathering before his return to the madness which he now seemed to be living in and he directed Joe to go here, despite a cautionary warning about the dangers of distorted doctrines and ideas. Joe wouldn't stop asking questions about spirituality and was constantly reminding Manny of truths that he wanted to ignore. Manny was trying to run away from his beliefs and he was confronted with his former reality through Joe's hunger and thirst for knowledge and experience.

For a church, the Street Mission and its community were unusually down to earth and most of them came from the Pollok area and particularly from Joe's scheme, Hardridge. As they tentatively entered the shabby old community council shop where the services were held, the Young Paka were received warmly and even joyfully which eased Joe's anxiety as he half expected stuffy, judgmental attitudes. This was dissimilar to his previous experience of church where the mood of the congregation seemed sombre and the authority of the building, the rituals and its leaders were intimidating.

Joe and a few of his friends showed up en masse-Bongo, Meeko, Gringo, Craigo, Weaso and a few of Joe's younger punters from the scheme. Some of the Street Mission community were slightly uneasy as they knew this group of boys and that they had a reputation as rogues. This suspicion wasn't put to ease when any of the boys moved about the room as they all followed each other as if they were joined at the hip. The congregation weren't half as scared of the boys' presence as the boys were at the fact that they were well outside of the comfort zone of drugs and criminality. *What are we doin' here? This is mental! The Young Paka in a church!* In the midst of broken projectors, the stench of stale ashtrays and a lingering whiff of alcohol stained chairs there was harmonious song, the weird lifting up of hands in what seemed to be celebratory praise and even some swaying of wavy, rhythmic bodies. Joe and his friends tried to slip in and hide at the back of the church. The contradiction of emotions was overwhelming. On the one hand they were in shocked awe and experienced a sense of reverential wonder at this strange group of zealous believers and their bizarre behaviour. On the other they were filled with the dread of exposure, and perhaps even criticism or rejection. Yet, this was a breath of fresh air and they didn't know why. It was insane. It was the last place that this band of broken brothers ever thought they'd find themselves. A memory of the Happy Hour broke over Joe like a cleansing wave. He felt his whole being trying to open to this other world; he also felt a pain in his heart rising to the surface. His fear swallowed every other feeling and guarded his heart. He wasn't ready for this. He wanted hope but not the change that he knew it would demand.

Joe wasn't entirely sure why he was there other than trying to understand some of the strange new thoughts and experiences he was having. He also thought he was looking for knowledge to make sense of the world and the persistent questions of the deepest parts of his being. He didn't really think that he was looking for God or anything to do with Him, or Her or It. He'd heard enough of that in school and church. But there was something different here. This wasn't cruel or dark. This somehow seemed relevant to their actual lives, addressing the reality of the broken soul. It wasn't accompanied by oppressive guilt and accusing shame but of an unfamiliar kindness and grace. This was all too much for Joe and for most of the boys. This was a scary new world and too much to take in.

Joe and his friends left and discussed the experience over a few joints. They enjoyed the social sharing of a joint but the hash wasn't dulling their minds as it used to. Rather, it was consumed by this fire which was burning within them. No matter how much they smoked they couldn't enter into the same journey of altered consciousness with the desired destination of unconsciousness. They were unusually all in agreement about the feelings it evoked and the faith that was growing in them. This didn't seem to be something that they were nurturing, but spiritual rain was falling on them and watering some seed which had been hidden in their hearts, perhaps even since they were children. God only knew whether the weeds in their lives would choke this seed and suffocate the energy which was accelerating in them. Over the coming weeks Joe and his friends intermittently returned to the Street Mission trying to find the right questions.

Weaso also came along to the Street Mission a couple of times and could see changes taking place in the rest of the Hardridge boys. He wanted to be part of it and had himself cried out to some unknown God as a child in the secret and painful places of his life. He had a faith in his youthful 'innocence' and had wholeheartedly believed in *something* in his pre and early teens. But for now this God of a childhood faith was distant and frightening to him. His heart had been darkened by drugs and he had no desire or intention to turn from the malice and pride that was in him. So when he arrived in the church on Bonfire Night he was surprised to find that Joe, Bongo and the others weren't there, but Jim was. Despite Jim's acknowledgment in the existence of this spiritual power he too had other intentions and hopes.

Weaso felt restless as the service unfolded. Anxiety crept and crawled through his heart despite Jim's occasional friendly glance and the radiant faces of the happy worshippers. Jim's lips smirked reassuringly but made Weaso feel that neither of them should have been there; the red rims of his eyes covered his revenge.

Near the end of the service a young girl from the scheme edged open the door of the church, poked her head in and motioned to Weaso to come out. She was looking for hash and didn't know where Joe and his friends were. Weaso went outside and the night was without light, except for the occasional blast and shimmer from an exploding firework in the starry sky. Yvonne, the young girl, asked for a half quarter and Weaso told her that he'd need to cut it. He didn't want to produce his knife in the street so he ran to the close facing the church. He heard a subtle thought warning him not to go into the close but he dismissed this as his conscience, which was in a more heightened state than usual after a night in church. As he stepped into the back-close his beating heart abruptly stopped as a ski-masked figure faded into the light from the shadows. He was so paralysed with fear that he didn't have time to scream or run before his eye caught the barrel of a gun.

Boom!

Time stopped as the gun blasted and the boiler suited gunman stood motionless before stepping over Weaso's writhing body. He held his groin and screamed in pain. In a calculated and determined stride the shooter sprinted behind the shops. A few seconds later the congregation began to pour out of the church, called by the sounds of screams and panic screeching from Yvonne's throat. The attacker turned round and pointed the shotgun towards the crowd, a warning not to follow. He jumped over the Railway Bridge and back into the sinister shadows just as he had appeared. Weaso lay screaming on the floor, his testicles in tatters, and his life in the balance. As the ambulance screamed into the street and the panicked crowd dwindled and dispersed, Jim went to visit his brother. Joe had been at home all night, playing cards with Bongo, Spock, Crums and Lovey. He had heard the blast of the shotgun through the back courts. The deed had been done; his alibi was secure, as was Jim's. No-one would ever suspect Gally. Jim and Joe discussed the vengeful act and rejoiced in their violence. The feeling of power and payback elated them and hooked them deeper into this world. They couldn't see the horror of this act for the pride which dulled their devastating deeds. This was the way of the world they lived in. *All knew the rules.* Weaso was rushed to the hospital and his family were distraught. They were quickly on the scene as the news spread fast in the scheme. Although Joe felt a twinge of shame tugging on his attention he would not allow it any room in his mind.

Weaso survived but he was never the same again. Not only the loss of a testicle and the prolonged period of pain, but the fear and paranoia of not knowing where this attack had come from was hell. His body and his nerves were shot to pieces. He suspected Joe and Jim's involvement although he knew they had water-tight alibis so he dismissed it. Gally never even entered his mind. However, Weaso had made many enemies over the years and Jim planted seeds of suspicion and betrayal everywhere. He remained confused, his mind and confidence broken. Weaso delved deeper into the pit of drug abuse to hide his fears and medicate his anxiety. Joe knew that he had cremated another bridge, that he had lost another friend, and as much as he was affected by the loss he was so used to ignoring it that it was just a part of his way of being. Bonfire Night left the church shaken by the arrival of this new group of boys. They had brought a darkness with them which raged against their comfortable light.

This wasn't the last battle; a new war had just begun.

Chapter 33
Captivity: Slaves to Themselves

There was no police interrogation for Jim and Joe as they had provided enough red herrings to seduce the scent of the law for months. The McShane brothers felt that Weaso's shooting had reinforced their position and encouraged their own belief that they could execute a higher level of violence and still avoid the law. Perhaps this was the reason for their careless arrest a month later when they took a local car thief to a West End leisure centre to 'borrow' a car for them.

Wee Rowany, was, despite his nickname about six feet tall, with a blonde mop of hair and a floppy gait not unlike Shaggy from Scooby Doo. He wasn't a specialist in stealing cars but considered himself a 'jack of all trades' when it came to crime. He believed he could put his hand to anything-the problem was letting it go. The brothers had known him most of their lives and they trusted his abilities. They needed a car to visit an employee from Pollok who had decided that his employment was no longer suitable. He had quit without telling Joe but had decided to go into hiding with the takings from his last batch of cannabis. This was to be expected from time to time as punters often mistook the lack of intimidation from the McShanes as a green light to rip them off. They didn't like to bark but they *were* going to bite.

So, Joe and Jim took wee Rowany in their blue transit van, to the car park of Scotstoun leisure centre, told him to go in and steal them a car, and promised that they would pay him when he came out. They didn't tell him that the car was going to be used in a violent attack as they thought this might un-nerve him a little. However, he was curious as to the holdall on the passenger seat, with overalls, ski-masks and machetes inside. He thought it best not to ask.

As Rowany lurked around the car park looking for a suitable vehicle he was unaware that the CCTV cameras had spotted him and the security guard had immediately identified him as a suspicious looking character. Perhaps it was his gangly appearance or his shifty glances or maybe it was the large screwdriver which he had used in an attempt to wedge open the window of a Ford Escort. Either way the police were immediately called and he was apprehended by two plain clothes officers before he even had the chance to run. As Joe and Jim wondered what was keeping him so long they began to get edgy. Had they known that they had also been spotted sitting outside the sports centre and that Rowany had been apprehended, they would have obviously abandoned the plan. Unfortunately, when Jim started the engine to drive into the car park a police car pulled up behind them. They knew that the old blue van wasn't going to provide them with a speedy escape so they hoped that their prepared alibi would be a suitable ruse.

"Hello Gentlemen. Can I ask you what you're doing sitting outside the sports centre here?"

The officer's politeness didn't really mask his deep suspicion.

"Aye, no problem officer. I was just givin' my wee brother a drivin' lesson and we thought this was quite a nice open road. Is that awrite?"

Jim hoped it was but the officers weren't remotely convinced. Their gut told them that there was something amiss here.

"Are you from this area?"

"No, we're fae the Southside… we just came through the tunnel."

"Could both of you step outside the van for a minute?"

O shit! As Joe and Jim got out of the van they knew this wasn't going to go well. One of the officers began to note down their details-names, addresses and the details of the car. The moment that he radioed in to do a police check Jim knew that they would be searched. The other officer began to prowl around the van and to his delight and horror he discovered the holdall, ski-masks and all.

"What the hell is this?" He asked Joe, sensing that Jim was the sharper of the two especially when dealing with the law.

"Eh…o that? That's my washin'. I was takin' it up to my Ma's?"

Joe hadn't realised that he'd looked inside it.

"You're Ma must be a right hard bitch if you've got tae take a machete up just to do your washin'!.. Turn roon…"

He immediately motioned to the brothers to stand with their hands on the van and began to search them. He found a lock-back knife on Joe and a quarter of cannabis. Jim put his head down, he was gutted; he would probably get a prison sentence out of this just for having knives in his possession. *Shit!*

They were handcuffed and taken to Maryhill Police Station. They refused to discuss the situation when questioned as they knew it was almost always better not to say anything which might incriminate themselves or each other. They were asked if they knew Rowany but they denied all knowledge of him, even when confronted with the information that he had lived in the next close to their Ma for ten years.

"We phoned Mr.Rowan's parents as he's only just turned sixteen. His Mum says that your family are quite close to his, you were good friends with his brother and that his Ma talks to you whenever she sees you in the street."

"Don't know him."

Joe's lies were beginning to infuriate the officers as they tried to piece together the evidence and information they had. They eventually gave up all hope of questioning and charged all three of them with *Conspiracy to commit an Armed Robbery.* Joe was affronted! They most certainly weren't going to rob the sports centre; they were going to steal a car and then slash someone. His sense of injustice was slightly skewed. A weekend alone in a cell gave the brothers space to think. Jim accepted the situation more readily than Joe, and wee Rowany was just worried that the McShanes would be angry with him. They weren't, they were mad at themselves for getting caught.

Joe sat in his cell and the forced aloneness of the grey concrete walls, with the light trying to break in through the dim lit barred windows grounded him in dismal reality. He remembered the first time he was ever in a police cell and the warning of an old officer to get off the path he was on. He thought of the sadness of Mary at that time and his own sense of failure. The recent contrast between violence and some sort of spiritual life, between deep impressions of love and fear flashed through his mind. He thought of his Da, although didn't know why. He thought of Marie, and did know why. He missed her. He also felt his spirit project imaginations into the future. He could see himself in prison, drugs being his only escape and violence his only protection. Now that he had come to believe that there might be more to life, some dynamic, some grace, some way of being other than the shit that he had always existed in, he felt a longing to be free.

"God…if you're there. Help me. I don't know whit to dae."

He felt stupid, like he was simply talking to the walls. There was no peaceful experience like Craigo had described, only the emptiness of this cell and his life. Unable to find any rest in the cold, hard cell, his mind tried to think positive thoughts. There were none. Eventually he fell asleep and drifted into the vast cavern of his subconscious. They were kept in over the weekend and duly let out on Monday morning. They discussed possible alibis and defences. There were none. They had been arrested with cannabis, a lock-back knife, ski-masks, overalls and a bag with two machetes. The evidence was overwhelming. As well as this, the detectives who questioned them told them that there were two witnesses who identified them and made statements, saying that they saw the three boys together, before 'the gangly one' made his way into the car park. The boys' lawyer wasn't very reassuring either.

"You could both be looking at least three years for this. We'll need to come up with something." Mr.Shield, referred to by Joe and Jim as 'the Cigar', was open to suggestions but the boys had none. Jim had been in prison and knew what it was like-he didn't want to go back. Joe had lived his life up until now as if he didn't care what happened to him. He felt that he had nothing worth holding onto. Up until now he was willing to risk prison or violence or even death as his heart had been filled with such a weight of despair. But his recent epiphany had moved this mountain ever so slightly. His consciousness had changed. He was being transformed whether he willed it or not. He was being led into a moment of decision and change. Life was accelerating and a dark day was drawing near. The time was coming and it was not to be taken lightly. This was nothing to do with religion or church or even much about belief systems. This was about what he would give his life to-his mind, his heart, his soul and his will. Whatever he chose would be the master of his life. Joe had the impression that he was being pursued by forces beyond his control but this was not clear to him. It would soon be made clearer.

Chapter 34
The Eleventh Hour

In the early morning of the early days of a Scottish November, as the autumn leaves began to crisp and freeze with the beginnings of winter frost, Craigo sat in his room, stoned, waiting for the dawn to awaken. He had been up all night reading, thinking and…searching!

He had recently moved away from the temptations of fascinating and seductive occult knowledge and was surprised to find himself exploring answers in ancient Scriptures from various religions. Craigo, like Joe, had also experienced an energy which seemed to permeate all life, something unchanging, some ground of all being which was gently but hastily calling him to a new life. He had always been fascinated by the symbols of religion and the knowledge promised in spiritual philosophies, as they pointed to some experience rather than attempting to describe it with language. His heart burned with a fire to go deeper into this experience.

Craigo's thirst to know and his hunger to discover something which would bring stillness to his restless soul consumed him. He was never one for patience and the depth of his spirit and mind compelled him to go to extremes, rather than waiting for life to unfold.

As his racing mind flicked through a tome of 'Renaissance Art' it stopped dead as he found an image of a crucifix created by a young nineteen year old Michelangelo; he discovered that it was found in a Florentine church-the San Spirito Basilica. He had seen many crosses and crucifixes in his visits to chapels and churches over the years, but he was mesmerised by the humility and simplicity of this naked Christ. This wooden carving did not have the grandeur of Michelangelo's later works but was a simple image of broken humanity-completely naked, bleeding, scarred, divine power carrying the weight of shame and human cruelty. Craigo couldn't take his eyes off this photograph as it seemed to melt the bitter frost which had grown over his fugitive heart from years of drug abuse. A gentle peace descended on him as he closed the book; the image had burned into his consciousness and a light rose from somewhere deep inside.

His whole being was awake and alive!

The heaviness of drugs ascended and a light and clarity filled his mind and emotion. The clouds of despair which had surfaced across the sky of his soul from his earliest memories seemed to fade into a satisfying nothingness. He felt free and safe. He was quickened by a prompting to let go of his tight grip and control of his world.

He couldn't let go.

The childhood pain hidden underneath his addiction to knowledge and drugs began to rise to the surface as the dawn shone through his venetian blinds. He opened the blinds and let the light of the rising sun radiate across his face and he breathed in the cool, crisp air of the morning.

Craigo had never felt so complete in his whole life and yet the pain of his own fractured soul on the outskirts of his consciousness terrified him. Like Joe had found recently, that with this unfamiliar light and healing grace, there came resistance and conflict, the need to surrender. Just like the falling autumn leaves, this new life required a letting go of the old, a dying to the old self to make way for the new. Craigo's hypersensitive spirit and his absorbent mind had taken in so much pain and fear growing up that he had lost all ability to completely let go-to trust. The feeling of losing control felt like an implosion, a consuming of his soul if he abandoned himself to anything which he couldn't categorise and contain. In some ways Craigo trusted Joe, Jim, Mooney, Meeko and Gringo with his life, but not his soul. Dread had taken his heart captive and the ability to close his eyes and allow the unknown to enter his soul was too much.

He knew this. God knew this.

He lay down on his bed and tried to calm the rising tide of emotion. He was filled with intense joy and yet was haunted by an untamed dread. He remembered that there was still half of a tenner bag of heroin in his jacket pocket which he was saving for an emergency. This seemed to be such an emergency. He told himself that after this he would never buy heroin again. This was true. He took it from his pocket and momentarily paused with hungry shame,

"God, if you're there, help me to stop takin' this shit…forgive me."

He entered the ritual and allowed the familiar numbness of heroin's fumes to bring him back into a state of unconsciousness. He lay down and went to sleep, praying and hoping, with the image of the Florentine Christ enveloping his mind. *Forgive me… Forgive me…Forgive me.*

Joe woke mid-morning to the sound of his mother wailing and of Gringo's muffled ranting at his front door. Mary's cry reminded him of his granny McDermott a lifetime ago when she lost her youngest son. He quickly pulled on his jeans and was met at the room door by Gringo. His amigo tried to speak but all that came out was pain and tears. He had never allowed himself to cry, even when Carol-Ann had died, but he couldn't contain the fountain of grief bursting the barred gates of his heart.
"Whit is it mate? Tell me?..Whit's wrang?" Joe's heart filled with panic.
Gringo slumped to the bed and sat with his head in his hands, trying to stop his mind from unravelling.
"It's Craigo…It's Craigo Joe…he's…" The pain of death stung his throat, "…he's dead Joe…he's dead…whit's happenin' Joe?" He shook his head in his hands as if trying to shake off the reality which invaded this moment.
Joe sat beside him on the bed, stunned into silence, unable to process what he'd just heard. It felt like he sat there forever but it was actually only moments later when he asked,
"Whit happened Gringo? How? When?"
"I went up to see him this mornin' about nine o'clock. His Da let me in and gave him a shout but he didnae answer. He told me just to go in…" He broke off in tears, "Why did it have to be me Joe?..I knew there was somethin' wrang when I saw the colour ae him. He was pale blue, just like…there was sick on his pillow…he wouldnae wake up Joe…he wouldnae wake up."
Gringo sobbed as if he would never stop. He didn't seem to care that Joe was there. The old scheme vow of never crying in front of other men, especially your pals, didn't matter. There was no restriction as the flood of pain poured out. Joe didn't cry. He couldn't. He felt numb and just allowed Gringo to come to the end of his pain, for the moment.

Apparently Craigo had went into such a deep state of unconsciousness when he smoked the heroin that he had choked on his own vomit and was too numb to wake out of his 'sleep'. The next few days were filled with talk of Craigo's death, mixed with reminiscent thoughts of his humour, his 'mad mind' and his great intelligence. It was like a flood of memories gushed out to stop the reality of his death from sinking in. When Joe told Jim, Meeko and Mooney it didn't seem real. Joe had the feeling that Craigo was going to walk into the room and that in some sick but satisfying way he was going to be told that this was all a hoax. At his funeral songs were sung and speeches were made. There was laughter and tears in the crematorium but Joe felt like a spectator peering into another world where it seemed that nobody had actually acknowledged what was going on.

His friend was dead.

A brother who had been part of his life for most of his childhood was gone. What was he supposed to do with this information? How was he supposed to simply adjust his mind and heart to a gaping hole? Like most of the traumatic emotions he'd experienced he would do his best to deny their existence. He left the funeral and got wasted. For the days and weeks to follow he got wasted. *I need to get out of my head.*

In December Joe's nineteenth birthday passed without a second thought. How could he celebrate anything now that his pal was gone? In the scheme it was business as usual on the surface but once again everything had changed under the shroud of words, activities and personalities. Gringo and Meeko were trying to move forward but the mountain of despair and shock which stood before them was impossible to move. Meeko threw himself into drugs and tried to numb all of reality. Heroin, vallium, temazepam and any other powder or pill which was available was swallowed with ease and indifference. Meeko didn't care what happened to him. Craigo's death wasn't a deterrent but a reminder of his own hopeless condition. Between heroin and hash he visited the church, hoping to find some answers. He did feel the longing for something greater, some richer existence than the one he was living in his daily life. He could see the genuine compassion of the community (well, some of them at least) and the message that they were expressing was one of love and acceptance, but the demon crouching behind the door of his heart was poised to pounce.

The pain of abuse, of living with addiction (his own and others) had pierced his psyche with shame and unworthiness. He hated himself and this was cloaked in resentment and hate for others. The spirit in the church, this power greater than himself, shone like a light and brought the conflicts within his heart to the screen of his mind. Sometimes he enjoyed this light, the poultice of love drawing the poison to the surface. At other times it was too much. The only way he could handle even listening to the message of Love, of surrendering to this Higher Being, was to come under the cover of darkness.

Heroin was his cover.

He could still hear the message and in some way he allowed it to go deep into his mind and heart, but he watched others with a suspicious eye, waiting for their rejection and condemnation. His ego was so fragile that it only took some fading comments overheard in a distant conversation to push him out the door.

"Well, I know that we're supposed to love others but I don't think we should be tolerating drug addicts to hang about the church. I mean…look what happened a couple of months ago when those boys all started coming about. One of them got shot! I mean…that could have been somebody in here. God Forbid."

"Aye, you're right, we should be tellin' them to come as you are but maybe not stay as you are."

Meeko knew that he couldn't stay as he was. He wanted to change, he really did. He didn't know if he could ever be like the people in the church or walk on anything remotely like a spiritual path or even if he really wanted to, but he knew he needed a new life. Not just a slightly improved one but a radically transformed one. He doubted whether he had it in him. He needed acceptance and a love that wasn't conditional. Was there a time limit on him coming without condition? Who decided when his time was up? Did God only give him a limited time? Was his time up, just as Craigo's seemed to be? He left the church hopeless, afraid and confused. He'd have to find his own way. As much as Craigo's death had been a shock, the lingering darkness didn't seem to fade with his funeral.

Death was hungry.

Joe knew that Meeko was struggling and trying to find his way to a better life. Craigo's death had drawn a clear line and the Hardridge boys were looking for a way to cross over, to escape from the pursuing darkness. Most importantly, Meeko and Joe were deeply concerned about Gringo as he had hardly left the house since Craigo's funeral. It had been two weeks and no-one had spoken to him. Bongo had seen him one day, early in the morning as he was on his way to work. He gave him a shout from the van.

"Gringo! Gringo! Awrite amigo!"

Gringo looked up and Bongo was horrified at the paleness of his skin and the skeletal expression on his face. His eyes were deep in their sockets and surrounded with a black shadow. His withdrawn, grey skin looked like it could easily fall from his face. He slowly nodded his head in acknowledgement but didn't seem to know who it was that was calling him. Bongo was worried and told Meeko, Jim and Joe. He'd been living with Kristy in his own flat in the scheme and they'd heard that she'd moved back into her mum's, as Gringo wasn't talking to her. She told them that he'd hardly spoken two words and was just getting wasted from morning till night; she was worried.

They decided to give him a visit to check up on him. It was late in the evening and as they approached the close they left the lights of the street behind and entered into the lightless, urine stained stairs. They climbed the two floors to his front door in silence and with foreboding etched on their foreheads. Even from the first chap on the door there was an ominous air. The silent response was met with their unanimous feeling of panic. There was no logic to explain it, only deep intuitions and fearful imaginations.

"Gringo! It's Jim!"

Jim's shout through the letterbox was met with more silence and a waft of rotting garbage.

"Gringo!...C'mon mate, open the fuckin' door! We just want to make sure you're awrite. Meeko and Joe are here as well."

Deathly silence.

"Fuck this!" Jim's impatience and fear lifted his boot as he volleyed open the door. He walked in with Joe and Meeko reluctantly following.

"Gringo! It's us. We were just worried mate. Where are ye?"

Images of the reaper which Jim and Joe had both seen in their dreams and visions flickered through their minds. After checking the empty bedroom they walked into the living room and a terrible image confronted and paralysed them- their eyes lifted from the discarded chair on the ground to the sight of their pal… hanging from the beam. His face was contorted and his neck hanging to one side. The horror of Joe's nightmares and Jim's deepest fears were manifest before them. The spirit of death wrapped itself around Meeko's heart and crushed it with terror and anguish.

"Aargh! O God no! O God no!"

Meeko squirmed and bawled but Jim knew that this prayer would not be answered. He hurriedly grabbed the chair from the floor and stood on it. He held Gringo's lifeless body by the waist and tried to untie the rope. Joe's wide eyes stared. *This isnae happenin'. This isnae happenin'.*

Jim tried to force the knot of the rope with all his might but it had been tightening with the weight of Gringo's body for almost two days. The frustration at his powerlessness to help, fuelled with the horrific grief and pain creeping up his back, exploded.

"Joe! Don't just stand there. Get me a fuckin' knife!"

Joe darted into the kitchen and returned with a large steak knife. Jim wiped the tear which had escaped from the cracked wall of his heart and cut his friend down. The rope was still round his neck. Meeko couldn't even look at him as he fell to pieces before his friends. Jim didn't want to cut it off as he knew the suspicions of the police would look for treachery if there was any blood. They got a neighbour to phone an ambulance and the police. God only knows what they hoped an ambulance could do.

Whit the hell is goin' on? If there is a God whit is he doin'? Why is everythin' goin' to shit?

In less than three weeks Joe and his friends had lost two of their closest brothers. They knew that Gringo was always a bit fragile and prone to deep mood swings but they never imagined this in their worst nightmares. This was the kind of thing you heard about in horror stories or watched in films. This was the kind of thing that happened to someone else. There had always been an unspoken hope, a small ember of light which made them believe that everything would turn out alright. This light had been tragically and suddenly snuffed out for Craigo and Gringo.

When Mooney was told a few days later he didn't cry. He just looked blankly as if he couldn't allow himself to even take this in to process it. He had to get away. When Jim and Joe left his house he packed a bag and sat on the edge of his bed. He knew he had to get away but he didn't know where to go. His fractured mind was falling apart and he feared being sectioned again. Being in the presence of others suffering from mental illness only confirmed to him that what he was experiencing was real. In as much as it was his experience it was real; whether it was based on any objective reality was another story.

He didn't say goodbye to his parents, to Jim, Joe or Meeko. He got on the bus to Central Station and still didn't know where he was going. When he arrived at the station he realised that he only had enough to get as far as Edinburgh. So he bought his ticket and headed to the capital. His mind was shouting with terror at the hustle and bustle of the station and he was sweating blood by the time he got into the carriage. He closed the carriage door aggressively and anxiously to shut out the noise in his head. He put on a set of headphones and told himself not to look at anyone.

If you look at them they'll know, they'll see it in your eyes.

No-one even paid attention to him but he was sure that as the train filled up and conversations murmured that his sick mind was the focus. His sense of exposure and fear of condemnation were tightly gripped as he held onto the zip lining of his jacket. Others looked at him and thought he was just cold and tired. Big Mooney used all the strength and will he had left just to hold on until he was away from Glasgow. Perhaps this place was the cause of his illness. After all, hadn't recent events shown him the danger here to his physical as well as his mental life? Craigo and Gringo were dead. He had to get away. A passing thought of Joe and Jim flitted across his crimson eyes and he wished he'd been able to say goodbye. He hoped he would see them again. He hoped that he would find some freedom from this demented mind. He hoped that hope wouldn't leave him.

Chapter 35
The Storm Returns

After Gringo's funeral something had died in Jim and Joe. They blindly threw themselves into their business and continued to make money, but it never even came close to any sense of satisfaction. The mortality of their closest friends had made all material gain in this world come sharply into focus for what it was-nothing. They knew that money could change their circumstances and make things a little easier in some ways, maybe in lots of ways, but what did it really matter? If they could have brought Gringo and Craigo back with all the money they had, or could ever make, they would have. Death was a common denominator which brought everything and everyone to one single reality- all things come to an end, and sometimes quickly! The illusions which had shrouded their hearts for years were falling off like grave clothes and they knew that life had to be so much more than this-or it was nothing. Joe, in particular, reflected on his life, and felt the weight of the world on his shoulders. He was ashamed of the life he was living and who he had become. He felt an emptiness inside which his friends' death prevented him from hiding from himself. The gale force of emotions battered against his soul, pressing in on every side. His mind was constantly aware of a growing consciousness of powers, energies and forces greater than himself and of a yearning within him for a better life-for hope instead of despair, love instead of fear and peace instead of chaos.

Yet there was still a rage in Joe and in Jim and the chaos would come again, sooner than they hoped. They had an impending court case in January and hoped to leave this year far behind them and start anew. So when the New Year approached they decided to gather as many of 'the troops' from Hardridge and have a party, or rather a serious session of drink and drugs. This would be a suitable manifestation f or their denial, but they needed an empty house to go to and they wanted to get away from the scheme. So when Jim said that his house was empty, as his Da was spending his first sober Hogmanay with Mary in her house, then they decided this would be the perfect location.

John's house was in Cranhill, in the East End of Glasgow and it wasn't exactly the plush side of town. Belrock Street was notoriously crime-ridden and potentially dangerous for any outsiders but Jim knew a few people from the area whom he had spent time with in prison. There wouldn't be any trouble. They were only looking for somewhere to go and enjoy 'the Bells' together. In fact, they decided not to go out at all. They would arrive in taxis about eleven, go straight into the house and not leave till the early hours of the morning. This was *their* plan.

On Hogmanay, therefore, John's house was filled with the boys from Hardridge and a few from Govan, friends of Jim and Joe. There was lots of drinking, drug-taking and even dancing, of sorts! A few of the girls from the scheme were there, Danelle ,who was once a girlfriend of Craigo's, Kristy ,Gringo's girlfriend, and a couple of others from Cranhill who had arrived just before the bells and claimed to know Jim's prison friends. There was hilarity and a brilliant atmosphere, a real sense of fun and even a hint of joy. Jim enjoyed playing the host, attending to his brother and their friends. He was the only one who didn't drink as he liked to keep his wits about him. So when the door rattled about half an hour after the New Year bell struck, he wasn't particularly alarmed to see two neighbours at the door.

"Happy New Year mate! Aw the best. Can we come in and share a wee drink wi' youse."

"Happy New Year…Eh…aye, c'mon in for one or two."

Jim invited them in not realising the extent of their inebriation until they stumbled through the front door. The two guys walked into the living room and wished everyone well but they seemed to be scanning the room more than trying to enjoy the party. This wasn't obvious as they were laughing and joking with those inside but Jim could see a deception in their eyes which instantly put him on guard. So, when, after about half an hour of drinking, one of them left to go to the toilet, Jim followed him out and found him snooping around John's bedroom. Jim really didn't want to spoil the party atmosphere so when he confronted this guy he was more than tolerant.

"Whit you doin' there mate?"

The prowler pretended to be so drunk that he'd mistaken the bedroom for the bathroom.

"O sorry man, I didnae know where I was goin' there."

Jim decided that it was time for them to leave and he took Joe aside to let him know the situation. They invited the two gentlemen into the kitchen and offered them one last drink, suggesting that they should leave as the party was coming to a close. Their guests reluctantly agreed, knowing that they'd been rumbled, but they'd heard of Jim through one of the Cranhill boys so decided it was best. Jim unclenched the knife behind his back and left it beside the dirty dishes as he escorted them to the door. He pleasantly wished them well and a safe journey home. He wished that this would be the end of trouble but his deepest gut told him it was not to be. Joe returned to the party but Jim was on edge for the rest of the night.

About an hour later the door rattled again and Jim looked through the porthole window in the kitchen to see who was on the landing at the door. He immediately recognised one of them as the brother of their previous guest and a local 'hard-man'. He decided to ignore it as he knew they wouldn't take no for an answer if they refused to let him in. They would hopefully leave when the door was ignored. They didn't. They rattled harder and started kicking the door.
"Open the fuckin' door'!
The violence rose from their voices and Jim knew that he would have to confront them. His mind flashed to his first childhood confrontation with violence. This time he wouldn't be slapped about.
"Joe!..Joe! C'mon into the kitchen a minute."
Joe left the party and immediately sobered up, sensing the presence of violence. Jim told him who was at the door and suggested that they ask them to leave before any trouble started. He knew it might not be as straightforward as this so he took a couple of precautions.
"Here, put this on."
He handed Joe a ski mask and put one on himself. He produced the shotgun from the holdall, the one that hadn't been used yet.
"This is just to frighten them, I'm no' gonnae dae anythin'."
Joe lifted a knife from the kitchen and swallowed his fear. Armed and ready they opened the booming door and the violent tones of their would- be gate crashers

grounded to a halt. They were stunned to see two ski-masked figures, let alone the barrel of a shotgun staring at them.

"Get tae fuck!"

Jim wasn't wasting time on a diplomatic solution.

"O…sorry for kickin' the door mate, we thought you couldnae hear us."

"Aye, I heard ye…now get tae fuck away fae the door and don't come back!"

Jim stepped slightly forward to make clear their position.

"Aye nae bother mate. We'll just go…sorry to bother ye."

As the two friends backed away from the door to the top of the close stairs, Jim edging them completely away, it seemed to Joe as if they'd diverted violence with violence, until he heard one of them murmur.

"Prick!"

A rage arose in Jim. He'd had enough. "Fuck it!"

In a split second Joe blinked and before his eyes were completely opened he was shaken with a thunderous blast.

Boom!

The shotgun exploded beside him and one of the men fell to the ground. Before thoughts had time to gather- Boom!

The other man fell onto the top of the stairs. Jim jumped over them and made his exit down the stairs and through the back close. In a panic Joe stepped back into the house and closed the front door. By this time everyone in the living room was in the hall.

"Whit the fuck was that!" Gally knew the sound but wanted confirmation that Joe or Jim weren't on the receiving end.

"Get tooled up! And when the polis come, we were all in here…no' a fuckin' word!" Joe directed them to put a large chair behind the front door as the flat was quickly surrounded, alerted by the blast of the gun and the screams of pain.

As the gathering mob outside couldn't get in through the front door they began smashing the kitchen and toilet windows. The girls inside the flat were screaming and Joe shouted,

"Get into the fuckin' bedroom and hide!" They duly responded.

The situation in the kitchen and toilet were like a distorted scene from 'The Shining', with ten psychotic Jack Nicholson's trying to burst through with an array of weapons. Ramie, a cousin of Joe and one of the Hardridge boys, smacked an intruder over the head with a hammer as he tried to enter through the toilet window but this didn't deter them. There were violent screams and vengeful shouts to the effect of "Youse are all fuckin' dead!" which Joe considered was a plausible scenario if the police didn't hurry up.

Joe and his friends had never been happy to hear the sound of police and ambulance sirens in their lives until now. As the siren got nearer and louder there was a simultaneous diminishing of bodies and screams from outside trying to hack their way into the house. There was a moment of silence and as the panic subsided there was another rattle at the door.

When the police came in they were met by Joe who explained to the officers that all he was aware of was the boom of the shotgun blast. He told them how this was followed by the attack on the house by local intruders.

"Naebody left the house. We've just been enjoyin' the party."

"Bullshit! Jack…Arrest everybody in the house under suspicion of attempted murder."

The detective in charge knew that lies were dripping from Joe's 'innocent' lips.

So, everyone in the house was taken to Pitt Street Police Station. All of the girls, Joe and his friends, even John as he'd returned promptly in the early hours of the morning in response to a call from the police. At the station they were all told to undress and given white poncho like garments as their clothes were being checked for shotgun spray. The police also had the ski mask which Joe had on. He was sure he was going to be charged. *Whit the fuck is goin' on?*

Joe wondered about Jim. *Had he gotten away? Did he make it out the close or out of Cranhill? Where was he?* The police also found a quarter pound of cannabis in the house and threatened to charge John with it as it was his house. John couldn't believe what was happening. How could his boys be caught up in this? He began to realise that his years of absence, alcohol and aggression were sending ripples through the lives of his sons. For the first time as a father he allowed himself to feel shame, guilt and failure.

Eventually, having been met with a six hour wall of silence, the police were frustrated and released everyone. Gally 'admitted' to the police that the cannabis was his so that John wouldn't be charged. He was a good friend, a loyal friend. Despite having a ski-mask and the clothes of all those in the house, the police were convinced that the shooter had left the house and escaped. Joe was relieved. He had 'dodged a bullet' so to speak. Jim's name did come up in their enquiry in the weeks that followed but they knew that without a gun, any witnesses, the clothes of the attacker or his presence on the night, they didn't have any substantial evidence. It wasn't what they knew that mattered, only what they could prove.

What a night this had been. Once again, not exactly a Happy New Year! And it wasn't over yet. John still had to live here and this was Jim's temporary home as well. The friends and family of his victim were not the type to forgive and forget. Jim returned to the house the next day and it looked like a bomb had gone off- broken glass sprayed across the floor, boarded up windows and every room turned upside down by the police looking for a weapon. John sat in the living room with his face cupped in his hands. Jim wasn't in the mood for conversation and John knew not to ask.

"Awrite Da?"

"Aye, well…are you awrite?"

"Been better…could be worse but."

Jim had been shot various vengeful growls and incredulous glances as he'd stepped out of a taxi and walked into the close. He was still in a heightened state of awareness and completely focused. The violence didn't seem to frighten him; in some ways it exhilarated him, kept him on edge and made him feel alive. He didn't exactly enjoy it but it was a rush, like a drug. The local criminals and gang members knew who was responsible. They knew that Jim had been in prison for violence but they really had no idea of what he was capable of. At this point no-one did, perhaps not even Jim. This battle wasn't over and it would have to be resolved.

Chapter 36
The Dominion of Darkness

On the first new day of 1989, mid-afternoon felt like any other for most people- hangovers of hazy minds, frothy tongues and dehydrated bodies. For Joe there was the added bitter taste of violence and fear. For Jim there was no haziness or bitterness, but clarity of responsibility and the need to protect- to make sure that his Da was alright. After all, he had shot two people at his front door in a scheme in which they were not accepted members of the community! He anticipated trouble for his Da and he wanted to be a good son. He also had a dis-satisfied unrest that the violence of the previous night wasn't over yet. This was confirmed to him as the day unfolded and there was a gathering of the local gang at his close and from a house across the street intermittent shouts of,

"You're gettin' fuckin' done!"

Jim and John were visited by a former prison friend, Big Spike. Spike warned Jim that there were rumblings of revenge and the day wasn't going to end without violence. Spike suggested that he and John should phone a taxi and leave just now, if they could. This was no surprise to Jim but it was a shock to Spike when Jim responded,

"I'll get my Da out but I'm no' goin' anywhere. I'm no' fuckin' leavin' here wi' ma tail between ma legs. We didnae start this, but we'll fuckin' finish it."

The controlled rage which seeped from Jim's words was a new form of violence to Big Spike. He was used to losing his temper, acting impulsively and lashing out in the moment. This was different. It was a premeditated preparation for battle, a willingness to face fear and death without drink or drugs to buffer it. This was a raw violence which he could feel was more brutal. Spike liked Jim but he felt that he had to warn him.

"Look mate, I know you're capable…and mental… but there's a team lingerin' about the street and about twenty guys in that hoose across the road…all waitin' for blood."

Jim smirked, "Good. Then they'll no' be disappointed."

Spike nodded his head and laughed at the boldness of his 'wee mate fae Govan'.
"I know whit you're sayin' mate. I appreciate it. If you happen to talk to them tell them we'll be here all night." Jim had a plan forming in his mind. He was shrewd enough to know that anyone wanting to make a violent attack would come in the darkness. He would get John out just now, alone. Spike left and passed Jim's message to the local youths, knowing that they'd relay it to the McPhersons across the street. They did and the plan was in motion. Jim told John that he'd have to leave and that he'd wait for Joe and the Hardridge boys to come over before he left. John was worried, not only for himself but for his boys. He should be protecting them, not the other way about. Jim didn't see it like this. He could see that John was trying to walk a straight and sober path and he could also feel a tension in the air and in his mind which told him that violence was on the prowl. He didn't want anything to happen to his Da; he had enough guilt tied around his neck like a noose.

"I'm no' sure I should leave ye here on your own Jim." John reasoned one more time.

"Listen Da, I'll be fine. Joe and the boys fae Hardridge are comin' over in a taxi anyway. We're no' gonnae cause any trouble. I just want to make sure your house an' your stuff don't get wrecked. You can leave in the taxi when they get here. We'll get your stuff out the morra."

With this last reassurance no-one was comforted or convinced but John got into the taxi when it arrived while Jim stood on the veranda to make sure he was ok. Joe and Gally, along with Meeko, and Jim's cousin Vinnie from Hardridge came out of the taxi holding a sports bags and jovially wished John a Happy New Year.

"All the best Da. Tell my Ma I'll see her the morra." Joe could see worry clinging to John's brow.

Jim knew the sports bags didn't have tennis rackets or a football in them but was relieved to know that reinforcements had arrived. It seemed as if the whole street was skulking and sneering at Jim as he stood and watched the taxi leave the scheme, but he didn't care. He was relieved. His brother and friends were here. At least he wasn't alone, although he did cherish a challenge when it came to violence.

"Is this the cavalry?"

Jim shook the hands of Joe and Meeko as they reached the top of the stairs. The image of a blood-spattered man from the night before flashed through Joe's mind as he saw the red-stained stairs.

"It's no' just us. Bongo and Crums are on the way as well as a lot of the young team- Lovey, Keenan and Geo…maybe a few others. Lovey was gatherin' them as we left."

Just as Joe said this, a fleet of taxis turned into Belrock Street and pulled up at the close. Eyes peered through the blinds in the house across the road and the street seemed to empty, like spiders and ants returning to their damp holes. There were five taxis in all and about twenty bodies poured out, with at least two holdalls per taxi. Jim had made a call to Govan so a few of the Teucharhill boys had come to provide support, just in case.

When they all got into the house they congregated in the living room. They were a rough-looking crew, not just as a result of their hangovers but over the years scheme life had impressed itself on their souls and faces. There was something old about them, eyes worn by years of deprivation and neglect. Yet they were only boys, ranging from sixteen to nineteen years old, and this was evident as joviality and camaraderie gushed out, the room filled with adrenalin, excitement and fear. The constant chatter and the passing of joints and booze were more reminiscent of a party than a preparation for conflict. They had all been involved in violence before, individual and gang battles, and they had a vague idea that they knew what was coming.

Jim, Joe and Meeko were noticeably quiet and cautious. Their lives had been touched twice by death in recent months and the dread they felt hadn't left. Violence was near and they anticipated its indiscriminate cruelty. It would have a victim tonight, and maybe many. Joe, Jim and Meeko were under no illusion that life could end quickly and that tragedy didn't just happen to others. So, it was no real surprise to Joe when Meeko took him aside and confessed openly,

"Look Joe, I'm obviously here to hander you and Jim, but when youse are awrite I'm out of here mate."

"Aye, Meeko, thanks for comin' mate. I know we've no' seen much of each other recently but...I'm glad you're here."

"I'll be honest wi' you mate, I'm shitin' maself the night and I don't even know how. You know me, I'm usually up for a fight but...I've no' got the heart for it anymore Joe."

This last thought clouded Joe's mind with a dark premonition.

I've no' got the heart for it anymore Joe.

"Well, you're here mate...that's all that matters, we'll be awrite." Joe could see the despair in his friend in a way he'd never noticed before.

"I've even been thinkin' about the stuff you were talkin' about...asking *Him* for help 'n' shit. No' just that... I had this mad dream...it was months ago... that I cannae get oot ma heid. We were all covered in blood but we were laughin'...freaky. It sounds mental but me and Gringo were talkin' about it when we left your house that night, remember?"

"Aye mate, I don't understand it but it's real. He exists. We'll talk about it later..."

Joe could see Jim getting agitated as he paced to and fro from the window and peered across the street, almost as if to observe the right time for battle.

"Right! Listen! Everybody grab a tool fae they bags. I'm no' sittin' here all night waitin' for an attack. They pricks have been shoutin' abuse all day, c'mon we'll invite them oot!"

Jim called the troops to arms and the bags were opened. Hammers, hatchets, an assortment of knives, a baseball bat and even a sledgehammer were produced. There was a rush of adrenalin before Jim gave them the plan of attack.

"Right, there in that house across there..." Jim pointed through the window to the tenement above the shops. "We'll split up and surround the house fae both sides so they cannae run down the stairs at the side. We'll go to the door and see whit happens. The Teucharhill boys go up the right side and we'll go up the left and meet youse at the top. Right?"

The energy and violence emanating from Jim was incredible and it was almost impossible not be infused by it. The force his spirit was generating was breathing through the others and they were charged for battle.

They left the house at a steady pace and as they streamed down the stairs they gathered momentum, no-one really wanting to be on his own, but to have at least one other by his side. Jim led the way brandishing a large machete at his right side and a dagger like blade in the other. He was followed closely by Joe, who held a hammer and a blade close to his side and his cousin Vinnie who had procured the sledgehammer.

"I feel like Thor wi' this thing!" He joked to Joe as he ran, his nerves and adrenalin didn't know where else to go. He'd been told that his job was to pummel the door if necessary and he'd never been in a close contact gang fight with such a lethal weapon in his hands. It would be necessary but not for the door.

Meeko was also by their side and held a baseball bat, with a knife in his other hand. He was scared, but loyal. Dread filled his soul as they bolted out of the close and darted across the street. As they ran up the stairs he made sure that he kept in line with Joe who was directly behind Jim. As they reached the top of the stairs, expecting to see the Govan boys appearing from the stairs on the other side, there was nothing but emptiness. For a few seconds there was a no-man's land of dim close lights and concrete, a landing about thirty feet long with four house doors to their right hand side. The house of their enemies was the third on the right. They seemed to stare at it in anticipation, feeling that a bomb was about to explode.

Sure enough, the door burst open and three figures burst out in a frenzy fuelled by alcohol and fear. They'd saw The Govan Team and The Paka running across the street. They couldn't miss them; the whole street saw them and took a sharp breath. Cranhill had never been invaded in the core of its own territory before. The character who seemed to be the central figure was armed with a large twelve inch blade and was either terrified or manic, or both. Either way he roared,

"Fuckin' come ahead!" and charged towards Jim.

Without hesitation Jim filled with violent power and sprinted towards him. As they neared, both men lifted their blades on the right side and struck the other full force on the side of the head. Jim's machete battered against the cheek and head of his opponent, McPherson, and blood gushed out. Jim was also struck and there was a two inch gash in the side of his head above his ear. He didn't have time to pay attention to it but immediately stepped back and instantaneously plunged a second blow with the dagger into McPherson's gut. The dagger pierced his clothes and sunk into his flesh but he remained standing, although swaying. The blood clotting on the side of Jim's head caused him to black out for a split second while still standing, motionless and exposed. Joe turned, trying to take in what was happening and to act in the frenzy of the moment. McPherson, seeing Jim's eyes closed and his body slump into the stunned, silent, second raised his eyes and his blade to strike Jim again.

In this instant something strange happened to Joe.

What could only be described as a sheet of stillness and peace fell upon him and his mind stood still in the midst of violence. He had never been so still in all his life. He didn't hear an audible voice but from somewhere deep in his spirit his whole being stopped as if someone held him tightly and said,

'*Look*!'

Not in a shout but as clear as a trumpet call. It was as if the scene had been freeze framed and he was able to look at all the elements to understand the reality of what was happening.

Look!

There is more to life than flesh and blood.

There is darkness in the hearts and minds of men.

Their thoughts are captive. No man is the real enemy.

Life is Spirit.

This gentle, but powerful whisper wasn't a voice or even a thought to Joe but it was a clear impression. It seemed to Joe as if they were all pawns being moved about by another energy. Once again he was aware that it wasn't that they were without choice but at some level they seemed unconscious of the reality which they were acting out. Whether this was the caution and revelation of a Higher Power, a heightened state of consciousness, a guilty conscience or a mental breakdown, Joe didn't know. He didn't question it; he just knew that he'd experienced something which he didn't will. This was coming from 'inside' him but simultaneously seemed separate from his own self. Time hadn't stood still on the outside but only on the inside. Joe could see Jim standing, stunned with a knife-wielding McPherson, his face demonically distorted and poised to strike a lethal blow. He was aware of Meeko, poised to attack and show his loyalty to his friends. He glanced at Vinnie's Scandinavian sky-blue eyes, his thick blonde hair and the weighty sledgehammer, unsure what to do, finding himself thrown into the midst of a level of violence which he'd never imagined or anticipated. He looked around at the clash of blades and hammers from the Govan team arriving at the other set of stairs to an angry, fearful mob. Everybody was trying to survive. No-one knew exactly what they were doing. They were in the midst of life in the only way they knew it-frenzied motion, intense emotion, the broken human spirit, fractured minds and craving bodies. And yet they were also in the presence of death- consuming violence, destructive fear and blind hatred.

In a fraction of a second, as suddenly and powerfully as it had arrived, the peace left Joe and the volume of outer screams and inner panic was his reality. Joe snapped out of this moment to the rushing sound of Meeko shouting, "Aargh!" whilst holding the bat with two hands and hitting McPherson's head like a large baseball. Unbelievably, held up by an energy not his own, McPherson remained standing. He'd been stabbed, slashed and struck with a baseball bat but seemed unable to knock down! He turned and stuck his knife straight into Meeko's neck. Blood streamed slowly and thick.

McPherson was still poised over Jim and as Joe moved quickly in the direction of his brother, he saw Vinnie dart past him with the sledgehammer raised and he swung it, Thor-like across his skull. Before he fell to the ground like a sheet of lightning, his blade flashed across Vinnie's head and ran down the length of his neck. Another bubble of blood burst forth.

At this moment there was a cry of 'There's the Polis' from one of the Govan boys and Jim, Joe and the others turned and sprinted down the stairs. As Joe was asking Vinnie if he was alright, knowing he clearly wasn't as his face was a mish-mash of blood and panic, he turned to see Jim and Meeko.

"Joe! Joe! You need to get me to the hospital." Meeko was trying to stop the rush of blood pouring from his neck and down his whole body. He looked like death as the life and colour drained from his eyes. A memory flashed in Joe's mind of Meeko standing on the piercing nail in the old railway signal house all those years ago. They weren't boys now; so much had passed in so few years.

When they poured back out onto Belrock Street there was no sign of the police but the blood-stained boys-Meeko, Vinnie and Jim-were badly in need of medical help.

"Joe, let my Ma know I'm awrite." This seemed like a last request from Meeko as Joe tried to reassure him.

"I will mate, listen get a taxi wi' Jim and Vinnie to the hospital. You'll be awrite."

Why does this seem like a lie?

Remarkably, all of the Hardridge and Govan boys got out of Cranhill alive. Jim hailed a taxi and motioned to Meeko and Vinnie. They got into the taxi and had the driver noticed the blood gushing from them onto his shiny floor he'd have stopped them. But they were in and he wasn't going to argue with them. He didn't know or ask if it was all their own blood staining their clothes.

"The Royal Infirmary mate!"

As they made their way to the Royal there was relief that they had survived. Jim told them to phone Joe if they got out of the hospital without arrest. He gave them Mary's number and having thought of all he could and should to prepare for the police he looked at them proudly. Here were two brothers who had saved his life. The three of them were using their sweatshirts to put pressure on their wounds, even the taxi driver threw in an old hand towel he kept in the front of his cab.

"Look at the state of youse two." Jim feigned a reassuring laugh and hoped that Joe got home safely. He looked at Meeko, slipping into unconsciousness and Vinnie as white as a ghost with the loss of blood and the trauma of violent shock.

"Meeko! Meeko, stay awake if you can!"

But he couldn't. The blood and the life were draining from him.

Chapter 37
Blood Redemption

By the time they arrived at the Royal Infirmary, Jim and Vinnie had to grab either side of Meeko and lift his unconscious body out of the taxi. Even though they'd put a lot of pressure and clots were beginning to form the blood was still slowly oozing from his neck as they walked through the doors of Casualty shouting,

"Somebody help us!" and again when the response wasn't instant. "Somebody, fuckin' help us!"

Two paramedics came out and took Meeko from his friends. He slumped lifelessly into their arms as they heaved his body onto a stretcher lying at the side of Reception. He was in a bad way. Vinnie and Jim weren't great either but at least they were conscious. Blood was still trickling through the gaps in Vinnie's fingers as he held the gaping hole in his neck. On the outside Jim's head wound had stopped bleeding but had a thick, dark-red blob of congealed blood forming on the surface. Both of them were covered in blood, some of it not their own. Jim was very aware of this thought and assumed that the police would arrive and question them, especially if their 'enemy' had not woken from his slumber.

Sure enough, once they had been initially examined Vinnie and Jim were separated for medical attention. As the nurses segregated them into individual cubicles, separated by pull round polystyrene sheets, they began to clean their wounds and a young doctor stitched their heads. After initial questioning by the doctor on duty, who discovered that they had been 'assaulted in an unprovoked attack in the city centre', the police were called as a matter of procedure. Vinnie was in a complete daze and the gentleness of the nurses and their tender attention began to bring him back into the moment. The shock and trauma of what he'd just seen and done shook his mind like an earthquake and sent tremors through his nervous system. This was comforted somewhat when the nurse said,

"Turn your body this way Mr.Collins so I can check the other side of your neck. I need to check that there's no other cut cos the blood's everywhere."

The proud smirk which started to form on his face at being referred to as

'Mr.Collins' for the first time in his life, drained away as he turned to see blood spattered eyes staring at him from the adjacent cubicle. This face glared unflinchingly with an angry smile as if to say,

"I'm still here…I'm no' dead yet."

It was McPherson, slashed, battered, bruised and stabbed. He looked insane. He stared manically, trying to intimidate Vinnie. It worked. The madness was manifest. Vinnie did what the nurse told him and turned round, wishing that Jim was beside him. No sooner had the nurse left him to go and check on another patient, the panic of being alone crept in. With great relief he heard Jim's voice a couple of cubicles away.

"Jim? Is that you?"

"Aye, you awrite Vinnie?"

Jim's voice was discreet.

"Well, aye, I think so."

Vinnie tried to whisper loud enough for Jim to hear,

"You'll never guess who…"

Jim abruptly interrupted.

"Ssh! Don't talk about anythin'. I know…I saw him."

Jim had seen McPherson coming in and immediately masked himself behind the polystyrene curtain. He would have the advantage if his enemy didn't know he was here. When the police arrived and questioned Jim and Vinnie they stuck to the story agreed in the taxi-they were attacked in the city centre after a night out. When the police left and questioned McPherson, Jim was angry and shocked to hear his name and the details of the previous events being relayed freely to the police. McPherson's mask of madness and gritty violence was covering his fear. He knew he was no match for the violent energy which had struck him this night. Jim was arrested and taken to Pitt Street. As soon as the nurses and police left the cubicle Vinnie sneaked out and phoned Joe, hoping that he was home.

"Joe…It's Vinnie. I'm up at the Royal…Jim's been huckled …they've just taken him away just now. I've done a runner before I get the jail. Jim told me to phone before I left."

"Awrite Vinnie, cheers for lettin' us know. Whit about Meeko?"

Vinnie paused; he had been so disturbed by the presence of McPherson and the police that he'd almost forgotten about Meeko.

"Eh…they took him into another room Joe. He wisnae lookin' too good mate. He conked oot in the taxi."

Joe worried.

"Awrite Vinnie, I'll see you when you get back to the scheme."

"Joe? Any chance of askin' somebody to come up and get us. I've nae money."

Vinnie was more worried about being attacked outside of the hospital than the five mile walk home to Hardridge.

"Aye Vinnie. I'll try and get wee Bongo to come up. Wait at the bust stop right outside the Royal, the one on High Street. If I cannae get him I'll come up in a taxi."

"Sound."

Joe quickly left Mary's and managed to get hold of Bongo who was reluctant to go near the hospital with the police presence.

"That's pure jailbait Joe. We might get nicked."

"We won't! I need to see Meeko…Vinnie said he's in a bad way. C'mon to fuck Bongo?"

Joe could feel something else slipping away. He had to see Meeko.

While Bongo and Joe made their way to the Royal, Jim was being questioned by two detectives. He said little apart from his rehearsed alibi and was duly released, for the time being. Vinnie hadn't left the Royal by the main doors but had made his way through corridors filled with the sick and suffering. As he skulked through the wards, hoping for a safe way out, he felt like he was the barely living walking among the waiting dead as they scowled at him, surprised at his agitated appearance. He eventually found a toilet with a window leading to an internal car-park. It was a tight squeeze but he squirmed through. He had to get out. He needed to get home. Vinnie was beginning to realise, as Joe and Jim had realised quite clearly in recent months that the viciousness of violence was without the glory felt in movies. It was raw and cruel, destructive and bitter. The retelling of its touch channelling through us or pursuing us might be glossed over but it always left its trail on the soul. It sowed fear and reaped destruction. So, by the time Bongo's blue Cortina swerved down High Street, he breathed properly for the first time in hours. Joe and Bongo smiled as they pulled up at the bus stop. He had earned their respect this night but he didn't care. He just wanted to go home.

"Awrite Vinnie? Good to see you… jump in mate."

Joe jumped out and offered him the front seat.

"I'll just sit in the back Joe."

Vinnie didn't want to talk he just wanted to hide.

"No…I'm gettin' oot anyway. I want to go in and see Meeko. Bongo will park round the corner an' I'll be round in about twenty minutes. I want to find out what's happenin'. If I'm no' oot in half an hour just go, I've got money for a taxi."

"Awrite, nae bother."

Joe went to the reception of casualty and asked about his pal.

"…Meechan, aye. I was told he came in last night."

"Ok son, just take a seat an' I'll see what I can find out for you. Who did you say you were again?"

"Eh…I'm his brother, Joe."

The nurse left and Joe sat in the waiting area scanning the victims of accident and attack who filled the hospital. He laid his head back on the wall. He was shattered, tired of the chaos that continually streamed into his life, tired of the persistent performance which he felt he had to maintain. He felt lost and alone. He couldn't keep this up. He needed help and for the first time in his life he had to truly admit it. He knew that all of his own efforts and will to stop the storm of emotion which had followed him all his days had led him to where it all began-he was powerless and afraid of life. Although he had been here before as a wee boy, it was different. This time he was surrendered inside, maybe because he felt he had Someone or Something to surrender to, Something to carry him on. He had come to the end of himself. The weight of responsibility which had entered his soul in youthful innocence had told him to fight the crippling fear, subtle shame and every obstacle in his path. He couldn't do it. He closed his eyes and silently prayed.

"I know you're there…help me…please."

In his exhaustion he let go and as he breathed deeply he began to drift into sleep.

It was a clear, bright New Year's Day and one of the few Glasgow days when the sky was without its overcast shadow of cloud. There was a party in Mary's house and John was there, sober. Jim and Joe were both there, together. There was a carefree lightness in the air and Joe laughed freely and loudly as if the past was forgotten, or at least forgiven. John opened the window to have a smoke as Joe breathed the frosty air gently blowing through the living room. There was a rattle at the door but no sense of alarm or foreboding which often accompanied it. Joe got up and as he walked down the hall to open the door John jokingly shouted after him,

"If that's your *amigos* tell them they're no' comin' in."

He knew John was joking but at this Joe was confused. *How could it be the amigos? They weren't…* Before this thought was finished he was already opening the door and sure enough he was met with a unanimous,

"Happy New Year!"

The amigos stood there beaming with joy and covered with a radiant light. They had never looked so young, so healthy and happy even in the pre-drug years. Craigo and Gringo hugged Joe and walked past him. He was stunned. He couldn't believe it but it was real, he believed his sight. He still hadn't spoken when Meeko shook his hand and simultaneously hugged him.

"Happy New Year Joe!"

"Meeko? Are you…?"

"I'm awrite Joe. Aye, I'm awrite."

Meeko walked in and left Joe standing at the door, stunned and confused. He could hear the New Year well-wishing burst into the living room. He stared up the hall,

"Meeko?Meeko?"

The world swirled for Joe as his eyes blurred in a sea of dizziness; the blood drained from his face and sickness simultaneously emerged as he fainted into unconsciousness. The echoing sound of an approaching kindly voice seemed to reach into him and draw him from his giddiness,

"Mr.Meechan. Mr.Meechan," he woke up into this reality that we call life.

The nurse looked at him with compassion and sadness in her eyes.

"Are you awake son? Sit yourself up." The nurse gently helped Joe to sit up from his slouch; she had important news.

"Aye, I'm awrite…eh, thanks. Did you find oot? Is he awrite?"

Joe read the hesitation in her eyes.

"I'm so sorry son…your brother did gain consciousness for a short time when he was first brought in, but…I'm afraid he passed away about half an hour ago. We were looking for the two boys who brought him in but one was taken by the police and we don't know what happened to his other pal."

Silence.

Life and time and hope stopped in surrendering stillness.

Joe couldn't take any more.

As much as he wanted to he couldn't stop the well of pain and tears from overflowing. He put his face in his hands and wept. A fountain of grief and loss and of the aloneness that a life of violence and drugs had brought broke the fortress he'd built up. He almost forgot the nurse was there until she put a hand on his shoulder and rubbed tenderly.

"I'm so sorry son… I'm so sorry."

For an immeasurable length of time Joe stayed inside his hands and wept a well of childhood feelings as memories, images, regrets and longings washed across the shore of his mind. He wished he could let it all go-this life and this pain was too much. When he returned to the moment he took his hands from his face and was surprised to see a different nurse standing there as only seconds seemed to have passed. She patiently held hankies in hand, ready to help him wipe away the tears. She handed him some tissues and quietly waited for him to wipe his face and blow his nose before she said,

"When your pal woke up…" she knew that Joe wasn't his brother but felt that he wouldn't or shouldn't be turned away, "he was smiling, even though he looked really weak. He asked me to tell you that he was alright. He just kept saying 'tell Joe I'm awrite' and 'tell my Ma I'm awrite'. Just before he slipped back into unconsciousness he also said 'tell Joe I've seen *him*… I've seen *him*…I'm awrite…I'm awrite'. "

He was told that Meeko had been given blood when he first arrived and then gained consciousness for a short time. Unfortunately, a blood clot had formed and pulled away from the wound and reached his heart. His heart couldn't take it.
I've no' got the heart for this anymore Joe.
Joe left the hospital and made his way home. Serenity strangely rested on his whole body and mind. The frantic performance of a previous life, of an uncomfortable dream was over. The curtain was closed.
Numbness.
He got into a taxi and gave the driver his destination,
"Hardridge Road… in Corkerhill."
He closed his eyes. He didn't have the energy to try and think any more. He didn't even want to try and understand it all. It was too much; he just wanted to go home.

Chapter 38
Restoration

What a start to the year this had been for the Hardridge boys: Meeko's death, Jim scarred and Vinnie slashed. Almost since the Bells welcomed in 1989 there had been bloodshed and chaos. There had been two shootings, three knife attacks, a drug charge and a flood of tears which Joe had held tightly to for many years.

In the first few weeks of January, as the storm began to settle and some calm returned, Joe sat in his room alone, smoking joints and reflecting on the previous year-Gringo, Meeko and Craigo's deaths, Weaso and Billy's shooting, the failed robbery at the bookies, a conspiracy to commit an armed robbery charge, a host of other 'minor' violent and criminal incidents- he sensed that these were all just the external weeds of some deeper roots. In the midst of all this Joe had also felt drawn to another life, some power (a spirit, an energy, a Higher Power) wooing him with gentleness and forgiveness with a promise of psychological or spiritual freedom. This wasn't some distant Being sitting on some obscure throne on some unreachable planet; this was silent and present in the very core of every Soul: the source of consciousness and life. He had a strong impression that this was more about a relationship than a religion, of connecting to a living encounter which could be developed and evolved, rather than a mere ritualistic morality set in stone. His experience growing up with organised religion had distorted his ideas and intoxicated his deepest feelings about himself and any notion of 'God'. Yet, there was a transforming feeling and power, a Grace embedding itself into his attention daily. He was aware that this new way of being he had encountered was nothing to do with his worthiness or his 'being good '- that ship had sailed a long time ago. He had come to see his own powerlessness over his past and the effects it had on him but had simultaneously came to believe that there was a power willing to help him, to love him and to transform him-if he was willing to surrender and trust.

Joe was by no means alone in being caught in this wave of change. Many others in the scheme had experienced their own Glasgow epiphany and were responding in their own ways- some searching in the secrecy of their rooms and hearts, some turning from drugs and crime, and some even opening themselves to ideas of a spiritual nature. There were too many to recount in the pages of this story. It became a standing joke in some parts of Glasgow's South –side that Hardridge was 'God's land'.

"Aye, if you go over to Hardridge for weed or kit you better no' stay there too long, you'll come oot 'reborn'."

Jim had also felt the call to turn. To turn away from violence and crime and to turn towards a different reality; but now was not the time. He had desires and plans, scores to settle and restlessness not ready to surrender. So, when Jim met up with his young brother, Joe confessed freely,

"I've had enough Jim. I'm chuckin' it. I don't want to punt any more. You and Gally can keep things goin' without me."

"That's too bad. I had plans for you as well." Jim gave a mischievous grin.

"Whit about you? Whit d'you think about all this stuff that's been happenin'? No' just the amigos…but all this…eh, I don't know whit to call it... 'God' stuff."

Joe hoped that his brother would be ready to open up to this new life. He worried about him.

Jim chose his words carefully as he had a reverence and an awareness of this spiritual power, even if he wasn't ready to submit to it.

"I think there might be somethin' in it Joe, an' if you want to gi' it a try then go for it…but it's no' for me."

Jim respected Joe's decision but firmly believed that turning away from one life to another would require gradual abandonment of all that he knew and held close. He was right and he wasn't ready for this. To give up the addiction of violence and the seduction of wealth were cloaks he wasn't ready to discard.

"I don't even know whit it means, I just know that I want a life that's better than this one. I believe that there's … somethin' in it…"

"Just remember we've got that trial comin' up. We might get the nick. The jail's no' an easy environment to be tryin' to be all spiritual."

Joe hadn't forgotten for a second. The upcoming trial was looming heavy on his mind and he had thought about being in prison without the cover of violence and lies to guard the fragility of his heart. He didn't know if he'd be able to do it. He feared that he wouldn't have the courage to resist violence. It would have been more familiar and less effort to keep the persona he'd always maintained. But it was gone now. He'd seen the truth of it; it was a false existence. Not only this, he couldn't wear this old life any more. The truth had made it lose its comforts and seductions. The fear and emptiness of this way of life was indeed something he wanted to be free from, but it was so much more than this. This altered perception which had come to him didn't just promise freedom from fears but he believed that it offered transformation. This was a new seduction, one which felt loving and compassionate. Joe believed that to be restored from his past (as he'd seen it recently catch up with him and try to destroy his life) he needed this Love, this Power and this Grace. He wasn't ashamed to admit this anymore, even if others thought it weak.

"I know…I've been thinkin' about that. I feel as if I just need to try and trust… in whit I'm no' quite sure."

Jim sat silently, wondering if Joe's resolve would be able to stand the test. He'd been betrayed once before at court and it had cost him his freedom. He trusted Joe but he knew that the thought of prison could bring many fears to the surface. Time would tell.

Later on that night as Joe sat in his room, stoned but never so aware or awake in his life, he thought about the trial. He thought about how the police had some extremely incriminating evidence-ski-masks, boiler suits, knives, a small lump of hash, witnesses and the arrest of Rowany in the car park with a large screwdriver!

Joe had told the police that the bag was his and therefore all of its contents. He'd already admitted this. There didn't seem to be any way out of this. They were caught and even though they'd been wrongly charged Joe knew that he'd managed to 'get away with' so many crimes and acts of violence. Their intentions on the night of the arrest hadn't exactly been noble. Joe had come to believe that ultimately he had to face his actions, if not to the justice system then to some Higher Law. He would have had no justifications, no arguments had he been sent to prison. Joe was ashamed of the life he'd lived. He had turned away from his conscience from a young age. He'd rebelled against his parents, teachers, authorities, church and every other voice which tried to tell him what to do or guide him in another direction, including any Divine authority. He'd spent years ignoring his thoughts and suppressing his feelings and now it had caught up with him. In his own eyes he *deserved* to be punished; that would have seemed like justice to him. This wasn't self-reproach; he didn't feel that he was worse than the rest of humanity, just the same. He'd gone his own way with self-will until he couldn't go any further. He believed that it was grace that had stopped him in his tracks and wooed him to another way of being, into relationship with the root of all Being. He was turning but he was also full of doubt and fear. A remnant stain on his conscience that it was 'God's will' to punish him was hard to remove with reason. In desperation he turned to this source of all life and asked for mercy; justice wouldn't be enough.

"I know I don't deserve to walk away fae this life, an' it would make sense if I had to pay for the things I'd done, but…"

Joe stopped, making sure that he never tried to lie to this all-knowing truth.

"I'm scared. Help me…forgive me…"

As he said this, a tear escaped, once again overwhelmed by the wave of emotion breaking through. As he opened his eyes his gaze was drawn to top of the chest of drawers beside his telly where a little 'Daily Reading' book sat unread. This was given to him by someone in his visit to the Street Mission before Weaso's shooting. He felt compelled to pick it up and was amazed at what he saw on the front cover. There was a picture of a set of handcuffs, lying open with the key beside it and a small quotation underneath.

'…there is now no condemnation…'

Joe immediately felt a warm peace and a reassuring calmness within.

Trust in Me.

He didn't really know what this meant but just felt that everything would be alright. He went to sleep, exhausted but feeling a reassuring safety.

The day of the trial came and the McShane brothers met wee Rowany and made their way to Glasgow Sheriff Court. Joe and Rowany were agitated; this could be their last day of freedom for a few years. Jim was also uneasy but he didn't allow himself anxiety. He had already begun preparing for prison. He was also watching his brother and friend to see if betrayal would play out in his life once more. Joe and Jim hated courts, as do most people, but especially those for whom the law and authority represented punishment. The authority of the law felt oppressive. The court was without humour and would soberly call them to account. How could they ever escape this without a prison sentence? It didn't seem possible.

As they entered the court and were told to go into the trial waiting room, the atmosphere was filled with foreboding. Numerous criminals who'd seen the inside of a court and a prison cell many times, first offenders and perhaps a few who were innocent, all with varying degrees of fear and guilt. The arrival of the Cigar, Mr Isaac Shield, in a grey pin-striped suit looking slick and relaxed did nothing to put them at ease either. Having reviewed the case and looked at the evidence against his clients his prediction wasn't promising. The pleasantness of his cigar smoke and the civility of his manner couldn't distract them from the reality they were about to face.

"It's not looking good gentleman. Along with the statements from the police I'm not sure how we can justifiably explain your, em…possession of machete knives and ski-masks. You might have to accept a custodial prison sentence for this."

He wasn't trying to frighten them but to negotiate a plea bargain.

"We should be up in about ten minutes as the court is running on schedule for a change. I'll just go in and see how the land lays as far as the trial going ahead today."

As Shield left them to discuss possible alibis, the boys just looked at each other, quite frankly a bit bewildered. In the past they had always managed to secure a way out of an accusation but 'It wisnae us' or 'We didnae dae anything' didn't seem plausible. They sat in uncomfortable silence, already feeling sentenced by their conscience, waiting to be brought to trial. After about fifteen minutes their lawyer returned with a rather confused expression etched on his wide brow.

"There's going to be a short delay gentleman as it seems the court is in a bit of confusion. The evidence for your case, aforementioned ski-masks and such, was put into the Evidence Room about half an hour ago, standard procedure." Shield frowned and nodded his head quizzically. "But it seems that the court officer can't find it.

This is really baffling as the evidence room can't be exited or entered unless through the court, meaning that someone would need to have walked by the Sheriff with the bag of evidence, which is obviously highly unlikely. I'm assuming that neither of you sneaked into the court in my absence?"

The cheeky grin was the first time Shield had remotely smiled at any mention or discussion of this case. He knew from Jim that Joe had turned from his life of crime and duly instructed them, tongue firmly in his cheek,

"Well, whatever you're doing… rosary beads or what not… keep it going, because it seems to be working."

The brothers and Rowany looked at each other, speechless, but a ray of hope was finding its way through. This couldn't be happening; it was too good to be true. They'd hold off on the celebrations for the time being, disaster had a way of striking unexpectedly. Ten minutes later Shield returned his mind strained with an expression of disbelief.

"I can't actually believe this. I've never seen a court in so much confusion… the confidence of the police had been so overwhelming! It seems that the two witnesses who made statements as to your presence at the Sports Centre and your association with Mr Rowan have not turned up. Nobody can explain their absence. Needless to say that the two officers who questioned you on the night of the arrest are in a state of disarray. The Sheriff isn't looking too happy either. He's told the court officer that if he doesn't locate the evidence within the next ten minutes the case will be thrown out. Let me go back in and see what I can find out."

The boys looked at each other and their lips were loosed with laughter and joy. They couldn't contain it. The foreboding which had clouded their thoughts when entering the court had completely gone. Faith rose up in Joe but he held it inside and treasured it.

A few minutes later Shield returned for the third and last time telling them with amazement,

"You're free to go!"

Joe felt that this was more than a freedom from the charge but from the accusation and condemnation which he'd stored up in his heart for years.

"The case has been thrown out. The police and court are in an uproar. The Sheriff is appalled at the lack of…" Shield's words and elaboration were irrelevant to Joe but he obviously needed some explanation to give to himself.

The train ride home to Hardridge from the town centre was jubilant, celebrated with the sweetest can of coke and the juiciest roll and chips ever tasted. The taste of freedom was great. Joe felt rich, like he'd been given back his life when an enemy had threatened to destroy it.

"Aye, they polis must be beelin'! I cannae believe this…" Wee Rowany was ecstatic.

"Well, that's what they get for lyin'." Jim laughed at the irony of his own words but believed that there was some 'justice' as he felt they'd been set up. The police were always the enemy.

For Joe it was not the police or the courts, nor any other human being that was the enemy any more, but he was beginning to see that the illusions we create from our damaged hearts was the real source of our grief. He didn't say much on the train home but he inwardly cherished this new release. He pondered his new relationship with the world and a spiritual life of his own understanding. This was not the one handed down to him from the mentors of his culture and childhood but a connection with a compassionate and merciful Being. He pondered the idea that the evidence had 'disappeared', mysteriously being removed from the court. He pondered the thought that this reflected his new spiritual existence- forgiveness was complete. Even the evidence stacked against him, in his own mind and often in the hearts of others had been removed, never to be held against him. This freedom from accusation and blame, from punishment and shame, powerfully and secretly began to work its way through the deepest parts of Joe's being. He had been made new and he was beginning to experience it.

In the months which followed the court case Joe rarely saw Jim or most of his other friends for that matter. They had gone to find their own way as he had to find his. Gally and Jim continued to make money and Bongo and Manny were still living the fast life, not ready yet to slow down or surrender. Their time would come; it seemed inevitable to Joe. *The amigos were dead and Mooney was gone*. This thought still filled Joe with sadness and loss but he had to break off old ties and the hooks which still held him to his recent way of life.

Drugs, violence and crime were all fading like shadows at the rise of the sun. Many from the scheme were experiencing and exploring notions of spirit or faith in their own ways. It was mad; no-one could understand it, but it was powerful and real. It wasn't always plain sailing. This world of spirit was more like a battle ship than a luxury liner. This was not a battle between men, but a wrestle between realities and comforting illusions; an inner conflict between a spirit and an ego. Joe hoped that he'd be able to keep to his resolve, to move further along this path that he was now on. He knew that there would be difficulties ahead and, like always, the past would try to return and haunt and occupy his soul again. The process of letting go had begun.

Scheme life continued but Joe felt separate from it. He began to develop a secret life, but this time it was not in darkness. He opened his mind and heart to a new consciousness and a new way of life. He would walk beside the River Cart in Pollok Park and open himself to this new spirit, listening, receiving, and welcoming this new inner experience. For the most part this was a hidden journey and often one which was travelled alone. He occasionally visited the Street Mission as he liked the people and found that most of them were genuine. He began to develop some close friendships with this spiritual community and even began to open up his life to them a little, sharing shameful secrets to those he really trusted. He would previously have been mortified to say it but he also loved the simple elation and the childish joy of singing spiritual songs, and felt like he was letting go of some hardened self-image which had encased his free spirit. He was losing his false image in something far greater than his 'self'. The Happy Hour was here again and this time the feeling lasted for more than just the hour.

On one occasion when he visited the Street Mission he was met with a double surprise, a pleasant shock almost. He sat down, at the back as usual, and as he looked about at the friendly faces, cheerful voices echoing off the walls, he was stilled. He quietly waited for the songs to begin and a baby girl perhaps seven months old, bounced joyfully on her mother's knee and peered over her shoulder beaming at Joe. He smiled back and her face surrounded by a white frilly bonnet lit up even more. She started to play a kind of peek-a-boo with Joe, hiding behind her mum and he found himself filling up with an unfamiliar joy. What surprised him even more was the quickness of the young, auburn-haired mother's reaction as she heard Joe's giggle, causing her baby to bend her weak puppy fat knees and bounce excitedly. She turned round, also surprised,

"Joe?"

"Marie? Goodness sake, whit you doin' here?"

This didn't come out right but Joe was so amazed to see Marie and to see her holding a beautiful wee baby!

"Och, it's a long story… but Danelle fae the scheme invited me along. Whit about you?"

"O…that's an even longer story… Anyway, who's this?"

"This is my daughter…"

Marie had never looked so radiant when she said this. She blossomed with joy and her well-being burst through her smile.

This wee baby had obviously brightened her life. Joe was surprised but the situation seemed so natural and right.

"She's absolutely beautiful."

He reached over to hold the extended grasping hand of the bouncing baby, who was still beaming for attention. "So, are you…?"

"Och no, we're no' together… another long story." Marie pre-empted any discomfort, particularly on Joe's part. She could tell by his happiness to see her that he still held a fondness for her. He looked different, lighter, brighter, and clearer? She was right; Joe could barely contain the gust of feeling blowing over him, and a refreshing affection for Marie, which he thought was lost, began to clear away some of the debris of grief which had recently littered his life. He didn't know how to continue the conversation but was allowing himself to be content with the silence when Danelle walked in and headed straight for them.

"Hiya, how are youse?" She smirked mischievously at Joe and Marie. "And how are you my wee lamb?" She instantly took the jumping baby from Marie's arms and started to speak to her in that baby language which some women seem to intuitively pour out whenever an infant is around. At this point two older women in the church who were standing nearby turned and joined in the baby talk and praising Marie for her daughter's beauty; it was evidently inherited.

"She is ab-so-lut-ely gorgeous. Look at her wee face. O…whit's her name hen?"

This seemed an important question but not only to the women, Joe's spirit waked to attention as if he was going to hear something profound. He felt like he was being carried along by a gentle but powerful breeze and that this whole situation was marked with perfect timing. Destiny and fate were inadequate words to describe the feeling of synchronicity as Marie gently, but adoringly responded.

"Grace."

She instinctively looked at Joe. His gaze was already fixed.

Printed in Great Britain
by Amazon